ROMANCES OF THE PLANETS. *No. 1.*

JOURNEY TO MARS.

THE WONDERFUL WORLD:

ITS

BEAUTY AND SPLENDOR;

ITS

MIGHTY RACES AND KINGDOMS;

ITS

FINAL DOOM.

BY

GUSTAVUS W. POPE, M.D.

" And wheresoever, in His rich creation,
Sweet music breathes,—in wave, or bird, or soul,—
' Tis but the faint and far reverberation
Of that great tune to which the planets roll."
FRANCES OSGOOD.

WITH A NEW INTRODUCTION BY

SAM MOSKOWITZ

HYPERION PRESS, INC.
WESTPORT, CONNECTICUT

P8253 ja

Library of Congress Cataloging in Publication Data

Pope, Gustavus W
  Journey to Mars.

  Reprint of the 1894 ed. published by G. W. Dillingham,
New York, which was issued as no. 1 of Romances of the
planets.
  I. Title.
PZ3.P81J9   [PS2649.P422]   813'.4
ISBN 0-88355-116-0   73-13262
ISBN 0-88355-145-4 (pbk.)

Published in 1894
by G. W. Dillingham, Publisher, New York.

Copyright © 1974 by Hyperion Press, Inc.

Hyperion reprint edition 1974

Library of Congress Catalogue Number 73-13262

ISBN 0-88355-116-0 (cloth ed.)

ISBN 0-88355-145-4 (paper ed.)

Printed in the United States of America

CONTENTS.

[iii]

GUSTAVUS W. POPE:
Creator of "The Scientific Romance"

By Sam Moskowitz

One of the most influential science fiction authors of the past fifty years was Edgar Rice Burroughs, the world-famous creator of the Tarzan books and a popular giant of science fiction, particularly in his novels about Mars, Venus, the hollow earth, the moon and various other locales where his imagination spawned colorful, action-packed, and thought-provoking scientific romances. Millions of readers followed his stories in magazines, books and paperbacks; inevitably, he could not help but make an impression upon many youthful would-be writers. A considerable number of authors have admitted their fondness for Burrough's works, particularly in the science fiction field. His admirers range all the way from Olaf Stapledon, that philosophical titan of the imagination who produced a history of the future of mankind in *Last and First Men*, to Ray Bradbury, whose poetic, emotionally evocative works are best typified by *The Martian Chronicles*.

In his lifetime, Burroughs created a school of science fiction writing, centered about the Frank A. Munsey magazines: *The All-Story, The Argosy*, and, to a lesser degree, in *Munsey's*, which very closely followed his formula for the scientific romance. Writers for these publications included such prominent names as A. Merritt, author of *The Moon Pool*, Charles B. Stilson, author of *Polaris of the Snows*, J. U. Giesy, author of *Palos of the Dog Star Pack*, Austin Hall and Homer Eon Flint, authors of *The Blind Spot*, Ray Cummings, author of *The Girl in the Golden Atom*, Ralph Milne Farley, author of *The Radio Man* and Otis Adelbert Kline, author of *The Planet of Peril*, to name but a few. For a quarter of a century the works of these authors were a major current in American science fiction; and their influence spread to the "comic" strips when Alex Raymond introduced *Flash Gordon* in 1934

Today, the novels and stories of Edgar Rice Burroughs are very much alive in hardcovers, paperbacks, comic books and motion pictures; and there now exists an entire school of researchers, scholars and devotees, supporting a half-dozen specialized publications, whose sole reason for existence is to ferret out every conceivable scrap of information about this author. Also, in hundreds of specialized courses in science fiction at colleges and high schools across the country, Edgar Rice Burroughs is now the object of serious academic study. It should also be noted that as far back as 1962 the Oxford University Press reissued his *A Princess of Mars* for a special study series, which included such established classics as *Robinson Crusoe, David Copperfield, Oliver Twist, Stories From Shakespeare, The Last Days of Pompeii, The War of the Worlds,* and others of similar renown.

All this by way of preface to *Journey to Mars* by Gustavus W. Pope, M.D., which unquestionably was a transition work between the schools of Jules Verne and Edgar Rice Burroughs and, conceivably, may have been read by Edgar Rice Burroughs himself. To date, little of a factual nature has been determined about the life and career of Gustavus W. Pope, a medical doctor practicing in Washington, D.C. who either found the time or set aside the time to do a great deal of writing. His earlier works seem to have been aimed at teen-agers. They included such action-packed titles as *The Mohawk Chief, The Rose of Shenandoah, The Boys in Blue, The Medical Student* and *The Merry Lunatics.* Among his non-fiction books, also written in a popular vein, were *Geology and Genesis, The Wonders of Psychology* and *The Terra Incognita.* He also wrote, and apparently published at his own expense, some pamphlets on religion. *Journey to Mars,* probably his first work of science fiction, was the first in a planned series titled *Romances of the Planets.* The second, *A Journey to Venus,* issued in 1895 by F. Tennyson Neeley, appears to have sold well in both a paperback as well as a hardcover edition.

The conscious purpose of *Journey to Mars,* as stated in Pope's introduction, was to prove that science fiction belonged in the mainstream of literature. In his introduction, Pope wrote: "It has been held by some persons that scientific romances, the scenes and *dramatis personae* of which are laid on distant spheres, are impracticable, owing to certain inherent difficulties of a scientific nature involved in the undertaking, and furthermore, such romances, being outside of, and beyond this mundane sphere, are necessarily beyond the pale of human interest and sympathy, like the lives of Mythological divinities, Loves of the Angels, creations of Faerie land and Oriental romance."

Pope, disputing this contention, maintained that "With a requisite amount of imagination and fancy, combined with other qualifications which constitute the *sine qua non* to the novelist, and also a reasonably fair acquaintance with physical science   in which latter many excellent writers of fiction are more or less deficient,   it is quite possible to construct romances appertaining to 'Other Worlds.' " The author of *Journey to Mars* did not have the literary qualifications of a William Dean Howells or Henry James; but by deliberately making a strong love interest pivotal to a fast-moving, colorful and imaginative adventure on another world, he anticipated the success formula of Edgar Rice Burroughs' later classic, *Under the Moons of Mars,* to an extent that can only be described as extraordinary.

Jules Verne sometimes displayed an admirable talent for good characterization, but love interest was rare in his works, and in many of them non-existent and hardly ever a motivating force. It was H. Rider Haggard in *She*, first published in 1887, who showed just how effective a strong love interest could be in a fantastic adventure. Some of the characteristics of Ayesha, who grew old before the horrified eyes of her lover when the flame of enduring life reversed itself, can be found in the character of Pope's Martian princess, Suhlamia. Pope reveals the origin of other elements of his story when his protagonist Lieutenant Hamilton, upon meeting the Martians on earth and trying to determine where they came from, puzzles: " 'They cannot live in the clouds nor on the moon; consequently I see no other habitation for them except down in the interior of the earth'. And in support of this opinion I announced that they might be elbow cousins to Bulwer's 'Vril-ya,' or an evolution from Verne's centre earth anthropoid apes, or astronomer Halley's hollow globe denizens, or lineal descendants of the chained Titans under Mount Aetna."

The utopian aspects and marvelous inventions of Bulwer Lytton's *The Coming Race* were both infused into Pope's story, as unquestionably were the spirit of exploration and the attention to versimilitude found in Jules Verne. In combining all of these elements, Pope created a new format for science fiction that would be carried to fabulous heights of popularity by Edgar Rice Burroughs.

It will not adversely affect the reader's enjoyment of *Journey to Mars* if I list many of the ingredients of Pope's adventure that later appeared in Burroughs' *Under the Moons of Mars* and the "sequels" that followed.

Like Burroughs' Mars, Pope's planet is a world where the seas have been drying up, where there are canals, and where there exists a group of fragmented, ancient and declining civilizations. There are red, yellow and blue races, and mighty giant natives. Though there is a high degree of science, the sword is still the weapon of hand-to-hand combat. People live for almost an indefinite length of time, and they never seem to age. There is a Princess of Mars, beautiful, bronze-hued, and courageous, who falls in love with a naval officer from earth. The officer, Lieutenant Hamilton, finds that the additional oxygen in the atmosphere of Mars gives him greater strength than the permanent inhabitants, therefore making him a mighty warrior. Among others, he meets a "mastermind of Mars." Pope's Martians ride gigantic birds, instead of the Thoths encountered on Burroughs' Mars; and a number of incredible monsters roam the planet.

As those who have read it know, the first Burroughs novel of Mars ends with a cliff-hanger. John Carter, too weak to walk, is trying to restore the oxygen plant that has ceased functioning on Mars. He falls unconscious before he can learn whether his Martian companion, who is crawling towards the pump room, can revive its function in time to save the planet. In the sequel, *The Gods of Mars*, John Carter watches his wife, the former Princess Dejah Thoris of Mars, being attacked by a jealous woman with a knife, in a chamber that closes in his face and cannot be opened again for a year.

The ending of *Journey to Mars* is also a cliff-hanger. A meteorite storm is about to wipe out the city of Mars where Lieutenant Hamilton's Princess reigns, and the reader will not know until the next book if she or the Martian civilization will be saved.

Whether Edgar Rice Burroughs ever read Pope's book has never been determined. He was attending college at Pontiac, Michigan when it was published. It is believed to have been reprinted at least once, possibly twice. The publisher, G. W. Dillingham, had good distribution, and through the years had a fair number of other science fiction, lost race and fantasy novels on his list. Speculation about that aside, however, this novel is so rich in color, adventure and concepts that it is worth reviving because of its own merits; and its place in the history of the development of science fiction will be judged primarily on that basis.

TO MY READERS.

In this day and generation,—pre-eminently distinguished for the rapid progress of science, mechanical arts and inventions, evolution of ideas and interchange of thought, when the advancement of yesterday is but the prelude to that of to-day, and the progress of to-day prefigures that of to-morrow—the World and Society are compelled to accept the dictum, "*Se temporibus accommodare ; tempori servire.*"

In the domain of current literature this progressive change is displayed ; many kinds of which vary with the opinions, manners, tastes and fashions of the times. Particularly so, is this seen in the field of popular fiction, in which regard, we, as a nation of readers, are not unlike the old Athenians of whom St. Paul speaks. —" For all the Athenians and strangers which were there, spent their time in nothing else, but either to tell or to hear some new thing."

It is generally admitted that, the day of the so called " sensational novel " and " sensational play " is drawing to a close. This is due, not so much perhaps, to the gradual elevation of what is termed " Moral tone," as to the fact that, the public are already surfeited with both.

Not a few careful and discerning critics have also expressed the firm conviction that, the so called " society novel " also, will ere long be numbered with things of the past, and that, what may be termed the "scientific novel" will appear, as a *desideratum* in the near future.

It has been held by some persons that, "scientific romances," the scenes and *dramatis personæ* of which are laid on distant spheres, are impracticable, owing to certain inherent difficulties of a scientific nature involved in the undertaking, and furthermore, such romances, being outside of, and beyond this mundane sphere, are necessarily beyond the pale of human interest and sympathy, like the lives of Mythological divinities, Loves of the Angels, creations of Faërie land and Oriental romance. It were perhaps needless to add that, the author cannot subscribe to this view.

It may be assumed, in strict accordance with the spirit of Science, Philosophy and Religion,—as well as analogy,—that, Humanity, created in the Image of God, must necessarily and always be the same · *in Esse*, in essential Being and Nature, on whatever habitable planet of our Solar system it may find its home, sphere of action and environment, and it is wholly contrary to reason and analogy to assume otherwise.

"Other Worlds than Ours" therefore, may present as rich and inviting fields to the philosopher, poet and romancist, as they always have, and always will, to the Astronomer and Scientist.

Fiction is simply that department of literary constructive art, whose creations appeal mostly to our emotions, feelings and sensibilities ; presenting its scenes and characters like pictures to the eye of the mind, as the creations of the painter do to the eye of the body.

With a requisite amount of imagination and fancy, combined with other qualifications which constitute the *sine qua non* to the novelist, and also a reasonably fair acquaintance with physical science,—in which latter many excellent writers of fiction are more or less deficient, —it is quite possible to construct romances appertaining to " Other Worlds." Neither is it necessary to resort, in such works,—so often the case with some writers,—to the fantastical, grotesque or monstrous creations of a crude and riotous fancy, nor, what is still more reprehensible, to any violations of the laws and principles of Science.

G. W. P.

WASHINGTON, D. C.
January, 1894.

INTRODUCTION.

"Look, how the floor of heaven
Is thick inlaid with patens of bright gold.
There's not the smallest orb which thou behold'st,
But in his motion like an angel sings,
Still quiring to the young ey'd cherubim."
MERCHANT OF VENICE, V., I.

Mars is the outermost of our terrestrial planets. Its diameter is about half that of Earth ; its day nearly the same length as ours, and its year nearly twice as long. Its volume and mass are about one-sixth that of Earth, while its density is nearly the same. Its orbit, like that of the other planets, is eccentric. Its distance from the Sun while in aphelion is about 154 million miles ; in perihelion, 128 million. It completes its orbital revolution in a little less than two of our years, its speed being over fifty thousand miles per hour.

A man weighing a hundred and fifty pounds on Earth, would weigh not quite sixty pounds on Mars, according to the terrestrial standard.

Once in something over two years it comes in what astromomers call " Opposition." At these periods our Earth is on a line between it and the Sun. During the early part of August, 1892, it was in opposition, and its distance from us was only a little over thirty-five million miles.   This was the nearest approach within the last fifteen years (1).

To give an idea of such a distance as thirty-five million miles—scarcely the breadth of a hair in comparison with the distance of many fixed stars,—were it possible to lay a rail road from Earth to Mars, and a babe of a day old should embark on a train of cars travelling day and night at the rate of sixty miles an hour ; if he survived the journey, he would be a white-haired old man of nearly seventy years, when he reached the Martian station.

This last opposition of the planet was of special interest to the Astronomical world, and awakened a degree of public attention never before known ; the press teemed with articles on the event.   The telescopes of all the great Observatories of Europe and America, were nightly pointed to the skies, and while cities and villages were quietly sleeping, the patient astronomer, seated in his chair, or perched on his ladder, was keeping his lone watch on our brother World.

Soon after sunset the planet rose like the Star of Bethlehem in the east, coursing along the Southern skies and as it majestically sailed up to its Zenith, it hung like a brilliant ruby among the glittering Stars, shedding its soft and rosy light o'er the celestial heavens.

This kingly orb, clothed in its robes of crimson fire, was the cynosure of all eyes.   'Twas watched by the mariner at sea.   'Twas oft the guiding star of the belated traveller.   In the soft and balmy summer nights, amid leafy groves and along the banks of streams, where the silence was unbroken save by rippling waters,—the notes of the whip-poor-will,—the cry of the night hawk,—the hum of the locust or chirrup

(1) The next nearest approach will be in 1909.

of the cricket—'twas oft watched by youths and maidens, as it glimmered among the leaves, or rolled in stately splendor in the deep blue vault above.

> "There is no light in earth or heaven,
> But the cold light of stars;
> And the first watch of night is given,
> To the red planet Mars."

Days, weeks, passed on. The rosy orb ceased its nightly reign ; departed on its journey, and disappeared in the vast realms of space.

* * * * * *

It was on the stormy and blustering evening of March 22nd, 1893, the vernal equinox, during which wide spread gales and tempests oft prevail o'er the lands and seas of northern latitudes, and many a stout ship and gallant crew are whelmed beneath the wild rolling billows,—weary with the labors of the day, I was sitting by my cheerful fireside, thankful for this brief respite from the professional cares and anxieties that constitute the daily life of the busy physician,—thankful even for the storm,—although I had often encountered many a worse one on my daily rounds,—and hoping I should not be called out again that night, when the sound of the office bell announced another arrival and a strong built, swarthy, sailor looking man of middle age entered the room. His countenance had a fearless, honest and good humored expression ; his voice was rough and powerful, like one accustomed to give orders amid roaring storms, yet kindly in its tone ; he was clad in a sailor's water proof, and carried a package wrapped in canvas under his arm. Doffing his cap, pulling his forelock and scraping his left foot in regular sailor style.

"Are you doctor ——?" he asked.

"I am ;" I replied. "What can I do for you, my good man ?"

"O thank ye, doctor ; much obleeged, but I dont need any overhaulin' in the way o' physic and surgery, just now. I'm sound as a dollar from keel to top-mast," replied he with a jolly laugh. " Tom Hallyard's my name ;—first mate o' the good ship White Gull—just hove into New York last week, strait from Australia— reckon you're the doctor I'm after, provided ye belong to this 'ere,"—handing me a letter which I read as follows.

"Off west coast of New Zealand, six hundred miles out. Tuesday night, December 27th, 1892.

" DEAR CAPTAIN,

An aërial ship and crew, in distress implores you, by all that is dear to the true sailor's heart, to take charge of this casket, and when by the blessing of Almighty God, you reach port, if you will kindly forward it with the contents inviolate, to either of the parties herein named—Commodore ——, No. —— street, New York City, or Doctor ——, No. —— street, Washington City, D. C., you will receive the heart felt thanks of him who commits it to your care and of those who receive it and also be liberally rewarded. May the hand of Almighty God protect you in this hour of peril and bring you all safe to port, is the earnest prayer of a brother sailor and his comrades."

As no name was affixed to the letter, I was at a loss to know who could be the writer.

"Show me the casket spoken of here," said I.

"Reckon you'll see somethin' ye never saw the likes 'afore," said he, then unwrapped the package and took out an elliptical shaped shell about two feet long by eight inches wide in the middle. It seemed to be com-

posed of some unknown, dark bluish colored metal;
was hard as steel, yet light as cork. It was surrounded
with a close net work of strong cords to which several
long cords were fastened with small buoys and steel
hooks attached to their ends. The material of the cords
was wholly unknown to me.

"Never's been opened you see," said the sailor. " Its
hollow,—somethin' inside."

I shook the shell : there was a sound like the rustling
of paper.

" How did you come in possession of this singular
looking article and this letter, written by some one who
evidently knows me, in a storm off New Zealand, ten
thousand miles from here, on the opposite side of the
globe?" I asked.

" Its a mighty queer story, doctor, and if I tells it, I'm
afraid ye'll fancy I'm spinnin' a sea yarn for the marines.
But its gospel truth, sure as my name is Tom Hallyard."

" O, I'm used to sea yarns ;—have heard many a wonderful one in my day ;" I replied.

" But ye never heard the likes o' the one I've got
coiled up in my locker. Shiver my jib if it are'nt
so."

" So much the better. Let's have it by all means. I
wouldn't give a fig's end for the best yarn ever reeled
off by any landsman that travelled. Of all the stories
told under the sun, a genuine sea yarn's the one for me;
and the tougher the better."

It was just the night for a rousing story. The window shutters were rattling lively. The storm was
roaring and howlihg outside and screaming down the
chimney. I told my sailor man to make himself at
home, and as hospitality of the spiritual sort is highly
appreciated by sons of the sea, I ordered up a brim-

ming mug of "hot Scotch" for my guest, and a cup of
Oolong for myself, and drawing our chairs up to the
board, we proceeded to discuss the respective merits of
inspiring, bold John Barleycorn, and the draught that
cheers.

"Take a cigar, Tom," said I, passing a box of fragrant Cubanos.

"Thank ye, doctor ; but if it's all the same to ye, I'd
prefer a whiff o' me old pipe,"—drawing out a rich
chocolate colored meerschaum, its bowl carved in the
form of a South Sea mermaid, combing her sea weed
locks and contemplating her beauteous physiognomy in
her hand glass, and the fumes of Lone Jack and Flor
del Fuma, gracefully mingling, ascended to the ceiling.

"Pretty rough night," said I.

"Pooh ! Nothin' but a fizzle. These 'ere land
storms are'nt no account. Bless yer heart, doctor, ye
ought to be out in some o' the rousers we have at sea.
Reckon you'd open yer peepers. The night I saw that
casket,—Blast my eyes, if I didn't think all hell had
broke loose !"

"Just the right sort of a night to uncoil a tip-top
yarn ;" said I, "go ahead, Tom, reel away."

"All right, doctor, you're just the sort o' chap I likes
to overhaul on a lee shore, and all's quiet, so I'll reel
off. Here goes. As I were a sayin'. I'm Tom Hallyard, first mate o' the good old ship White Gull, a tip-
top sailor are she,—weathered many a rousin' blow
off Cape Horn, Caribbean Sea and Hatteras. In the
iron, hide and wool trade, 'twixt New York and Australia. Took in a full cargo at Melbourne two days afore
Christmas last, put out from harbor, made good sea
way for a while, then ran smack into a terrible gale
from the sou-west off Van-Dieman's land. Tried to
keep course around Zealand, but weren't no use,—ha-

to clew up and scud afore it. Was drove away off New South Wales, on night of 27th December. Lord bless you! How it did blow. 'Twas black as pitch,—couldn't see an inch beyant the jib-boom,—lashed the steersmen to the wheel and some o' the deck hands to the railing. Captain Goodman were sick in his cot,—shoulder broke by a falling spar—Poor Jack Peterson went up the fore top to watch ahead for bergs. Lost his ballast and pitched overboad strait to Davy Jones' locker. I climbed up and took his place,—mighty tough crawlin', I tell ye. By Jingo! How that gale did yell, and the billows chasin' us like hungry tigers as we flew on ; the thunders rattling and the lightnings flashing. Bye and bye, Bang!—Off went an alarm gun on the port quarter. 'It's a ship in distress,'—says I to myself—' God help her now.' Of course we couldn't put about and lay to, in that terrible sea,—much as we could do to keep our ship from foundering any minute. We had to keep our eyes skinned, I tell ye. I skewed my head around, and what d'ye think I saw, Doctor ?"

" The polite and dignified old gentleman in black ?"

"Worse nor he and all his imps, I tell ye. Three cable lengths off the port quarter were a great iceberg five times higher than my top-mast, heavin' and tossin' in the waves. On the lee side of it were a terrible lookin' thing, bigger than any fin back whale. It had a long sharp nose like a pike, two shiny green eyes big as cart wheels and three big wings like an eagle's on each side, and shone all over like silver. It were hoverin' high above the waves, and looked like one o' them big flying monsters they tell about as lives in the moon. All at once it dashed right out from the berg and made straight for my ship. I never was skeered afore, doctor, but my heart stood in my mouth when I saw that terrible thing a comin'."

"Pooh ! Tom, that was nothing but a flying ship.
Yankee inventors have got the patent out, and are
beginning to manufacture them by the wholesale. One
is going to take a trip to the North Pole next summer,
so they say."

"A flyin' ship ? Where in thunder did that monstrous
big fellow come from, that were aboard of her ? Shiver
my timbers, but he were never born on this 'ere earth.
He looked like one o' them giants they tell about as
lived 'afore the flood. I saw him plain enough by the
lightning flashes as he stood alone on deck, holdin' on
to a great iron chain, while she was reelin' and plungin'
in the storm. He were over ten foot tall, and looked
big and strong enough to fling an elephant over his
shoulder. His face and hair were yellow as gold and
terrible to look upon. He were whirlin' this 'ere casket
'round his head by the cords like a lasso. ' Ship ahoy !'
—he calls out. By the Eternal !—what a voice. It were
like a thunder clap, and made the spars and riggin'
rattle. On came that flyin' ship whirlin' like a leaf in
the wind. I thought he'd be flung overboard, but he
hung on to the chain like grim death. As she flew past,
he hurled the casket right into the riggin' like a shot
out of a cannon. It caught by the hooks and held fast.
Then he calls out again in pretty good English—
' Hello ! there. Foretop man,—take good care o' that.
Good bye ship-mate—may Almighty God bring us safe
to port.' Then he stamps on the deck, and shouts out
again like thunder,—' All right Captain ;—Go ahead !'—
and the flyin' ship flew like a cannon ball straight up
in the clouds out o' sight. What d'ye think o' that,
Doctor ?"

"It is the most wonderful story I ever heard, Tom."

"Gospel truth I'm tellin' ye, Doctor. Now I've reeled
off my yarn, I'll coil up and stow away. As I were

sayin', the storm blew over in two hours. I got down
from the fore-top, took the casket to Capt. Goodman, he
read the letter and I put 'em in his sea chest. We made
good voyage home ; stopped at Rio, Havana and New
Orleans on the way to change cargo ;—got into New
York last week—Captain had to go to the hospital ;—I
took the casket,—made a bee line for the Commodore's
house—all shut up,—family gone to Europe."

" He was an old friend of mine,—on the retired list,—
died some months ago," said I.

" Then I conceited the casket b'longed to you ; so as
I were comin' on for to visit my old Mother as lives
down in Maryland, I brought it along."

"We'll find out what's inside of it ;" said I, and I
ordered my servant man to go for a clever locksmith
near bye. He came with his tools. After some trouble,
he found the screw joint and opened it. The walls were
an inch thick, and harder than the toughest steel. I
took some of the filings and submitted them to a thorough chemical and microscopic examination. The
metal was wholly unknown to me and seemed to be
united with some peculiar adamantine siliceous base.
The casket contained a voluminous journal written in
clear fine hand, with many notes in short hand, a few
letters addressed to friends ; one to the late Commodore
and one to myself, as follows :

" Off West Coast of New Zealand.

" Tuesday, Dec. 27th, 1892.

" DEAR DOCTOR,—You have known me ever since my
childhood, and were the old and valued friend of my
honored father. You have carefully watched over me
during my youth. You have been almost as a father to
me, have done many acts of kindness for which I beg
you to accept all my gratitude. If my father's old

friend, Commodore —, is not living, I commit the contents of this casket to your care ; dispose of them as in your judgment seems proper. Since I last saw you, I have been through many strange scenes and adventures, as you will discover on perusal of this journal. Kindly do me the favor to forward the accompanying letters to my friends, and my dear sister Madeleine. Heaven only knows whether I shall ever again see the faces of those near and dear to me.

"Sincerely and gratefully yours,

"FREDERICK HAMILTON."

It is impossible to express my astonishment at this extraordinary news. After examining the papers—

"Tom," said I, "These papers are of great value to friends of mine. We owe you many thanks for taking such good care of this casket and you must allow me to reward you substantially for it."

"Thank ye, doctor ;—but I couldn't think of takin' a reward for doin' the fair thing by a brother sailor in distress."

"Are you married, Tom ?"

"Married. Bless yer heart, doctor, poor sailors like me can't afford to get married now a days. The gals are gittin' altogether too expensive. Never saw the likes o' one yet, I could take a shine to, no how. All they cares for is gew-gaws, finery, and havin' a good time. When one of 'em marries a sailor man, she always gets a gang o' land lubber spoonies sneakin' round her with their monkey shines, and soft-soapin' her with taffy and sich like, when he's off on the broad sea. My dear, good old Mother,—I'm her only boy— and my brave old White Gull and shipmates, are all I cares for in this world. Mother runs a little farm down

in Maryland, and I'm workin' hard to pay off the mort-
gage on it,—Bless her dear old soul, won't she be glad
to see me again after a year's voyage."

"What's the amount, Tom ?"

The sailor told me.

"You are a good son, and God will bless you," said I,
drawing up a check on my banker for the amount.
"You must accept this for your Mother, with my compliments and kind regards to her."

After considerable hesitation, Tom accepted the
check with many thanks. He was my guest for the
night and during the long stormy evening related many
interesting scenes and events connected with his numerous voyages, and the next morning took his departure.

A short explanation of the papers in the casket is
necessary. I had known Lieut. Frederick Hamilton
since boyhood ; he was an officer in the U. S. Navy ; his
father was Col. William Hamilton, one of my oldest
and most valued friends, an officer in the Army and
served with high honor during the late War. He died
in 1876, leaving two children, Frederick a boy of ten,
and little Madeleine a child of nearly two years, over
whom Commodore —— had been appointed guardian.
Madeleine, now a young girl of eighteen, was pursuing
her studies at the Convent of Notre Dame in Paris.
She was distinguished for her great personal beauty,
and loveliness of character. Frederick, after several
years of study and travel abroad, graduated with high
honors at the —— Naval Academy. He was one of the
most splendidly educated young men I ever knew ; of
brilliant intellect and accomplishments, magnificent
physique,—handsome as an Apollo,—of noble bearing,
elegant manners, and what was far better, he was the
soul of honor, and his character without a blemish.
His mother, who died early, was a remarkably bril-

liant and beautiful woman, from one of our oldest and
best blooded Creole families of Huguenot descent, in
New Orleans.

Capt. William Anderson was Frederick's great uncle
on the maternal side. He was a bold and skilful sailor,
had followed the sea all his life, and when a young man
was attached to the crew of the renowned French navigator, Baron Dumont D'Urville, in the ship Astrolabe,
during the Antarctic polar Expedition of 1840, in which
year the British Expedition under Sir James Ross, and
the American, under Capt. Wilkes, were also engaged
in their explorations in these wild and inhospitable
regions. Capt. Anderson was a man of extraordinary
courage and enterprise. In 1890, he had planned an
expedition to the South Pole, which his wealth and
the facilities under his command enabled him to organ-
ize in the most thorough manner. A strong and swift
brig rigged screw steamer of seven hundred tons burden and five hundred horse power, was built under his
personal supervision at the —— ship yards. She was
thoroughly adapted in every detail to encounter the
perils of a long polar voyage. Her bows were encased
with heavy steel sheathing for protection against the
impact of ice. She was manned with a crew of thirty
seamen, officers, engineers etc. trained and experienced
men, also scientists, provided with a complete outfit of
apparatus. Lieut. Hamilton, at the earnest solicitation of
Capt. Anderson, joined the expedition, having obtained
a furlough. The vessel was christened the Albatross.
Early in the fall of 1891, she sailed from New York to
Australia, took in fresh supplies at Melbourne and on
the morning of Nov. 10th, set out on her voyage to the
South Pole.

JOURNEY TO MARS.

———◆———

CHAPTER I.

"And now there came both mist and snow,
    And it grew wondrous cold ;
    The ice mast high, came floating by,
    As green as emerald."

ANCIENT MARINER.

Nov. 10th, 1891.—Our ship the Albatross, put out
from Melbourne harbor and after two weeks sailing
reached the Antarctic circle which sweeping in a ten
thousand mile circuit around the South Pole, marks the
boundary line between the south temperate and frigid
zones. It was the beginning of the Antarctic summer ;
the sun was approaching his greatest southern declination, which he reaches on the 21st December. Revolving in a spiral circle around the horizon he diffuses,
save when mists or tempests prevail, his cheerful,
though feeble light through the Antarctic summer
which continues six months. It was now midnight,(1) and

(1) At the polar regions, the terms morning, noon, evening
and midnight are inapplicable, as it is either continual day or
night for half the year.

the solar luminary presented the usual extraordinary appearances displayed in these regions. It hung about ten degrees above the horizon ; its disc was oblate,— the effect of atmospheric refraction, of a deep, blood red color and traversed with parallel bands resembling those sometimes seen on the planet Jupiter. It was surrounded with magnificent parahelia and its great crimson halo poured radiant beams across the waters tinting the waves with rosy and golden hues. The sky presented a beautiful appearance ; over head, a deep, indigo blue ; to the south a brilliant red ; to the north it seemed hung with shadowy veils of gorgeous purple, mingling with the misty vapors that floated o'er the sea. Our ship was sailing in the midst of a scattered floe and under steam, the wind being adverse ; as the volumes issued from the funnel they were condensed into an icy mist falling in little showers on the deck. One of the sailors on the look out in the foretop cross trees now called out—

" Ice bergs ahead."

" Where away ?" asked Captain Anderson, who stood with his officers on the quarter deck.

" Two points off the weather bow."

The bold navigator who seeks to explore the polar regions is confronted with many obstacles and dangers unknown in other parts of the world. Dame Nature, like man, has her variable moods. She can be rude, rough and inhospitable as well as genial and inviting. Like the god Janus, she wears two faces, one for peace, the other for war, and like the eastern magician, can blow hot or cold with the same breath. She is exceedingly jealous of any intrusion on her savage polar domain and whenever man seeks to penetrate her regions of eternal frost, she obstructs his course with drifts and barriers, blinds him with fogs and mists, buffets him with freezing tempests of snow and sleet, and assaults him with bergs and billows.

And now a great chain of ice bergs came looming up in one unbroken line from the southern horizon. As they elevated their towering crests above the waters they looked like frowning giants arising from the deep to guard the frontiers of the polar monarch. These stupendous masses, which are the disrupted fragments of vast shoreline glaciers, are, in the antarctic regions, of far greater dimensions than those around the north pole or North Atlantic Ocean. Floating in the tow of the great polar drift currents, their foundations immersed to a depth six times their altitude above the surface, they advance majestically forward in spite of winds, waves, or tide. In these regions they are sometimes seen from one to two miles long and four to six hundred feet high.

" Now, boys,"—said the Captain," you'll see the most magnificent sight in the world."

Captain Anderson was a splendid specimen of the old time sailor, few of whom are seen now a days. He was about seventy ; of medium stature and herculean frame, a massive head clothed with iron gray hair, bronzed complexion, deep set, penetrating steel gray eyes, such as are seen among men born to command. A voice like a lion, a courage and daring that would face the devil himself. All on board swore by the grand old commander of the Albatross.

As the long line of bergs arose in full view, a panorama of wondrous beauty was displayed before us. Brightly illumined by the sun, it seemed as if a chain of glittering gems o'erspanned the deep. Sometimes they reflected from their crystalline surfaces dazzling sheens of light, or like immense prisms, scattered the solar rays in gorgeous rainbow colors over the waves.

As they drew near, they gradually underwent extra-ordinary transformations of shape, and resembled a metropolis of giants. Stupendous castles, temples, and pavilions apparently of marble, alabaster and porphyry, with soaring pinnacles, minarets, battlements and vaulted portals, floated in stately grandeur o'er the waters. Colossal towers mingled with floating mountains, whose interiors were hollowed out in tremendous caverns.

We stood in silent wonder as this magnificent pageant advanced toward us. We carefully steered the ship through the narrow and tortuous channels lying between them, they were like cañons cut through floating mountains and their hollow caverns re-echoed the sounding waves like thunder. After a few hours we passed through the line, which floated to the north and finally disappeared from view below the horizon.

We had now reached the 70th, parallel, and entered that broad bay bounded on the west by the shore line of Victoria land (1) and on the east by immeasurable ice fields—and which, according to our present knowledge of these regions, offers the only accessible route to the south pole. This bay, beginning at Cape North penetrates to the 78th, parallel, a distance of six hundred miles due south. With a bright sky, propitious wind and clear sea we made full sail and entered the bay, passing Cape Adair, Mount Sabine and the Admiralty range. The coast line is illy defined ; enormous ice cliffs and low ice fields obscure its boundaries. We passed Mount Melbourne and Prince Albert's Mountains (2) with other ranges from whose summits the

(1) Discovered by Sir James Ross in the south polar expedition of 1840 and named in honor of Queen Victoria.

(2) Discovered by Ross and named in honor of the Prince Consort.

descending glaciers swept over valley and shore, abruptly terminating, far out at sea, in stupendous ice cliffs. On the fourth day we came in full view of that famous Antarctic volcano, Mount Erebus. (1) From its snow clad summit, nearly fifteen thousand feet high, issued vast volumes of flame and smoke. Near by was Mount Terror (2) an extinct volcano, forming by its projection into the sea, Cape Crozier.

We had now advanced nearly to the 78th parallel, where the great ice barrier discovered by Sir James Ross rose before us. " A massive and perpendicular wall of ice with a sea front from a hundred and fifty to two hundred feet high, flat and level at the top, stretching to the east as far as the eye could reach." The façade of this tremendous barrier resembles a solid wall of azure tinted crystal crowned with a battlement of frosted silver. Impregnable to the assaults of tempests and billows, it has stood from the immemorial ages, built of the glacier, cemented by the frost and nourished by the everlasting snows. We coursed along this barrier many miles to the east, far beyond the limits of Captain Ross' sailing, where his progress was prevented by the ice.

The sky now became overcast, the crimson halo surrounding the sun disappeared, and his light changed to a dull and angry glare. The splendid hues that glowed from the face of the barrier and surrounding icebergs died away like the colors of a dissolving view, and a dense fog settling over the sea immersed everything in gloom.

" There's a storm brewing, boys "—said the Captain,

(1) In the South Polar expedition of 1840 and named after his Ship.

(2) Named after Captain Crozier in command of the Ship Terror.

"and it will be a rouser. Keep your peepers wide awake and be lively on your pins when it comes."

We clewed up sails and prepared for it. The wind soon began to blow a gale from the north east bringing loose masses of drift ice down on us. Ere long we were completely beset and had no sea room ; further progress was impossible and we were compelled to lie close-hauled to. A blinding storm of snow and sleet sprang up, and the deck, spars and rigging were speedily encrusted with ice. The storm increased in violence and the wind shifting to the north, forced us to leeward. We got up steam, veered the ship about, head to the wind. For a while she held her position but the sea gradually drove her backward in dangerous proximity to the barrier.

CHAPTER II.

THE STORM.

"There's tempest in yon horned moon,
There's lightning in yon cloud,
And hark, the music, mariners !
The wind is piping loud."
                    ALLAN CUNNINGHAM.

Our ship was now immersed in a tumultuous ocean of ice masses, grinding and crushing around us on every side.

"It is impossible to keep her head to the wind ;" said the first mate to the Captain.

"Let go the port and starboard anchors ;" he replied.

This was done, and the loud rattle of the chain cables

announced that the anchors had plunged to the bottom of the sea. The backward drift of the ship ceased, and she was brought up.

" She rides hard ;" said the Captain, as the Albatross tossed from side to side in fearful lurches.

" The chains hold well ;" said the officer. " They are forged of the best Swedish iron, their proof is sixty tons."

A shade of doubt passed over the Captain's face as, leaning over the railing he watched the huge chains rising, falling and clanking amid the waves.

" Hark !" said he. " The ring of the iron is crystalline, a hundred tons won't hold her in this sea."

Crash ! Both chains snapped short off at the ports, and reeling and staggering like some wild and wounded animal broke loose from its fastenings, the ship rapidly drifted stern-wise toward the barrier.[1]

" D—n the chains !" growled the Captain. " They snap, like pipe stems. Hemp is better than iron around here. Let go the sheet anchor and be spry about it. Blast my eyes ! she's got a hemp cable on her with a twist in it that'll hold a man o' war in a hurricane."

Faithful and true old sheet anchor. How the last hope of the storm beat mariner clings to that crucial iron mass, fit symbol, amid the tempests of ocean, of that sacred cross to which the last hope of the christian clings, amid the storms of life. She springs from the cat head, dragging her huge cable through the port and plunges beneath the waves ; her mighty flukes grapple the sea bottom and bury themselves to the shank.

What a grip is that ! The ship is brought short up

[1] The intense cold of high latitudes often produces a crystalline state of the iron rendering it easy of fracture. This is sometimes seen in the axles and flanges of railroad car wheels in winter.

like a wild bull suddenly lassoed by the ranchero. In vain she plunges and leaps, straining and tugging at her tether which holds her with the elastic tenacity of steel.

" She rides easy," said the officer as the billows gathering in front, lifted the bows of the Albatross high on their foaming crests.

" And there's music in twisted hemp, too," said the Captain as the elastic vibrations of the great twenty inch cable poured forth a deep and mournful tone like the sound of an immense bass viol.

" We'll weather it yet, Captain."

" Provided the anchorage ground holds."

There was a frightful burst of the storm and the ice masses pouring forward with irresistible momentum, forced the ship backward.

" She drags," said the officer.

" D—n that sea bottom," growled the captain. " It crumbles like rotten muck under the anchor's grip."

Again the anchor bites and the ship is brought up ; again she drags, and the ship drifts, once more she bites, then drags and bites again. The brave old anchor strove to fulfil her office ; she bit and tore the treacherous foundations of that marauding sea with many a furrow ; had the anchorage ground been firm, she would have held her, but the overmastering sea still forced the ship backward. The struggle was in vain.

" Captain," said the first mate, " we're drifting on the ice barrier and unless steam can keep her off, she'll strike in thirty minutes."

" Crowd on more steam," replied the Captain.

The engines were put to their fullest power. Their throbbing shook the ship ; for a short time she held her way. Suddenly a loud crash was heard at the stern, one of the engineers rushed up the companion ladder, his face pale as a corpse.

"The propeller has broke loose," said he.

At this terrible news many of the crew uttered cries of despair and all was in confusion ; some clung to the rigging ; others stood with folded arms, calmly awaiting the dread summons to death, for the ship seemed doomed to destruction.

At this awful moment the Captain's lion voice arose high above the din, penetrating every part of the ship. It was like the voice of some fearless spirit whom no emergencies could perplex nor terrors appall.

"All hands,—every man to his station !"

Anchors, cables, engines and steam had been beaten in this contest with the elements and human muscles and daring seamanship were now called upon to enter the lists. The inspiring tones of that voice shook off the paralysis of fear,—the boatswain's shrill pipe echoed the call and the officers and crew obeyed it.

"Every man to his post.—Prepare to ware ship."

The keen eye of the Captain had descried through the gloom a narrow cove or inlet penetrating the ice barrier about two furlongs off the starboard quarter, the entrance of which was faced by a stationary iceberg and thereby screened from the storm, and he had determined to put the ship right about and run her into it.

To "ware" or veer a ship—in other words to put her right about and on an opposite course under such dangerous surroundings is a manœuvre of the most delicate kind. It requires great skill in seamanship and the exercise of the utmost caution and circumspection on the part of captain and sailor. Every man must thoroughly understand his duties and implicitly obey each order as it is given, or the ship may be swamped and sink to the bottom.

The officers and crew quickly gathered around, awaiting their orders.

"Lay aloft and stand by to loose fore tops'ls.—Clear away fore and storm stays'ls" shouted Captain Anderson. The boatswain's pipe sounded high and shrill ;— with a loud cheer the seamen ascended the slippery shrouds, grappling the ice crusted spars, sails and rigging. After a few minutes—

"All ready there, aloft?" again shouted the Captain.

"Aye. Aye. Aye!—" resounded from the rigging like faint voices from the skurrying storm clouds, then turning to the deck hands—

"Man top-sail sheets and halliards."

The men stood ready, the Captain again shouted to the riggers aloft.

"Stand by,—let fall,—sheet home and hoist away."

The boatswain's pipe echoed each order, which was obeyed to the letter. The sails cleared, the riggers swiftly descended to the deck ; as the sails filled with the wind, the bolt ropes, clews and reef bands creaked with the strain and the sheets flapped as if they would tear to ribbons ; the Captain now called to the seamen in charge of the anchors.

"Slip cable."

"Aye Aye !"—resounded from the hold. Two strokes of the sharp axe,—the great cable was severed in twain, —rushed through the hawse pipe with a loud whiz,— coiled and writhed in air like an immense serpent, then sank beneath the waves. Released from her tether the ship for a moment staggered to and fro helpless.

"Up helm !"—shouted the Captain.

The steersman put the helm hard up. As the ship veered about, she fell into the trough of the sea, careening almost to her beam ends, the waves breaching over her, but the storm sails paid her head off and she righted, trembling from keel to topmast.

"Square yards.—Right helm.—Make for the inlet !" Again shouted the captain, and like a hound loosed from his leash, the ship sped swiftly towards the cove— the billows and ice masses dashing against her from behind—it seemed as if her stern would be torn to pieces.

The Captain had discovered a current skirting the foot of the barrier and running into a narrow defile between the ice cliffs and communicating with the cove ; it was scarce a ship's length across, was filled with surf, ran with great velocity and terrible as was the alternative he determined to plunge the ship into it. The crew were astonished at his courage and hardihood, but it was the only chance for the ship. The roaring sea flung its mighty billows to the summits of the cliffs and louder still resounded the thundering cannonade of the ice masses, as uplifted by the waves they were hurled like battering rams against the upright wall of that awful barrier that loomed up between sea and sky. It seemed as if the death knell of the doomed ship was sounding.

"Hard a-port helm !" shouted the Captain.

Down rushed the ship into the gorge, reeling from side to side—her yards almost grazing the ice walls—the billows breaching over her decks—the spray hissing around her, then veered about—staggered into the cove —shuddering like a weary and wounded bird escaped from the fangs of some beast of prey.

"Well done, my brave old sea bird !" said the Captain, as leaning over the prow, he patted and stroked the scarred and weather beaten figure head of the Albatross, one of whose wings was knocked off in the dread struggle.

CHAPTER III.

THE OPEN POLAR SEA.

" The fair breeze blew, the white foam flew,
    The furrow followed free ;
  We were the first that ever burst
    Into that silent sea."

ANCIENT MARINER.

In a few days the propeller was repaired, the axle
pins and one of the blades only being broken. We left
the cove, sailed eastwardly many miles along the barrier, and entered a broad bay stretching to the south,
comparatively clear of ice. After a run of sixty miles
we reached a great glacier stretching across it from
shore to shore, connecting the slopes of two opposite
mountains about twenty miles apart. We got out two
boats, manned with six men each, pushed our way
through the pack, reached the foot of the glacier,
moored up and began the difficult ascent. After a
journey of ten miles we reached its summit, over two
thousand feet high. The view was magnificent, measureless ice fields stretched on either hand and mountain
ranges whose snow clad peaks glittered under the bright
sun like polished marble. Directly in front stretched a
boundless expanse of waters till they were lost in the
far distant southern horizon. It is impossible to express
our delight as we gazed on this Antarctic polar sea, and
we broke into loud huzzas. After a short rest we
retraced our way back to the ship and announced the
great discovery.

" Lieutenant Hamilton—" said the Captain, whose arm

had been injured by a falling spar,—" you will don your uniform and take possession of that open sea in the name of our country. Plant the stars and stripes there, and long may they wave."

Among the ship's crew was a young fellow about twenty-five, a native of New Zealand, whom the Captain had picked up as a boy on one of his voyages to that island. He was a grandson of a distinguished Rangatira or King of the brave, warlike and once powerful Manoa Tanehoka tribe, now reduced by disastrous wars against other tribes to a few hundred souls. He was of medium stature, his frame well-knit, active and supple as a leopard and possessed extraordinary muscular strength ; his skin was a rich olive brown color, his well shaped head clothed with glossy black curling hair ; his fine cut nostrils, splendid teeth, winsome dark eyes, open and happy expression of countenance, combined to produce as handsome and engaging a specimen of the South Sea islander as one would find in any tribe. According to the custom of his country he was tattooed on the breast and arms with New Zealand mythological figures, and on his cheeks a pair of little sun fishes, the tails meeting at the chin. This was the insignia of his rank as prince of royal New Zealand blood. He was an excellent sailor, uncommonly bright and intelligent, an expert hand at many things. A devout Christian, he unconsciously mingled with his faith some of the superstitions of his race,—belief in fairies, witches and demons. His disposition was affectionate and he was devotedly attached to me, he had been christened John, and was very popular with the officers and crew who had dubbed him the title of Corporal. As sailors not unfrequently have their pets on board ship,—parrots, owls, monkeys, cats, etc.,—John had his particular ornithological favorite in the person of a tame raven, a splendid specimen of the corvine tribe with jet black beak and legs, black glossy plumage tinged with green. Like the generality of his tribe, this fellow was pugnacious, fearless, thievish, a terrible fighter, cunning as a fox, highly intelligent, his collo-quial abilities were wonderful, surpassing the most accomplished parrot ; he could outswear any pirate that ever roamed the seas. His name was Jack, to which John had prefixed the title of Commodore, and Commodore Jack was the especial pet and at the same time, terror, of the whole ship. He and John, like Dickens' Barnaby Rudge and Grip, were inseparable. He was jealous as Othello and woe betide any unlucky cat, owl, or monkey that came within reach of his pow-ful claws and beak. His style of business was like his conversation, brief, always to the point and he never spared expletives. He addressed his master as Corp, and myself as Cap. Both are introduced here as hav-ing their necessary, though perhaps humble rôle to play among the dramatis personæ of this narrative.

The next morning our crew got out the boats pro-vided with the necessary articles for the trip ; canned food, arms, nautical instruments. One of the ship's flags and my naval uniform, to do honor to the cere-mony ; also a few cans of gunpowder and sticks of dynamite to try some experiments in blowing up ice. Our first mate, David Roberts took command, and accompanied by John and the raven,—perched firmly on his master's shoulder, we embarked, pushed through the pack, reached the glacier, mounted the boats on sledges, dragged them with much labor up to the sum-mit ; then descended the opposite slope, and night com-ing on, pitched our tent, took supper, wrapped ourselves in our blankets and went to sleep. Next morning we re-embarked, rowed several miles along the shore which was skirted with ice, till we reached a long narrow strip of land projecting out into the sea. Its shores consisted of rugged precipices rendering it impossible to land. It was flanked by a large ice berg. We moored our boats along side, climbed the steep slope and reached the summit, which commanded an extensive view of the open polar sea, over which numerous bergs and floes were floating towards the south.

I planted the flag on the highest part of the berg, and the star spangled banner waved over the south polar ocean. I made a short speech in honor of the event ; we fired a salute from our carbines and revolvers, then began the descent by a shorter route. It was difficult and dangerous. Our shipmate David lost his footing and fell into one of the deep crevasses of the berg from which he was rescued with great difficulty. His lower limbs were broken, besides severe injuries in other parts of his body. It was impossible to convey him to the ship in either of the boats. I ordered the crew to go back in one as quickly as possible and return with larger boats, and the ship's surgeon. They departed and rowed swiftly over the waters. John and I bound up poor David's limbs as well as we could with splinters of wood and pieces of rope and patiently awaited the return of the crew till night, during which our wounded shipmate suffered extreme pain.

The next day and night passed with no sign of the boats. John, whose eye was keen as an eagle's, often climbed the berg and scanned the horizon. The weather now changed, announcing a coming storm. In the face of the berg, and about twenty feet above water, was a large cavern which had been hollowed out by the waves. With great difficulty we raised David from the boat, drew him up into the cavern, and made him comfortable as possible. We drew up most of our boat gear, food, blankets, arms, instruments, etc. The raven perched himself silently in a corner of the cave. We partly closed the entrance with blocks of ice to screen off the wind. I was filled with torturing anxiety in view of our deplorable situation and feared that the crew on their passage to, or return from the ship, had been lost in the ice drift. During the day a heavy gale sprang up from the northeast, and it grew freezing cold. The bergs and floes were heaving and tossing in all directions over the sea. By night fall the storm increased in violence, and the waves dashing high up against the face of the berg forced streams of water into the cavern. Worn out with fatigue and anxiety we sank to sleep in spite of the uproar. Suddenly a loud and appalling sound aroused us. We hurried to the portal. The fierce gale shrieked through the cavern. Beneath us rolled a tumultuous ocean of billows and ice masses, and as the black storm clouds flew across the sky, the fitful light of the moon disclosed to our terrified gaze an immense ice berg bearing down upon us. For a moment its dark shadow loomed over us, then its mighty wall—crushing our boat to atoms, dashed down upon the cavern's mouth like thunder. The shock hurled us back on the floor—it was dark as midnight—the air grew thick—the roar of the tempest was heard no more—the bergs were frozen together and we were buried alive in an icy tomb!

CHAPTER IV.

THE ICE DUNGEON.

"For all was blank and bleak and grey;
It was not night—it was not day;
But vacancy absorbing space,
And fixedness, without a place,
*　　　*　　　*　　　*　　　*
But silence, and a stirless breath,
Which neither was of life, nor death.
Prisoner of Chillon.—BYRON.

The ice berg had been torn from its station by the tremendous collision and was slowly oscillating to and fro, evidently floating along a current toward the south. This continued many hours, finally a heavy grinding and crushing sound announced that it had stranded on some rocky shore and the motion ceased. What was to be done? Nothing. Helpless, far from all human aid on this wide and desolate ocean. The full horror of our situation now flashed upon me; death in its most dreadful form, by slow suffocation or starvation was our doom. I sank down on the icy floor and prayed that our sufferings might not be prolonged. John lit the lamp, its feeble rays alleviated the darkness and we sought by cheerful words to encourage each other with hopes of release. Delusive phantom of hope, when we knew full well that there was no possible escape for us except by miracle. In a short time we found to our great joy that the air penetrated the crevices in the cavern and we were relieved from the fear of suffocation. Three days passed; my watch having run down, reckoning of time was lost. Poor David suffered extreme pain, became delirious and refused food. I could scarce touch a morsel and even John ceased to prepare his daily meal. Fortunately we had saved a small cask of water from the boat. After a few days the lamp gave out and we were immersed in darkness. Time passed on unheeded ; we suffered from long periods of sleeplessness alternating with uneasy slumbers. The raven, who had remained speechless in his corner, suddenly started up, flapped his wings and uttered a loud whistle.

"Hello !—Commodore,—what's up ?" asked John.

"Bang !—Bang !—Bang !—" croaked he in tones deep and solemn as a bass drum. We listened and in a few moments, felt a slight tremor vibrating through the cavern. John arose and put his ear against the wall.

"Hark, Cap'n Fred, me hear queer noise."

I placed my ear against the wall and heard a faint rumbling sound. It seemed to come from the bowels of the earth.

"Is it thunder, or the roar of distant waves ?" I asked.

"Bang !—" replied Jack.

"No thunder, no wave ; muchee like big gun powder blast what blow up coal mine," said John.

The idea of mining operations conducted by the hand of man in these regions of ice and darkness, was so absurd, I burst into a fit of laughter, in the midst of which poor David in his delirium began to sing—

> "I see them gather o'er land and sea
> The banners and arms of races three,
>   Of races three the terrible men ;
>   The red, the yellow, the blue.
>
> They come ! They come ! I see them fly,
> On winged ships far o'er the sky ;

They wend their way from an unknown land ;
They gather along the polar strand ;
    The red, the yellow, the blue."

" All ready.—Take aim.—Fire !—Bang!— " roared the
raven, giving his orders like a drill sergeant.

Time passed on and soon those fantastic hallucina-
tions so often the prelude to insanity, enthralled my
brain. Of the workings of my mind—what was thought,
said or done, I knew nothing. In such a situation all
idea of time, place, or succession of events is lost;
there is no memory of the past, no hope for the future;
a never ending and dreadful present is the only idea
of which the mind is conscious. I must have become temporarily insane, for I babbled of green fields,
flowers, home, books, ships, philosophy, music, and
have dim recollections of raving and tramping like a
wild beast around my den, shouting and singing in concert with my poor delirious comrade his never ending song of "the red, the yellow, the blue " and often
restrained amid my frenzy, from self violence by
John's firm hand.

Meanwhile the mysterious sounds continued to penetrate the icy walls of our dungeon, gradually growing
louder and more frequent until I began to regard them
from a scientific point of view and gravely announced
to my fellow prisoners that we should ere long enjoy
the supreme pleasure of witnessing a great geological
upheaval on the grandest scale, with a general smash
up of the Antarctic continent ; when suddenly a tremendous concussion seemed to upheave the very
foundations and our dungeon rocked as if by an
earthquake.

" Bang !—Bang !—Bang !—" roared the raven, louder
than ever.

" Hi!" shouted John. " No earthquake, Cap'n Fred,

old Commodore, he know big heap. That be muchee big gunpowder blast !"

"Fact, d—d if it ain't," emphatically responded Jack.

"Guess we gettee blown out o' here, terrible quick. By Jingo !"

"All ri—" complacently croaked the raven, settling himself quietly in his corner.

Up and down, to and fro, round and round we whirled, as if in the rapids of Niagara. We threw ourselves on the icy floor dizzy and sick with the gyrations. Another tremendous concussion accompanied by a frightful ripping and tearing overhead and our dungeon roof was split off as if by the axe of the Norse god Wodin ; the walls upheaved and we were thrown out on a ledge of rock under the open sky, breathing the pure air of heaven and murmuring prayers of thanksgiving such as they only can breathe who have been snatched from the jaws of death.

The raven—considerably discomposed by his hasty ejectment—scrabbled up the ledge, mounted the highest point, flapped his wings, and gave a rousing crow. We were momentarily stunned by the shock, then recovering ourselves, carefully bore our wounded companion up the ledge, and as the fragments of our icy dungeon whirled away over the waves we looked wonderingly around. We stood on a solitary rock in the midst of a boundless sea overspread with dark storm clouds : here and there over the broad expanse, flashes of flame and long curved lines of fire sprang up amid the darkness accompanied with loud explosions and detonations like cannon. Suddenly the raven, who had flopped around the other side of the rock yelled out—

"Hello !—Cap.—Hello !—Corp."

"What's up now, Commodore ?" yelled John.

"Devil's to pay ! Hurry up !"

We hurried around the other side of the rock as the most tremendous spectacle ever seen by mortal eyes burst on our terrified gaze. Rolling tumultuously over the waves were huge ice bergs and floes all on fire ; all blazing ; some were enveloped in great roaring masses of flame ;—some were shooting up long fiery columns ; others were bursting like gigantic bombs scattering their fragments in all directions. As they rolled along, heaving and tossing, the very billows shrank back from the contact and fled away in showers of hissing foam. Clouds of vapor whirled over-head. I shook with affright at the awful spectacle. John fell on his face crying out, that the day of judgment had come, and it seemed indeed as if the " Dies Irae," that dreadful day of wrath had dawned upon us and that the very rocks and mountains, the sea, yea, the solid globe itself might melt with fervent heat and be wrapped in whirlwinds of fire.

Here and there appeared small boats with lights glancing over the waters. All at once amid the uproar, cries of alarm arose ; one of the boats, struck by a floating ice mass, was overturned and its crew thrown into the water a short distance from the rock. I aroused my terror stricken companion and fastening the bight of a long rope over a projecting crag we grasped it and rushed down to the water's edge. Several men were struggling in the surf. Among them was a young man in advance of the others ; he seemed almost exhausted. Suddenly John cried out :

" A shark ! A shark !"

Close behind the young man I saw the long sickle shaped fin of the ravenous " tiger of the sea " glancing amid the surf. Fortunately I had my long knife in my belt. I snatched up an iron ice spike lying on the rock and plunged through the breakers. The shark had turned on his back—his huge mouth armed with its terrible saw like teeth, wide open. In another instant the body of the young man would have been severed in twain. I dashed forward, seized the monster's snout with one hand and thrust the sharp spike crosswise within his jaws. He snapped them together, driving it through his upper and lower jaw, pinning them together. I drew my knife and stabbed him repeatedly under the breast fin—the only vulnerable place in a shark's body ; the blood spouted out in jets. The monster dashed furiously to and fro amid the surf, at times raising me bodily out of the water, or plunging me to the bottom. I held firmly to the spike, striking blow after blow with all my strength. The monster was over twenty feet long and it seemed as if I could never reach his heart.

Finally after a prolonged struggle he floated away dead. John was already by my side pounding the monster's head with a hammer, but making no more impression than on wood. We grasped the young man and after a hard struggle against the undertow, bore him up the rock and laid him down. He was apparently dead. I applied the usual method of resuscitation and in a few moments to our great joy, he began to breathe. His features were the most beautiful I ever beheld in man, resembling in their contour, Leonardo da Vinci's painting of St. John. His complexion was the color of gold, softened to a delicate magnolia hue. His dark lustrous hair hung in heavy curls down his neck ; his form was lithe and a perfect model of manly beauty. His dress was of dark blue cloth of a peculiar pattern and unknown fabric. In a few moments he revived, raised his dark and beautiful eyes wonderingly to mine, faintly murmuring in a sweet and melodious voice a few words in an unknown tongue, then noticing my inability to comprehend, he feebly pressed my hand and placed it on his breast. I raised him partly up and placed his head on my knee. In the meantime John fastened the rope around his waist and plunged into the sea, rescuing several men from the breakers. Boats now drew up and a band of men of strange complexions and attire, gathered around me. They wore helmets surmounted with pointed crests emitting lights of different colors and bore strange implements in their hands. One, whose helmet gleamed with a brilliant crimson light and who was evidently their chief, sprang forward and clasped the young man in his arms, spoke to him in a low tone, then turning to me.

"*Kosi twam ? Sva naman ? sva lathiliam sva rhazotram ? Brafi*"[1] said he and removed his helmet disclosing his features. His complexion was a deep bronze, his hair snow white and his eyes piercing as those of an eagle. I threw back the hood of my capote which partially concealed my features and stepped out from the shadow of the rock. As the lights shone o'er me, he looked me full in the face with an expression of astonishment, then turning to the throng.

"*Guara asi tasmayal. Nilakshini tasmae santi baruza tasmayal aya janasti, so'sti Avani Samtanaza .*"[2] He then took my hand, placed it to his breast, thence to his forehead with a graceful gesture ; then motioning to his retinue, they advanced one by one, going through the same ceremonial. Their complexions were of red, yellow and blue colors, their stature rather below the medium, their forms exceedingly graceful. As they looked at me with wonder, talking in their strange language, the delirious song of David seemed a prophetic

[1] "Who art thou ? What is thy name ? thy language, thy country ? Speak."

[2] "Behold this young man, his face is white ;—he has blue eyes and fair hair. He is of the Earth born race."

description of the scene. The young man now arose and throwing his arm affectionately around my neck drew me to his side. Then the whole band raising their faces and hands upward toward the heavens, burst with one accord into a grand choral. The theme seemed to express thanksgiving to the Most High for deliverance from death. The harmony was sublime and the voices powerful and melodious beyond aught I ever heard from human lips. As I stood on this lonely rock in this unknown sea, surrounded by this human throng whose forms presented the highest types of manly beauty and whose faces displayed naught but the nobler attributes of the soul, as I listened to those sweet and majestic voices whose choral song rolled in waves of harmony o'er the deep, it seemed as if I were in the presence of beings of another world. The tide of my emotions overcame my weakened frame, staggering to the spot where lay my wounded companion, I sank down. The young man rushed forward with a loud cry and clasped me in his arms, my senses suddenly gave way and I fell prostrate in a swoon.

CHAPTER V.

THE DOCTOR.

"This is your devoted friend, Sir ; the manifold linguist."
    All's Well that Ends Well.—Act IV. Sec. 3.

When I recovered my senses I was lying on a bed and clad in the habiliments of an invalid. John was by my side bathing my face and hands.

"Thank God !" he fervently murmured. " Dear Cap'n

Fred. Do you know me?" and tears stood in his eyes. I could only reply with a feeble pressure of his hand ; my lips were dry and I was parched with thirst. John gently raised my head and gave me a drink of cool water ; in a few moments I felt refreshed.

"There now ; dear Cap'n Fred begin to lookee like himself. Me feel so muchee proud happy to see that."

" What's happened to me ?—What makes me so weak ?"

"Muchee bad luck, Cap'n Fred ; you been terrible sick, long time, twenty-one days," counting his fingers.

"Good heavens ! Is it possible ?"

" Yes, indeed. Terrible fever allee time. No sleepee, no eatee, most gone die.—If dear Cap'n Fred die, poor John die too."

I was greatly astonished to hear this. I looked at my hands, they were white and thin, I looked around the room ; it was a commodious apartment, the walls and ceiling of a bluish color. There was a cot, a table, a few chairs of red and yellow wood and peculiar shape. In one corner stood an upright cylinder of metal communicating an agreeable warmth ; on the opposite side of the room were two windows ; a fresh sea breeze wafted through the lattice, mingled with the bright and cheerful rays of the sun. On a small table near by were glasses ; spoons and what seemed to be a medicine case.

" Where are we ? What place is this ?" I asked.

" On small island in middle of sea. Canno say where, —must be near south pole.—Muchee strange peoples around here, some with face like shiny brass, some red like Indians, some blue like indigo ; talkee such queer lingo. O Cap'n Fred, so many strange things. Me feel muchee troubled ; seems as if we had fallen on

Rienga land([1]) since was tumbled out of ice berg on little rock long way from here."

" The ice cavern !" and I shuddered as the dim recollections of that living grave came over me like the fragments of some dreadful dream. " My ship, my comrades, David, where are they ?"

John bowed his face on his hands, sobbing like a child.

" O dear Cap'n ; a'most break me heart, when tellee you. Poor David he die next day after we came here in little boat. Good doctor try hard to save him, but canno do it. Everybody so kind. Poor David lie in little grave yard outside. No news from ship, muchee 'fraid we never see her no more."

At this dreadful news I sank back, overcome with grief and despair.

" O dear Cap'n, please no thinkee 'bout that ; makee you feelee so bad ; must thinkee 'bout own's self, and nothing else, so can gettee well right soon."

" How long were we shut up in the ice cavern ?"

" Four weeks."

" The watch ran down, how did you calculate time ?"

John produced a small pine stick covered with notches. " When sun come round in front of ice cave, me see little light shine through cracks, then cuttee notch for day ; when go around behind, all gettee dark. When come round again can see light, that be another day ; then cuttee another notch. Hab cuttee one notch every day since," handing me the stick.

We had entered the cabin on the 1st Dec. 1891. There were twenty eight notches on one side, and twenty four on the other. To day was therefore 22nd

([1]) A fabled land of Enchantment in New Zealand Mythology.

Jan'y, 1892, fifty three days had passed since we left the ship.

"Guess Cap'n Fred can settee watch all right now. Sun go all around sky just like cork screw ;([1]) when he gettee up high, that be noon, when sinkee down, that be midnight," said John, as he opened a closet, took out my chronometer and handed it to me : it seemed to be in good order.

"Look at the sun and when it reaches meridian, let me know," said I, winding up the watch. John opened the lattice, the sun shone full in the room and was steadily ascending—after a few moments,—

"Sun tip-top-high in the sky," said he. I set the hands at the hour of 12 M. and lost time was restored at the south pole.

"Handsome young gentleman what Cap'n Fred pullee out of sea 'afore shark eatee him up. O Cap'n,— you be bravest gentleman in this world, any how. He bring old yellow face man, muchee big doctor, so kind,—takee good care of you allee time."

"Where is the doctor ?"

"In next room."

"Call him in : I would like to thank him."

John left the room and in a few minutes returned accompanied by a man of advanced years and clad in a long grey robe ; his silver hair flowing to his shoulders. He was below the middle stature, of slender form, bright orange complexion, refined and intellectual expression of countenance.

"This is the good doctor,—Cap'n," said John withdrawing respectfully aside.

The doctor approached with a dignified salutation,

([1]) The apparent course of the sun around the pole is in a spiral, like a screw.

took a seat by my side, fixed on me his keen eyes, felt my pulse, looked at my tongue, according to the usual professional style, nodded his head with a satisfied look, then taking a small vial from the medicine case, poured a few drops of a ruby colored liquid in a medicine glass of water, and presented it to me. I drank it. In a few moments the potent medicament seemed to penetrate my veins like a draught of wine and new strength was infused into my weakened frame. The doctor viewed the change with manifest pleasure, then made a sign to John, who hurried out and brought in a steaming bowl of nourishment and proceeded to feed me, his eyes glistening with pleasure as I appropriated one spoon full after another. It tasted like some peculiar kind of bouillon rich and palatable, and I took a goodly supply. This concluded, he arranged the pillows so that I could sit up, and the doctor addressed me in a kind and gentle voice as follows.

" *Jana-yuvan.   Atmuja samtanasya aryuna : mahyam brafi lathilam tava.*"(¹)

In these words I recognized that same unknown tongue I had heard in the grand choral sung on the rocky ledge.

" Doctor wish talkee with you, Cap'n ;" said John.

" So I perceive, but I'm sorry to say I don't understand a word of his language."

" Doctor no speakee English. He be foreigner, I reckon."

"Yes ; he appears quite foreign."

" Cap'n can speakee muchee foreign lingo. S'pose you try him on that."

If there was any one thing on which I prided myself

(¹) " Young man, son of the earth born race, speak to me in your native language."

more than another, it was my linguistic acquirements. I had a natural gift for that line of study from youth and my travels in foreign countries had largely facilitated my attainments in that direction ; I could converse with tolerable fluency in nearly all the European languages, some of the Asiatic, and also the classics ; so bracing myself up, I began.

"*Bon jour, Monsieur, comment vous portez vous ?—Parlez vous Français ?*"

"*Buenos dias, Señor ; come lo pasa ? Habla usted Español ?*"

"*Buon giorno. Come sta questa mattina ? Parlate Italiano ?*"

"*Guten morgen, mein Herr ; wie befinden Sie sich ? Sprechen sie Deutsch ?*"

"*Taler de Dansk ?*"—"Do you speak Danish ?"

"*Taler herrn Svenski ?*"—"Do you speak Swedish ?"

"*Spreekt gij Hollandsch ?*" — "Do you speak Dutch ?"

"*Gavaritji la we pa Russki ?*" — "Do you speak Russian ?"

The Doctor smiled and bowed negatively.

"Doctor no understand white gentleman's lingo— never travelled abroad I reckon. He hab yellow skin. 'Spose Cap'n try him on lingo what yellow faced peoples talkee."

"All right ; I'll try him on Turkish, Persian, Arabic and Hindustanee."

Then addressing the Doctor with the usual salutations of those races.

"*Waktinez kair olsum. Mazage sherif ? Seuilemisin Turkjah ?*"

"*Dumaughi shuman chauk est ? Ahwauli koosh est ?*"

"*Sabah alchire ya sidi. Allah yosallimak. Salaam aleikoum, Hal tatacallam lisan Bilcarabi ?*"

" *Tum hari kya halat nai ? Tum kaum ho ?   Tum Hindus-tanee bol sukte ho ?*"

But the doctor seemed no wiser than before.

"He no Turk,—no Arab,—no Hindoo gentleman,—'Spose Cap'n try him on dead lingo."

" What do you mean by dead lingo ?"

" What school gentlemans learn in college book, and talkee big proud to makee grand show of lingo learning and mystify, but never talkee in business, nor makee love by, nor swear by."

" Your definition of the ancient classics is quite original and not far from the truth, so I'll try him on Latin, Greek and Hebrew." Then addressing the Doctor with a scholastic flourish—

" *Salve domine ! Quomodo te habes ? quid tibi nomen est ? Sciesne Latine ?*"

" *O chaire Kyrie ! Pos echeis ? Ti soi onoma estin ? Hellenisti ginoskeis ?*"

" *Shalom leka adoni ! Hashalom lak ? Mah shimka ? Hayadatta shephath ever ?*"

The doctor shook his head emphatically.

" Humph !" muttered John. " He never been to college, no how."

The doctor now rose from his chair, took from his pocket an elegant little card case, opened it and drew out a small card on which was engraved strange looking characters totally unlike the letters or symbols of any language, living or dead, known on earth ; then tapping his chest significantly, and handing the card to me—

" Therios zar Hamival," said he.

Comprehending that he was announcing his name, I took a pencil and wrote my signature on the back of the card and handing it to him—

" Frederick Hamilton, at your service," said I.   The

Doctor looked at the signature with much curiosity, turning the card upside down, etc. then shook me warmly by the hand.

By this time I was quite exhausted and threw myself back on the pillow. The doctor gave me another dose of his tonic which revived me considerably, then going to the door, opened it and a young man of medium stature, bright red complexion, broad forehead, strongly marked features and remarkably penetrating eyes, entered the room.

" Phero zar Hypnotos," said the Doctor introducing him. The young man bowed, sat down by my side, and taking both my hands in his, fixed his brilliant eyes on mine. In a few moments I began to feel a wonderfully magnetic and soothing influence·creeping over me. I knew that he was a magnetizer, and feeling some apprehension, endeavored to resist his powerful influence, but in vain ; his gaze seemed to penetrate my very soul and my will was held captive ; indescribable sensations passed through my frame. The magnetizer now gently placed his right hand on my forehead. I suddenly became benumbed and sank into insensibility.

CHAPTER VI.

COMMODORE JACK.

" In there stepped a stately raven, of the saintly days of yore."
POE.

When I awoke, John was by my side ; his face had a puzzled and somewhat anxious look.

" Hi ? me muchee glad to see Cap'n Fred wakee up all right."

"Really," said I, "it seems to me, I've had a good long nap."

"Indeed you hab, Cap'n. Two days and nights, right strait, just like little babby when mamma give 'em paregoric."

"Good gracious, John ; why didn't you wake me up long ago ?"

"Me try, but you no wakee up at all. Muchee queer things going on here. When red face gentleman makee you go sleep, little blind man come in ; muchee funny looking fellow : blue face like indigo, hair white like old Doctor ; he sat by your side, hold your hand,—he sound asleep too,—talkee with you and you talkee with him allee time, O, it was right funny, makee me laugh ; seems to me he learn how talkee English ; muchee queer way for to learn, any how."

I was considerably astonished at this piece of news and expressed myself accordingly.

"You must takee nourishment now. Hab little more soup ?"

"No more soup—I'm hungry, and want something substantial,—let me get up !"

"Hi ! Hi !"—jumping up and down with joy—" Cap'n shall hab nice hot breakfast right off "—then rushed out of the room, gave the order, hurried back and with all the skill and gentleness of a professional nurse, gave me a sponge bath, prepared my toilet and I sat down by the table in an easy chair near the open window and enjoyed the genial sunlight and fresh sea breeze. Two boys of red complexion attired as waiters entered with well laden salvers and laid the cloth ; the service and menu were unique. The dishes, platters, cups, etc. were composed of some brilliant metal and fine porcelain, tastefully decorated with pictures of birds, fruits, flowers, etc. The knives, forks and spoons were of highly polished red, blue and yellow colored metals wholly unknown to me. The food consisted of hot rolls and crisp cakes prepared from some peculiar kind of flour ; a vegetable, resembling the yam ; little fishes baked and broiled ; a singular variety of preserved fruit, with other appetizing viands. A fine flavored beverage resembling Ceylon tea, served from a richly carved breakfast urn ; a pitcher of fresh milk, with several peculiar flavored condiments and spices, but there was no meat, game, nor fowl of any sort on the table.

"Splendid breakfass, Cap'n," said John, with a look of pride. "First class New York hotel canno gettee up half so good."

"Is there no meat market around here ?" I asked.

"Bless your heart, Cap'n, this island be one big solid rock ; no grass, no tree, nothin' but stone houses and peoples what live in 'em."

"But here's fresh milk. They must keep a cow."

"No cow, no horse, no pig, no chicken, turkey, duck, dog, cat, rat, fly, musquito, 'round here. Sea bird fly in sky, big whale swim in sea."

"O, yes, I'd forgotten, we're near the pole."

"Folks in kitchen gettee up breakfass, dinner and supper, muchee queer style. Hab no wood, no coal, no fire."

"How is that ?"

"They put the vittles inside shiny brass box, set little machine a going ;—boil, bake, roast, stew, fry, fricazee all tip top style, in ten minutes."

"What a wonderful saving of worry and tribulation to an anxious housewife ;—how do you communicate your orders to the cook and head waiter ?"

"Me stir em up regular sailor style."

"What's that ?"

"Caboose ahoy! Tumble up there; you lazy lubbers. Bring on your horse tack and be d—d to you !
—Cook no understand, but he hurry up right smart."

John's energetic illustration of his culinary orders
almost paralyzed the red faced waiters with fright and
they slid out of the room.

"Now Cap'n, you must eatee all you can ; nice
breakfass do you heap good ; me be head waiter ;" putting on a white apron.

I donned my napkin, drew my chair up to the table,
when a gentle tapping was heard at the door and a deep
sepulchral voice croaked out—

"Corp?"

"That's the Commodore," said I.

"Yes, Cap'n ;—had to lock Jack out, while you was
sick, he makee terrible fuss ; cry allee time just like
poor little babby. Reckon he want to say good mornin'
to Cap'n."

"I had no idea the Commodore loved me so well ;
invite him in."

John opened the door and in marched Jack with
measured and stately step, like Poe's raven ; advanced
leisurely toward us, hopped on the back of a chair,
arranged his plumage, made a dignified bow, cocked
his head knowingly to one side and winked at me with
his sharp black eye—

"Good mornin', Cap."

"Good morning ; Commodore. I'm delighted to see
you. How are you ?"—holding out my hand.

"All ri—" he replied, standing on one leg, seized my
hand in his iron claw with a grip like a blacksmith's
vice.

"Cap, sick ?"

"Have been, so they say, quite ill. But I'm getting all right now."

"Hurray!—Hurray! Never say die," flapping his wings and uttering a rousing crow.

"Hope to have the pleasure of your company at breakfast, Sir," said I.

"All ri—," and Jack flopped to the edge of the table, squinting his eye around the menu with the air of a connoisseur.

"Let me help you to some soup, Commodore," dipping out the consommé into a plate.

"Slops," sneered he.

"What will you have, Sir?"

"Rats;"—with great emphasis.

"I regret to say, there's none on the bill of fare."

"Blast my eyes!" then after a pause, glancing around the table—

"Horse tack.—Hurry up!" snapping his iron beak.

John tied a napkin around the Commodore's neck, filled his plate liberally and set it before him; taking his fork in his claw, he carefully selected and appropriated the nice tit bits, with all the genteel decorum of an extra-superfine gourmand, wiping his beak with his napkin and sustaining a lively table talk with his host. Breakfast concluded.

"Now Commodore, will you take a nice hot cup of tea:—chocolate,—glass of milk?"

"Dish water,"—with great disdain

"What will you have to drink?"

"Glass o' grog."(¹)

"No grog 'round here, Jack," said John.

"D—n lie."

"Hab no grog since we left ship; Cap'n Fred and me be temperance, now."

(¹) Sailors often teach monkeys, ravens, etc. to drink grog and smoke a pipe.

"D—n yer eyes !—you're a hog.—Glass o' grog.—
H—ll of a row.—Fact, d—d if 'taint.—Dish water.—All
ri—. Stingy cuss.—Devil's to pay.—Hurray !—Rats !
Rats !—Rats !"—screeched the Commodore, jumbling up
his expletives pell-mell,—tearing off his napkin,—scattering the dishes right and left,—dashed over the table,
—grabbed up half a dozen spoons in his claws and
sped out the window.

"By Jingo ! Old Commodore go pawn 'em for
drinks,"—said John, then touching a bell, the waiters
entered and cleared the cloth ; he then opened a closet
and to my great joy, drew out my nautical instruments,
charts, uniform, fire arms, etc., which he had saved
from the boat wreck.

"Me pick 'em all up when was blown out on rock ;—
shiny up little tools t'other day." The instruments
were in good order. He then brought out my pocket
cigar case, which, with many other little articles left on
board the ship were parting gifts from my dear sister
Madeleine. It was filled with choice regalias selected
by her own fair hand. My eyes filled with tears as I
looked at them.

"Takee a little smoke, Cap'n ; Do you heap good,"
said John, striking a match. I lit a cigar and enjoyed
the fine flavor.

"Where's the Doctor ?" I asked.

"In next room, with young blind man."

"Say to them I should be happy to see them."

"Me no talkee, me makee motion.—Walkee in,
gentlemens, Cap'n Frederick muchee 'bliged for to see
you "—and he opened the door.

CHAPTER VII.

THE MIND READER.

"It is the soul itself which sees and hears, and not those parts which are, as it were, but the windows to the soul."

CICERO.

Doctor Hamival entered with a young man of extraordinary personal appearance. He was below the medium stature, of slender form, large and intellectually developed head covered with a profusion of snow white hair. His complexion was a bright blue, his features delicate, the expression pleasing and good humored. He was blind and his sightless eyes had a pathetic look : he was clad in plain attire, like that of a student. The Doctor greeted me cordially, seeming pleased at my improved personal appearance, but opened his eyes somewhat at sight of my cigar, which John laid carefully aside. The young man advanced as I arose, bowed courteously and in a gentle voice :

"Lieutenant Hamilton, I am indeed proud to enjoy the honor of an introduction to you and beg your kind acceptance of my congratulations on your recovery."

"Good heavens !" I exclaimed, "can it be possible that I meet a fellow countryman here ? I am indeed delighted,"—then as I noted his extraordinary colored hair, complexion, etc.—

"Pardon me, Sir—Your peculiar appearance "—

"Doubtless surprises and puzzles you, and I do not wonder ;"—he replied with a pleasant smile. "Permit me to introduce myself. My name is Ascopion zar Vidyumat and I belong to what is called the Nilata, or blue race. This gentleman," turning to the doctor, "is

Therios zar Hamival, of the Arunga, or yellow race.
He is one of our most eminent physicians; holding a
distinguished rank among the medical profession of
our country,—the name and situation of which, however, I am not permitted at present to make known to
you. When you and your wounded companion were
brought here from the little rocky island,—where you
so bravely rescued from imminent death one very
dear to us all, you were seized with a severe inflammation of the brain and for a long time your life hung on a
thread. But Dr. Hamival's skill and devoted attention
were the means, under God, of saving your life."

Recovering somewhat from my astonishment at hearing this remarkable looking young man,—belonging to
a race wholly unknown on earth, conversing in my
native language, I replied,—

"Will you do me the favor, Sir, and convey to Dr.
Hamival my sincere thanks for his great kindness, and
my high appreciation of his medical skill."

Ascopion spoke to the doctor, evidently translating
to him my words, and the doctor replied with a courteous expression of thanks to me.

"I will now briefly inform you," continued Ascopion,
"the process by which I have acquired your language.
I am what is called a Mind reader. Many in my country possess this gift. I was brought here two days
ago, when you were thrown into what you would call
the mesmeric sleep by my friend, Phero Zar Hypnotos,
who is one of our most distinguished mesmerists or
magnetizers as you call them—although we employ
quite a different word to express the phenomena, I was
then thrown by him into the mind reading trance. I
took my station by your side, and occupied the whole
time in reading your mind and memory, studying out
your language, in other words, your vocal method of

expressing your thoughts and ideas. I have now become thoroughly acquainted with it, and shall be most happy to officiate as interpreter between yourself and our friends here."

I had occasionally witnessed a few experiments in what is called mind reading by self styled professors of mesmerism, psychology, etc., but this wonderful exhibition of his power in acquiring my language within forty eight hours considerably surprised me.

"While you were studying my language," said I, "did you ascertain any thing else relating to me,—my race, country, or how I came here?"

"I did not; I was occupied solely in acquiring your language; I know nothing of your race, your nationality, whence you came, or how you arrived here. Our friends were perfectly astonished when they found you on the little rock in the midst of this great ocean around us. During the delirium of your illness you talked of many things, but none of us understood your language. Your companion intimated by signs that you had come from some far distant country to the north. Will you kindly inform us who you are and where you came from?"

"I am a citizen of the United States of America and an officer in the U. S. Navy."

Ascopion translated my announcement. The doctor spoke a few words to him, and he replied.

"Doctor Hamival requests me to say that we know nothing whatever concerning the country you speak of."

"Can it be possible that you have never heard of the greatest and most glorious Republic on the face of the Earth, whose name is honored in every land and whose Star Spangled Banner floats over every ocean on the globe?"

" We regret to say, we have not."

" Nor of Christopher Columbus,—World's Fair,—Democratic party ?"

" We grieve to announce, we never have."

" Nor of Washington afternoon teas and the New York four hundred ?"

" We are very sorry indeed," he replied with an expression of intense interest, as I announced these latter objects of such vital importance among our superfine kid gloved *haut ton.*

" Good heavens !" I involuntarily exclaimed. " What stupendous ignorance !"

" Hi," giggled John, " these folks ain't a bit fashionable, no how."

These statements seemed so outrageously incredible, I concluded he and the doctor were indulging in a little pleasantry or were trying to deceive me for purposes of their own, and I determined to ascertain the truth if possible, by a test which I thought would be satisfactory.

" You say that I was in the mesmeric sleep and you in the mind reading trance, when you acquired my language ; are you in that trance now ?"

" No, I am in my normal wide-awake state as you all are."

" Well, if you are out of the trance, how can you possibly read my mind ?"

" The ice once broken, I can read your mind as easily while out, as in the trance."

" That is quite beyond the abilities of any mesmerized or clairvoyantized subject I ever heard of. They can only manifest the power while in the clairvoyant trance ; when out of it, and in their normal state, they are wholly unable to do so."

" The powers of our clairvoyants are not limited that

way,—the mind once read, can be always, and at any time, read, for a month to come."

" Really, do you pretend to say that you are able to read my thoughts ?"

" Pardon me, my dear sir. I make no pretence about it, I simply say that I can read your thoughts on any subject you may choose to think about.

" Tell me, what I am thinking about, this moment."

Ascopion laid his delicate hand gently on my forehead and fixed his sightless eyes on mine. Their glance was mysterious,—indescribable,—almost terrible, —for a moment I felt almost unnerved,—then withdrawing his hand—

" You are thinking of a ship," said he.

This was the fact, and I was not a little staggered at his announcement of it.

" And of her name also ;" he continued.

" What name ?"

" The Albatross."

" True, but I may have uttered that name in the delirium of my illness, and any quick witted person could connect it with a ship, so this, after all, may be merely a species of probability gymnastics, or a lucky guess on your part."

"Thanks for your compliment, Sir," he replied with some little hauteur.

Although somewhat nettled at this polite rebuke, I felt that it was not quite undeserved ; nevertheless, I determined to continue my test ; then turning to John—

" Have you ever spoken, or intimated by signs, or otherwise, to any one here, anything about ourselves, or our ship ?"

" No indeed, Cap'n Fred. Me no gabble 'bout private business to no body,—know heap better than that, no body gettee anything out o' me, no how," he replied emphatically.

I was quite satisfied with John's discretion in the matter, then, to Ascopion—

" Have you ever seen or heard of my ship ?"

" Do blind persons see ships with their bodily eyes ? I never heard of your ship until this moment."

" If, as you say, I am thinking about a ship, I must have some sort of a picture of her in my mind."

" So you have ; that is the way with all mental operations with reference to natural objects. They are presented as pictures before the eye of the mind and the accuracy of those pictures depends upon the clearness and precision of the mind. There is a very great difference between minds in that respect."

" Can you perceive that picture in my mind ?"

" I perceive it perfectly with the eye of my own mind ; in other words, my spiritual eye."

" In that case you should be able to give a description of what you see."

" Certainly ; and if it pleases you, I will do it."

" It will please me, greatly," I replied.

Ascopion paused a few moments as if in deep thought, then slowly, as if observing in detail—

" I see pictured in your mind what you call a brig rigged screw steamer, seven hundred tons burden and five hundred horse power, built evidently for a polar voyage. She is encased with steel sheathing, fully supplied with all the necessary equipments, has a crew of thirty seamen, officers, engineers, surgeon. Her prow is ornamented with a carved image of an albatross ; one of her, wings broken off, has lost three of her anchors, —appears to have passed through a severe storm, and many parts of her hull are battered as if from blows of ice masses. On her stern in gilt letters, is inscribed her name, The Albatross. You are now thinking of her commander ; his name Captain William Anderson, a relative of yours, great uncle,—a first class sailor. You are now thinking of a glacier, an ice cavern, you and two men shut up there. But this is foreign to the subject. Well, Sir, is my description correct ?"

" Perfectly correct in every particular," I replied, thoroughly astonished.

" Now, if you like, I will show you something better than this, and much more satisfactory to you. I am blind, as you perceive,—was born so, consequently my ideas of light, color, shade, form, dimensions, distance, etc., of all material objects, are—as in the case with blind persons—entirely different from those who are blessed with vision. Your ideas about all these things are derived by means of your senses of sight and touch, aided also, by hearing. Mine are derived by touch alone. Now, I am something of an artist, and I will make a sketch of your ship drawn from your mind, as you last saw her, if agreeable to you."

Here, surely was a test offered which would have thoroughly satisfied any committee of examiners in the mysteries of mesmerism or psychology and I gladly accepted it. Dr. Hamival placed a large sheet of drawing paper and different colored crayons before him on the table.

" And in order that you may be thoroughly satisfied as to the impossibility of any trick or deception on my part," continued he, " I request you to have my eyes blindfolded."

John wrapped a pair of handkerchiefs around his eyes, and drew his sailor's woolen cap completely over his head.

" Hi ! Me reckon you canno see through this night cap, no how."

"Well, John, ' we'll see about that,' as the blind man says," then—

"Are you all ready, Lieutenant ?"

"Yes ; I have a pretty clear picture of my ship, delineated in my mind."

"You must hold it there steadily, and don't let your mind wander from it while I am making the sketch or I shall get things mixed up. Begin at the hull, then go up to her deck, then to her masts, rigging and other appointments,—officers, crew, surroundings, etc. and any other necessary details in regular order, as I progress."

"All right."

Ascopion drew the sheet before him, took up his crayons one by one, making the sketch,—filling up details, color, light, shade, etc. his hand swiftly flying over the paper. I watched with breathless interest ; all at once he paused.

"Please go on," said I.

"Your mind is wandering from the subject."

"Indeed, how do you know that ?"

"You are thinking of a big hotel,—a church,—menagerie,—a mill pond,—a base ball game,—a tea party,—a naval review,—an iceberg five hundred feet high—and a national convention, considerably mixed up. Do your polar navigators usually carry that sort of freight on board ship ? If so, I'll put them all on deck, but it strikes me there'll not be much room left for your crew."

This was the fact ; I had purposely allowed my thoughts to wander off on those subjects merely to test his powers and I felt rather cheap at being detected in it.

"Please keep your wandering thoughts on board ship where they belong, at least for the present, till I get through ; then you are at liberty to wander on fancy's wing where'er you please."

"All right, I'll never give up the ship," and I stuck close to the Albatross.

Ascopion's hand flew over the paper with amazing speed, snatching up and throwing down the crayons one by one, without making a single mistake or erasure. In less than thirty minutes he completed what would have required at least four hours unremitting labor by the hand of the most rapid and skilful artist I ever knew, then presenting it to me :

" How do you like the picture ?"

To say that I was perfectly astounded, is a weak expression. Here was my ship, every detail from stem to stern, from keel to topmast, delineated with the accuracy of a photograph, as I last saw her moored up near the glacier, the steam pouring from her funnel, her figure-head the Albatross, with broken wing. The stars and stripes streaming from her foretop mast. Captain Anderson and officers on the quarter deck, her crew on the forecastle or scattered among the rigging, watching our party passing across the glacier. The delineated figures were necessarily so minute I examined them with my pocket microscope. They were drawn and colored to the life. Over head was a polar sky, the sun hanging low in the horizon. In front was the great glacier, and the sea, with its scattered floes ; in the distance loomed up the great icebergs.

John, who had watched the performance with open mouthed amazement, whispered in my ear.

" Cap'n ;—he be terrible witch man."

The cap and handkerchiefs were removed, the doctor now resumed conversation, Ascopion acting as translator.

" Well, Lieutenant," he asked. " What's your opinion of our friend's mind reading and picture making abilities ?"

" I never dreamed it possible that any human being could be endowed with such powers," I replied. " It seems almost like a miracle."

" This is working, so to speak, on the surface of the mind only. We have experts in our country who pos- sess far greater powers and can make far deeper re- searches in the mind. Who can find out everything about a person's whole life, who can fathom the whole mental and moral character, all its proclivities and tendencies toward good or evil, virtue or vice, truth or falsehood. Who can find out every secret thought, desire or act, done any time in the past, or proposed to the mind for the future. In short, can turn the whole man inside out as it were, and disclose him to the world."

As I reflected upon this tremendous psychological power, before whose infallible search, " nothing is secret that shall not be made manifest ; nothing is covered that shall not be revealed and whatever is spoken in darkness shall be heard in the light ;"(1) as a prophecy, that might,—in the not far distant future, be fulfilled to the letter, by the cultivation and advancement of psychological science among us terrestrians, I realized how exceedingly useful such a mode of inquest might be to the world in general and society in particular, although many high-toned members might seriously object to having their moral closets overhauled in this style.

But leaving that class out, if we turn to what are called the lower orders of humanity, who generally do their wicked things open and above board, and don't care to steal the livery of heaven to serve the devil in, the

(1) St. Luke viii. 17, xii. 22.

establishment of such a psychological tribunal would be highly valuable in many ways. The whole paraphernalia of our criminal courts, with their judges, juries, lawyers, witnesses, police detectives, etc., might be dispensed with, and there would be no courts, except for adjudicating equity or punishment ; all dishonesty, hypocrisy and lying would be worse than useless, the rogues, cheats, swindlers and criminals would not only be instantly detected, but compelled to confess their evil intentions beforehand.

At this moment one of the servants entered and spoke a few words to the Doctor.

"Lieutenant Hamilton," said he, "a distinguished visitor has arrived whom you will doubtless recognize," then to the servant—

"Admit His Highness."

CHAPTER VIII.

PRINCE ALTFOURA.

"A combination and a form indeed,
Where every god did seem to set his seal,
To give the world assurance of a man."
Hamlet, Act iii. Sc. 4.

The door opened and the young man whom I had rescued from the sea, entered the room. Even amid that terrible scene, as he lay senseless on the rock, I was struck with his appearance ; now, I was highly impressed with his distinguished air and princely bearing. He was of tall stature and his form a perfect model of manly beauty. His countenance was the most remarkable I ever beheld in man. His features were exquisitely moulded and their expression lofty, ingenuous, and engaging. His dark and beaming eyes were perfect mirrors of a pure and noble soul : their expression was wonderful. A monarch would have coveted their look of imperial command. A despot would have sold his sceptre for the magnetic power of that glance, which could detect a foe, unmask a hypo- crite, or overawe a savage, and with it, was a look of winning gentleness, a queen might have envied. His lustrous purple hued hair was tinged with a sheen of resplendent gold and hung in heavy masses down his shoulders. He was clad in a close fitting dark gray jacket and falling collar decorated with brilliant insigniæ, indicating his rank ; gray trousers and high boots reaching to the knee. A ruby of resplendent lustre, cut in the shape of a human heart and sur- rounded with a glittering cluster of star shaped dia- monds and emeralds, was suspended on his breast. He wore a black plumed chevalier hat and a short dark blue mantle over his shoulder : His whole appear- ance and bearing, would have elicited the greatest admiration among the proudest courts of Europe. We all arose as he advanced with quick and graceful step.

"Altfoura Yuvaraja Thullivarrh, Basileus Mandal-Uttima,"[1] said the doctor, making the ceremonial intro- duction which was translated by Ascopion. The eyes of the Prince sparkled with animation and his counten- ance was wreathed with a bright smile. He clasped my hand, placed it on his forehead, thence to his breast, with a graceful gesture.

[1] Altfoura Raja Thullivarrh, Prince royal of the kingdom of Mandal Uttima.

"With what pleasure do I salute you, my preserver. Accept, I pray you, my sincere congratulations and my heartfelt wishes for your speedy restoration to health," which was translated by Ascopion.

I responded to the Prince's salutation in terms as polite as I could command.

"His highness has been a constant attendant at your bedside," said the doctor ; "manifesting the greatest anxiety during your dangerous illness."

"At the risk of his own life, and after a desperate battle, he rescued me from the sea and the shark," the Prince replied. Then turning to me, his countenance glowing with gratitude :

"Lieutenant Hamilton, to your intrepid courage and devotion I owe my life, not that I prize it so much for its own sake, but for the sake of my kindred and friends, who love me. From what grief and despair you have saved them and what a debt of gratitude we owe to you, that can never be repaid."

"Honored Prince," I replied, "I beg you not to speak of obligation. I am only too proud to have been able to render you any service."

"From this hour," continued he in tones of deep feeling—"you are knit to me in friendship's most sacred ties. Receive, I pray you, this slight token of my gratitude and esteem,"—and the Prince removing the jewelled ruby from his breast, placed it around my neck ; then calling John, he pinned a splendid medal on his breast. "Wear this in behalf of my companions, whose lives you bravely rescued," said he, as the poor fellow in the excess of his admiration and delight, dropped on one knee and kissed the hand of the Prince.

We sat down and engaged in conversation, Ascopion interpreting. I gave a full narration of my voyage, and the incidents connected with it. I also described the efforts of former navigators to explore these inaccessible regions.

"Enclosed within these icy barriers," said the Prince, "our people have had no definite knowledge of the great world beyond. We have believed however, that it is inhabited by great and populous nations, highly advanced in power and civilization. Your presence among us confirms it. Can you not favor us with a short description of your world ?"

I briefly described its countries, races and nations, enlightened, civilized, and barbarous ; the wealth, power, progress, and wonderful achievements of the dominant white race. The different forms of government and wound up with an enthusiastic eulogium on my native land, the greatest and happiest republic on the face of the globe, to all which my audience listened with absorbing interest, expressing their astonishment at my recital. I then asked the Doctor to explain the extraordinary phenomena connected with my rescue on the rocky ledge. The burning ice bergs and terrible explosions. "To tell you the truth," said I, "my comrades and I thought the end of the world was at hand."

"We had a little fire ship cruising around this polar sea," he replied, "and the Captain was instituting a few experiments in the way of destroying ice bergs," etc.

"Your mode of accomplishing it is certainly wonderful and unknown to any other nation." I then described the mysterious sounds heard in the ice cavern and the breaking loose of our berg from its connection with the shore.

"Our vessel was cutting a channel through a glacier at that point. As your berg floated down the current it fortunately was not set on fire or blown up in common with the others ; had such an accident happened we should not now be enjoying the pleasure of your company."

"Very fortunate, otherwise we should have been blown to atoms or boiled alive. Please explain how we were saved from such a catastrophe and how the sixty foot thick roof of our icy dungeon was split off over our heads as by the axe of the Norse God, Thor?"

"As your berg rolled down the current, our ship fired a shell at it."

"That lucky shell did excellent service; tore off the roof, upset the berg and threw us out on the rock in the nick of time. Pray inform me your object in cutting this channel?"

"To make a direct communication with the great open sea lying beyond to the north."

"I fear you will find it impossible. Your channel, cut in the summer, will freeze up during the long winter. These great icy and rocky barriers, extend in a circle of ten thousand miles around the pole and reaching nearly fifteen hundred miles beyond it."

"We are aware of this; still, we do not despair of finally overcoming these obstacles. The operations of our fire ship have been suspended for the present. When they are resumed, you will have an opportunity of witnessing them."

In a few days I was able to go out. My first visit was to the grave of my shipmate David, which had been prepared by the kindness of the Prince. It was hewn in the solid rock and surrounded with a railing. At the head was a plain slab of stone on which had been engraved by one of the workmen under John's directions, this simple inscription.

To the Memory of DAVID ROBERTS,
1st mate of the ship Albatross.
Aged 30 years.
The first discoverer of the Antarctic Polar Sea.

"We tried hard to save your brave shipmate," said Altfoura. "But Heaven willed it otherwise." As I knelt by the grave of my departed comrade, tears came to my eyes at the sad thought that, on this cold and barren isle, in this unknown sea, far from home and kindred, poor David's mortal remains had found their last resting place, with no green sod nor tender leaf to deck his lonely tomb.

We had been provided with new clothing made after the pattern of our old suits. The material was a peculiar variety of wool, finer than any cloth made in our factories. The undergarments were softer than silk and woven without seam. The boots and shoes were made of some unknown material, finer and stronger than our best leather. The caps were like those worn by naval officers and sailors. We took frequent walks over the island. With my nautical instruments, I found its position, 82° 45′ South, lat. by 150° West long. or about five hundred miles from the pole. It is about three miles long by a mile wide, of igneous rock, being one of a small group communicating with the southern shore of the so called Antarctic continent which consists of several large islands or continents surrounding the pole and separated from each other by great bays, or inlets, more or less filled up with ice.

The air is pure and bracing, the temperature from 40° to 50° F. Storms and cold winds occasionally visit us but they are always from the north ; the winds from the south, strange as it may seem, are generally warm and pleasant. The island is barren and destitute of vegetation, except moss and lichens such as are indigenous to polar regions and is a great resort for sea-gulls, penguins, etc. who build their nests among the rocks. The waters abound with fish. Our house is large and commodious ; built of the same rock, one story high

and roofed with a metal resembling copper ; no
wood of any kind enters into its construction. It is
warmed by a singularly constructed electric apparatus
and steam ; the culinary operations are conducted by
the same method and the kitchen utensils are of some
unknown metal. It is occupied by the superintendent
in charge of the island and the servants ; men of dark
red or bluish complexions ; two other houses near by,
are occupied by workmen. On the north shore is a
ship house, machine shop, and stone pier. Our diet is
simple and nutritious, consisting of fish and other
articles, before described, which are evidently brought
from a distance, but there is no meat, fowl or game of
any kind. The Prince remained with us several days ;
one evening he announced that he should depart early
the following morning ; in the meantime he would
leave us in charge of the doctor and superintendent
until his return. His departure was mysterious ;
whither he went, or how he was conveyed over this
polar ocean I was not informed, and politeness forbade
me to inquire.

Time passed on. It was now the close of Feb'y. The
sun was gradually descending toward the horizon.
The Antarctic summer was passing away, and soon the
long night of polar winter would begin her dark reign.
In the mean time I had applied myself diligently to
the study of this remarkable language, which is totally
different in its alphabet and grammatical construction
from any other known on earth, and I was astonished
to find that, in respect to majesty and power, beauty
and harmony, elegance and precision, it surpasses
all other languages ancient and modern. In this I was
greatly aided by Ascopion and was soon able to dis-
pense with his clairvoyant translations. John also made
good progress. The books furnished for the purpose

were elegantly bound ; the paper and imprint surpassing any thing of the kind I had ever before seen. Ascopion took his departure early one morning toward the mysterious south, Hypnotos had departed with the Prince.

The mystery surrounding this remarkable people continually deepens in my mind. Their peculiar physical appearance, so different from that of all other races on earth ; their red, yellow and blue complexions, their high civilization and knowledge of science, their cultivated manners, mild and gentle demeanor. This youthful Prince with his noble countenance, splendid physique, manly bearing and polished manners, and presenting in his *ensemble* so striking a contrast with the pampered scions of royalty, who inherit the "Divine right" and tainted blood of their ancestors, many of whom spend their lives in frivolity and pleasure amid the luxuries and corruptions of European Courts. Oft the delirious song of my poor shipmate in the ice dungeon comes to my mind, and that song indeed seems a prophetic realization of what now transpires around me. Oft I ask myself the question. "Who are these mysterious people ? Whence came they ? Where is their country ? Shut up within these narrow confines, separated by these tremendous barriers from the great world beyond. Is their country at the centre of the pole, only five hundred miles distant ? If so, it cannot be larger than the states of New York and Pennsylvania. And their climate ?—according to all known climatological laws the Antarctic pole is certainly the coldest spot on earth, a region of utter desolation, and its confines uninhabited by man or beast." I often asked the Doctor to explain these paradoxes, and also the geographical situation of his country, wherever it might be, and as oft received his courteous, though evasive reply, " Be patient, my friend, when the proper time comes, all these seeming mysteries shall be explained to you."

It was now the 21st.Mch., the autumnal equinox of the Antarctic. The sun had disappeared below the horizon; summer was gone and the long polar winter was at hand. The work shops were closed, the workmen had departed. The superintendent and a few servants only, remained. The circumpolar constellations, Centaur, Argo and Southern cross, with many others not visible in the northern hemisphere, now shone in full effulgence, giving the heavens an incomparable splendor, while the full moon, circling around the horizon for ten days every month, shines in this clear atmosphere with a brilliancy unknown in other parts of the world. The heavens are often illumined by the Aurora Australis which in vastness and splendor wholly surpasses those of the north polar regions.

" As the period of our departure from this island draws near," said Dr. Hamival, " it is necessary for you to go through a preliminary acclimative process in order to be prepared for our climate."

" Is your climate different from this ?" I asked.

" Its atmosphere is quite different in many respects; it contains certain elements and forces not existing here; it also contains a larger proportion of oxygen.

" What !" I exclaimed, " do you mean to say that the atmosphere of your country is so chemically different from the great aërial envelope surrounding the globe ?"

" So much so that it would be highly dangerous for you to be transferred to my country without a previous preparation."

For a moment I was almost stupefied. Said I, " What mystery is this ? In the name of heaven, where is your country that has such an atmosphere as you describe ?"

" Some distance from here, as I have oft told you ;

its character and appearance are quite different from yours."

At this extraordinary announcement a feeling of apprehension and almost of fear came over me.

" The atmosphere of these regions," continued he, "lacks many qualities of our native air, and although we have become more or less acclimated to it, still, it is enervating and depressing to our people. I shall have prepared for you an artificial atmosphere corresponding with our own, and you must take daily inhalations so that you may gradually become accustomed to it, then you can visit my country with safety."

The doctor prepared a generator and reservoir in the house, charged with the chemically prepared air. John and I were provided with respirators and took daily inhalations. The effect was at first quite stimulating, not at all resembling however, that of oxygen, nitrous oxide, or any other exciting gas ; finally that effect passed off and was succeeded by more agreeable sensations. What chemical influence it had, if any, on the blood, or vital processes, I cannot say, but it certainly produced a greater activity of the bodily and mental functions, with increased physical vigor and powers of endurance. One day while we were industriously pulling at our respirators, John said.

" Cap'n, where you thinkee these queer folks live ?"

" That's the very thing that puzzles me. They don't live any where on earth outside the pole ; they cannot live at the pole, for their summer is not warm enough to grow a single blade of grass, and their winter is six months night, with freezing tempests of snow and sleet. They cannot live in the clouds nor on the moon ; consequently I see no other habitation for them except down in the interior of the earth." And in support of this opinion I announced that they might be elbow

cousins to Bulwer's "Vril-ya," or an evolution from
Verne's centre earth anthropoid apes, or astronomer
Halley's hollow globe denizens, or lineal descendants
of the chained Titans under Mount Ætna.

"Hi! Cap'n, if these folks live down there, how do
they gettee outside?"

"Through a great opening at the pole, according to
the theory of Captain Symmes."

"They creep in and out like flies from bung hole of
empty beer barrel?"

"That's the only way they can get in and out."

"Cap'n; be these folks, a going to takee you and me
home with 'em?"

"Highly probable;—we're getting ready for the
transfer."

"Me no wantee go down there, and no lettee you go,
if me can help it."

"Why not?"

"Devils, witches and bad peoples live down there—"
mysteriously.([1])

"They can't be bad peoples, they are so kind and generous;—they can't be witches because they don't ride
on broom sticks, and as for devils—they are altogether
too fine looking, well bred, gentlemanly—"

"Hi! Cap'n Fred, don't you know that sort be the
cunningest devils of all?"

I was constrained to admit the force of John's argument, and that the horned and tailed gentry might
find their compeers even in polite society.

After several days, the doctor having made a careful
physical examination of our lung capacity, respiration,

([1]) According to all South Sea Island mythologies, as well as
the ancient Greek and Roman, the infernal regions are situated
within the interior of the earth.

circulation, etc., announced that we were sufficiently acclimated, could pass muster, and were ready for transfer.

"I am rejoiced to hear it," said I. "These regions are
gloomy enough, and the sooner we're off, the better."

"Humph!" muttered John. "If old yellow face doctor reckon on me and Cap'n Fred a going with him
down big hole under ground, where bad peoples and
devils live, he muchee mistaken. By Jingo!"

---◆---

CHAPTER IX.

THE POLAR AXIS.

"And the well balanc'd world on hinges hung."
Hymn on the Nativity.—MILTON.

On the morning of April 18th, to my great joy the
Prince arrived on the island.

"Good news, Frederick," said he; "I have come to
escort you to my home. The journey is interesting
and you will witness some pleasant scenes on the way."

We hastened to get in readiness, packed our clothing,
instruments, etc., bade adieu to the superintendent, left
the house and walked to the pier, where a small vessel
lay moored. It was about eighty feet long by twenty
abeam, constructed of bright copper colored metal,
and had no masts, sails, nor rigging. Its motor power
consisted of electro-magnetic batteries and propellers;
it was manned with a Captain and crew. We embarked; the vessel got under weigh and sped over the
waters at the rate of twenty miles per hour, directing
her course to the pole about five hundred miles distant.

After several hours sailing I saw with great surprise that, the sea horizon around us,—instead of sinking from view a few miles beyond, as is the case on all other oceans of the world, gradually extended, until 'it stretched out on all sides as far as the eye could see and stars which before were below the horizon, now rose one by one above it ; the sky also, seemed expanded to almost twice its former dimensions.

Although I knew these peculiar phenomena were due to the flattening of the surface at the poles, where the diameter of the earth is twenty six miles less than at the equator, still, the appearance was none the less startling ; there were no waves, surf nor foam, only a slight undulation of the great watery expanse.

This is in consequence of the diminished speed of the earth's rotation, which at the poles amounts to nothing. The electric lights on deck illumined the waters to a great distance around. They abounded with fish and numerous fin-back whales,([1]) cachelots, and other denizens of the polar seas raised their huge heads above water, staring at us in amazement or fled away with loud bellowings. All day we sailed over this silent sea and by nightfall([2]) we moored along side a floating ice berg. Next morning we resumed our journey and by evening had advanced nearly five hundred miles. Soon we reached a small island of igneous rock about three miles square, on which stood two stone houses and a machine shop. We moored up to a pier, debarked and were received by another superintendent and several

([1]) This species of whale are found in the Antarctic seas far larger than at the north pole ; some are nearly ninety feet long, and exceedingly dangerous.

([2]) At the poles, the terms, morning, noon, evening and night are inapplicable. Time is measured not by the sun, but by the chronometer.

assistants, who escorted us to his residence, where we took supper. After a short rest we walked to the shore, where a long vessel of black metal lay moored ; its hull was pierced with port holes. This was the fire ship which had been employed in destroying the ice bergs, etc. The doctor informed me that the operations would be resumed the ensuing spring.

We now passed to a broad, rocky platform extending a long distance out in the waters. Close by, was a low roofed building, evidently a station. The whole surface of the sea was flat and level as a floor, as if a great circular segment of the polar surface had been sliced off. This was due to the flattening of the pole. A short distance in front of the platform was a great circle several thousand feet in diameter where the waters were upheaved in great swelling eddies, revolving and clashing against each other.

During the last few hours of our journey the heavens had been illumined by flashes of the Aurora, which were rapidly increasing until the whole horizon seemed girdled with a cordon of fire, resembling a vast conflagration. Gigantic pillars, columns and spires were shooting up to the heavens all around us. They were crossed by rainbow colored arches, and surmounted by the magnificent auroral clouds. Streamers of all colors flapping like immense banners, and huge fiery cables coiling and writhing like serpents, chased each other from sea to sky, mingled with whirling clouds of crimson flame and black streaks. Flashes of lurid lightning spread a ghastly glare over the sea and it seemed as if we were looking upon a combat of mighty aërial forces and as if we could almost hear

> " The silent tread of phantoms dread
> With banner, spear and flame."

And now the great eddying circle of waters was thrown in a terrible tumult. Huge spouting masses of foam and spray flew high in the air while the billows were lashed and torn as if by the explosions of a submarine volcano. The needle of my compass flew round its pivot as if under the influence of conflicting magnetic forces.

"The Aurora is unusually brilliant to night," remarked the Prince.

"And the polar magnetic streams seem to be in full force," replied Dr. Hamival.

"What is the meaning of that extraordinary phenomena over the sea and the disturbance of my compass?" I asked.

"The south polar axis is exactly in the centre of that boiling circle," replied the doctor, "and the turbulence of the waters is caused by the tremendous energy of the electro-magnetic forces centred there. The earth is a vast solenoid, in other words an immense electro-magnetic battery, and the electric currents running through its crust in a direction parallel with the equator, produce the magnetic phenomena at the poles of which the aurora is the visible manifestation. The disturbance of your compass is produced by the same cause."

"Come, doctor;" interrupted the Prince. "Please defer scientific explanations for the present. Time presses and we must be off;" then addressing the superintendent:

"Signal my Ethervolt car."

"And in the mean time catch me a few of yonder sea-gulls, Mother Cary chickens and penguins, as I wish to stock my aviary;" said the Doctor.

The men ran around the rocks and caught a dozen of these polar birds and stowed them in a basket. The

superintendent fired off a signal rocket which flew high
in air and exploded with a loud report, throwing off
showers of brilliant sparks.

"Here she comes !" said the Prince.

I looked up and saw a little crystal globe swiftly falling through the air like a meteor from the very midst
of the auroral flashes over head. In a few moments
its speed slackened and it gently descended to the tossing waves in the circle, then floated toward us and
paused close to the edge of the platform.

"This is our Ethervolt car," said the Prince.

The shape of the car was parabolic, resembling that of
a pear. It was thirty feet high, by twenty feet wide at
the base, constructed apparently of crystal and brilliant as polished silver. A row of small circular, double
windows ran around its circumference and a circular
door communicated with the interior; a long, slender
metallic staff projected from its summit tipped on the
end with a bright green ball. The car rested lightly
on the water, close to the rocky platform. The door
opened, a young man stepped out and advanced toward
us. He was of slender form, strikingly handsome
countenance and about twenty five years of age. His
complexion was a bright azure of delicate tint, giving
him an almost ethereal appearance ; his expression was
noble and ingenuous, resembling that of the Prince,
who greeted him with the warmth and affection of a
brother. His fine dark eyes had a far off look, like
those accustomed to see long distances in space and
their glance was like that of an eagle.

"Lieutenant," said Altfoura, "I take pleasure in
introducing my friend and fellow classmate, Helios
Zar Asterion, our distinguished polar navigator and
Captain of our Ethervolt car. Asterion, this gentleman is my esteemed friend, Frederick Hamilton,

an officer in the navy of the United States of America, situated about nine thousand miles from here. This is his first visit to these regions ; he has accepted our hospitalities and will be our honored guest."

Asterion's greeting was highly courteous and winning ; his manners were polished and dignified, and I soon discovered that he was a man of extraordinary genius and high intellectual attainments.

" I am indeed proud and happy to meet for the first time one of your favored race, concerning whose power and progress I have been informed," said he ; " and I cannot sufficiently express my admiration of your courage and daring in penetrating these regions."

" Is the car in readiness for our departure ?" asked the Prince.

" It is, your highness ; the Cosmo-magnetic forces are in full power to-night," he replied.

" Well, then, we will get aboard. Come Lieutenant."

" Whither are we bound ?" I asked, feeling some hesitation in going aboard this singular looking craft.

" Bound for home," replied he, then entered the door with Asterion. John had been observing the car with a mingled expression of astonishment, doubt and curiosity. The raven perched on his shoulder, his head almost buried in his feathers, was also watching it with quite a suspicious look.

" Cap'n Fred," whispered John, " don't you gettee aboard that glass balloon no how."

" Really, John, what are you afraid of ?" asked the doctor.

" Me no 'fraid for self, but heap 'fraid for Cap'n Fred. Muchee queer things going on 'round here, me no like 'em."

" Nonsense John ; come get aboard with your raven."

"You please tellee me aforehand where you're going?"

"We wish to give the Lieutenant and yourself a little surprise,—you'll see when you get there; come."

"O me no lettee Cap'n Fred go where you live; you wantee carry him down big hole under ground."

"Pooh! John, we're not going down, we're going up."

"Hi! Up to the moon? Terrible cold place, nobody live there but old man, old woman and dog."

"Bow-wow-wow! Get out!" growled Jack, who had a special spite against dogs.

"We're not going to the moon; we're going higher up than that."

"Up in the sky?"

"Yes."

"Phew! nothin' there, but the stars and heaven; heap long way off."

"We're not going to the stars."

"Where the d—l you peoples live any how? Do you live in heaven?"

"We all hope to go there, surely, some day."

"O me no great hurry to go there just now. 'Fraid canno gettee in. Me heap bad fellow. Old Commodore heap worser. Swear like pirate. Fight like the devil. Doorkeeper no lettee him in no how. Reckon we have to go to bad place."

"Fact. D—d if it ain't," complacently remarked Jack.

The Prince and Asterion now stepped out on the platform.

"Come Frederick; all's ready; get aboard."

"Really, Prince, travellers generally like to know something about their destination before going on a journey."

"Certainly, I thought you knew. Has not the Doctor informed you ?"

" He has not."

" We are bound for the planet Mars."

" The planet MARS !" I almost shouted.

" Of course we are."

" Good God ! have you lost your senses ?"

" I think not, Sir."

" Well then,—are you indulging in a bit of a joke ?"

" No, Frederick, I am in earnest."

For a moment I could not speak. My voice seemed to stick in my throat—finally I gasped out.

" Is Mars your home ?"

" Yes. We're all Martians here, except you and John."

" Martians !" I almost shrieked.

" Martians. To the manor born. Our ancestors dating back countless centuries."

" By Jupiter ! Saturn ! Mercury ! and all the gods of Olympus and Infernus ! how did you ever get here ? On the tail of a comet, or a falling meteorite ?"

" On this little car, and we're going back just now. Come, step aboard."

My brain was in a whirl, I involuntarily shrank back.

" It's only about one hundred million miles from here ; a mere trifle," quietly remarked Asterion.

I could not speak ; an indescribable fear seemed to crawl through every fibre of my frame, my very blood ran cold ; John fell on his knees,—wringing his hands ; his gestures were frantic : " No, no," he cried, the tears rolling down his cheeks. " Dear Cap'n Fred, don't go, for God's sake, don't. You be carried off to witch land, and poor John never see you no more."

At this moment the auroral flashes and flames faded

away like a dissolving phantasm, and the glittering stars again shone in the deep blue vault above.

"Look yonder !" exclaimed Altfoura, pointing to the east, "there lies our world ! our home ! our native land !"

Far, far in the distant horizon, and cradled on the bosom of the deep, appeared the planet Mars. Beautiful and sweet, it lay like some new born god of the Empyrean, throbbing with young and vigorous life. Its rosy beams caressing the waters with a soft radiance, seemed gently to invite me ; the twinkling stars seemed to beckon me : suddenly a brilliant meteor shot across the eastern sky and scattered its showers of bright sparklings over the blushing orb like a halo of glory. It seemed an auspicious omen from the celestial spheres.

"O, thou beauteous gem of night !" I murmured, "I accept thy signal," then to the Prince.

"I'll go with you to yonder new and untried world."

"'Tis a much older world than yours," said he ; "but whether 'tis a wiser or a better one, remains to be seen, and rest assured, my friend, you shall receive from the denizens of Mars a cordial welcome ; commensurate with that honorable distinction which you, as a representative of the younger Earth born race, are entitled to receive."

"All aboard !" said Captain Asterion.

Our baggage and the birds were taken in ; the superintendent bade us *bon voyage ;* John clung to me like a frightened child. We entered the car and the door was shut. It moved lightly over the waters to the centre of the polar axis, swaying to and fro, amid the tossing waves and whirling foam like a chained balloon shaken by the wind, and struggling to be free.

I blush not to say that, on my bended knees I

breathed a prayer for our safety, to the Almighty Framer of the skies, who holds the Universe in the hollow of His hand.

------------◆------------

CHAPTER X.

DEPARTURE FROM EARTH.

"Look how I go ;
Swifter than arrow from the Tartar's bow."
Midsummer Night's Dream.—Act I., Sc. ii.

The interior of the car was a circular room sixteen feet in diameter and twenty feet high ; the walls of a bright-blue color and two feet thick ; the floor of dark-blue metal ; a large circular window in the roof and six small, double sliding windows of transparent crystal, extending around the room ; three were provided with powerful telescopic lenses. A cushioned seat around the room ; beneath it were hampers of provisions, water and extension cots. An air generator and instruments for measuring altitude, speed, temperature, etc., affixed to the walls. A few chairs and centre-table, on which were books, astronomical charts, maps and instruments. The room was lighted by an electric burner and warmed with a calorific apparatus and electric cook-stove. Captain Asterion introduced his two assistants, Bhuras and Vidyuna, young men about his own age and of bright-blue complexions. They were seated near a complex mechanism of highly polished metal communicating with the floor. We took our seats. The raven stepped around the room, closely inspecting every thing with his sharp eye, then paused near the basket of polar birds that were sticking their heads from under the cover. They stared at him and he at them, for several minutes in blank amazement, then in a tone of deep commiseration :

"Poor devils !"

Then flopped up on top of a clock fixed to the wall, arranged his plumage, cocked his head on one side, winked his eye ; then to John :

"Corp ?"

"Well, Jack ?"

"All ri—?"

"I reckon."

"Cock-a-doodle-doo ! Hurray !" Then squatting down like Poe's raven, 'perched and sat, and nothing more.'

"What is the material of this car ?" I asked, passing my hand over the polished walls.

"A peculiar Martian metal called Alektron, lighter than cork, a hundred-fold stronger than steel and possessing remarkable magnetic properties," replied Asterion ; then addressing his assistant :

"All ready. Start the batteries."

Bhuras and Vidyuna moved the levers of the machinery, the green ball on the summit of the staff threw off a shower of electric sparks with a loud snapping sound, enveloping the car like a fiery halo ; it rose slowly and gracefully from the spouting masses of foam, rapidly ascending, and within fifteen minutes attained an altitude of twenty thousand feet in the air. As there was no balloon, such as is employed in aërostatic navigation, I was considerably astonished.

"What mysterious power elevates this car ?" I asked.

"Underneath the floor," replied Asterion, "are the Ethervolt, or anti-gravitation batteries, which generate a peculiar Martian force called Maha-Dunamos. This force is so powerful as entirely overcomes the force of gravity, and elevates our car above the surface of the earth, notwithstanding its weight. I might explain it that, the magnetism of the earth has such a powerful antagonism against that of the batteries it repels or drives the car upward just as a frictional electric machine at first attracts and then repels a pith ball or bit of cotton brought near it."

" Our scientists have no knowledge of any such wonderful power as this," said I.

" Really, I am surprised to hear that. They have something new to learn in the field of terrestrial physics. By the way, you have of course noticed in the orbital revolutions of comets around the sun, that the tail of the comet always keeps away from the luminary. When the comet is approaching the sun, its tail streams out behind ; when it goes around the sun, the tail sweeps around sidewise, and when the comet retreats from the sun, the tail always goes foremost. How do your scientists explain that phenomenon ?"

" Many explanations have been offered, none of which appears to be satisfactory. One is, that the sun at first exerts a powerful attraction on the comet, which, when it arrives close to it, becomes charged or saturated with the solar electricity, and on the well known principle that opposite electricities attract, and similar electricities repel each other, the sun repels or drives the comet's tail away, until it gradually loses that electricity in its journey through space, and is again attracted by the sun and so on. The phenomenon, however, is regarded as one of those many astronomical enigmas, the solution of which is yet unknown."

" And which I shall have the pleasure to explain to you hereafter. And now we come to another subject relating to our mode of interplanetary travel. Your scientists are of course familiar with the theory of the magnetic influences existing between your Earth and ours, and also between the other planets ?"

" The powerful magnetic influence of the sun on his attendant planets is well known," I replied, " but that your planet and ours should sustain any particular magnetic relations with each other is not even dreamed of."

" Is it possible ? Your scientists have a new and untried field teeming with wonderful phenomena awaiting their investigations. Not only our planet and yours, but every member of the solar system is united in one common bond of brotherhood by Cosmomagnetic currents running from one to the other. These currents are generated at the poles of each planet, and flying with immense velocity across the great spaces lying between, join them together in one fraternal bond of union. The currents running between our planet and yours, form a closed circuit connected at the poles. When we make our interplanetary journeys, we always have to start from the poles where the streams are generated and also land on the same places. We cannot start from, nor land upon any other part of the planet. We are now in the return current which is bearing us to Mars ; we can regulate our speed along it at pleasure by our batteries ; when we have reached a certain distance above the earth and are out of its attraction, I will put the car under the full influence of the current and we shall fly at a speed that will surprise you."

We had now ascended six miles and began to experience the usual sensations of fullness about the head, oppression of breathing, etc., caused by the rarity of the air at these high altitudes (¹) Asterion opened the

(¹) The highest recorded balloon ascents are those of the distinguished French aëronaut, Gay Lussac, five miles. Messrs.

valves of the air generator, letting in a supply of fresh air in the room and the electric heater kept it a comfortable temperature. In a few moments we reached the height of twenty miles. The barometer hanging outside one of the windows had run down to nearly two inches.

" The atmospheric pressure which at the surface is about fifteen pounds to the square inch," said Asterion, " is reduced here to less than two ounces. Were any of us outside the car, all the fluids in the body would ooze through the outlets and pores of the skin."

" Which I will illustrate," said the Doctor, then taking one of the penguins out of the basket, and carefully opening one of the double windows to avoid the escape of air, he placed the bird outside. It gave one gasp, the blood oozed from its nostrils, its eye balls burst open, its plumage dripped with blood and its body collapsed like an empty bag. We now ascended with great rapidity.

" What is the estimated height of your terrestrial atmosphere ?" asked Asterion.

" Our astronomers are not agreed on that point. Some place it at about forty-five miles, others at a hundred, or more," I replied.

" How high have we ascended ?" he asked.

" Seventy-five miles," replied Vidyuna, consulting the instrument for altitude.

An aëronaut at this altitude over the United States, could command a view extending from Boston to

Glaisher and Coxwell, in England, 1863, ascended nearly seven miles. Mr. Glaisher almost perished from extreme cold and his companion became insensible from the extreme rarity of the air. Mr. Glaisher was unable to use his hands in order to pull the valve rope, and grasped it with his teeth, letting out the gas and they descended from their perilous situation.

Colorado on the one hand, and Lake Superior to the gulf of Mexico on the other. Long curved lines of light and brilliant flashes now began to appear, springing out of the darkness and shooting around us in various directions, with loud hissings and occasional explosions like distant musketry.

"We are in the region of meteors and must keep a sharp look out to avoid collision ;" said Asterion.

The showers came from all directions, and the idea of running a gauntlet through this aërial artillery, some of which might reduce our car to powder in an instant, was not pleasant to contemplate.

"How do you avoid collision?" I asked Asterion who was affixing an instrument resembling a photographic camera to one of the windows and arranging the lenses and plates.

"I photograph their approach and lines of curvature on the plates and calculate accordingly. By checking, or accelerating our speed, can get out of their way. I don't mind the small meteorites, but the large ones might injure the car by collision."

The assistants now paid close attention to the machinery, regulating the course and speed of the car during her passage through the meteoric shower, as a mariner carefully steers his ship through an ice floe.

"Here comes a big fellow right ahead," said Asterion, who had been closely watching through the window. "Check off the batteries."

Vidyuna and Bhuras moved the levers and the car stopped. Asterion looked through his camera.

"I have calculated its curve ; it will pass by about half mile to the left."

The next moment a great glare of light streamed in the windows. We looked out and watched the swift approach of the aërial monster. Its terrible appearance, would have made the stoutest heart quail. It was a huge blazing mass of white hot metal or rock, big as the pyramid of Cheops, and with a fiery train at least twenty miles long. It flew by with the rush and roar of a hundred railroad trains. In a few seconds it exploded in the far distance. The sky was illumined with showers of sparkling fire, and our car rocked as if on the waves of a stormy sea.

"The speed of that meteorite was five hundred miles a minute," said Asterion. "It is a wise provision of nature that such huge masses burst to fragments or are consumed to ashes while passing through the atmosphere, else had it fallen in any of your terrestrial cities, imagine the frightful scene."[1]

The car now ascended more swiftly and in a few moments, Bhuras, who had been consulting the instrument for altitude, called out:

"Two hundred miles."

"We have passed through the limits of the Earth's atmosphere," said Asterion, "and are entering the great gaseous envelope surrounding it, which is several hundred times lighter than hydrogen and about eight thousand miles deep."

I looked through the window in the battery room below the floor. The great disc of the south pole was black as night. Through the window in the roof the stars shone with indescribable splendor, their discs appeared larger, and their twinkling—the effect of

[1] Great masses of meteoric matter weighing from a hundred lbs. to several tons have frequently fallen on various parts of the Earth's surface, particularly in Southern Mexico and certain parts of Asiatic Russia. There are several enormous specimens in the Smithsonian Institution and National Museum in Washington, D. C.

atmospheric diffraction, had disappeared. And now the full moon arose in all her glory.

Through this attenuated gaseous medium her appearance was far more grand and beautiful than viewed from earth. Through the lenses of the windows her dimensions were greatly enlarged and every detail of her topography brought out in bold relief; her mountains, precipices, gulfs, craters, dried up ocean beds and arid plains, fissured and honeycombed in all directions, plainly showing the long past epoch of volcanic outbursts and geological upheavals of whose extent and tremendous power the mind can form but a feeble conception.

" What think you, Lieutenant," asked Asterion ; " was your dead satellite ever inhabited by human beings ?"

" Fancy has pictured in glowing details the once happy denizens of that world, long since passed away ; the theatre of human greatness and glory, the scene of human hopes, joys and sorrows," I replied.

" Hi !" giggled John. " There's the old man with his bag, the dog and tree, old woman gone to bed, can see her nose and toes stickee out from under blanket."

" Joking aside," laughed Altfoura, " as the past history of your moon is written on her fire scarred face, it would almost seem as if those shadowy forms were indeed the ghosts of the lost Lunarians."

" Must have been terrible big peoples ; old man and woman pretty near a thousand miles high," said John.

" Four hundred miles," called out Bhuras.

Suddenly a flood of blinding light poured through the windows, so intolerably bright, we shrank back and covered our faces with our hands. It seemed as if a flaming volcano had suddenly opened before us.

" Hi !" exclaimed John, " see the big sun ! Whew ! he shine terrible hot."

We had reached the point where the sun's rays grazed the earth at the Antarctic circle and through this attenuated medium poured the full power of their light and heat directly upon us. The thermometer rose, to 150° and the room became hot as an oven ; we were panting for breath. Vidyuna screened off the windows, Asterion sprayed an evaporating lotion around the room which cooled off the torrid heat. He then inserted a smoke tinted lens in one of the windows, which cut off the heat rays and subdued the light.

" Come and take a solar observation," said he.

I looked through the lens and to my astonishment the luminary presented all those phenomena that are seen in annular eclipses by the moon, with this extraordinary difference that, whereas in eclipses, these phenomena are shown only in the ring outside the moon's dark disc, here they were shown all over the polar surface. What influence this thin gaseous medium had in producing this effect I know not, but all the tremendous explosions, fiery cyclones, hydrogen flames and spires, the huge spots or abysses—some of which could engulph a score of worlds like ours at once, were displayed all over the surface, and with them appeared all the varied colors shown in the solar spectrum flashing and glittering everywhere, so that the luminary looked like a vast star shaped rose, gleaming with a grandeur and beauty impossible to describe.

" It is now midnight, according to the clock, but midday according to the sun," said the doctor, " I propose we retire for the night."

" And in the meantime, Asterion, please traverse this gaseous envelope speedily as possible, and when you have reached the Interplanetary space, let us know," said Altfoura.

"I will do so," replied he, then to Bhuras, "Put a little more tension on the batteries."

The cots were drawn out and we prepared for the night. The Prince, Doctor and John were soon wrapped in the arms of Morpheus, but sleep was effectually banished from my eyes as would have been with respect to any denizen of Earth flying at such a rate and bound for another world. As the hours passed on, the silence was unbroken save by the subdued whispers of Asterion and his assistants announcing to each other, the rates of speed and distances in miles, as the car flew silently onward.

"1. o'c, 4,000 miles," "2. o'c, 8,000 miles," "We have passed through the gaseous envelope and are now entering the Interplanetary space."—"Shall we wake up the Prince?" "No, let him sleep on with his friends," "3. o'c, 30,000 miles." "4. o'c, 60,000 miles"— "Put a little more tension on the batteries."

"Asterion," I whispered, "how fast are we going?"

"A thousand miles a minute."

"A hundred times as swift as a cannon ball!—Heavens! What a tremendous speed."

"Our Ethervolt is merely taking a quiet walk."

"A walk? Great Scott!—How is he on a trot?"

"Makes pretty fair time."

"On a run?"

"You can time his paces when he takes the home stretch for Mars."

"The home stretch," I muttered and dropped to sleep.

CHAPTER XI.

WONDERS OF THE HEAVENS.

" Ye stars! Bright legions that, before all time
Camped on yon plain of sapphire, what shall tell
Your burning myriads, but the eye of Him
Who bade through heaven your golden chariots wheel?"
The Stars.—CROLY.

We were aroused by the voice of Asterion.

" Awake !   Arise !   Behold the glories of the starry Universe !"

" Have we traversed the great ethereal envelope ?" asked the Prince as we sprang from the cots.

" Long ago. We are now two hundred and fifty thousand miles above the Earth and floating in the vast lumeniferous ether, which fills all space and in which the stars, suns and planets roll as in a boundless, infinite ocean."

Asterion withdrew the screens ; we sprang to the windows, speechless with inexpressible wonder.

The heavens were one universal blaze of glory ! From heights immeasurable, from depths unfathomable, gleamed millions of suns ! The stars in the constellations Perseus, Southern Cross and Centauri, to observers on the earth, have been compared to thousands of jewels strown on a ground of black velvet ; but here, the whole measureless expanse seemed powdered with precious gems. There were great diamond, ruby, emerald, amethyst, sapphire and chrysolite suns. Countless stars and clusters unknown on earth now sprang into view. Galaxies, before whose mighty splendors even Sirius, Arcturus, Aldebaran, the Pleiades and Hyades paled their ineffectual fires, now gleamed before us, and giant nebulæ, in comparison with which, Orion, Argos, Lyra and Andromeda, seemed like faint misty vapors, now hung their vast and gorgeous curtains, half concealing, half disclosing still greater glories beyond, while the Milky way, that—

> " Broad and ample road
> Whose dust is gold, and pavement, stars,"-

spread its mighty arch over all. It almost seemed as if the gates of Paradise had opened to disclose the infinite splendors of Deity and the grand words of the psalmist came to mind.

" The heavens declare the glory of God, and the firmament sheweth His handy work."

" Look at the planets, the worlds we inhabit and whose magnificence we expatiate so much upon," said Asterion. " They present rather an insignificant appearance."

Sir Edmund Burke says, " There is but one step from the sublime to the ridiculous ;" and never was the aphorism so strikingly illustrated as now. Here were the members of our wonderful and beautiful planetary system, Mercury, Venus, Mars, Jupiter, etc., looking like little black insects slowly creeping around their orbits, what feeble reflected light they could boast of, absolutely turned to darkness in the surrounding effulgence, like the light of a candle held up to the sun.

" We mortals have little to boast of in our earthly habitations," said Asterion.

Through the window under the battery room we saw the earth, two hundred and fifty thousand miles below. Its shape was like the half moon although many times larger. On the illuminated eastern hemisphere we could see the Antarctic continent and ocean, part of the South Pacific and Atlantic oceans and the southern portions of Africa and Australia. The western hemisphere was in darkness. The spirit thermometer hanging outside was frozen solid long ago.

" I wonder how cold it is outside ?" asked Altfoura.

" So cold, I fancy, a piece of ice would feel like a coal of fire, beside it," replied the doctor.

" Place the frigometer out on the shady side," said Asterion.

Vidyuna placed a peculiar looking instrument outside one of the windows. It registered what would be equivalent to 300.° below zero of the centigrade.[1]

" Place the calorimeter out on the sunny side."

Vidyuna did so ; in a few moments it ran up to 500.°

" Which shows the enormous power of the sun's direct rays," said Asterion.[2]

" The moon must be more than twice as hot as boiling water," remarked Altfoura.

" On the sunny side for half the month only. During the other half she has a chance to cool off."

" What protects our car against these violent alternations of cold and heat ?" I asked.

" Its brilliant surface reflects the solar rays like a mirror. Its walls are absolutely non-conducting, and do not permit the escape of the warmth inside."

" What protects our planets from this terrible heat ?" asked Altfoura.

" Our astronomers say their atmospheres perform this office," I replied.

[1] It has been mathematically demonstrated that, at this degree of temperature, the atmosphere would become fluid.

[2] The great power of the sun's direct rays is well known to aëronauts, and illustrated on the summits of lofty mountains. Prof. Tyndall states that on a journey to the top of the Alps, he held out his naked hand in the sun, the back of it was nearly blistered, while the palm was cold.

" Only partially," said Asterion. " The outer gaseous envelope, whose depth equals the diameter of the planet, strikes down, or absorbs about seventy-five per cent of the hot rays ; the atmospheric vapor absorbs a great portion of the remainder, allowing merely enough to reach the terrestrial surface for the necessary purposes."

" What if some stray comet should happen to come along and brush away that envelope with its tail ?"

"All animal and vegetable life would speedily die under the intense heat of the sun's rays."

" What if the coma should completely surround the Planet, or come in contact with its atmosphere ?" asked Altfoura.

" The whole surface of the planet would be enveloped in flames."

"How can that be ?" said I. " Many years ago the coma of a large comet became entangled among the moons of Jupiter and remained there four months without producing any perceptible effect on them."[1]

"Jupiter's moons have no atmosphere and consequently no perceptible effect would be produced," Asterion replied. " The comas of many of the comets are composed—in addition to fine meteoric matter—of hydrogen gas and certain compounds of carbon,[2] which, as you know, are highly combustible ; now if the coma of one of these comets should happen to surround one of our planets—the earth, for instance, the hydrogen would at once unite with the oxygen of the atmosphere, for which it has a powerful affinity, and

[1] Lexell's comet of 1770. It had an elliptical orbit and a period of 5 years. That comet has never been seen since. Showing that Jupiter's moons must have exerted a great disturbing influence upon it.

[2] Shown by spectroscopic analysis.

take fire ; this would immediately ignite the carbon and the planet would be wrapped in flames."

At these words, the prediction of the Apostle came to my mind : " But the day of the Lord shall come as a thief in the night ; in which the heavens shall pass away with a great noise and the elements shall melt with fervent heat ; the earth also, and the works that are therein shall be burned up."[1]

"As this interplanetary space is practically a vacuum," said I, " the out-pressure of the air in this car must be enormous."

" Amounting to several thousand pounds to the square foot," replied Asterion.

" If it should happen to burst open, what would be the consequences to us ?"

Asterion took one of the penguins from the basket and carefully opening one of the double windows placed the bird outside. It instantly burst to atoms, flesh, feathers, bones and all, as if blown up with dynamite. The instantaneous disappearance of the unfortunate penguin sufficiently illustrated what our fate would be.

" Have no apprehensions of our car bursting," said he. " It can sustain a tenfold greater out pressure than this."

John fed the polar birds from a hamper of fish caught on the island and they took a hearty meal in which the Commodore, who appeared to have taken quite a fatherly interest in them, condescended to join, at the same time teaching them a few lessons in table etiquette. Asterion renovated the air from the generator, Bhuras put the batteries to higher tension, and the car flew onward at the rate of two hundred thousand miles per hour, three times the velocity of the earth in her orbit around the sun.

[1] 2nd Peter, Chap. iii.

I now inquired what was the object of the Martians in visiting Earth.

"We have known for a long time past, by our telescopic observations that your Earth was inhabited, and we very naturally desired to ascertain something about you," replied the Doctor.

"We terrestrians have always supposed our Earth to be the only inhabited planet in the solar system," said I.

"Which brings to mind the fable of the caterpillars in the gooseberry bush, who believed their own bush to be the only inhabited one in the garden," replied he.

"Our astronomers having recently discovered in your planet, certain features somewhat resembling our own, some of our people have been willing to accept the idea that your planet might possibly be the abode of life, although not under the same conditions as exist on Earth."

"And what kind of life have you terrestrians imagined our planet to contain?"

"Some of our novelists and romancers of the sensationally fanciful school have taken that subject in hand and peopled your world with all sorts and varieties of fantastical beings, human, animal and vegetable." I then briefly described a few of their extraordinary and whimsical conceptions, and monstrous absurdities, which would almost make Captain Gulliver and Baron Munchausen jump out of their graves with amazement.

"Your terrestrial romancers are gifted with wonderful imaginations and we Martians should feel highly complimented at their pictures of our world and society."

"Some of our people, in consequence of certain peculiar appearances, seen on your planet, have thought it might be inhabited by intelligent beings like ours, and that they were trying to communicate with us by some kind of signals, and a few of our astronomical enthusiasts have suggested that our governments undertake the great labor and expense of replying by display-. ing huge letters or geometrical figures by means of electric lights covering many hundred square miles of territory."

" It would be impossible for either of us to interpret each others' signals and I doubt whether they could even be distinguished ; for we can see only the bright side of each others' planets and any such signals would be swallowed up in the powerful solar reflection. Whatever unusual appearances your astronomers may have seen are wholly natural. And now as to our object in visiting your Earth ; being convinced that it was inhabited and having made great advances in interplanetary navigation, we decided to pay you a visit, and made our first many years ago, but we found it impossible to land anywhere on your globe except at the poles, where the cosmo-magnetic currents are centered. A few journeys were made, which were accompanied with great danger and several of our navigators lost their lives. Some landed on your North Pole, during your arctic winter and in respect to cold weather your planet is quite ahead of ours. Your freezing winds and terrible tempests drove us away. Asterion is the only one who has succeeded in accomplishing safe transit. He has made several journeys and landed on your south pole where the cosmic currents are more powerful and uniform than at the north pole. These trips were made during your Antarctic summer. He brought over his workmen, engineers, machinery, etc., built the houses and workshops, out of your polar rocks. He also transported the fire ship and vessel in which you crossed the polar sea. This required a small fleet of Ethervolts ; he has now

made your south pole the base point for future operations. He is investigating the electric and magnetic
forces of your Earth, its atmosphere, etc., which in
many respects are so different from ours. Soon as the
necessary arrangements are completed, he will bring
over a few of our air ships in order that we may make
aërial voyages over your globe and visit your different
countries. How will your people receive us?"

" I cannot answer for other countries," I replied,
" but I assure you that, the people of the United States
of America, who are the most open hearted and generous, as well as the most powerful and progressive nation
of our globe, will receive you most kindly, and extend to
you those courteous hospitalities for which they are re
nowned among the nations and kingdoms of the Earth."

" We are indeed truly delighted to hear that," said
the Prince.

" There's my hand on it," said I, " and promise me
that your first visit shall be to our great and glorious
Republic of which I am proud to be an humble representative."

" We shall certainly make our first visit there," he
replied.

" And may that happy day soon come," said Asterion
with enthusiasm, " when Earth and Mars shall join
hands in friendship and cement their bond of brotherly
union across the planetary spheres."

By evening we had made two million miles. We
took supper and retired for the night, Vidyuna and
Bhuras taking turns at the machinery. Next morning
Asterion informed us that we were five million miles
from Earth and were rounding the great elliptical curve
in the direction of Mars at the rate of six thousand
miles per minute, the Earth's attraction continually
diminishing in direct proportion with our flight from it.

Day after day passed on, as our car, impelled by the mighty cosmic currents, sped her swift flight through the measureless realms of space. New stars, constellations and galaxies unknown and undreamed of on earth, rose around us on every hand. We felt almost overwhelmed and crushed amid these awful infinitudes. Human reason and sense could no longer endure these never ending grandeurs and glories of Deity, in the presence of which poor finite Man is but a worm of the dust. We were compelled to screen the windows, and seek relief in the contemplation of our own infinite littleness.

"We are now approaching that point where the Cosmo-magnetic stream running between Jupiter and Venus, crosses our pathway to Mars," said Asterion. "Jupiter lies to the west, about four hundred and seventy five million miles from the Sun. The orbit of Venus, being within our own, she lies only about thirty million miles distant on the east. How would you like to take a look at her?"

We all eagerly assented.

"All right. When we reach that point, I will change the magnetism of our car and batteries to correspond to the magnetism of the stream running between those planets, we will take that stream and reach Venus within three days. We will return by the same current till we reach the intersection again, then change our magnetism to the Martian and continue our journey."

In a few hours the cross stream was reached. Asterion charged the batteries with the Venusian magnetism. Our car turned to the east, flew with increasing speed along this new current and on the morning of the third day we came within five hundred thousand miles of the planet, which was revolving at a mean distance of about sixty seven million miles from the Sun.

CHAPTER XII.

VENUS.

" Fairest of stars, last in the train of night,
    If better thou belong not to the dawn,
    Sure pledge of day, that crown'st the smiling morn
    With thy bright circlet."

Paradise Lost.—Bk. 5.

"Look !" exclaimed Asterion, pointing through the window, " behold yon beauteous orb, that ushers in your terrestrial day dawn and evening tide."

" And which we Terrestrians have named Venus, the bright star of love, whose eternal sway all the race of men obey," said I.

" And which we Martians have named Bhama Kis-zulia or the ' sweet kissing one.' "

" Quite a kissable name and exceedingly appropriate to her."

The orb was in her third quarter ; viewed from our position, and as we were within half a million miles of her, she appeared more than eight times the size of our moon. Her illuminated hemisphere shone with great brilliancy. Through the window lenses we could plainly see the topography of her oceans and continents, which are arranged entirely different from those of Earth. The former are of a deep blue color, the latter a brilliant green, mingled with a coppery hue ; this is owing to her dense vegetation. The snow caps of her poles shone like polished marble ; her atmosphere is laden with dense clouds of various colors produced by the varying sun light, and the great inclination of her axis to the plane of her orbit necessarily produces extreme vicissitudes of her climate. Asterion took several fine photographs with his camera.

" If we had one of our great Martian telescopes here, we could view her landscapes as plainly as if we were on top of one of her mountains," said he.

"Have you ever paid her a visit ?" I asked.

"I have not," he replied. "One of my ancestors, a renowned planetary navigator, made three trips there and lost his life on the last. His discoveries were important and confirm our telescopic observations. The journey is highly dangerous in many respects, and no one has had the courage to undertake another. I intend to take one, however, sometime this year, special precautions are required."

"Is she inhabited ?"

" By the lower orders of vegetable and animal life only. She has passed through her first two geological epochs, and is now at the close of her third, preparatory to her last, during which she will be fitted for the abode of man."

" May we all live to hail that glorious day when the Venusian Man, shall walk over those primeval plains, monarch of all he surveys," said Altfoura.

" I fear we old Martian grey beards will never have a chance to participate in the festivities of that great event," said the Doctor.

"Nor their descendants either, to remotest generations yet to come," replied Asterion. " Long before humanity ever dawns on yonder planet, her present orders of vegetable and animal life must disappear to make room for higher and nobler forms, fitted for the use of man, and that may not take place for many ages to come."

" What is its present aspect of life ?" I asked.

" Its continents and islands are covered with dense

forests, jungles and morasses teeming with that rank, and luxuriant vegetation which forms the immense coal beds of our older worlds. Its oceans and seas are crowded with countless myriads of the infusoriæ and molluscs which form all the vast calcareous or limestone deposits of our worlds. Its atmosphere is dense, hot, loaded with carbonic acid and watery vapors, while both land and seas are peopled with huge and terrible monsters and reptiles, whose appearance is frightful to behold."

"Splendid!" exclaimed Altfoura, his eyes sparkling with anticipated pleasure. "What a magnificent hunting ground. When you take that trip, Frederick and I will go with you. We'll have some rare sport."

CHAPTER XIII.

A BURNING WORLD.

> "O'erwhelmed
> With floods and whirlwinds of tempestuous fire."
> *Paradise Lost.*—Bk. V.

We had now approached within two hundred thousand miles of the planet. All at once a red ball appeared floating out from behind her disc over the dark side of her hemisphere.

"Venus moon looks more angry than usual, to-night," said Dr. Hamival.

"What!" I exclaimed, "has Venus really a moon?"

"Certainly," said Asterion. "Did you not know it?"

"The opinions of our Astronomers are greatly at

variance on that point," I replied. "Some positively
assert they have discovered a satellite and have even
calculated her elements.([1]) Others positively deny it.
The planet has been diligently searched for years by
many Astronomers."

"Venus has her moon as well as Earth. It is somewhat larger than yours, further away from the planet
and rotates more rapidly. The reason why some of
your Astronomers have failed to discover it, is, because
there is as great a difference in the power and penetra-
tion of their eyes as in those of certain animals and
birds. Great visual power is a natural gift which can
be cultivated like any other.([2]) One reason why the
objectors denied the existence of her moon, is because
she shines by her own light fitfully, and often much
obscured, and not by the solar reflected light as your
moon and all our planets do."

"Shines by her own light? I do not exactly understand."

"Because she is on fire."

"What! On fire?"

"Yes, going through a prodigious conflagration.
When we arrive within a thousand miles of her, check
off the batteries," said Asterion to Bhuras.

In about an hour we reached the point and the car
stopped.

"I'll show you the grandest and most terrible sight
ever seen by mortal eyes," said he, inserting a lens in
one of the windows. "This lens brings the moon within the apparent distance of ten miles to the naked
eye."

([1]) Cassini, Short, Montaigne, Baudowin, Rodkier, Montbaron
and many other distinguished Astronomers.

([2]) The celebrated Dawes and Schiaparelli are called "eagle
eyed" because of their superior powers in this respect.

I looked through the glass and my very blood ran cold as I gazed on the tremendous horrors of a burning world. It seemed as if the pit of hell itself were yawning before me. This vast orb, six thousand miles in circumference, was one mass of liquid fire. All over its molten surface the red hot mountains, precipices and plains—broken fragments of her crust,—were heaving and tossing amid the blazing surges. From the craters of innumerable volcanoes spouted vast columns and jets of lava mingled with pillars of smoke. Fiery whirlwinds and vortices swept o'er the surface. Great black clouds and vapors hung like vast canopies high above, ripped and torn asunder in all directions, at times enshrouding the hellish pandemonium in cimmerean darkness, while ever and anon great sheets and flashes of cosmic lightning threw a ghastly glare over the awful scene.

"You now behold the last act of a tragic drama which closes the career of a dying world," said Asterion. "When Venus was still a small sun, thrown off from our great parent luminary, yon burning orb was her little world, basking in her genial light, the abode of human beings, the theatre of human progress, and like your moon, having had her rise, glory and downfall, she is now passing through the throes of her final dissolution. When in future ages Venus shall have become fitted for the abode of man, this burning world shall have exhausted her fires and become a cold and lifeless moon, like yours, shining by reflected light and filling her appointed sphere as queen of the Venusian night. Such has ever been, and such ever shall be, the history of our worlds, and the same fate that has befallen her, awaits us all."

"Who shall say that the instrument of yonder world's destruction might not have been the fiery coma of some passing comet, for the nearer our planets are to the sun, the greater is their danger from the swift perihelion flight of these terrible messengers," said Dr. Hamival.

"And who shall say that these dead worlds and moons may not in future ages, touched by the Almighty hand, spring into new life ?" said Altfoura.

"And as according to what we know of Nature's laws," said I, " we may safely assume that, as all matter is indestructable, continually reappearing under various forms, that what has been, is now and ever shall be, why may not all created things in the world of life, as well as the world of matter, continually pass through never ending changes and transformations, throughout the grand cycles of Eternity ?"

CHAPTER XIV.

TOTAL ECLIPSE.

" Methinks it should be now a huge eclipse
Of sun and moon ; and that the affrighted globe
Should yawn at alteration."
Othello.—Act V., Sc. 2.

Passing the burning moon, we sped toward the planet which was moving in her orbit at the rate of seventy five thousand miles an hour. Our car flying more than five times faster, soon came near, and drew up within twenty thousand miles of her, opposite the dark side of her hemisphere, she being in inferior conjunction, or nearly on a line between us and the sun, which was about sixty seven million miles distant.

The transits of Venus across the sun, having relation

as they do to one of the most important problems of astronomy, *i. e.* the determination of our earth's exact distance from the luminary, are looked forward to with the greatest interest by our terrestrial astronomers, and government expeditions are sent out to various parts of the globe for the purpose of making correct observations of this important planetary phenomenon, and we were certainly in the most favorable situation for observing it.

"We will now witness a total eclipse of the sun by Venus," said Asterion.

Of all the phenomena in Nature ever seen by man, a total eclipse of the sun is the most grand and imposing. The extraordinary appearance of the skies, the changes of color in all natural objects, the reduction of temperature, the gathering darkness, the funereal, and often ghastly aspect of the landscape, the magnificent and wonderful appearance of the sun with its flaming columns, upshooting pillars and jets of fire, its rosy sierras, crimson photosphere and golden corona, the general solemnity felt by all observers, the loudly expressed terrors of almost all barbarous races, the fears and frequent outcries of birds and animals,[1] and what is even still more impressive, the swift and awful rush of the moon's black shadow across continents and oceans, like some vast demon of night borne on wings of darkness ;[2] all attest the sublimity of the phenomenon. But a total eclipse, or rather occultation of the sun by one of the planets witnessed by an observer in the interplanetary space, and within twenty thousand miles

[1]   Interesting accounts are to be found in many works on Astronomy.

[2]   This terrible umbra which almost overwhelms the observer with awe, has been often witnessed by observers on the tops of mountains within range of its transit across the earth.

of it, is a phenomenon so awful and fraught with such unspeakable horrors as would make the blood of any man who witnessed it almost freeze in his veins.

In a few moments the great black disc of the planet, nearly eight thousand miles in diameter, and from our position appearing more than two hundred times larger than the full moon, began to move slowly across the sun, step by step, carving, or gouging out as it were, a huge semi-circular excavation, right into the very bowels of the luminary, until it almost seemed,—according to the superstitious terrors of certain barbarous races,—as if some gigantic aërial monster was actually devouring the fountain of light. Soon we were immersed in its umbra—an immense black cone stretching hundreds of thousand miles in space. None of the usual phenomena attending eclipses seen on earth appeared, but in an instant the great solar luminary was utterly blotted out, and in place of it, a huge gulf, black as ink, and apparently more than a million miles across, was hollowed out in the celestial vault right in front of us, its vast mouth sweeping above, beneath and all around us. It is impossible to describe the horror of the scene. It seemed as if we were sinking into an infinite abyss, swallowed up in a vacuum of absolute nothingness, prefiguring the bottomless pit of perdition, the dreadful realm of "Outer darkness," into which the rebellious angels and damned spirits of wicked men are forever doomed at the day of Judgment. The aspect of the burning world wrapped in whirlwinds of flame, was almost cheerful compared with this, for it had light, although infernal ; but this was the darkness of death itself, the Erebus of annihilation. An overwhelming horror seemed to seize us. John trembled, Altfoura and the Doctor grew pale, while the spirituelle countenance of Asterion had an expression of triumph like some mighty magician who had called up the tremendous scene.

"Move on, in heaven's name," said Altfoura; "the sight is too awful to look upon."

"After a few trips, your highness will become accustomed to it," said Asterion.

In a short time Venus completed her transit; and the sun again shone forth in all his glory.

"Captain," asked Bhuras, "shall we go ahead?"

"Yes, at double speed."

Bhuras moved the lever and we flew faster than ever. Taking the cosmic stream toward Jupiter, and reaching the intersection on the second, day we took the Martian stream.

"We shall now make ten million miles per day," said Asterion.

"How far off is Mars?" I asked.

"Sixty million miles."

"We should reach him in six days."

"In less time than that."

On the evening of the second day we had made twenty million miles.

"Now, gentlemen," said Asterion, "we are approaching that neutral point between our respective planets where Earth's attraction ceases and that of Mars begins. In our previous journeys we have shot by that point. I will now slacken up speed and approach gradually. When we reach it, you will witness some interesting phenomena."

Bhuras carefully checked the batteries and the car slowed up.

"What's our speed now?" I asked.

"Almost as fast as the hour hand of your watch."

"At that rate, in a day's journey, we could make nearly five inches."

"We must approach very carefully. The variation of a single hair's breadth would throw us beyond the line," replied he, consulting an instrument which registered distance and space to the minuteness of a spider's thread, while Bhuras closely watched the register of his machine.

In a few moments the faint tinkling of a bell sounded from the instrument.

"Halt," whispered Asterion.

Bhuras touched a key and the car paused.

CHAPTER XV.

GRAVITY ANNIHILATED.

"Tekel. Thou art weighed in the balances, and art found wanting." *Daniel*, Chap. V.

"We are now exactly at the middle point where Earth and Mars mutually balance each other and their respective attractions are neutralized," said Asterion. "At this point all gravity ceases to exist; there is no such thing as weight here."

He then placed a ten pound weight on a pair of spring scales affixed to the wall. They did not move.

"Could a hundred million Ethervolt cars be placed on a pair of great scales outside, they would not turn the balance a single hair," said he.

"Then a mountain weighs no more than a grain of sand," said the Doctor.

"Neither of them weigh any thing."

Asterion held up a few books, papers, maps, etc., high above the table, then let go, they remained motionless, poised in the air. Although I quite understood the scientific theory of non-gravitation, I was none the less surprised at this practical illustration of it. We threw up our pocket knives coins, handkerchiefs, feathers, cotton, small pebbles ; all floated around for a moment, then hung motionless.

"Cap'n Fred," whispered John mysteriously in my ear. " Witches around here."

"Looks somewhat like it, although they have travelled a long way from witch land," I replied.

" Hi ! Witches can fly heap long way up the sky on broom sticks."

" As every thing weighs nothing up here," remarked the Prince, "our bodies must be almost as ethereal as our spirits."

" So they are," said the Doctor, " I begin to feel the etherealization already."

" How do you like the sensation ?" asked Asterion.

" It is delightful. I feel as if I were in Elysium."

" How is it with respect to yourself, Lieutenant ?"

" My feelings coincide with the Doctor's."

" And you, John."

" Me feelee as if me could fly like little bird."

" How would you like a still higher elevation ?" asked the Prince.

" O, me wantee go way up, high."

" And you, Doctor ?"

" I should enjoy a higher elevation immensely."

" And you, Frederick ?"

" I agree with the Doctor and John *in toto*."

" Your aspirations shall be gratified," replied the Prince, as taking us by the coat collars with his thumb and finger, he lightly lifted us high over the table, where we hung suspended, sprawling our legs and arms among the books, papers, etc., like a trio of dancing jacks.

"Your highness has illustrated the higher elevation in quite an original and striking manner," said the Doctor.

"I hope you enjoy it all the more," replied Altfoura.

"Hi," giggled John. "Me feelee lively as a hop-toad; reckon could jump to the moon."

"So you could, if you had anything to jump from," said Asterion.

"Prince, I must confess I don't feel quite as comfortable up here as I expected," remarked the Doctor.

"Really, I am sorry you are so disappointed," replied he.

"In fact it is becoming rather irksome."

"Well then, why don't you come down?"

"I find it quite impossible to do so," vainly trying to hook his foot in the arm of a chair.

"Jump down," suggested Asterion.

"Which way shall I jump? there's no up nor down, top nor bottom, right nor left, forward nor backward, in these non-gravitative regions. Besides, I have no foundation to jump from."

"I deeply sympathize with you, in your unfortunate situation," said the Prince, rising from his chair.

"I may as well enjoy the sympathy of your highness' company in the meantime," replied the Doctor as reaching down he took the Prince by the coat collar and pulled him up; but lost his balance in the effort, turned a complete summersault and hung with his head downward and his heels upward.

"Good! Doctor," laughed the Prince, "you have made a total change of base, and can dive strait down to your chair."

"But I shall have rush of blood to the head, and die of apoplexy before I get there."

"No danger," said Vidyuna, "the blood weighs nothing, and circulates as freely through the lower extremities, as the upper."

"If you will kindly inform me which are my upper, and which my lower extremities, in this position, I shall be much obliged to you."

"The question is a poser, I'll admit," replied he rising from his chair.

"Perhaps we can solve it better up here," said the Doctor, reaching down and pulling him up alongside.

"The more counsellors, the merrier," said Vidyuna, catching Bhuras by the coat tails, pulled him up, and there we six hung, helpless as beetles on their backs, sprawling our arms and legs about, and shouting with laughter; while the raven flapped his wings, and hur-rahed himself hoarse.

"Well, gentlemen," said the Prince, "here we are, all balanced, like Earth and Mars, head to tail."

"Yes, and you've got yourself in a pretty fix," said Asterion.

"How so?" asked the Prince.

"Because you can't get out of it."

"Is that a fact?"

"It is indeed."

"But you can help us out, when we get tired of the fact."

"I regret to say, I am not able to help you out."

"Reach up your hand and pull us down."

"I'm afraid to risk it, I cannot pull you six down here, but you six could easily pull me up there, you would then be in a worse fix, than you are now."

"Well, then, start the car out of this non-gravitation place, and we'll all float down."

"I cannot start the car alone; I need Bhuras' and Vidyuna's help, you have got them up there."

"We're rather in an awkward fix," said I.

"D—l of a fix," croaked the Commodore.

"You are both quite mistaken," continued Asterion. "Nothing is fixed in Nature. Everything is in motion ; atoms, molecules, bodies, all. After a while our car will begin to revolve in an orbit of its own, around the sun."

"As a new asteroid, or baby planet, to be the observed of all observers in the astronomical world," said the Prince.

"And inhabited also," said I.

"And all locked up inside. The other planets, will swear a floating jail has come among them," said the Doctor.

"And like all celestial bodies," continued Asterion, "our car will begin to revolve on its axis, and each of you will revolve on your own individual axes, and around each other at the same time. It will be quite a lively waltz, and I believe the Doctor is morally and religiously opposed to waltzing."

"So I am," replied the Doctor emphatically. "Prince, see what a ridiculous predicament you have placed yourself and all of us in, with your mischievous prank. A sedate, dignified old gentleman like myself, whirling around on my axis."

"The car has started in her orbit already, and is beginning to revolve on her axis," said Asterion, consulting his instrument.

"And we are also beginning to revolve on our axes, individually and collectively ;" exclaimed the Doctor.

"Gentlemen," said the Prince. "The ball has opened, take your positions for the waltz."

"And I sincerely hope you will enjoy it," said Asterion, composing himself in his chair and consulting his book on astronomical logarithms.

CHAPTER XVI.

THE DANCE OF DEATH.

" The dancers are dancing and taking no rest,
  And closely their hands together are press'd ;
  And soon as a dance has come to a close,
  Another begins, and each merrily goes."
                    Dream and Life.—HEINE.

We were revolving on ourselves and around each other
in lively but irregular style.   The Commodore, who had
often taken a prominent part in the sailors' dances on
board ship, and knew the fiddlers' calls by heart, viewed
our performances with a severely critical eye and
determined to bring us to order at once ; so blowing a
shrill blast of his whistle, he roared out with the full
power of his brazen lungs :

"Shipmates Ahoy !—Blast yer eyes !—What the d—l
ye about ?—Swing right.—Swing left.—Swing corners.
—All hands round—Change partners—Up—Down—
Outside—Middle.—Promenade all.—Hurry up.—Lazy
lubbers.—D—n yer eyes.—D—l take the hindermost ;"—
as we whirled round and round, knocking and banging
against each other right and left.

" Bravo !—Bravo !"—applauded Asterion.   " You're
doing splendidly, gentlemen.—Hope you enjoy it."

" Immensely," replied the Prince ; " although I must
confess it is rather monotonous without any music."

"And without any pretty girls to recline their sweet
heads on your shoulders, while you steal your arms
around their dainty waists, and whisper soft sentiment
in their pretty ears.   What a pity !" replied Asterion.

"O, me don't want no women folks 'round.   Long

skirts heap bother. Me likee jig, hornpipe, double
shuffle.—Wish had toot-horn, drum and fiddle up here
and somebody for to play 'em.—Reckon could jump sky
high," and John tried to cut the double shuffle, but having no waxed floor to start from, made rather a poor
show.

"My dear Prince," puffed the Doctor, "will you
kindly do me the favor to keep your shoe leather out
of my eyes?"

"My dear Doctor, your heels are drumming a lively
tattoo on my nose, so I fancy it's about even."

"Asterion," said I, "the devotees of the dance generally like a little variety in their evolutions. Can you
not favor us with a change of programme?—a polka;—
schottische;—galop;—quadrille?"

"Nothing could give me greater pleasure than to
gratify your laudable desire, but you're booked for
the waltz and nothing else."

"How long will it go on?" asked the Prince.

"It will always go on."

"Always?"

"Yes, in other words it will never stop, day or
night."

"Is that a fact?"

"'Tis a scientific fact."

"Distressingly scientific," said I.

"Scientific facts are often distressing, but they cannot be helped."

"Then this is a regular dance to the death?" said I.

"According to science, it is."

"Asterion," anxiously queried the Prince, "can't
you help us out of these inconvenient scientifics?"

"No man can circumvent science."

"Well, there's one comfort; death stops all dancing,
however lively, then there's rest."

"My dear Prince, you are laboring under a delusion ; death stops nothing ; motion is the great law of Nature. With these mighty cosmic and atomic forces playing around us, there's no such thing as rest. You will waltz till you die. Your corpses will waltz, till all the flesh drops off. Your skeletons will waltz till the ligaments drop off. Your bones will revolve around each other till they fall to dust. Your dust will revolve till it separates into its ultimate atoms and molecules, and they will continue to revolve around each other forever and ever. The great laws of Nature are in full force around here, and you must submit to them, however inconvenient it may be to you."

"The surrounding chaos is beginning to revolve already," said the prince.

"Getting in order for the dance, and Order is Heaven's first law," replied Asterion.

The great cosmic laws of Motion, Revolution, and Attraction were now manifesting themselves in a lively manner. For more than an hour we continued revolving around each other, the miscellaneous chaos of books, knives, coins, pebbles, etc., whirling around us, thumping against our heads and faces. In vain we essayed to fight them off, they rebounded from the walls of the car back to the centre of attraction, striking us in all directions. The old Greek philosopher Leucippus' theory of atomic collisions, and Professor Helmholtz's and Sir Wm. Thomson's theory of elastic vortex motions were illustrated in a most striking manner. The raven flapped his wings, hurrahed and cock-a-doodle-dooed ; the gulls, Mother Careys and penguins strutted around, whooping and gabbling in perfect delight, as if the performance had been gotten up for their especial entertainment. By this time we were perfectly desperate and cared not a straw what we said or did. In the meantime, on went the dance, like the waltz of the Infernals in " Robert le Diable."

" Gentlemen," puffed the Doctor, " shall we free born citizens of Earth and Mars consent to dance ourselves to death, or be knifed, stoned and booked to death, according to Asterion's science ?"

" No, no, no," we all puffed in reply.

" Death being inevitable, it strikes me that, the proper course for us to get rid of this disagreeably scientifical mode of dying is, to shuffle off our mortal coils at once. What say you ?"

" Our old stoic philosophers," said I, " esteemed suicide the greatest privilege whenever they happened to get in an unpleasant situation and couldn't get out of it."

" Their example is worthy of commendation, and I propose we follow it," replied the Doctor.

" The question is before the society, and open for debate," said Asterion, taking the chair.

" Mr. Chairman," said I, " I quite coincide with the Doctor's views, and move that we proceed to commit *felo de se*, individually and collectively."

" Gentlemen, you have heard the motion," said Asterion. " All in favor of it signify by saying ' Aye.' "

" Aye." " Aye." " Aye," we puffed, *una voce*.

" All those opposed to it, signify by saying ' No.' "

" No !" thundered the Commodore. It was evident he didn't want any interruption of the waltz.

" The Ayes have it," announced Asterion.

" D—n 'em," growled Jack, scowling like Mephistopheles baulked of his prey.

" *Felo de se* being decided on," said Asterion, " the next question before the society relates to the *modus operandi*."

"Asterion," said I, "please open my portmanteau and get out my revolvers."

"Thanks ; but I don't propose to allow you to get up revolving fire works inside this car."

"Have you any cold poison aboard ?" queried the Doctor.

"This isn't a drug shop, Doctor."

"Our situation is indeed deplorable," said I—"No pistols allowed ; no poison on hand, what's to be done ?"

"Take courage, Lieutenant," said the Doctor. "I see a deadly weapon. Asterion, please pass up that ivory paper cutter lying on the table."

"But who'll undertake the job ? I'll oversee this business. It must be neatly done. I'll have no botch work," he replied.

"O, we'll suicide ourselves all around," exclaimed we all.

"I'm a little doubtful on that point, the Doctor is too old and feeble to undertake it ; the Prince is too tender hearted ; the Lieutenant, with the *esprit du corps* of the Navy, is quite too chivalrous to assassinate a fly. Vidyuna and Bhuras are not accustomed to the butchering business," said Asterion, laying down his logarithms.

"O, me first class butcher," exclaimed John ; "me stickee good many roast piggy on board ship for dinner."

"Who will you begin with, John ?"

"Me stickee meself 'fore hand, then stickee 'em all 'round."

"Good !" said the Doctor, "I have great confidence in persons who are willing to institute experiments on themselves, before experimenting on their neighbors. Asterion, pass up that mortal ripper."

Asterion passed up the ivory, John took it with a grin and broke it to pieces.

"John ; you have broken your word," indignantly exclaimed the Doctor, "you're a trickster, and I despise you."

"Me no care. Me heap good dancer any how."

"Doctor,"—said the Prince, "now's the time to bring in requisition that calm philosophy for which you are so eminently distinguished."

"Really, Prince, I fail to see what philosophy has to do with this situation."

"It may console you in this evil plight and enable you to rise above it."

"A fig for philosophy. It easily enables us to rise above past and future evils, but I'll be hanged if it can enable me to rise above this infernal predicament."

"Jump up to the roof and get out of the window," suggested Asterion. "Your exit would be like that of the penguin, quick as a flash."

"Excellent," replied the Doctor. "Of all modes of shuffling off this mortal coil, I prefer the penguin style. Pop.—And all is over, no need of coffin, parson, nor graveyard ; but philosophy won't help me up to the window."

"Asterion," said the Prince ; "the situation is becoming desperate ;—a crisis is at hand."

"And the dance will go on all the same, crisis or no crisis," replied he.

"But you must get us out of this scientific muddle," said I, "some how or other,—by Jupiter !"

"Is it possible, Lieutenant, that I hear you using profane language ?"

"Great Scott ! Isn't it enough to make a saint swear ? But the tallest kind of swearing isn't equal to the situation,"

"Call the Commodore. He's equal to it."

"Hello! Jack;" called out John. "Come and help Cap'n Fred swear."

"Not by a d—d sight!" snapped the Commodore emphatically.

"The heartless villain wants this infernal dance to go on," groaned the Doctor.

"There is only one way to get you out of it," said Asterion.

"In heaven's name, out with it," we all shouted.

"You can blow yourselves up with a bomb. Your dance will be stopped. Your atoms will fly forever through space."

"Illustrating the Atomic theory of Democritus," said I. "Come, get out your bomb."

"I grieve to say I have no bomb on hand at present." It is impossible to describe our disappointment.

"Hi!" giggled John, "you wantee stuff for to blow up? Me got 'em in portmanteau."

Asterion drew out the portmanteau, opened it and took out a can of dynamite carefully wrapped in cotton.

"What is this singular material?" he asked, and I explained its uses among the terrestrians.

"No need for to blow us up," said John. "Puttee can under bottom of car, touch 'em off—car boom along like shot out of big gun."

"John's plan seems feasible. I'll try it," said Asterion, then carefully attached the can outside the window underneath the floor and connected it with a wire to an electric battery.

"Now, gentlemen, are you all ready?"

"Take aim.—Fire.—Bang!" said the Commodore.

Asterion transmitted the electric spark; the dynamite exploded with a force sufficient to upheave an iron clad on any planet; but in this empty space the recoil on the car was hardly equal to the touch of a feather, sufficient however, to move it beyond the neutral point.   Gravity was restored and we all six gracefully floated down to our chairs and the revolving chaos gently descended to the floor.

"Three cheers for John!" exclaimed Altfoura.   "His clever wit has saved us," and the applause made the windows rattle.

"And the dynamite has started us ahead.   We are now under the gravity of Mars," said Asterion.

"How far off is he?" I asked.

"Forty million miles."

"Four more days and nights of tedious travel," said the Prince.

"Not so.   We'll take the home stretch," Asterion replied.

———◆———

CHAPTER XVII.

TWENTY MILLION MILES A MINUTE.

"Swifter than lightning flashes, or the beam
That hastens on the pinions of the morn."

PERCIVAL.

"Now, gentlemen," said Asterion; "I have news for you.   For many years, as you know, our scientists and planetary navigators have been earnestly at work seeking to devise some mode of more rapid transit through space, and the problem has thus far defied all their efforts.   I have recently given much attention to the subject and am happy to announce to you that I have solved the problem."

" Is it possible !" exclaimed the Doctor. " Then you have made one of the greatest discoveries of the age."

Asterion modestly acknowledged the compliment.

" And while you were investigating that profound subject," said the Prince, "you shut yourself up in your scientific laboratory, refused all callers, and took not a morsel of food, nor a wink of sleep, for two weeks."

" In such researches, where it is necessary for the mind to grasp and hold a multiplicity of details continuously and keep them in order, food clogs the brain, and sleep interrupts the train of thought. I lived on ideas and cold water, the best diet for any man engaged in that kind of work," replied Asterion with a smile.

" Nothing but your wonderful constitution and powers of endurance took you safely through such prolonged and intense concentration of mind," said the Doctor. " Most men would have gone insane over it."[1]

" Asterion has the coolest head and steadiest nerve of any man in our kingdom," said the Prince.

" I have found that these cosmo-magnetic currents running between the planets fly with a velocity far greater than light or electricity," continued Asterion.

[1] The great astronomer Kepler, while engaged in the solution of intricate problems, sometimes secluded himself for two or three weeks at a time, allowing no one to enter his study and subsisting almost entirely on bread, milk and water, and very sparingly. The renowned mathematician, Euler, frequently did the same, and on one occasion solved a problem proposed by the French Academy, within three days, for the solution of which other eminent Mathematicians had demanded several months' time ; but the immense effort nearly cost him his life, and he lost the sight of one eye. Sir Isaac Newton, and other distinguished Astronomers and Scientists not unfrequently secluded themselves for weeks when engaged in profound scientific researches.

" What !—" I exclaimed. " Swifter than light ! whose speed is nearly two hundred thousand miles per second ?"

" Yes," he replied. " There's no known limit to their speed. Before their mighty rush, Time and Space seem to be annihilated. Swift almost as imagination, which doth glance from heaven to earth, from earth to heaven. Swift almost as thought, which roams through the infinite universe and leaps from star to star, so these cosmic vibrations leap from planet to planet quickly as the molecular vibrations between the atoms of a mote that floats in the sunbeam."(1)

" This is pre-eminently the age of progress, great discoveries and inventions," said Dr. Hamival. " Nature, which has so long been almost a sealed book to Man,—

(1) The instantaneous action on the magnetic needle of great solar storms, and the magnetic streams emanating from the sun spots, are well known phenomena, and frequently associated with the prevalence of great auroras. The late Richard A. Proctor states that he witnessed a magnetic undulation passing through the tail of a comet, over 30,000,000 miles long, within two seconds. This is about SEVENTY FIVE TIMES THE SPEED OF LIGHT ! M. Pingré, a distinguished authority on comets, states that these vibrations resemble those of the aurora borealis, and often traverse the whole length of a comet's tail within a few seconds, furthermore, that " these pulsations are in some instances ALMOST INSTANTANEOUS and hence cannot be the result of electric action, which would require several minutes to reach us as they pass along the tail." The tail of Donati's comet during the different observations made of it, varied from 15. to 40,000,000 miles in length. That of the great comet of 1680 was 100,000,000 miles long. Of 1811, 130,000,000 miles, and that of 1843 200,000,000 miles. The tail of this comet increased at the rate of 35,000,000 miles per day ! If the coma is able to evolve its cometary material at such a prodigious rate, no wonder its magnetic undulations or vibrations are almost, if not quite, instantaneous.

which has locked up her secrets in her strong citadels, guarding them with jealous care,—has at last been compelled to yield them up, for Man has opened those prison doors with the keys of Science."

"Aye," continued Asterion, "and he has snatched from Nature's grasp those great forces, hitherto wielded by her blind and unreasoning hand. No longer her slave, he is now her master. How grand the thought. O, Man, what mighty powers are in thy hands ! What greatness and glory await thee ! The light that beams from yonder sun,—the thunderbolt that rends the gnarled oak,—the tempests that rage o'er land and sea, —the billows that lash the trembling shore,—shall bend to thy will and kneel in submission at thy feet ;—yea ; thou'lt harness to thy chariot the invisible powers of Earth, Air, Sea and Sky, and they shall bear thee in thy triumphant flight through the realms of the Universe !"

As Asterion spoke these prophetic words, his countenance glowed almost with the light of Divine inspiration.

"Now gentlemen," continued he, "prepare yourselves for great news. I have found that we can travel on the currents of these mighty cosmic streams at the rate of TWENTY MILLION MILES A MINUTE !"

At this tremendous announcement we shrank back almost aghast, while Asterion's fine eyes gleamed with an expression of triumph impossible to describe.

"And we can make the trip to Mars, forty million miles distant, within two minutes."

"Nearly twice the speed of light," said the Doctor, with an expression of profound awe. "Asterion, have you made known this wonderful discovery ?"

"You are the first to whom I have announced it, and I have reserved its practical application to this import-

ant event,—the first journey of an inhabitant of Earth
to Mars."

I acknowledged my appreciation of Asterion's great
compliment to me.

"In order to accomplish this almost miraculous
flight," continued he ; "certain conditions are required,
which if strictly fulfilled, will insure absolute safety,
but if neglected, or disobeyed in the smallest degree,
bring instant death to us all. Are you willing to accept
the conditions ?"

"We are ;" all replied.

He now drew out a metallic casket and opening it,
carefully removed a globe of transparent, sky blue
crystal, about two feet in diameter and containing an
intricate and delicate mechanism.

"This is my Cosmic Motor, by means of which our
car can fly along the magnetic streams with a velocity
almost equal to their own. 'Tis my latest invention."
Then ascending a short ladder he affixed the globe to
the lower end of the metallic staff which projected
above the roof. A long slender wire wrapped with
silk and fastened to a glass handle hung from the globe
down to the floor. Attached to the globe were a pair
of dial plates with rows of figures and revolving hands
or pointers like those of a clock. One dial was numbered from 1 to 20, each figure indicating a million
miles ; the other dial was marked with figures indicating seconds.

"We will now put on our non-conducting armor,"
said Asterion.

Vidyuna took from a chest seven suits of close fitting
flexible armor, constructed apparently of crystal and
some unknown metal, the color of steel, with helmets,
vizors, opticals and gloves of the same material.
Bhuras unrolled a flexible circular plate of crystal

about eight feet in diameter, and spread it in the centre of the floor.

"This armor will protect us from the Cosmo-mag- netic streams which will pass through the adamantine walls of the car when I put the Cosmic Motor in action," said Asterion. "The slightest exposure of any part of our persons to these streams would produce instant death. Put on the armor, take your stand on the crys- tal plate, take hold of each others' hands and don't stir from your positions till I give the signal."

We removed our garments, put on the armor, helmets, etc., and stepped on the plate. Bhuras shut up the birds and raven in a box of non-conducting crystal.

"Discharge the Ethervolt batteries of their electricity. Check off the heat and air generators. Screen the win- dows and put out the light, as all these interfere with the Cosmic streams in the car. When I give the signal, close your vizors,—the joints are hermetical, but there will be sufficient air in your helmets to support you for a few moments. Watch the dial plates and figures for time and distance, and don't move hand or foot."

Bhuras and Vidyuna fulfilled the orders and took their stand on the plate.

"Are you all ready?" asked Asterion, taking the handle of the wire in his hand.

We nodded our heads.

"Close your vizors."

We closed them,—then joined hands.

"8 o 'c. We'll now take the home stretch for Mars," then closed his vizor and took his stand on the plate. I glanced at the dials ; the hand for distance pointed to figure 1. That for time pointed to 8 o'c. precisely. I glanced through the window and saw Mars, a little black speck, floating along the bright celestial vault, forty million miles away.

Asterion now gently pulled the wire.

A long flash, like watery vapor or mist, instantly shot from the green ball surmounting the staff, strait out into space. It was not like lightning nor a beam of light, for the speed even of these swift messengers is appreciable to the eye and sense, but the speed of this was wholly inappreciable. The instantaneousness of its appearance might perhaps be expressed by the words in the first chapter of Genesis, describing the Creation. " *Et factum est ita.*" At the same instant, a lurid phosphorescent glare permeated the room, showing that the Cosmo-magnetic streams had passed through the adamantine walls of the car. A peculiar nervous thrill impossible to describe, ran through every fibre of my frame. As we looked at each other in this ghastly light we seemed like human spectres, hovering as it were on the brink of eternity.

The pointer for speed was moving around its dial. I looked at Mars, it was rapidly expanding to the size of the full moon. The pointer on the time dial, moved around from one second to another, each one indicating our flight at the rate of nearly 400,000 miles for every second that flew. Sixty seconds passed and our car had accomplished its 20,000,000 miles. The misty emanation from the ball stretched like a slender wire, spanning the abyss of space. The disc of Mars grew larger and larger, rapidly expanding like a huge inflating balloon ; and now its strange topography of continents and oceans ; its polar snowcaps, its bright spots and cloud like patches, its two little moons, Diemos and Phobos, flashed before our eyes like the figures in a revolving kaleidoscope. Larger and larger it grew, until it swept in one vast circle as far as the eye could see all around us and it seemed as if we were dashing right into the very heart of the planet.

The pointers completed their revolution. Asterion dropped the wire. The flash disappeared from the ball. The phosphorescent glare passed away. Asterion stepped from the plate, raised his vizor, and pointed to the clock with a smile.

It was two minutes after 8 o'c. precisely.

" 40,000,000 miles in two minutes !" shouted Altfoura, as we stepped from the plate and threw off helmets and vizors. " Now let the beams of light that fly from the sun and the lightnings that flash from the thunder cloud, forever hide their diminished heads. Three cheers for Asterion. Commander in Chief of the Celestial highways. He shall have the highest honors our kingdom can bestow."

Asterion modestly acknowledged the compliment. Vidyuna and Bhuras took their stations ; the car paused in her tremendous flight and gradually reversed her position, with the base pointing downward.

"We are now entering the gaseous envelope surrounding the atmosphere of Mars," said he. " I checked off our speed before reaching it, for had we entered at that rate, car and all would have been consumed to ashes in an instant. We shall pass through it in thirty minutes, descend through the atmosphere at leisure and land near the south pole."

We took off the armor, and resumed our clothing. The light was lit, the air generator and batteries re-charged ; Asterion carefully removed his Cosmic Motor from the staff.

" Well done, my brave planetary racer," said he and kissed the smooth surface of the shining little globe. " You have made splendid time on your trial trip." Then placed it carefully in the casket.

" Asterion," said the Doctor, " please make for me a little Motor, so that when I want to do some swift thinking, I can wear it in my hat."

" I am afraid your ideas would fly so swift you couldn't hold them, and they would run away with you."

" Hello ! Corp ;" croaked a sepulchral voice from the glass box. " Lemme out o' here, d—d quick."

John let the birds out. The raven emerged from the box with stately step and began poking around under the chairs as usual.

" What's up, Jack ?"

" Gone chick'n."

" Hi !"—exclaimed John. " Somebody been a pickin' these chickens,"—holding up a pair of Mother Careys, who had crawled out of the box some how. They were stripped clean of their feathers and their bodies reduced to a pulp.[1]

" Which shows the power of the Cosmic stream," said Asterion. " Had it not been for our armor, we should have been served out in the same style."

We swiftly traversed the gaseous envelope and entered the atmosphere. We were on the dark side of the planet and the Martian night was gathering o'er us. Beneath lay the great polar snow cap, shining like white marble, while the snow clad plains and mountains stretched on either hand far as the eye could see. Lights gleamed here and there o'er the broad expanse.

" We shall land on one of the magnetic centres, not far from the pole," said Asterion.

The car took a westerly direction and in a short time several large stone buildings, brightly illuminated, came in view. We passed over them and came to a great

[1] Severe electric storms often produce these effects on fowls.

circular amphitheatre, large as the Roman Coliseum and surrounded with lofty walls of red stone ; the car ceased its flight and slowly descended, then paused motionless in the air.   A concourse of people were assembled below.

" This is our polar Ethervolt station, where we start on our planetary journeys," said Asterion.

" Now, Frederick," said Altfoura ; "you and John must conceal your faces with these veils, for should our Martian friends catch a glimpse of you, they would be full of curiosity and probably suspect from whence you came.   For the present you must appear incognito."

John and I tied the veils over our faces, Bhuras opened the windows and threw out long ropes which were seized by some of the people below who drew the car gently downward to a frame work standing on a large platform near the centre of the amphitheatre.   Asterion opened the door and we all stepped out on the platform.

"Welcome, ye men of Earth,—thrice welcome to Mars !" said he.

We landed on the planet, Sunday, May 1st, 1892, terrestrial time, which nearly corresponded with the Martian midsummer.   The planet was in the constellation Sagittarius.

CHAPTER XVIII.

ARRIVAL ON MARS.

" My thoughts and I were of another world."
Every Man out of his Humor.—BEN JOHNSON, Act III., Sc. 3.

The amphitheatre was brilliantly illumined with many colored lights.   A crowd of yellow, red and blue complexioned men gathered around us with loud cheers.

They were clad in suits of armor similar to those we had worn, and bore strange implements, emitting fine electric sparks. Several, who seemed to be the leaders, courteously greeted the Prince and Asterion. We descended the platform and were escorted by the superintendent of the station, through the gates of the amphitheatre to his residence, a commodious building of red stone, where we took quarters for the night. Altfoura informed me that he should depart early the next morning for home, to arrange for our reception. In the meantime he would leave us in care of the Doctor, for a few days, until we heard from him; during which we were to observe strict incognito as to our names and nationality. The next morning we donned our veils and accompanied by the Doctor and superintendent, took a walk about the place. It was a small village of dwelling houses and machine shops, containing a few hundred inhabitants, engineers and workmen with their families. It is situated on the shores of the Antarctic continent, about two hundred miles from the pole, which is surrounded by the Samudra Iozan, or South polar sea, corresponding to the so called Mare Australe on our Martian maps and which communicates with other oceans, separating the continents and lands of the south temperate regions.

On the following day, Asterion, who had been engaged in making preparations for another planetary journey, informed us that he was about to take a trip to the Asteroids, that vast belt lying between the orbits of Mars and Jupiter.

"My dear Asterion," expostulated the Doctor. "In the name of heaven, why do you not take some rest. You need it. You take no proper care of yourself, and as for recreation, you never allow yourself any."

"My enjoyments and recreations are in these jour-

neys," he replied. " You know I am in love with my
profession, and never so happy as when roaming among
the planets."

" But the strain on your nervous system is exceedingly severe ; you'll wear yourself out, in spite of your
wonderful powers of endurance ; you'll be shipwrecked
some day. Your life is too dear and valuable to us for
you to risk it in these dangerous pursuits. Remember
the sad fate of your renowned ancestor. Besides,
Prince Altfoura expects you to participate in the festivities celebrating the arrival of our guest from Earth ;
and the Princess Suhlamia will honor the event with
her royal presence."

A faint blush overspread Asterion's countenance.

" I deeply regret that I shall be compelled to deprive
myself of the pleasure. I have many important investigations to make in those regions, and this is the only
season for it."

" But you are to receive the especial commendation
of the Grand Duke, and high honors from the royal
College of Scientists for your wonderful discovery, the
greatest of the age. Prince Altfoura and all, will be
exceedingly disappointed at your absence," urged the
Doctor.

" As you well know, Doctor, I care nothing for
worldly honors and applause. My aspirations find their
highest gratification in whatever discoveries I may
make in the noble science to which I have devoted my
life, and which may be useful to my fellow men. I
seek for no reward here, and live only in the hope that,
when my mortal life is ended, I may be permitted to
pursue, in higher spheres, the calling I so dearly love."

" We do highly honor your truly noble sentiment,
Asterion, but 'tis not right that you should permit yourself to incur such dangers in the pursuit of science."

"As to perils, my dear Doctor, while I never unwisely incur them, as you know, I never permit them to interfere with my duty."

"But the journey is long and tedious."

"The belt is only about fifty million miles from here, and less than three hundred million miles wide," replied he with perfect nonchalance.

"'Tis nothing but a huge, revolving chaos," said I. "An interplanetary desert, consisting of a few hundred planetoids and thousands of mere fragmentary meteorites."

"And I am interested in that very subject of planetoidal and meteoroidal consolidation. By the way, Lieutenant, what is the opinion of your astronomers in regard to the origin of this great Asteroidal belt?"

"They are not in agreement on that point," I replied. "Some entertain the opinion that, they are the fragments of a former planet destroyed by a terrible explosion, or a collision with some other celestial body. Others hold that, they consist of partly consolidated cosmical matter, which originally formed one of the great nebulous rings thrown off by the sun in past ages and which has not yet been rolled up into a solid planet."

"They are the fragments of a once glorious world ; the most resplendent in the planetary hierarchy ; its name Luzio-Avani Dhramza, or the 'Great Shining One,' the history of whose awful destruction is recorded in the annals of our royal library. Many of the revolving remnants of this planet are surrounded by atmospheres,([1]) which could not otherwise exist, unless portions of the original great planetary atmosphere had not clung

([1]) Pallas for one. About 280 Asteroids have been already catalogued, and the list is being increased by new discoveries. Some have already been lost to view, perhaps having been united with others.

to them after the explosion. In future ages all these fragments will be reunited by mutual attraction, and consolidated into a new planet."

At these words, the scriptural prophecy came to mind. " For behold, I create new heavens, and a new Earth, and the former shall not be remembered, nor come into mind."(1)

Toward evening the superintendent announced to Asterion that his Ethervolt car was in readiness, and we all entered the gates of the station, which was built over one of the polar magnetic centres. It was a thousand feet in diameter, surrounded by massive walls of red stone and its pavement resembling blue crystal. On the platform, elevated a few feet above the floor was a large Ethervolt car supported on a metallic framework. Underneath were immense magnetic batteries, connected with conductors penetrating deep in the earth, and which evolve the great Cosmic streams originating at the polar centres and which propel or attract the cars on their planetary journeys ; near by were other platforms and cars. A pungent odor, resembling ozonized oxygen, and a peculiar electric aura pervaded the air, producing a singular tingling sensation over our faces and hands. Crowds of workmen

(1) Isaiah LXV. 17. The word "heavens," in the original Greek plainly indicates not HEAVEN,—the place of final beatitude, but, the firmament or atmosphere, which is used in the plural, signifying the atmospheric and cloudy envelopes of the habitable planets. See Poole, "Genesis of Earth and Man," and other eminent writers by whom this subject has been admirably and exhaustively discussed. All through the prophetic books as well as the Apocalypse, the phrase has this significance although many theologians fail to perceive it. HEAVEN, the place of final rest, once created, exists forever, is never changed or destroyed, and needs no new recreation.

clad in complete armor, stood around the platform, near the batteries.

"Yonder is my old favorite, which brought us here," said Asterion, pointing to one of the cars. "I have named her My Lady, Terrestrio-Martialis, Queen of the Martio-Terrestrian highways. She made splendid time on her return trip when my little Cosmic Motor took the reins, and I shall let her rest till my return. My old Asteroidal Ethervolt was pretty badly battered up on her last trip. This is a new car built under my personal supervision by the most celebrated car builders in our kingdom, and has many improvements of my own."

As the car rested lightly on its platform, it was a model of beauty, fifty feet high and glittered like burnished silver under the rays of the setting sun ; it was fully manned with the necessary appointments for a long planetary voyage. Vidyuna now came forward with the casket and motor.

"How rapidly will you travel ?" asked the Doctor.

"At my usual speed, from ten to twenty million miles per day, reserving my motor, for strait shoots along the Asteroidal belt, as occasion or necessity requires."

"How long will you be absent ?" I asked.

"From two, to three months, depending on circumstances. I have special investigations to make on many of the larger planetoids."

We ascended the platform, and Bhuras opened the door of the car.

"Farewell ; dear friends ;" said Asterion, warmly pressing our hands.

"And please accept my sincere wishes for your safe and prosperous journey," said I.

"And may you also enjoy the festivities in honor of your arrival," he replied.

"And to which your presence, now denied us, would give the greatest éclat;" said the Doctor, almost reproachfully.

"Doctor," replied he, "please convey to the Grand Duke, and members of the Royal College, my highest sentiments of loyalty and esteem, and present to the Princess Suhlamia the respectful salutations of her honored and devoted servant Asterion."

As he spoke these words, his voice trembled and an expression of deep sadness o'erspread his countenance.

"Farewell, Asterion," said the Doctor, placing his hands on the young man's head as he bent before him, while a tear stood in his eye. "May He who holds the Universe in the hollow of His hand, who guides the Stars, Suns and planets in their course through the Infinite Realms of Space, watch over and shield you and your companions from all harm, through this long and perilous journey, and restore you safe again to your friends and all of us who love and esteem you."

We descended the platform to a distance. Asterion, Vidyuna and Bhuras entered the car, and closed the door. The engineers worked the batteries. A profound vibration seemed to arise from the depths of the solid ground, and the crystal floor and lofty walls of the amphitheatre trembled as if shaken by the commencing undulations of an earthquake. Showers of sparks flew from the summit of the green globe. The car rose from its platform, rapidly and gracefully ascending in mid air, throwing off resplendent prismatic colors in its upward flight, and was soon lost to view in the distant clouds. It seemed like the flight of an Ethereal chariot to the celestial spheres.

"Asterion is the most high minded and chivalrous young man in our kingdom, Prince Altfoura alone excepted," said Dr. Hamival. "His courage is heroic, his genius unsurpassed and his devotion to science and his arduous profession unparalleled. All our scholars and men of science have the greatest regard and affection for him. Prince Altfoura loves him like a brother, and the Princess Suhlamia entertains the highest esteem and admiration of his truly great and noble qualities."

"And the Princess?" I asked.

"Suhlamia Angelion, the Juvan-indra, or Princess of the blood royal of the ancient line of Thullivarrh Kings and sister of Prince Altfoura," he replied. "She is the pride and glory of our kingdom and universally beloved. Her beauty is matchless; her accomplishments of the highest order, and what is far better, her nobility of soul, amiability and gentleness of disposition and perfect ingenuousness of character, endear her to all."

We left the amphitheatre and returned to the house. That night I dreamed of those intrepid voyagers winging their swift flight through realms where chaos reigns supreme, to other worlds than ours. And amid these dreams, floated a vision of transcendent female loveliness, such as mortal eye hath never seen among the beauteous ones of earth, and with it too appeared the sad and noble countenance of Asterion, gazing on that angelic vision with a mingled look of adoration, hopeless love and despair.

CHAPTER XIX.

BOMBARDING THE POLE.

"Cannon to right of them,
    Cannon to left of them,
    Cannon in front of them,
    Volley'd and thunder'd."

Charge of the Light Brigade.—TENNYSON.

The next morning I was awakened by the booming of heavy artillery from a great distance.

"Our fire ships are cutting a channel through the ice barriers, from the sea to the pole," said the Doctor. "Would you like to see the great work?"

I assented, and after breakfast we got ready for the trip. As the weather was cold, we donned our Martian overcoats, fur caps and veils, the latter screened our faces from recognition and protected them from the wind and it is the custom for persons visiting the poles to wear them. In company of the superintendent, we left the house and passed through the town. The surrounding country is rocky and barren; resembling the shores of Greenland; ice and snow fields extending on every hand. We walked to the sea shore where a pier was built out in the water. Here lay a small vessel similar to the one in which we had made the trip over the polar sea of Earth; it was manned with a captain and crew. We embarked and sailed up the coast several miles and entered the mouth of a great channel twenty miles wide.

"This is one of the sea canals cut by the fire ships directly toward the pole," said the Doctor.

We sailed a few miles along the shore and reached a

pier ; the vessel moored up and we debarked. Here was an immense quadrangular tower of red stone, three hundred feet high and nearly a thousand feet long. The superintendent escorted us up a winding staircase to the summit, a broad and level stone platform on which stood a battery of fifty cannon, bright as polished steel and of enormous dimensions. They were from one to two hundred feet long, and five to ten feet calibre, and mounted on moveable carriages. Huge conical shells from ten to twenty feet long, and immense globular bombs, ten feet in diameter, were piled alongside the guns, with powerful machinery for loading ; the guns were manned with crews in uniform. The Doctor introduced us to the captain, Zar Fulminax, a young man of bright red complexion in charge of the battery.

"It will give me pleasure to exhibit to your guests our mode of destroying ice," said he. "Our fleet has been at work several months at the head of the channel and large quantities of bergs and broken ice masses have been sent down the current this way."

Our elevated position commanded a view of ten or twelve miles over the channel along which large masses of disintegrated ice were floating. In a short time an immense ice berg appeared ; we waited until it had approached within a mile. It was full three hundred feet high, and two thousand feet long.

"I will now show you how we blow up ice bergs," said the Captain, then ordered three of the long guns to be loaded. The gunners worked the machinery, one of the conical shells was raised and placed in the gun ; Captain Fulminax levelled and fired it with a small electric battery. I expected a tremendous report, but a slight puff, only, like that of a steam pipe was heard. The shell flew across the water and plunged deep in the berg ; the explosion was terrific, and tore the whole upper part to pieces; the submerged part rose heaving and tossing above the surface; this was also blown up, and another discharge destroyed the remainder. The fragments covering several hundred acres, floated down the current.

After a while, a great ice floe appeared looming on the waters at a great distance up the channel. It was fully three miles long, by a mile or more wide, consisting of irregular fragments piled up together, and frozen in a solid mass. In the arctic regions of our world these are called hummocks; are wholly impassable to ships and when skirting land shores, are crossed with difficulty by Esquimaux dogs and sledges.

"This floe has been disrupted from some great glacier," said the Captain. "I will set it on fire."

Forty of the large calibre guns were loaded with the great ten foot bombs. The gunners worked the elevating machinery and as the huge yawning muzzles rose upward pointing to the skies, they looked almost like the weapons of the Mythological Titans, ready to assault the throne of Jupiter Olympus. Soon as the floe had approached within three miles, all were fired simultaneously. The enormous shells rose in great curves high in air and falling in a shower over the floe, burst open, setting it on fire in all directions. Repeated discharges were continued till the whole mass was enveloped in flames. The sight was terrible, resembling the conflagration of a great city. The firing was kept up and in a short time the entire floe was consumed.

"What are your guns loaded with?" I asked.

"With water," the Captain replied.

The idea of loading guns with water, struck me as savoring of a joke.

" By means of a chemical," continued he, " the water is decomposed into its two gases with such force as can throw a shell ten to twenty tons weight, from twenty to fifty miles. The shells are made of materials so strong they can penetrate several hundred feet in solid ice or rock, and they are charged with a fulminate of terribly explosive power. A few gallons of water only, are required for a gun. The bombs are charged with a peculiar gas condensed to a solid. This gas has a powerful affinity for oxygen ; when the bomb bursts, the gas is let loose, decomposes the ice, sets the hydrogen on fire, and the mass is speedily consumed."

" Why does not this gas also set fire to the water, and throw the whole ocean in a blaze ?" I asked.

" Sea water contains salt, as you know. When it freezes, the salt is expelled. The gas acts on the water in its frozen state only ; when the flame touches the salt water, it is extinguished."

We bade adieu to Captain Fulminax, descended the tower, embarked on the vessel and continued our course up the channel. It was cut through glaciers, rocks, hill slopes and plains, strait almost as a canal. We sailed about fifty miles up to its terminus, where it was crossed by a long line of precipices and ice barriers, several hundred feet high, which formed the slope or spur of a great mountain chain stretching to the south.

An astonishing spectacle was here displayed. Directly in front of this stupendous barrier and extending in compact line for twenty miles, lay a fleet of immense ships, each one from fifteen hundred to two thousand feet long, and of corresponding dimensions. Their hulls were bright as polished copper. They had no masts, sails nor rigging. Their decks were covered with high, sloping roofs of metal, supported on pillars. The decks and port holes bristled with enormous cannon

similar to those on the tower, and manned with crowds
of seamen and gunners with their officers. They were
bombarding the barrier with the full power of their
gigantic artillery, firing point blank at the upright
walls of the precipices, or at their foundations, or the
surrounding reefs, or at the ice bergs and glaciers, the
enormous shells blowing them to pieces in all directions. Some hurled their bombs, which, falling in
showers on the summits of the ice barriers or floes,
burst open and set them on fire. The sight was terrible and the uproar deafening. The explosions were
like the volcanic outbursts of Vesuvius or Stromboli.
Icy and rocky fragments, mingled with columns of
water and sheets of flame were hurled high in the air,
thence falling almost like cataracts from the sky, the
surrounding sea was converted into a seething cauldron of whirling waves, foam and fire. The downpour
of rocks on the pent roofs of the ships was like the rattle of whole brigades of musketry. Thousands of seamen in barges and floating dredges gathered up the
debris and carrying them down the channel sunk them
in the deep waters of the ocean. On other parts of the
mountain slope and surrounding plain were enormous
engines boring deep shafts in the solid rocks and blowing them up, while immense ploughing machines ripped
and tore the earthy crust in all directions, and the fragments were swiftly conveyed on great tramways many
miles distant and deposited over the surface of the surrounding plains.

Our vessel now sped over the channel to the fleet,
reached the flag ship and we went aboard. The
Doctor introduced me to the Admiral, Tangeo Zar
Erumpitos, a stout built man of deep bronze complexion, iron grey hair and about sixty years of age, who
received us with a hearty sailor's greeting and showed

us the appointments and armament of his ship. She was a prodigious naval monster, built of metal, two thousand feet long, three hundred feet abeam, sailed by electro motors, was nearly two hundred thousand tons burden, and her speed from sixty to eighty miles per hour. Twenty of our largest Atlantic steamers could lie side by side athwart her deck. Such a stupendous Oceanic giant, sailing among the combined navies of our world, might be compared, in respect to speed and power of destruction, to a shark amid a shoal of herring, and the combined artillery of all the iron clads in the world, could make no more impression on her adamantine hull, than a child's pop-gun on the hide of an elephant. A single one of her shells could blow the pyramid of Cheops sky high, and a dozen such ships lying off London, Paris, or New York, could reduce them to ashes within twenty four hours.

" We have cut sixteen great canals from two to three hundred miles long and ten to twenty miles wide, directly from the sea to the pole," said the Admiral. " We cut straight through all barriers, precipices, hills, or mountains, that happen to lie in our way, besides excavating them to a sufficient depth for the passage of our largest ships and floating ice masses. We are also engaged in cutting a great circum-polar sea three hundred miles wide, right over the polar centre, where the canals meet. We have been engaged in the work many years. Similar operations are being conducted at the north pole. Our average speed in cutting is from four to six miles a year."

" How do you prevent them from freezing up during the winter ?" I asked.

" By establishing steady currents through them ; running sea water never freezes, and we prevent the ice from accumulating along the shores by breaking it up."

We were compelled to decline the Admiral's polite invitation to partake of a collation in the magnificent saloon which was large enough to seat comfortably a thousand guests, as it would have required the removal of our veils. We bade him adieu, re-embarked, sailed down the channel and reached the superintendent's house by night-fall. I asked the Doctor what was the object in constructing these immense polar canals.

"As you doubtless know," he replied, "our years and seasons are nearly twice as long as yours, although our days are about equal, and in consequence of the greater inclination of our planet's axis to the plane of its orbit, it experiences greater vicissitudes of climate than your earth. During our six months summer the heats of the equatorial and south temperate zones, are greatly prolonged and intensified, and during our six months winter, in the polar and north temperate zones, the cold is correspondingly prolonged and increased. We are also subject during the spring months to extensive floods and inundations from the rapid melting of snow and ice. These canals are cut for the purpose of producing a more steady and uniform circulation of the waters of our oceans from the equator to the poles, the equatorial waters communicating their warmth to the polar waters and they, in turn, cooling those of the equator. This mutual interchange, also produces corresponding influences on our wind currents, thereby equalizing our climate and temperature from equator to poles. Furthermore, by removing as far as possible these vast accumulations of polar snow and ice we greatly mollify the severity of the climate in those regions, and reclaim a great part of the lands, rendering them habitable and productive. Similar canals have been cut on a much larger scale, over many of our continents in both hemispheres for the purpose of establishing communications between the seas and oceans all over our planet which renders our climate more salubrious and uniform than it would otherwise be."

CHAPTER XX.

THE AIR SHIP.

" I come
To answer thy best pleasure ; be't to fly,
To swim, to dive into the fire, to ride
On the curl'd clouds."

Tempest.—Act I., Sc. 2.

On the following morning we received a dispatch from the Prince, that his special messenger would soon arrive to escort us to his country.

" As we have a journey of nearly five thousand miles to make," said the Doctor, " in order to escape public curiosity your terrestrial complexions must be concealed, and as veils are inconvenient, you and John must have your faces painted, in the Martian style, in order to keep up your incognito."

" Cap'n," queried John, " what that foreign lingo word mean, any how ?"

" It means we are to assume a character that does not belong to us ; to take an alias, the privilege of thieves and princes, to play a part like a stage actor."

" Hi ! Me can paintee face just like big Tanehoka war chief when he go a courting his gal, when he gettee married ; when wife die, when he go after anudder wife, when he go on war path, and when he go die. Can paintee Cap'n any style he likee."

" All right," I replied, " and as all the world's a stage, and all the men and women merely players, and one man in his time plays many parts, we may as well put on the stage paint, and play our aliases, but no New Zealand war chief for me ; paint me like a peaceful Martian."

One of the children in the house had a box of colors. We retired to a private room. I resigned myself to John's clever hands and in a short time my complexion was changed to a bright golden hue, and my hair, mustaches and eyebrows to a jet black shaded with blue. I looked at myself in the glass and for the life of me could not tell whether I was myself or somebody else.

" Excellent !" said the Doctor, " your incognito is perfect, you are now a genuine Martian, all except your stature, which is quite above the average, and your eyes, which are bright blue, and there are no blue eyes among the Martians."

" Eb'ry body hab black eyes 'round here ; canno' give Cap'n Fred black eye, no how," remarked John.

The Doctor produced a pair of dark tinted spectacles.

" Wear these. You are a professor of philosophy and very near sighted,—you understand."

I took the hint, donned the glasses and assumed the rôle of the professor.

" Me fixee up meself like war chief, by and by," said John, then painted himself in genuine Martian red, his coal black hair needing no extra tint, then wrapped himself in a striped red blanket like an Indian.

" You can now make your entrée into our fashionable society with flying colors," said the Doctor.

" It is to be hoped these colors are not fast," said I, " for before I enter your polite circles in this masquerade, I'll fling myself into a coal pit."

" They can be removed with a harmless chemical in ten minutes," replied the Doctor.

In a short time a man of bright bronze complexion, piercing black eyes and strongly marked countenance, entered the room ; he was clad in uniform.

" Good morning, gentlemen," said he. " I am Halis Zar Volanto, and am commissioned by His Highness, Prince Altfoura, to escort you to the Kingdom of Mandal-Uttima." Then he handed the Doctor a letter, who opened and read it.

" Captain," said the Doctor, " this gentleman is Professor Hamiltoneus of the chair of philosophy in the North polar college, and this gentleman,"—pointing to John,—" is—is—really, John, I have forgotten your title."

" Julius Cæsar, Pompey, Hannibal, Napoleon, George Washington, Ulysses S. G. Corporal John, Prince of New Zealand and King of the Cannibal Islands !" vociferated John with a grand flourish.

" And I'm Commodore Jack the giant killer ;" bellowed the raven as he flopped up on John's shoulder, cocked his head on one side with a knowing look and winked both eyes at Zar Volanto.

" I am delighted to meet you, gentlemen," replied Volanto with a profound salutation, at the same time looking very hard at the raven, " but your stature, breadth of shoulder, etc., are somewhat in advance of the general run of hyperboreans, and as for this extraordinary bird, I must confess I—"

The Doctor hastened to explain that we had lived close to the pole so long, we had grown very tall and that the raven was an unknown species of educated bird supposed to have flown from one of the Asteroids, on a voyage of discovery.

The Captain now announced that it was time to

depart. We hastened to get in readiness, packed up our baggage, arms, instruments, etc. John stowed the raven and birds in the basket ; we put on our overcoats, left the house and walked down to the pier where a very singular looking vessel lay moored.

"This is my Nai Filius or Air Ship," said the Captain.

It was about eighty feet long by twenty abeam, shaped like a spindle and constructed of bright blue colored metal. Its deck was flat and surrounded by a high railing. Its prow projected out like the nose of a pike, or sword fish, and was tipped on the end with a small green ball like that on the Ethervolt car. Its stern was obtuse and its rudder resembled the tail of a bird. It was pierced along the sides with small circular windows, and two at the prow resembled the eyes of a fish. Three great wings, each twenty feet long and shaped like those of the frigate bird, projected from port holes on either side. Several men in uniform stood on deck.

"Are you all ready, boys?" asked the Captain.

"Aye, aye," they replied.

"All aboard," ordered he.

We bade farewell to the superintendent, and got aboard with our baggage. The ropes were cast off ; the captain gave the signal, a low rumbling sound was heard in the hold and to my astonishment, the ship rose from the waters in spiral circles, her wings waving to and fro, till she had ascended three hundred feet in the air.

"Steer to the north east," ordered the Captain.

The great propelling wings waved gracefully to and fro like the wings of an eagle and the ship flew onward with a swift and steady motion.

"What power elevates her?" I asked.

" The aerovolt batteries, similar to those on the Ethervolt cars," he replied.

" What's her speed ?"

" From a hundred to a hundred and fifty miles per hour, generally, but she can go much faster."

We descended the hatchway to the cabin which was commodious and elegantly furnished. The machine room occupied the forward part. Beneath the floor were the aerovolt batteries and electro motors. The propelling machinery was of intricate and delicate construction, combining the greatest degree of tensile strength with lightness of weight. The wings were composed of some unknown metallic membranous material, and their strength, lightness and ease of motion, were marvellous. The molecular structure of the metals being altered in some peculiar manner by the Martian machinists, so that, their cohesive strength, or toughness, is increased a hundred fold beyond our strongest steel.

The ship flew swiftly over the blue waters of the polar sea, and the great ice cap soon disappeared from view. The appearance of the horizon was surprising. On our earth, the eye of an observer elevated six feet above the surface, commands a view of about three miles either way (1) Here, it is only about a mile and a half, Mars being about half the circumference of Earth, his horizon is correspondingly shortened. The clouds also appeared much nearer, and their colors were more pronounced and bright owing to the lesser depth and density of the Martian atmosphere as compared with that of Earth.

During the day we crossed the Mare Australe, or Antarctic sea, and by evening had advanced nearly a

(1) The Earth's curvature on the sea board is about seven inches to the mile.

thousand miles corresponding to about 60° south latitude as designated on our Martian maps and were coursing over Leverrier sea beyond which lies the continent
of Copernicus (1) The sky became overcast and the
wind began to blow a gale ; the propelling wings were
furled and laid back in their grooves in the sides of the
ship, the shorter storm wings were projected from their
ports and their swift and more powerful motion bore us
ahead for a while, but the gale steadily increased and
it was difficult to make headway.

"How high is the storm belt?" asked Captain
Volanto.

"Five miles," replied the first officer, consulting the
instrument for altitude.

"Ascend above it to the region of calm," ordered the
Captain.

The ship's prow was directed obliquely upward and
she began to ascend in great spiral circles toward the
clouds. She had arisen about six hundred feet and
while I was admiring the ease with which she was
surmounting the gale, suddenly one of the wings broke
loose.

"Hold fast !" shouted the Captain.

The ship tilted sidewise and almost capsized. We
clung to the railing ;—a cry arose.

"Man overboard !"

John, who had been carelessly leaning against the
railing, was thrown over and fell six hundred feet
down into the sea. Captain Volanto quickly cast a belt
around his shoulders, snatched up a short metallic staff

---

(1) The names of the Martian Continents and Oceans vary on
our Martian maps, according to the nationality of their discoverers, several of whom lay claim to prior discoveries ; the
French and German maps differ from the English and American.

to which was attached a small crystal globe, hooked it firmly to the belt, and taking up an instrument resembling a small folded parasol, secured it to the strap, threw off his cap and overcoat, then shouting to the crew.

"Clear away the broken wing and follow me"— stepped on the railing, sprang over and disappeared.

I was overwhelmed with horror and felt that even if John reached the water alive, his breath would be knocked out of him when he struck. The daring act of the Captain amazed me.

"Does John know how to swim?" asked the Doctor.

"He is the most expert swimmer and diver I ever saw. I have often seen him jump from the main top gallant mast down to the sea, for mere sport and swim for miles. But of what avail are any man's powers from this awful height: he will be killed at once, or stunned into insensibility and perish in the waves."

"If the blow does not kill him, he will be saved. We must hope for the best. As for the Captain, armed with his aerostat and gyral, he wouldn't mind jumping from the ship if she were ten miles high."

The engineers now reversed the batteries; the ship righted, and with her fore wings only in motion, descended in a long spiral toward the sea; then coursing slowly to and fro just above the waters threw out a powerful electric light, illumining them to a great distance and blew loud whistles; in a few moments a solitary light was seen glimmering in the darkness, a faint "hallo," was heard, and the ship came to.

An extraordinary spectacle now appeared. Captain Volanto was suspended a few feet above the waves, upheld by his aerostat, which shone like an electric light, John was clinging to his waist. The Captain was holding his gyral by the handle, strait in front; it resembled a small Japanese parasol thrown open and was swiftly whirling on its handle like an electric fan, drawing them rapidly through the air. In a few moments they reached the ship and descended to the deck. John presented a ludicrous appearance, with his jacket swollen out all around him, the Captain unscrewed a button in the collar, the confined air rushed out and he shrank to his original dimensions. I expressed my sincere thanks to the Captain for his noble and daring act.

" 'Tis a mere nothing," he replied ; "no man was ever lost from an air ship flying over the ocean, although many have fallen over board. The jackets with which we are clothed contain within the lining a small quantity of the crystallized chemical elements of the atmosphere which are decomposed when the water comes in contact with them, and evolve large quantities of air which swells the jacket out, forming a perfect life preserver, supporting the body above water."

I examined the aerostat. It was a crystal globe about a foot in diameter containing a small aerovolt battery and fastened to the straps around the shoulders. By touching a spring in the handle, the wearer could increase or diminish its elevating power, and thereby ascend to any required height, or descend at pleasure. The gyral was a flat, parasol shaped air fan about three feet in diameter when opened. Its framework was composed of delicate metallic vanes arranged at the required angle around the staff, or handle, within which was a small electric motor. It was held in the hand or attached to a belt around the waist. When put in motion, it revolved with immense velocity, and when the wearer was upheld by his aerostat, it could draw him through the air swifter than a horse on full gallop.

" Well, John," facetiously remarked the Doctor, " you

descended from the ship with rather more haste than dignity. Please relate your adventures by the way."

"When tumble overboard,—heap big fool for that,— me draw knees up close to chin,—clap hand over nose, hold breath tight,—fallee down terrible swift,—if strike water flat,—knock breath all out,—but me know better, —no lettee arms and legs sprawl about,—strikee water head first, or bottom side first, don't care which,—go in water just like a wedge, down deep,—water gurgle and hiss all around, jacket swell out,—canno go down any more. Next minute me come up, pop! like cork out of beer bottle. Me likee big rolling sea, but no likee jacket what swell out like balloon. Canno swim, no how,—float around like a frog when you blow up his belly with a pipe. Now when storm go down, you go up five times higher than top mast of biggest ship in the world; me dive down head first, and swim ten miles. Bettee a hundred dollar on it. Will any gentleman takee bet?"

As no one volunteered to accept the challenge, John was voted the champion swimmer and diver of the day.

"As the waves are running high," said the Captain, "although our ship can make good headway against them, I will take the opportunity to show our guests how easily our air ship can swim under water," then to the engineers.

"Withdraw the wings, reverse batteries and descend beneath the surface."

We entered the cabin, the hatchway was closed, a loud gurgling announced that the ship had plunged beneath the waves; the light was lit.

"Start the propeller and head light."

This was done; a slight oscillation announced that she was moving through the water. I looked through the circular glass windows in the prow and along the sides, the sea was brightly illumined all around by the light. Sea fish of all varieties and shapes, such as I never saw before among the oceans of Earth, attracted by the light, clustered around the ship, some gazing curiously at us with their glassy eyes, or rubbing their noses against the windows. One huge monster, whether shark or whale I could not make out, opened his jaws, rushed forward and repeatedly bit at the ship's side, his teeth grating against the metallic hull like the sound of a stone crushing machine.

"Well, old fellow," said the Captain, "are you trying to get the toothache?" The monster finally gave it up and disappeared.

"How deep have we descended?" I asked.

"About a hundred feet, which is deep enough to avoid the perturbations of the most violent storms," replied he.

"How deep can you sink beneath the surface?"

"About half a mile only. We have ships which can descend to far greater depths where the water pressure amounts to several tons per square foot. I hope to have the pleasure some day of escorting you to certain parts of our oceans where the depth is so great that the water feels like quick silver."

"I should think the hulls of your ships would be crushed by this enormous pressure. How do they resist it?"

"By their style of build, etc. They are constructed of the strongest metals expressly adapted to resist the greatest amount of aqueous pressure; besides, their interior being filled with air, materially aids their powers of resistance."

"How long can you remain under water?"

"As long as we please, a week, or a month, if necessary. We renovate the air by our generators," and the Captain touched a valve in the generator, letting in a supply of fresh air in the cabin, then opening a valve in the roof, the confined air rushed out with a loud hiss.

A terrible sound now rang through the cabin ; it was like the roar of the rapids of Niagara.

" What noise is that ?" I asked.

" It is the rush of the ship through the water."

" How fast is she going ?"

" Sixty miles an hour."

Notwithstanding this tremendous speed there was only a slight oscillation of the ship.

" What time do the polar magnetic engines fire up ?" asked the Doctor.

" Nine o'c. precisely," replied the Captain, looking at his watch. " It is now the hour."

" We must try to reach Angosta bay by to-morrow morning."

" It's nearly three thousand miles distant, but I think we can make it in spite of the broken wing." Then to the engineers—

" Withdraw the propeller and head light,—get out the storm wings and ascend to the surface."

A rattling sound was heard in the hold, the prow of the ship was directed upward, a slight rocking took place, as she shot high above the surface, upheld by the swift motion of her storm wings. We looked through the windows ; the night was dark,—the rain fell in torrents and loud above the roaring of the billows, arose the shriek of the gale.

CHAPTER XXI.

DEFYING THE LIGHTNING.

"To be exposed against the warring winds,
  To stand against the deep dread-bolted thunder,
  In the most terrible and nimble stroke
  Of quick, cross lightning."
                King Lear.—Act IV., Sc. 7.

"Captain," called out the first officer, "the ship can make no headway."

"What's the speed of the wind?" he asked.

"It's blowing eighty miles an hour, and dead ahead."

"Charge up the magnetic cathode and withdraw the storm wings," ordered he.

The officer touched the key of a battery, the green globe at the prow threw off a shower of fiery sparks. The wings were folded in their grooves, the helmsman turned the rudder, the ship wheeled about, head to the wind and hung poised, swaying in the gale as if held by an invisible cable.

"What wonderful power is this that holds the ship?" I asked.

"Immense magnetic engines stationed on the summits of lofty mountains at the north pole, five thousand miles distant, pour their magnetic currents over the planet and attract the air ship toward the north. Similar engines stationed at the south pole attract the ships in that direction," replied the Captain.

"They resemble the interplanetary cosmic currents on a miniature scale," said Dr. Hamival.

The ship now began to move ahead and in a few

moments, drawn by the mighty power of the streams, flew like a whirlwind right in the teeth of the storm.

" How fast are we going ?" I asked.

" Five miles a minute," replied the Captain.

In a few moments a low murmuring sound arose which gradually increased to a loud and horrible scream resounding through the cabin.

" What frightful noise is that ?" I asked.

" 'Tis the rush of the ship through the air. She is flying ten miles a minute."

" At that rate she could circumvolate Mars in twenty hours."

" Sooner than that if necessary."

The loud scream now gradually ceased and silence prevailed.

" Are you slacking up ?"

" O, no, we're flying faster."

" How fast ?"

" Twenty miles a minute."

Swift as a bullet shot from a rifle ! The silence was explained. The sound waves, whose speed is only about eleven hundred feet per second, were outstripped in this race and could not reach the ear ; yet in spite of this immense velocity, not the slightest motion of the ship was perceptible.

" Can you fly faster than this ?"

" Certainly ; from fifty to a hundred miles a minute if necessary, but the friction of the air makes the walls of the ship too hot for comfort, and sometimes the deck railing is swept off by the rush."

I placed my hand over the metallic walls of the cabin, they were warm as the flue of a chimney.

" Theoretically, there's no limit to our speed along these polar magnetic currents," said the Captain, " but practically there is ; and that, consists in air friction ; a ship flying six hundred miles per minute would become red hot, and at much higher rates would be consumed to ashes by the enormous friction heat, like a falling meteorite."

From time to time I saw through the windows, great numbers of air ships, shooting by, almost like flashes of lightning.

" They are bound for the South pole, attracted by the engines stationed there," said the Captain.

" How do you check off this tremendous speed ?"

" We withdraw the positive magnetism from the cathode at the prow, and charge the anode at the stern with negative magnetism. This acts like a break and checks the ship up."

We were now among the storm clouds and immersed in the very heart of the furious tempest. The dreadful thunder peals seemed to split the heavens. The lightning flashes flew hither and thither, illumining the dark abysses and fathomless gulfs of this cloud ocean with a hellish glare. It is impossible to describe the awful grandeur of the scene.

" Is there not great danger of these lightning flashes striking our ship ?" I asked.

" None whatever," replied the Captain, " her magnetism is powerfully antagonistic to the cloud electricity, and she tosses off the thunder bolts as a lion shakes the dew drops from his mane."

I could scarce believe my eyes, as looking through the windows, I saw many of these fiery, zigzag flashes, aimed by the Storm King strait at the ship, the instant they came near, flew off in tangents, or were dashed into millions of harmless sparks, overwhelmed and crushed by an imponderable foe more potent than they.

In an hour the gale went down, the clouds fled away and the stars shone in the Martian sky with a brilliancy unknown on Earth. This is owing to the diminished depth and density of the atmosphere, compared with that of our globe.

Drawn by the magnetic streams we had swiftly crossed Leverrier sea and were coursing over the continent of Copernicus which forms the southern part of Kepler's continent. We flew over mountains, lakes, rivers and plains, the whole country was illumined by brilliant lights in countless thousands. At midnight we retired to our cots ; Captain Volanto posting his engineers for the night, during which we crossed the Storm Sea and a part of Kepler's continent and were advancing toward Angosto bay running into Tycho sea, which communicates directly with Airy sea lying between Galileo continent and Rosse's land as laid down on our Martian maps. We had crossed the equator and were in the sub-tropical regions of the planet.

———————◆———————

CHAPTER XXII.

S U N R I S E O N M A R S.

" This earth of majesty ; this seat of Mars ;
This other Eden, demi-paradise,
This happy breed of men ; this little world ;
This precious stone set in a silver sea."
Richard II.—Act II., Sc. 2.

At dawn of day I was aroused by the Doctor.

" Awake ! Behold our Martian sunrise !" said he.

" I have checked off our speed that you may enjoy the view," said Captain Volanto as we ascended the deck.

Sunrise on Mars ! The glorious orb of day was rising in the east with a splendor unknown in the terrestrial world, and language is wholly inadequate to describe the magnificent scene. Mounted on our aërial ship we were flying o'er an ocean of emerald, flecked with crimson and gold. How sublime this matchless Empyrean ! far transcending the " deeply beautifully blue " that o'erspreads the Mediterranean, the isles of Greece, or the Vaie of Cashmere, so oft the theme of the poet and romancer. The Martian skies are infinitely more lovely. Their prevailing hue might be compared to a delicate heliotrope. In the zenith float the soft and fleecy cirri, white as the driven snow. The horizon is bedecked with gorgeous clouds. All along the circular sweep of mingled sea and sky, what a wealth of glory is lavished there ! They hang in masses of brilliant scarlet, green and gold ; in draperies of crimson and purple, festooned with silver, fringed with pearl, and shaded with softest greys. These resplendent hues are mirrored upon the waters as if the sea and sky were wooing each other in love's embrace. The wave crests glitter with such dazzling coruscations it seems as if the jewels of ocean had risen from their deep caverns and were joyously floating and sparkling there.

How pure and soft this Martian air ! Its wondrous electric and vital properties thrill through every fibre of the frame, mantling the cheek and enkindling the eye. As the heaving bosom breathes these ambrosial draughts, it almost seems as if the swelling soul panted to burst its earthly confines—

> " To mingle with the Universe and feel,
> What it can ne'er express, yet cannot all conceal."

These are the skies,—the seas,—the air, of Mars, and I gazed, absorbed, entranced, on the beauteous scene.

" How compare they with those of your great world ?"
asked the Doctor.

" Compare !" I exclaimed. " In vivid flights of the
imagination, or the rapt visions of the devotee who
dreams of Paradise, such scenes may be displayed to the
eye of the mind ; but splendors like these were never
yet seen by an inhabitant of Earth."

" I deemed your world, which is so much larger than
ours and so nearer the sun, far more beautiful than our
little globe," replied the Doctor. " These scenes are
ever present in fair weather and heightened by almost
endless variety of form and color. The glimmering
dawn and bright noonday, the even-tide and night,
have each their own peculiar charms. Like you, we
also have our gloomy skies and lowering clouds ; were
it not so, even these beauties would, by continual repetition, pall upon the eye."

We were coursing over the broad Angosta bay which
penetrates Kepler's continent to the southward several
hundred miles, nearly to the equator and which communicates to the north with the great Tycho sea separating Galileo's and Madler's continents. The shores of
this bay are lined with dense forests, and luxuriant
vegetation such as are seen in the tropical regions of
South America. They are skirted with low lands,
morasses and sandy beaches ; the color of the latter
were bright yellow, red or dazzling white. Back in the
country were plateaus and mountain ranges. The
foliage of the trees is in many respects different from
that of Earth, and presenting to my unaccustomed eye
fantastic forms and great varieties of color ; the brilliant
and gorgeous hues of the flowering trees and plants
were almost dazzling to the eye. Numerous species of
birds unknown on Earth, were flying amid the forests
or over the waters and shores in search of their food ;

their plumage was often of great beauty, and the shores resounded with their shrill and musical cries.

Our ship now took her course toward the eastern shore of the bay, and descended to the quiet waters of a little cove penetrating the land. We took breakfast and Captain Volanto announced that necessary repairs to the machinery and broken wing would delay our journey a few hours. In a short time a beautiful little vessel which had been sailing over the bay in company with several others, now changed her course toward us and drew alongside our ship. She was built like one of our top sail schooner yachts about a hundred tons burden ; her hull, masts and yards entirely of metal, presenting a brilliant appearance. Her Captain and several of his crew came aboard. They were fine looking and athletic young men of bright yellow or red complexions. Captain Volanto introduced John and myself, as the Prince and Professor, and the Captain invited us to take a short trip over the bay which we accepted and got aboard, John with his portmanteau and raven in his basket. Captain Volanto announced that when the repairs were completed, he would overhaul us. The yacht coursed along the shore a few miles, then put out over the bay under a strong breeze. The appearance of the waves is different from those of our seas and oceans. They are of a bright green color and roll in longer undulations, often rising in lofty combers crowned with great masses of surf which flew before the wind in showers of spray ; this is owing to the lightness of the waters as compared with those of Earth, being nearly two thirds less in weight. We passed several islands clothed with luxuriant verdure and drew alongside one, as the Doctor wished to collect some botanical specimens. We took boat and went ashore ; the island was inhabited by birds and several varieties of harmless little animals, such as would have puzzled our terrestrial naturalists to name and classify. After a while we returned to the yacht. It was noon day ; the sun shone with great power and the heat was like that of our tropics. The wind died away ; the sails hung motionless on the masts and the vessel was becalmed. The waters glittered under the sunlight with a glare almost painful to the eye. The crew slung hammocks and awnings over the deck. The Captain retired to the cabin, to await a fresh breeze, and we laid down in the hammocks for a short siesta. We were just falling into a doze, when suddenly a loud and terrible roar burst upon the air. I sprang from the hammock and looked around, but there was nothing to be seen. A few moments passed and again that dreadful sound arose as if from the foundations of the deep ; the deck trembled, the masts shook and the binnacle glasses jingled in their frames, as those thundering tones rolled in long echoes o'er the sea.

" Look ! look !" shouted John, pointing to leeward. " *Taniwha! Taniwha!* "[1]

A gigantic sea-monster was rushing through the waves toward the ship with the speed of a railroad train. His long neck was curved high in the air. His enormous eyes glaring from under the brows of his eagle shaped head like the open doors of a fiery furnace. His jaws were wide open, displaying rows of long, sharp, glittering teeth. A smoky vapor streamed from his nostrils. From his shoulders two long, wing shaped paddles rose and fell amid the waves. His vast chest ploughed through the waters like the prow of a great ship, while ever and anon, his tail, reared high in air, flapped like a mainsail in the wind.

[1] In the New Zealand Mythology " king of the sea monsters."

"Great God !" I almost shrieked, springing to the Doctor's side. "See,—see that terrible monster !"

"Pooh !" replied he, hardly condescending to look up from his plants. "That's our gay and frolicsome little sea horse."

Again that thundering roar shook the sea and the monster was bearing swiftly down upon us. I shouted to the crew but they heeded not my call. Anticipating our instant destruction, I seized the Doctor by the collar, dragged him across the deck, intending to plunge with him into the sea and swim ashore, when suddenly a tremendous voice called out—

"Ship ahoy !—Hello there !—Tumble up out of your hammocks, you sleepy heads."

I looked around, as the monster, bigger than any ship afloat, and on whose back stood crowds of Martian men in strange attire, sped o'er the waves with the mighty rush of a great ocean steamer ; then checking his onset, drew up quietly alongside the yacht, while a man of gigantic stature stood on top of its head, holding a pair of reins fastened to its jaws, flourishing an immense whip, and roaring out his horseman's orders with the voice of a lion.

The crew sprang from their hammocks with loud cheers, which were answered by scores of laughing voices. A ladder was thrown out and several men in bright green uniform came on deck. The Doctor introduced me to the Captain, Ronald Zar Samadron, and officers, who received us with hearty sailors' greetings. The Captain invited us to take a trip on his ship. We bade adieu to the Captain and crew of the yacht, and ascended the ladder to the deck. It was of metal, surrounded by a railing and spread here and there with awnings. Crowds of officers, engineers and seamen, stood in groups on the deck. Captain Samadron blew a loud whistle. Officers and seamen took their stations. The monster wheeled his vast bulk right about, raised his enormous paddles and tail high in air, smote the waves with a sound like thunder and sped swiftly onward, a long wake of tossing foam trailing behind him, while the colossus mounted on his head, shook the reins, snapped his whip, and in a voice like ten Stentors rolled into one, sang his rollicking sea song.

" Here comes Leviathan!
   O'er the billows bounding.
Gaily he dashes on,
   'Mid thunders resounding.

What cares Leviathan,
   For lightnings flashing ;
Tempest and rolling waves,
   O'er the sea dashing ?

" What cares the ocean King,
   For storm clouds low'ring?
What cares Hartilion,
   For hurricanes howling ?

" Ho ! Ho ! my jolly boys,
   Dangers defying ;
Gaily we'll laugh and sing,
   O'er the sea flying."

" Captain," said I, " what is the name of your ship ?"
" Leviathan," replied he.
" Who is that gigantic horseman ?"
" Arozial Zhang Hartilion, Leviathan's master."
" Is he a Martian ?"
" He is a Plutonian ; a prince of blood royal descended from one of the seven great kings of the lost planet, ' Luzio Avani Dhramza,' or ' The Great Shining One.' "

CHAPTER XXIII.

LEVIATHAN.

"Canst thou draw out Leviathan with a hook, or bore his jaw through with a thorn? None is so fierce that dare stir him up. I will not conceal his parts, nor his power, nor his comely proportions. His teeth are terrible round about. When he raiseth himself up the mighty are afraid. He esteemeth iron as straw and brass as rotten wood. The arrow cannot make him flee; sling stones are turned with him into stubble; he laugheth at the shaking of a spear. He maketh the deep to boil like a pot. Upon earth there is not his like, who is made without fear."

Job. Chap. XLI.

What is LEVIATHAN?—Is he a fish, reptile, or whale?

The mighty monster on whose deck we stood is neither. He belongs to no order of beings ever seen on Earth, ever enrolled in ancient mythologies, or conceived in the wildest dreams of imagination. He is a special and distinct creation, akin to no other, yet combining within himself all the more noble and beautiful characteristics seen in the higher orders of the animal kingdom. His graceful and supple body is the exact similitude of man's in the chest, shoulders and loins, and his neck is like that of the horse. His head and beak are shaped like that of the golden eagle. From his shoulders project two great pectoral fins or paddles shaped like the wings of the frigate bird. His tail, serpentine in form, is terminated by two immense flukes like those of the fin back whale. His body is encased in a flexible cuirass of jet black horny scales, fringed with white on their edges. His voice possesses three different qualities of tone ; sometimes he utters musical sounds, sweet as the tones of an Æolian harp, when in company with his mate, or moving quietly over the waters ; at other times he pours from his vast lungs a deep and ponderous roar which shakes the sea like thunder, and when enraged, or at the approach of great storms he utters a piercing and terrible scream, or cry, which almost seems to split the very heavens. As to dimensions, he is four hundred feet long from the tip of the beak to the extremity of the tail ; his head is forty feet long from beak to occiput ; he is sixty feet broad across the shoulders, his paddles are seventy feet long and thirty feet wide, his tail flukes fifty feet across from tip to tip and his weight avoirdupois, thirty five thousand tons.

As this monarch of the ocean moves o'er the waves with a presence so majestic and terrible, yet beautiful, he seems like some great mythological deity incarnated in earthly form.

The name of Leviathan in the Martian language is "Maha-Raja Bhuvazon, or Supreme King of the Ocean."

Captain Samadron conducted us to the quarter deck which was shaded with awnings. We took refreshments and spent a short time in conversation. Having become somewhat accustomed to the novelty of my situation, I accompanied him over this living ship. The officers and seamen numbered about two hundred men of the three different complexions. The deck was of dark blue metal, about two hundred feet long by forty feet wide, and secured upon Leviathan's back with stanchions and great brazen bands surrounding his body. Near the railing were chests of provisions, water casks and a number of large crystal coffers. Near the centre of the deck were several electro-galvanic batteries manned with operators.

"We sometimes employ electricity to control and guide Leviathan's movements," said the Captain. "Although he is generally docile and obedient to his master, yet sometimes his fiery spirit hurries him beyond bounds, and we are compelled to curb him ; this is accomplished by the batteries, the wires of which are connected with certain parts of his body and communicate with his muscles and motor nerves, stimulating or repressing them as occasion requires. His anatomical and physiological structure are thoroughly understood, and we have him under better control, than any ship afloat. On some occasions he plunges to great depths beneath the water during hurricanes or tidal waves ; we then take refuge within the coffers which are transparent and we can see what is going on around us."

In the meantime Leviathan was rushing over the waters with tremendous speed, far outstripping that of the swiftest ocean steamer. His mighty paddles smote the billows with thundering sound and hurled them back in masses of spray. His enormous tail flukes sculling from side to side, sweeping the waters up into great whirling eddies, or spouting masses of foam, literally making the " deep to boil like a pot." We now passed to the fore deck where Leviathan's neck, towering up eighty feet high, was swaying to and fro under the tremendous impetus of his paddles like a giant oak under a gale. It was clothed with an immense mane, the hairs—if hairs they might be called—from forty to sixty feet long, thick as hemp cords and of a reddish yellow color. As they streamed out in the wind they resembled a great waving mass of flame. A long rope ladder hung from the top down to the deck.

" We will now go up and pay our respects to Arozial

Zhang Hartilion, our renowned Leviathan tamer," said the Captain.

We ascended the ladder to Leviathan's head which was covered with great scales, black as ebony and hard as iron. It was encased with a close fitting framework of steel bands, on the summit of which was a circular metallic platform about fifteen feet wide covering the top of his head like a morion, or skull cap and surrounded with a chain railing. Through an opening in the centre projected the great horny buckler, shaped like the crest of a Grecian helmet, curving forward and upward over the eyes and backward over the occiput. It was black as ebony and smooth as polished marble. We stepped over the railing and stood on the platform holding to the chains.

Seated astride the crest and mounted on a saddle firmly secured to it, was a young man whose magnificent form and prodigious muscular proportions would have awed the Grecian Hercules, or the Giant of Gath. He was over ten feet in stature, his complexion the color of red gold and his short, curling hair a rich Tyrian purple. His large and deep set eyes surmounted by heavy black brows, were like glittering steel, piercing as those of the falcon and had a resolute and commanding expression. His features were cast in a grand and colossal mould like those of the Capitolean Jove, but their expression was laughing and jolly as a young Bacchus. He was clad in a flexible suit of shining crystal armor with helmet and gauntlets. From his belt hung an electric wand and a huge mace, shaped like a sledge hammer, its solid iron head weighing at least five hundred pounds. In his left hand he grasped a pair of long steel chains fastened to a great ring perforating the monster's nostrils and in his right, he flourished an immense whip, like a cat o' nine tails, its long lashes armed with sharp glittering barbs. Seated on his saddle like a monarch on his throne, whirling his fiery whip, every crack of which threw off showers of electric sparks, he looked like Olympian Jove, playing with his thunderbolts.

"Good day, Hartilion," said the Captain, " I have the honor to present to you Professor Hamiltoneus, a distinguished philosopher from the North Pole."

The colossus glanced at me good humoredly with his fierce looking eyes, leaned over and took my hand in his mighty palm with a gentle pressure.

" I am proud to make your acquaintance, sir," said he, in a voice deep and ponderous as the contra-bass pipe of a great organ. "You have come from a climate cold enough to freeze the marrow in an elephant's bones. You must be a pretty tough customer, sir. I hope you enjoy these genial regions where the sun is warm enough to roast eggs,"—then bending down and whispering in my ear, "Your incognito is pretty good in its way, but I see through it in spite of spectacles, paint and hair dye. I know all about you, my little professor, but mum's the word, you understand," laying his finger significantly across his nose. "Our Prince has told me all about how you whipped that twenty foot shark in a square fight. Splendidly done. By Pluto !"

Hartilion looked quite competent to tear any shark to pieces with his bare hands in two minutes, as Samson did the lion.

"What do you think of my sea horse?" he asked, snapping his whip with a crack that could have flayed a rhinoceros alive.

" He certainly is a tremendous specimen of the breed," I replied. "How did you manage to catch and tame him ?"

"I didn't catch him. I only took him in training
after he began to grow up. Have you any sea horses
in your oceans?"

"Yes, but they don't grow much larger than your
thumb."

"Is it possible? The breed must have miserably
degenerated."

"Undoubtedly. Does this frolicsome species of hip-
pocampus flourish around here?"

"O, no. They come from another planet."

"Which one, pray?"

"From Venus."

"Venus?—Great Scott! How did you ever get him
here?"

"On board an Ethervolt car."

"Your car must have been considerably larger than
the Treasury Department at Washington."

"Never having heard of the shop, I cannot quite
appreciate your comparison. Asterion's ancestor, on
one of his trips to Venus, found a nest of little Leviathans. They were not much bigger than alligators.
He caught them in a net; as good luck would have it,
their big papa and mamma were off scouring the sea
after other monsters at the time. He put them in a
water tank on board an extra-sized Ethervolt and
brought them over; several died on the passage, but
he managed to save a couple of pair and deposited them
in our Zoo gardens. They were well taken care of and
grew finely as you see. This fellow is a mere boy,
hasn't got his full growth. I've had him in training
about three years. He is a clever pupil, obeys me
implicitly and loves me like a faithful dog his master."

"Asterion informs me there are all sorts of land and
sea monsters on Venus."

"Yes, that would frighten the devil himself to look

upon. Prince Altfoura and I propose to take a trip there with Asterion, this summer. You must go with us. We'll have splendid sport."

"Are there any monsters on Mars?"

"Most of them were cleared off ages ago by the early Martian races, but near the equator we have sea serpents a few hundred feet long. Octopuses with arms long and strong enough to pull over an ordinary sized ship. Leviathan and I have had many a tussle with them, but we always lay them out cold, and they generally show great deference for him and keep at a respectful distance. Now and then, we meet shoals of sharks or sword fish who are fools enough to show fight, but my sea horse always gives them a sound thrashing; perhaps we'll meet a gang of them and you'll see how he lays them out."

"I should be happy to witness the operation. By the way, Hartilion, I am informed that you are a Plutonian."

"I am of that race."

"And descended from one of the seven great monarchs of that lost world."

"True, but I am not over proud of it."

"And a Prince in your own right."

"With naught but a barren title."

"When was that great planet lost?"

"About six thousand years ago, according to our annals."

"That is about the date of terrestrial man's first appearance on Earth, according to our chronologists."

"Quite a remarkable coincidence, the creation of inhabitants on one world, corresponding to the destruction of inhabitants on another."

"Why was your world destroyed?"

"Because it was accursed for its wickedness, so the

theologians say ; because it had grown old and lived out its allotted period, the scientists say ; because it met with an accident, the thoughtless crowd say."

" Please relate the circumstances connected with the awful catastrophe."

" Our world was the greatest and most magnificent of all. Our race the mightiest and most highly favored in knowledge, wealth and power, but as time passed on we became inflated with pride, love of self and the world, forgot our Creator to whom we owed all, became immersed in pleasure, plunged into all manner of excesses, and sank into the depths of sin and corruption. We were often admonished to turn from our evil ways but scoffed at the rebuke, and although warned of the dreadful doom hanging over us, we paid no heed, and hurried on from bad to worse, singing, dancing and carousing over the slumbering volcano beneath us. Some of my ancestors who had not wholly gone over to Satan, and who were familiar with interplanetary navigation, organized a fleet of Ethervolt cars and fled hither ; many were lost on the way. The few survivors who reached this planet, were received with great kindness and hospitality by the Martians and taught them many of our useful arts and sciences."

" How was your planet destroyed ?"

" Some of my ancestors think it was set on fire by the coma of a comet. Others that one of our moons, which for several hundred years had been gradually drawing nearer in its orbit, at last fell down upon it. Still others affirm that it was blown up by a tremendous explosior. Asterion says the Asteroids are the fragments of it."

" What was its population at the time ?"

" About six hundred thousand millions ; the population, however, had been frightfully decimated by long and destructive wars."

"Were they a tall race like yourself?"

"Much taller, larger and stronger every way. Our race has greatly degenerated since we came here."

"Are there many Plutonians here?"

"But few. There is something in the air and soil of Mars, so different from our world, inimical to the propagation of our race. What it is, we know not. While we owe everything to the kindness and generosity of our Martian friends, who succored us in our great affliction, and while we love them as members of one happy family of brothers, still, we cannot help lamenting the loss of our once glorious world, and we have nothing to look forward to in the future, but the final disappearance of our race from the stage of humanity."

As Hartilion said these words a look of deep sadness came over his countenance, and a tear stood in his eye.

"But I must not yield to these feelings." Then in cheerful tones, "Away with melancholy, say I. Toss dull care to the dogs. While we live, let us live," and in a voice whose mighty tones rang over the sea, he burst into his rollicking song. All at once to my great astonishment Leviathan joined in with a soft, sweet musical sound, now rising, swelling and dying away like the tones of an Æolian harp ; they consisted of a series of rhythmical chords, seeming like an accompaniment to Hartilion's grand song, swelling louder and still louder, pouring forth their deep and sonorous vibrations, like some vast organ swept by a master hand. Now majestic and commanding, now joyous, and now sad and plaintive. The effect was thrilling and I never before knew what magic power lay in a few simple chords, as I listened to these wonderful tones uttered by this stupendous monster of the deep.

"Leviathan is a great lover of music," said Hartilion,

"he has a fine and appreciative ear. It always quiets his turbulent moods and he is never so happy as when conveying a gay party with musicians, on some pleasure excursion. We will now take a look at his eyes."

Hartilion dismounted from his saddle, gave the reins and whip in charge of the Captain, and taking my hand we cautiously descended from the platform along the nasal ridge and took a seat astride the beak near the huge nostrils, traversed by a steel ring big as the driving wheel of a locomotive, and to which the reins were fastened. The air rushed through them like the blowing off from the pipes of a steam ship. The immense eyes, four feet in diameter and eight feet apart, were overhung by great black, bony brows. The pupils were a deep green, the great circle of the iris, golden yellow. Leviathan regarded his master with a pleased expression, then discovering in me some unaccustomed object, converged his eyes like a pair of convex mirrors directly upon me. It is impossible to describe the sensation that awful gaze produced ; an overwhelming magnetic fascination, such as is ascribed to the serpent on birds, seized me. I trembled, grew faint and would have fallen had not Hartilion's arm upheld me. He waved his electric wand in front of the eyes ; they withdrew their terrible gaze and fixed their look beyond.

"Leviathan's eyesight is wonderful ;" said Hartilion. "He can detect a friend or foe at almost any distance, and his eyes possess both telescopic and microscopic vision. Would you like to look at his mouth ? It is a curiosity."

I assented.

"Then we must go inside of it."

"Is it safe ?"

"Perfectly." Then touching Leviathan's masseter muscles with his wand,—

" Open your mouth," said he.

The monster noiselessly expanded his vast jaws, Hartilion fastened a short rope ladder to the ring, we descended to the lower jaw, clambered over the huge tusks and stood upon the tongue,—an enormous red, fleshy mass, covered with prickles. Twenty feet over our heads hung the arched roof of the upper jaw, around which projected the row of immense molars, incisors and fangs, like those of the lion. They were white as ivory, and resembled the stalactites hanging from the roofs of subterranean caverns. The monster's breath blew over us like a gale of wind. I looked down the throat, a deep red, yawning chasm, large as the opening of a great water-main ; on either side were the huge tonsils resembling a pair of great battle shields worn by the mediæval warriors, and between them hung the rose colored palate, projecting forward like the stump of a ship's bowsprit.

We left the mouth and ascended to the forehead. Hartilion resumed his seat and took the whip and reins in his hands. All at once Leviathan uttered a tremendous snort like a startled moose when he perceives a concealed foe.

" He scents an enemy," said Captain Samadron.

" Good !" said Hartilion ; " we'll have some sport."

" You and he are always ready for a fight."

" Of course. By Pluto ! things have been dull enough, lately. Leviathan hasn't had a square fight for six weeks."

" If you discover anything worth notice, let us know."

" All right," laughed the giant, whirling his whip through the air, like the whizz of a wind mill. The Captain and I descended the rope ladder to the deck.

CHAPTER XXIV.

BATTLE WITH SWORD FISH.

"And having routed the whole troop,
With victory was cock-a-loup."
Hudibras, Pt. I., Canto iii.

All at once Leviathan snapped his enormous jaws together like the crash of two colliding locomotives, raised his paddles high in air, flapping them like a ship's mainsails, uttered a thundering roar that shook the sea and dashed forward with tremendous speed.

" Hoa !—Bhuvazon !—Hoa !—Hoa !—" shouted Hartilion, tugging at the reins with a power that would have thrown a dozen horses back on their haunches.

" Hollo !—Hartilion. What's up ?" shouted Captain Samadron.

" Look yonder—there's a big fight going on !"

" Sharks ?" queried the Captain as all on board sprang on the deck railings.

" Sword fish and narwhales."

" Pull up your sea horse."

" By Jupiter ! That's easier said than done. He's crazy for a fight. Your whole crew couldn't hold him," —bracing his legs in the stirrups and sawing the reins right and left through the monster's nostrils with a sound like the grinding of a quartz crushing mill, but Leviathan hurried on faster than ever.

" He's getting unmanageable," said the Captain.

Hartilion grasped his five hundred pound sledge hammer, whirled it aloft with a terrible sweep and brought it down on Leviathan's bony brow with a stroke that would have smashed the skull of a whale. The monster shook his head, uttered a deep guttural growl like the muffled roars of a thousand lions, and paused in his career.

A short distance ahead, the sea was thrown into a frightful tumult, as a great piscatorial battle waged before us.

A colony of narwhales, or sea unicorns, in the course of their migration over the ocean, were attacked by a fierce horde of xiphians or sword fish. The narwhales had assembled themselves in a circle, in the centre of which were collected their females and helpless young, while the outside was occupied by the males, in a compact ring, bristling with their spirally twisted ivory tusks which project forward from the snout and are from five to seven feet in length. Outside the ring myriads of sword fish in tumultuous masses hurled themselves against the narwhales and the clashing of their long bony spears against the tusks, resounded like the hammerings of thousands of anvils. The fury and persistence of the assault was equalled only by the unflinching bravery of the defence. The force and impetus of the collisions often threw whole ranks out of the water. At each successive charge of their foes, the narwhales dashed them back as from the walls of a rampart, or fenced them like skilled swordsmen, their strong tusks snapping off the bony spears, while those beneath,—the ring being in layers one above the other,—plunging their tusks upward, ripped up the bodies of the xiphians. The outlying crowds of sword fish, unable to reach the narwhales because of the press, leaped over each other in all directions, in their blind rage plunging their swords into each other and all over the field, fratricidal combats were raging with unexampled fury. The waters were converted into a seething cauldron of crimson foam, and writhing combatants, while the lashing of fins and tails, the hammering of spears and tusks, mingled with the enraged bellowings of the narwhales combined to produce a piscatorial pandemonium utterly frightful and indescribable.

" These sword fish infest this part of the sea," said the Captain. " Leviathan hates them as we do snakes. The creatures are from twenty to thirty feet long, fierce and voracious as sharks, and although their spears cannot deeply penetrate his scaly armor, yet they worry and annoy him beyond endurance."

Leviathan uttered repeated roars and his excitement was so great, Hartilion could scarce control him.

In the mean time the piscatorial battle was raging with more fury than ever. Leviathan waited his master's orders. Hartilion threw the reins over his shoulders, secured his wand and hammer to the platform, clasped his legs firmly around the cranial buckler, and grasped a great brass ring on the pommel of the saddle in his left hand.

" Captain," said he, " Bhuvazon and I are going to walk into that fight."

" What ; mounted on the saddle as you are ?"

" Of course."

" But you'll be whirled right and left, tossed up and down amid the waves, perhaps flung from your seat."

" Ha ! Ha !" laughed the giant. " Have you forgotten the sea-serpent and the devil fish ? How Bhuvazon and I served them out ?"

" Well, then, as you're bound to have your own way, all I can say is, go ahead, and may the eagle of victory light on your banner."

" As she generally does," replied he, waving his terrible whip, then shouted at the top of his voice.

" Hola ! Hola ! my brave Bhuvazon !"

The monster sprang half way out of the water, with a scream of rage that seemed to split the very heavens. His fiery mane bristled all over his head, giving him a terrible appearance, and his eyes seemed to emit sparks of fire ; then tearing madly through the waters, he dashed into the thickest of the battle. The narwhales, instinctively conscious of the approach of a friend, dove down *en masse* to the depths of the sea, while the sword fish, enraged at the loss of their prey, gathered around their gigantic foe, hurling themselves in thousands upon him, their long spears rattling against his scaly armor or snapping off in their furious onset. Leviathan rushed through their masses like a tornado, every stroke of his enormous paddles and tail smashing whole ranks at once ; darting hither and thither, snapping his terrible jaws, crushing them with a single bite, or tearing them to pieces and flinging them high in air. But his gigantic master was even more terrible to behold. Swaying to and fro on his saddle under the tremendous surgings of his steed, he lashed them with his mighty whip, its fiery barbs throwing off showers of electric sparks, every stroke cutting to the bones, ripping up, tearing to pieces or skinning from snout to tail, dozens of sword fish at once ; showers of spray and fragments of flesh rained down on the deck ; lacerated bodies, broken spears, and crimson surf swirled around us. It was like a battle of the gods, and as this terrible horseman and charger rushed over the ensanguined field, Leviathan looked like some incarnate genius of vengeance crowning his mission of destruction with a grand and bloody carnival, while Hartilion was like Jupiter Olympus hurling his Vulcanean thunderbolts at the Titans.

The carnage was brief and the army of sword fish was annihilated. The scattered remnants fled in terror from the field. Hartilion resumed his post, the crew cleared the deck, Leviathan sped o'er the sea with thundering roars of triumph, while the grateful nar-whales followed in his wake as fast as their fins and tails could carry them. In a short time we drew up to an island, on which stood a number of dwellings. We were greeted by a crowd of people, and Leviathan moored alongside a stone pier.

Hartilion now descended from his station, his eyes sparkling with pleasure and his face flushed with his exertions. As he strode forward among the officers and seamen who greeted him with cheers, he looked like Hercules receiving the ovations of the Argonauts.

"Well, Captain," said he with a jolly laugh, "victory perched as usual on Leviathan's crest."

"We all hope you enjoyed the battle," replied the Captain.

"So, so. I like to thrash the vermin with my whip, but, pooh! it's like fighting musquitoes. Give me a genuine Vodra Nakarips(1) two or three hundred feet long, and big enough to swallow an elephant ; give me an octopus that can pull over a ship, for my game, they're worthy Leviathan's notice. But it's time for his dinner," and taking out his silver pipe he blew shrill whistles. A number of barges manned by sailors and laden with large quantities of a nutritious variety of sea weed mixed with the chopped up bodies of fish, drew up to the pier. Leviathan under his master's directions, dipped his beak into the barges and partook of his repast with decorum such as would have done credit to a gentleman seated at his dining table.

"What is his daily allowance?" I asked.

"He takes his regular three meals daily, with lunches whenever he likes," Hartilion replied. "He usually

(1) Sea Serpent.

consumes about nine hundred tons of food per day. He is a very small eater."

Other barges drew up containing great tanks of fresh water, Leviathan dipped his beak into them, raising his head and swallowing after the manner of birds. As the streams ran down his throat, the sound was like that of a mill sluice. Having swallowed enough to quench the thirst of two hundred thousand men, he curled his head over his shoulder and went to sleep.

"He always takes a short nap after dinner," said Hartilion.

The crew now opened the provision chests, spread tables under the awnings and loaded them with Martian viands in profusion. We all partook of the repast, which was enlivened with the philosophical disquisitions of the Doctor, the jolly good humor of Hartilion, and the drolleries of John. The repast concluded,

"Come, Corporal," said the Doctor, "give us a specimen of your war chief performance."

"All right," he replied, and disappeared behind the curtains of his private awning. In a short time he sprang out, completely transformed into a magnificently ferocious New Zealand warrior chief, his face, breast and arms painted in fiery colors with figures of owls, bats, devils and imps, his hair standing up in spikes all over his head which was surmounted with tufts of sea gulls' feathers ; his ears, nose and neck decorated with rings and necklaces of sharks' teeth and birds' claws ; a striped red and yellow blanket flapping over his shoulders ; a vicious looking knife stuck in his belt ; he grasped a long toasting fork in one hand and a cudgel, its head stuck full of sharp nails, in the other. On top of his head perched the raven, tricked out like a Methodist parson, clad in a long black gown, shirt collar up to his ears, a white wig plastered over his head, a stove pipe hat, spectacles on his nose, and holding in his claw a long sermon. John had occasionally amused us by getting up this character while on the island. He sprang forward with a tremendous war whoop, glaring ferociously around the assembled throng, brandishing his cudgel and toasting fork.

"Brethern and sistern," croaked the parson in sanctimonious nasal tones. "Let us pray."

"Excellent ; my pious but somewhat carnal minded brother," said the Doctor. "'Tis always proper to open theatrical performances with prayer."

"All ri— Cock-a-doodle—"

"*Tenora Koko ! Pohe mai anako ! Karebok wylie be tea ! Kabo wry koa ban awyali !*" yelled John, ripping out a perfect volley of high class New Zealand oaths. "Me big Tanehoka war chief ! Hab killee, cookee and eatee one, two, three dozen enemy chiefs. Who dare say,— d—n lie?" looking fiercely around. "Nobody ? All right ; reckon you be heap 'fraid. Me killee you all one, two, three minutes. By Jingo !—Me no hurtee Cap'n Fred, nor old Doctor,—" looking at us benignantly. "Me love 'em big heap. Me scalpee that big fellow over there."

"Hooray ! I'm Jack the giant killer !" vociferated the parson glancing fiercely at the big fellow.

"All right, Parson,—we'll scalp 'em all around right off ; hab heap fun,—cookee 'em by and by,—hab heap good dinner."

"Roast beef,—horse tack,—hurry up !" ordered the parson, flapping his wings and snapping his beak.

"Whoop ! Me big war chief ! Look out !" tossing his war club and toasting fork up in the air and adroitly catching them as they fell.

"Rats ! Rats ! Bow, wow, wow ! Scat ! Scat !" screeched the raven, as John jumped six feet in the

air and tore over the deck in a ferocious war dance,
rattling his cudgel and fork like a pair of castanets,
scowling and yelling like a high class New Zealand
devil, while all on board almost split their sides with
laughter ; then throwing down his weapons and placing
his arms akimbo, he dashed off into a regular sailor's
hornpipe, in which he was joined by the parson and
they skipped around each other, pirouetting, kicking up
their heels, mincing and ogling coquettishly at the
audience in a style that would have astonished the
corps de ballet of the grand opera, amid the tumultuous
applause of all on board, Hartilion vowing that he
would put them at the head of the coryphées of the
Martian Theatre Comique, then with sweeping bows
and smiles to the audience, the war chief and carnal
minded parson, retired majestically to their awnings.

CHAPTER XXV.

ARMORED CITIES.

"Work on at your cities and temples, proud man,
  Build high as ye may, and strong as ye can
  But the marble shall crumble, the pillars shall fall,
  And Time, Old Time, will be King, after all."
            Old King Time.—GEORGE P. MORRIS.

In a short time our air ship appeared high in the sky,
flying swiftly toward us and in a few moments
descended to the water, alongside the sleeping Leviathan. Captain Volanto came aboard and the usual
greetings over, announced that repairs were completed.

Bidding adieu to Leviathan's officers and Hartilion, we re-embarked and continued our journey to the north west, over the bay. By evening we had crossed the great Tycho sea and a long shore line appeared in the distant horizon.

"That is the continent of Mandal-Uttima, our destination," said Dr. Hamival. "It is twenty five hundred miles long, by fifteen hundred wide, containing an area of about three million square miles."

"About the size of the United States of America," said I.

On our Martian maps it is designated as Galileo continent, and is situated in the northwestern hemisphere of the Planet. The evening shades were gathering, as we crossed the shore line and advanced several hundred miles in the interior toward the north.

"At what hour do the cities light up?" asked the Doctor.

" Eight o'clock precisely," replied Captain Volanto.

"It is within fifteen minutes," looking at his watch. "We would like to witness it."

"Shoot the ship five miles above the surface and check her up," ordered the Captain.

The prow was directed upward and she rose in great spirals to that height, then paused with a gentle motion of her wings. We ascended the deck. The stars shone bright in the clear sky ; our elevation commanded a view of nearly two hundred miles all around. The landscape beneath was immersed in darkness, here and there a few lights only were seen.

"Our moons are not up. So much the better for the view," said Dr. Hamival.

"8 o'c.," said the Captain, looking at his watch.

Instantly three long narrow streaks or bands of brilliant light shot like flashes of lightning across the dark

landscape from north to south as far as the eye could
see. One was immediately beneath us ; the others
spanned the horizon on either side, two hundred miles
away. The next moment three other bands shot from
east to west crossing the former at right angles. They
looked like white hot wire screens of open lattice work
several miles wide, and hundreds of miles long. As
the ship flew onward new bands arose in view one by
one, crossing the country in all directions. The dark
spaces lying between them, resembled immense
geometrical figures, triangles, parallelograms, etc.,
traced out by these lines of fire ; we were directly over
one which stretched from east to west, and was full
twenty miles wide.

"Lower the ship," ordered the Captain, and she
slowly descended to within three thousand feet of the
surface and to my astonishment a vast panorama of
countless roofs, rows of magnificent buildings, towers,
domes, etc., burst into view, all in a style of architecture
unknown on earth, and brilliantly illuminated with
myriads of many colored lights. There were broad
streets thronged with people and vehicles, canals over
which sailed pleasure boats, flocks of little air ships and
quaint looking aërial chariots flying to and fro in all
directions. As our ship flew onward, we passed over
gardens, orchards, cultivated fields, little lakes, woodlands and long stretches of forests, interspersed with
country houses and villas all over spanned by these
bright meshes of lattice work resembling immense
ribbons of fiery lace. The whole was elevated high
above the topmost trees, buildings and towers and
supported by countless rows of lofty pillars.

"You behold one of our great linear cities," said the
Doctor, " which includes within its domains the charms
and beauties of rural scenery, as well as the works of

man's industry, science and art. It is two thousand miles long, by twenty miles wide, containing an area of forty thousand square miles and a population of twenty five millions."

" Nearly equal to half the population of the United States of America," I exclaimed in amazement. " Is it not greatly over crowded ?"

" Not at all. The citizens enjoy plenty of air, light and elbow room. Over crowding of population is unknown on our planet. Twelve great linear cities from one to two thousand miles long, and fifteen to forty miles wide, traverse our continent in crossing lines, and accommodate the great bulk of our populations without including our smaller cities country towns and pleasure resorts, occupying the intervening land spaces, mountain slopes and sea shores."[1]

" What is the population of your continent ?" I asked.

" About five hundred millions."

" More than one third that of our globe, with its enlightened, civilized, barbarous and savage races."

"Is it possible that your great world, nearly four times as large as ours, is so thinly populated ?"[2]

" Certain parts of it are very densely populated, and

---

[1] In the great linear cities are found the true explanation of the so called " double canals," or parallel and crossing lines discovered by the distinguished Italian Astronomer, Schiaparelli, many years ago, and the existence of which has been denied by other Astronomers. The recent observations of Mars during its opposition in August, 1892, seem to confirm the existence of these lines, particularly the observations conducted at the great Lick Observatory in California. See Proctor's " Old and New Astronomy," London Ed., Part 9.

[2] In consequence of the relatively greater proportion of land on Mars as compared with Earth, it has about five million more square miles of territory.

in many of our cities the inhabitants are packed almost cheek by jowl together, and often in a condition of great poverty and suffering."

"Can it be that your governments and municipal authorities permit such a state of things?"

"They seem quite unable to prevent it."

"You spoke of half civilized, barbarous and savage people in your planet."

"Hardly one quarter of our populations are enlightened or civilized, more than half are half civilized, the remainder are barbarous or savage," I replied.

"Your Terrestrians are truly in a deplorable state; such a phenomenon as a half civilized, barbarous, or savage race or individual, is unknown on our planet. Do you all speak the same language?"

"No. There are about twenty six hundred different languages and dialects spoken on our globe."

"What a perfect Babel your world must be. One universal language only, is spoken on our planet."

"And there are also about a thousand different religions professed among our races and nations."

"You Terrestrians evidently flatter yourselves there are many roads to heaven."

"By no means. Each sect asserts its own religion to be the only true one, and declares that all the others are in error."

"What a chaotic state of religious and spiritual affairs. Cannot your wise men set it to rights?"

"Our philosophers and scientists do not interfere with those questions, which appertain to the province of theology."

"Cannot your theologians adjust them?"

"They seem unable to do so. Our barbarous and savage races are immersed in gross idolatry; many of our half civilized nations are equally wedded to their peculiar forms of worship. Among our enlightened and civilized nations many warring creeds prevail, which theologians are wholly unable to harmonize, and denounce each others' forms of religious belief and worship in unmeasured terms. Many of our enlightened and intelligent people worship God according to the dictates of their own consciences ; while others reject all so called religious faith and belief, and embrace agnosticism, materialism, spiritualism or atheism."

" I am quite ignorant of the meaning of those terms. Please explain."

I favored the Doctor with a brief description of the so called "advanced and progressive thought,—" the " fashionable philosophy of the day,—" so much affected by a certain set of easygoing and luxurious worldly folk ; scientific amateurs, intellectual fools, philosophical idiots, flippant women, brainless fops, *et id genus omne*, floating around among the literary coteries, clubs and fashionable circles of our so called polite society.

" Many centuries ago a similar amusing class of individuals gifted with more conceit than brains, appeared in our Martian society and gathered around them circles of weak minded ones, who joined themselves into coteries, clubs, etc., vaporizing their whimsical fancies and absurd conceits for a while, then quietly sank into oblivion. With us Martians, true religion, true science and true philosophy, go hand in hand, forming one grand and indissoluble Trinity. Although our different races and nations, have each their own different forms of government, laws, internal policy, etc., and entertain their own peculiar opinions on other minor subjects, still, all are in strict agreement on the one great subject, and that is, Supreme love and adoration to the Almighty Creator and Ruler of the Universe, and strict obedience to His commands. By observance of this one great law of life in our relations to God, and to each other, as nations and individuals, we can truly say, that we are preserved from many evils, and rewarded with many blessings."

" You seem to have attained the true philosophy of living, which is really the greatest blessing that can possibly appertain to man in this lower sphere."

" True, and our great populations are happy and enjoy life in all things save one."

" What is the population of your planet ?"

" About eight thousand millions.

" Nearly seven times that of Earth. How can you possibly support such vast numbers of people ?"

" Our planet is abundantly able to support many times that number. There is no crowding. Every man lives under his own vine and fig tree so to speak. Every citizen of family owns his own house, garden and grounds, although their extent and cultivation depend upon the taste of the occupant. Such a thing as poverty or struggle for bread, is unknown in our world ; every one has enough to eat, drink and wear, labor of every kind is light and pleasing, with plenty of time for recreation, and every facility for the enjoyment of our honorable desires and inclinations."

" Your Martians seem almost to have reached the *summum bonum* of human happiness. What is the one drawback to perfect enjoyment of which you spoke ?"

" Observe those immense frame works covering the whole length of our linear cities, with their gardens, fields, woodlands, etc."

" I was just about to inquire the object in constructing your cities in this geometrical style, and covering them with these great frameworks."

" They are for the protection of our lives, sustenance and property."

" Protection ?   From what ?"

" From terribly destructive meteoric showers."

" Is it possible that those celestial phenomena, so harmless and beautiful in the skies of our world, are so dangerous in yours ?"

" Your Earth in its yearly revolution around the sun, encounters the outskirts only of one of several great meteoric belts traversing our solar system. As the showers fall through your atmosphere, which is twice the depth and density of ours, they are for the most part consumed to ashes before they reach the surface. Our planet passes through the centre of one of the largest belts, which is more thickly strown with much larger meteoric masses and as our atmosphere is only half the depth and density of yours, they nearly all fall to the surface.   During the periods when these showers take place, certain parts of our planet are exposed to terribly destructive downfalls of masses weighing from many pounds to several tons.   Thousands of our people have been killed, buildings and public works destroyed, crops annihilated and forests levelled. After one of these awful downpours, hundreds of square miles of land on our continents look as if they had been swept with tornadoes of fire, for many of these masses descend red hot and sometimes in streams of molten metal. This linear mode of arranging our cities for the bulk of our populations, our gardens, forests, etc.,—which latter have been transplanted from other parts of the country, is the only means of protection.   Our smaller cities, towns, country villas, etc., are similarly protected, as also those of all the continents and islands of our planet.   Before the expected shower takes place, its exact date is always known, the frame works are covered with metallic plates sufficiently strong to resist the heaviest down-pour. The whole population and all the domestic animals are safely housed, even the birds from the sur-rounding forests and sometimes wild animals, the few we have, instinctively seek shelter under these roofs from the storm. The downpour is utterly awful and indes-cribable. It seems like a furious cannonade from the heavens. When it is over, our people emerge from their coverts, the roof plates are removed, the meteoric debris is gathered up and conveyed over great rail-ways to the sea shores. Many hundred miles of shore line have been built out, ravines and valleys filled up, road beds laid, etc., with these masses. Many of the great land spaces lying between the city lines, some of which cover several thousand square miles of territory, are practically of little value for high cultivation, sub-jected as they are to the destructive showers."

" How often, and at what periods are you subject to them ?" I asked.

"Once a year during our fall months always, and sometimes also during the spring. We have recur-rences of them on a gigantic scale, and far more destruc-tive, at periods of about every sixty six years."

"Which corresponds to our thirty three year period of recurrence, according to our terrestrial astrono-mers."(1)

By midnight we re-crossed the shore line and entered

(1) Professor Newton has traced the historical records of these November showers back to a thousand years, confirming the observations of the great German Astronomer Olbers. They occur once in thirty three years. The great showers of 1799 and 1833, were visible in Europe and America. The last great one was in 1866. The next may be expected in Novem-ber, 1899.

the great Airy sea([1]) separating Mandal-Uttima from Rosse's land([2]) on the east. Our vessel descended to the water and moored up to the rocky base of a lofty headland near the bay of Gulomezal, which penetrates the continent for many miles, and we retired for the night.

CHAPTER XXVI.

THE STARS AND STRIPES FLOAT O'ER MARS.

" Flag of the free heart's hope and home,
    By angel hands to valor given ;
  Thy stars have lit the welkin dome,
    And all thy hues were born in heaven."
                    The American Flag.—DRAKE.

Early next morning, before I was up, Altfoura rushed with his usual impetuosity into the cabin.

"Awake ! Arise ! Thou sluggish son of Earth," he exclaimed with a merry laugh. "Get yourself in readiness to meet our friends of Mandal-Uttima, and participate in the little reception I have arranged for the occasion."

We arose, dressed, took breakfast and went on deck. The sun was rising in the east, shedding his glories of light and color o'er sky, cloud and sea. Our ship unmoored and entered the mouth of Gulomezal bay, situated near the Martian 41st parallel, north lat., according to the terrestrial geographical standard and nearly corresponding to the harbor of New York. The

([1]) Named after Professor Airy, Astronomer Royal of England.

([2]) Named after Lord Rosse.

entrance is five miles wide and adorned with a magnificent work of art, infinitely surpassing any thing of the kind on Earth. In the centre is an immense fountain a thousand feet high and three hundred wide at the base, consisting of four terraces rising one above another and of different colors. The lowest a sea green, the second crimson, the third golden and the topmost snow white. Innumerable rainbows gleamed amid the spouting columns of water and showers of spray.

" Enormous hydraulic engines sunk deep in the sea, propel the waters through colored tubes of crystal, which communicate these different hues to the fountain," said the Captain.

Four colossal statues, each two hundred feet high and mounted on splendid carved pedestals of igneous rock, surround the fountain. In front, facing the east, is a female figure of brilliant gold, appropriately draped, one arm resting on a harp, the other raised in invocation to the heavens, from her girdle are suspended various emblems. This represents religion, poetry and music. On the north is another female figure of bright crimson, holding in one hand an open scroll and with emblems at her girdle. This represents history, philosophy and art. On the south, another female figure of bright blue, holding a cornucopia filled with sheaves of grain, fruits and flowers. This represents the seasons of nature and the plenteous fruits of earth. On the west is the figure of a man in jet black marble surrounded with implements of tillage and machinery. This represents agriculture, the useful and mechanical arts. Beyond these are two other figures of still more colossal dimensions. One, of brilliant silver, is a man clad in armor, holding in one hand a lighted torch, and in the other a sheaf of forked lightnings, mounted on a great sea monster the exact similitude of Leviathan.

This represents man's progress in civilization and his conquest over the elements and forces of nature. The other is of pure, snow white marble ; a man clad in royal robes with a crown on his head, holding in one hand a globe and in the other a sceptre, seated in a chariot drawn by four winged horses. This represents the triumph of man in the realm of mind.

Leaving this magnificent work of art, our ship rapidly passed up the bay which penetrates the continent many miles, expanding in a circular form on either hand. The waters glittered under the bright sunlight with the lustre of sparkling gems. Its shores consist of lofty promontories of red or ochre colored rock, alternating with bright green grassy slopes and white or yellow sandy beaches. In the interior country are plateaus, fields and gardens under the highest cultivation, in many parts covered for miles with the great metallic frameworks, the hill tops and mountain slopes were adorned with stately trees and forests. Sweet and aromatic odors, like the perfumes of the rose gardens of Persia in the blooming time of flowers, were wafted on the soft and balmy air. A rich and sub-tropical flora flourishes in profusion every where. Some resembling that of Southern Europe, South America or the Indian Isles, while others of different species display a beauty of form and gorgeousness of color unknown on Earth. The waters abounded in fish of almost infinite varieties, such as I never saw before, and birds of strange form and plumage flew through the air in all directions, frequently alighting on the deck and permitting themselves to be caressed and fed by the crew. It was evident, no implement of destruction had ever been turned against them.

"These harmless and beautiful creatures," said the Doctor, " recognize a friend in every human being."

A long line of snow white sails now appeared, skirting the distant horizon.

"Our friends are coming ;" said the Prince. "We will prepare to meet them. Your incognito will now be laid aside."

We descended to the cabin, the Doctor removed every vestige of my Martian paint and dye, and I began to feel that I was really myself again.

"We will now appear in our official capacity in accordance with our rank and title," said Altfoura. "You, as Lieutenant in the United States Navy, John as Prince of New Zealand, and I as Lieutenant in the royal life guards of Mandal-Uttima."

The Prince put on his uniform which had been brought aboard by a subaltern officer. It was a light flexible coat of chain armor, shining like burnished silver and decorated with brilliant orders ; sword and helmet with waving plumes of crimson and gold ; over his left shoulder a short chasseur's mantle. Splendid specimen of youthful manly beauty as he was in his ordinary attire, in this dress he looked like young Mars fresh from Olympus. I donned my uniform, which John had furbished up in good order, while he put the finishing touches to his war chief attire and looked as splendid a specimen of a New Zealand Prince as one would wish to see. The raven divested himself of his canonicals, sprang on his master's shoulder, flapped his wings and uttered a ringing cock-a-doodle-doo, before which the most vociferous Shanghai would have hung his diminished head.

"Lieutenant Hamilton," said Altfoura, doffing his helmet with a princely salutation, " I am happy to make your acquaintance, sir. I hope you are well, and how goes the United States Navy, sir ?"

" As well as can be expected, considering the munificent appropriations voted for its enlargement by the government of the United States in congress assembled. We feel quite competent to whip the combined navies of Earth, Mars and Jupiter singly or collectively in less than half a dozen rounds each."

"And may your stars and stripes wave in triumph over them all." Then looking over me critically. "Really, Lieutenant, you are a magnificent looking fellow and I shall be proud to present you to my friends. What a pity we have no Anglo Saxon type of man or woman on our planet. With your six foot, two inches stature, splendid physique, fierce looking moustache, handsome blue eyes and altogether elegant style and manner, you will create a perfect furore among our Martian beauties."

As we passed up the bay a beautiful spectacle was displayed. A fleet of two hundred yachts with streaming pennons stretched on either hand in a long crescentic curve. As their snowy sails flecked the horizon, they looked like a flock of white winged eagles flying o'er the waters. Another stupendous oceanic monster, the counterpart of Leviathan, was leading the van.

"That is Zeuglissa, Leviathan's mate," said the Prince.

This Queen of the ocean was the beautiful consort of her royal spouse and well might he be proud of her. She was perhaps a third smaller and her proportions were elegant. Her neck arched gracefully like that of the swan. Her scales were a bright green edged with crimson. A broad band of white extended from her throat down her breast. She was destitute of mane, but in lieu of it, her head was ornamented with a crest of towering crimson and golden plumes like the coiffures of *les grandes dames* of the court of Louis XVI., giving her an exceedingly stately appearance. As she majestically moved over the waters, her haughty head high in the air, she seemed fully conscious of her own dignity and importance in this imperial display. A man of gigantic stature and clad in shining armor was seated on her cranial buckler, holding his glittering whip and reins in his hand.

"That is Zhang Benoidath, Hartilion's younger brother," said the Prince.

All at once the deep toned roars from an army of lions arose from her deck. Zeuglissa threw back her head, opened her enormous jaws and uttered a thundering roar as of triumph, completely drowning the voices of the lions ; this was followed by the ringing cheers of men.

" They are the morning salutations of our friends," said Altfoura.

The fleet of yachts rapidly sailed toward us. They were perfect models of naval beauty, with their graceful lines, sharp cut water, tall masts and great spread of canvas. Their hulls shone like polished silver ; their decks of dark green wood, masts and spars like ivory, rigging of light blue woven silk and sails white as snow. They were manned by officers and cadets in naval uniform. High over their masts, beautiful little air chariots with streaming banners and decorations were flying in circles. Zeuglissa leading the van, rapidly advanced and drew alongside our ship. The moment she caught sight of the Prince she uttered a sweet and low sound of recognition, and bent her head down over the deck, while he caressed her enormous beak. It was indeed a grand and fearful sight to see this mighty monster, her vast eagle shaped head towering above us, her immense eyes blazing with a terrible light, and her enormous jaws, which, with one single snap could have crushed our ship in twain.

"Good morning, Benoidath," said the Prince, "and how does Zeuglissa comport herself to day ?"

"She greatly grieved at Leviathan's long absence, but is now perfectly happy at having the pleasure of escorting your highness and friends," replied the colossus, bowing in his saddle.

We left the ship and stepped on her bright blue metallic deck which was fastened to the great silver bands encircling her body.

"Your first introduction shall be to my comrades in arms ;" said Altfoura.

Zeuglissa's deck presented a scene so imposing, and at the same time so formidable, that for a moment I drew back in apprehension. Standing in rows on either side, and facing each other were a hundred magnificent horses which, in symmetry and beauty of form, surpassed the finest equine specimens on earth. Their coats were a bright golden color and their manes and tails, which swept the deck, a dark blue ; they were decorated with military trappings. Mounted on the back of each was a Martian officer clad in brilliant silver armor with plumed helmet, and armed with strange looking weapons. In front of the horses stood two rows of magnificent lions, compared with which our largest African or Asiatic species seem as mere pigmies. Their coats were a bright tawny color and their long thick manes dark red or jet black. Standing by the side of every lion and with one arm around its neck was a beautiful child clad in the costume of a sylvan shepherd, holding in hand his little rustic crook and a silken cord tied around the lion's neck.

"Comrades of the army of Mandal Uttima," said the Prince, making the Martian military salute, " I have the honor to present to you Lieutenant Hamilton of the Navy of the United States of America, the greatest

Republic on the Terrestrial Globe. He has taken this long and perilous journey of one hundred million miles through the trackless realms of space to do us honor, and is the first inhabitant of Earth who has ever visited our world. Let us bid him welcome and extend to him those hospitalities and courtesies which he, as a representative of the younger Earth born race is entitled to receive. The members of our glorious planetary. system, tho' widely separated, are a band of brothers. On the deck of our Ocean Queen, let Earth and Mars join hands in fraternal union."

The warriors gave the military salute, dismounted from their steeds and led by their commander, Captain Zar Armozan,—a handsome and gallant young cavalry officer and intimate friend of the Prince, assembled around us with cordial greetings, Prince John and Commodore Jack receiving their full share of distinguished attention. The warriors re-mounted and escorted by Armozan we passed through their ranks. The shepherd boys greeted us with happy smiles, waving their little crooks in salutation. The lions raised their royal crests, majestically regarding us with their kingly eyes and sniffing around us with deep breathings. We passed forward and took seats on a military chest under an awning of flags surmounted by a magnificent grey and black eagle. Benoidath flourished his immense whip ; Zeuglissa wheeled gracefully about and moved slowly up the bay surrounded by the yachts in close circles.

And now from their decks arose the loud roll of innumerable tenor drums mingled with the shrill and piercing tones of fifes. These are the sounds that thrill the soldier's heart. They speak of the fiery spirit and dauntless valor of war. O'er many a bloody field they have marshalled the forlorn hope and desperate charge to victory or death. That military ardor, which none but the soldier knows or feels, inspired us all. The warriors waved their helmets, shook their swords and uttered ringing cheers. The steeds champed their iron bits and uttered shrill neighings. The thundering tones of Zeuglissa mingled with the loud roars of the lions and the triumphant cries of the children.

A magnificent naval spectacle now appeared. A fleet of a thousand war-ships massed in solid phalanx, spread its wings like a vast crescent o'er the sea. Their enormous hulls, which shone like burnished steel, bristled with military engines whose terribly destructive power is unknown on Earth. Their decks were thronged with the élite of the Martian Navy and Army in countless thousands. Their glittering arms and uniforms flashed under the bright sun in mingled streams of crystal, silver and gold. The clamor of fifes and drums ceased. The fleet drew near and expanding its vast wings enfolded us in one great circle. It is impossible to describe the beauty and grandeur of the scene as this forest of ships, their lofty masts and streaming pennons seeming to sweep the clouds, silently gathered around us. Strains of sweet music arose from the bands on their decks, playing the Martian national anthems and filling the air with waves of harmony. The flag ship of Mandal-Uttima advanced from the circle and drew alongside. The towering head of Zeuglissa scarce reached her gunwales. Her dimensions were immense and her appointments superb. She seemed a floating palace and citadel united in one. We ascended her deck which was thronged with the highest naval and military officers of the realm. Admiral Zar Walthovian, a noble looking man of advanced years, bronzed and weather beaten complexion, received us with distinguished courtesy. We ascended to the quarter deck, the throngs gazing on us with wonder and curiosity. The Admiral gave a short address of welcome to which I briefly responded in behalf of my native world and country. The Prince then introduced us to the officers of the fleet. The ceremonial concluded, the chief artillery officer gave a signal and the united thunders of thousands of cannon rent the air, rolling in long echoes o'er the sea.

"Look!" said Altfoura with a smile, pointing over my shoulder.

I looked around, and there, side by side with the royal standard of Mandal-Uttima, floated the same old flag I had planted on the ice berg of Earth's polar sea. My heart swelled with joy. I grasped the dear folds and pressed them to my bosom, kissed them o'er and o'er again. O, what sweet memories they brought to me of home, friends and native land! Every star and stripe, every thread of that dear old flag seemed redolent of my native breezes. Once more those deep toned thunders shook the sea, and from every mast and spar, from every swelling sail of the fleet streamed thousands of Martian banners, and elevated high above them all, on the summit of the flag ship's top mast, waved the STAR SPANGLED BANNER, its beauteous folds mingling as it were, with the soft and fleecy clouds. My eyes filled with tears of joy when I thought that, the banner of liberty which waves o'er the land of the free and the home of the brave, honored in every nation and on every sea of Earth's broad domain, should have been borne through the trackless realms of space, amid that shining galaxy of orbs that wheel around the sun, and UNFOLD ITS BROAD STRIPES AND BRIGHT STARS OVER ANOTHER WORLD!

And now from the united bands of that vast fleet, amid the roll of innumerable drums and the clarion tones of countless trumpets, arose the majestic strains of the "Star Spangled Banner," rolling in mighty waves of harmony o'er the deep. Higher and still higher rose that glorious anthem, seeming to greet the HEAVENS OF MARS WITH THE SALUTATION OF EARTH !

" O, say, can you see by the dawn's early light,
    What so proudly we hailed at the twilight's last greeting."

It seemed as if my heart would burst with ineffable joy, and overwhelmed with emotions impossible to control, I sank almost fainting in the arms of my friend.

CHAPTER XXVII.

THE PRINCESS SUHLAMIA.

"She walks in beauty like the night
    Of cloudless climes and starry skies ;
And all that's bright of day and night,
    Meet in her aspect and her eyes."
                        Hebrew Melodies.-- BYRON.

When I recovered myself, Altfoura was by my side.

" I appreciate your keenly awakened feelings," said he, " aroused by the sight of your national flag and the tones of your grand national anthem. 'Tis truly an inspired lyric outburst of the purest patriotism enshrined in the hearts of a great and free born nation."

" The high honor you have bestowed on me by this magnificent reception," I replied, " and which the monarchs of Earth might be proud to receive, I accept as a tribute to the greatest republic of Earth, the home of liberty, the asylum of the oppressed and the hope of our nations. O, tell me, shall I ever see my native land, my home, kindred and friends again? At times the sad thought comes o'er my soul, that I have trod the soil, breathed the air, and gazed on the skies of Earth for the last time."

"Dismiss these sad thoughts from your mind," he replied. "The same skies, the same stars, that shine o'er this our world, shine also over yours, although so widely separated from each other by these awful abysses of space. I promise you that, whenever you so desire, I will escort you through those vast realms again, back to your native world and home. In the meantime rest assured that you are among true friends upon whose kindness and hospitality you can in good faith rely," and he warmly pressed my hand.

"How did you secure my flag? which I planted on the summit of my icy prison? I deemed it lost long ago in the waters of Earth's polar sea."

"We found it floating amid its fragments. I brought it hither on my return, as a memento of the great service you rendered me, and as a royal trophy from your World; which I felt would gladden your heart to see floating on the breezes of Mars."

"And the national anthem of my country, whose grand harmonies rolled o'er land and sea, rising e'en to the very skies of this other world?"

"In the delirium of your illness you talked of friends and bygone scenes. You seemed to hear sounds from home, so dear to us all. You oft sang old songs, many of which were beautiful. Really, my friend, I had no idea you were so fine a singer. We could not understand the words of course, and when you sang your Star Spangled Banner with such force and feeling, we felt that it must be your national anthem ; being somewhat of a musician myself, I copied it from your lips and gave it to the leaders of our military bands. We Martians have our national hymns and anthems, but deem it no flattery when I pronounce your Star Spangled Banner, unsurpassed by any thing of its kind on this planet. Whoever of your Earth born poets was the author, deserves to be immortalized for all time."

"His name is already immortalized in the hearts of the American people," I replied. "Thè Star Spangled Banner is played on every national celebration of the United States of America, and its strains have re-sounded o'er every land and sea on Earth's broad domain."

We were seated in a beautiful sea chariot resembling the illustrations of that in which the mythological sea god Neptune rides o'er the waves. Its prow was sur-mounted by a figure of the Ocean monarch armed with his trident, and drawn by his steeds, half horse, half fish, with silver scales, coral eyes, golden manes and brazen hoofs. It was surrounded by a band of young Tritons, blowing their conch shells. Around these were bands of Oceanides mounted on sea unicorns and blowing their cytheriums. It was evident that the Martians, as well as the Terrestrians, had a mythology, and its striking resemblance to our old Grecian, surprised me.

"Humanity," said Dr. Hamival, "is the same on whatever planet it may happen to be created and find its home, and all its intellectual manifestations and ideal conceptions are, in the main, similar, though varied some what by their natural surroundings. Long before your Earth born races were created, our old Martian races had passed through their periods of Sun, Moon and Star worship, deification of natural objects, heroes and ancestors, although they never sank to the gross idolatry of yours. The early Martian ages of poetry and romance, had also their mythological conceptions and ideals, which were more or less associated with religious worship. These idealities are beautiful, and like you, we still retain them as pleasing and graceful creations of the young and vivid poetic imagination, although of course they are wholly divested of the powerful religious element they once held in the hearts of men."

The fleet with the yachts and Zeuglissa leading the van were sailing down the bay. Our chariot now drew near the shore, which was clothed with a dense forest to the water's edge. From its depths a little river flowed into the bay. Its banks were lined with giant trees unknown on Earth, their trunks towering up like ship's masts and crowned with dense masses of bright red or green foliage, with scarlet or bright yellow fruits. The sward was clothed with strange and fantastic shrubbery and flowers. Strains of sweet music like the sounds of harps and viols issued from the leafy depths. The Tritons and Oceanides blew answering blasts from their shells and cytheriums. Our chariot passed through their parting ranks and paused in its course.

And now came a pageant so faërie like and beautiful, so chaste and classical in every detail, as seemed like a dream of Oriental romance. From the depths of those leafy bowers and floating on the rippling waters, came a band of young maidens attired as Nereides, Sea Nymphs and Mermaids, mounted on dolphins, physeters, and other strange fishes, whose brilliant colors made the watery expanse appear like an emblazoned field of gorgeous tapestry. They wore crowns, necklaces, bracelets and girdles of coral. They held their

little mirrors in their hands, combing their long green
locks, or scooping up little fishes in their nets and play-
fully pelting each other with asterias, sea hedgehogs,
porcupines, jelly fish, etc., amid peals of merry laughter.
Following them, came a band of young girls attired as
Naiads, Potamids, and Lymnads,—nymphs of lakes,
rivers and streams,—mounted on giant nautiluses with
their sail-like paddles and shells the color of silver, or
pearl ; on chetodons and pipe-fish, throwing up jets and
sprays of water from their bottle shaped mouths.
Some were mounted on great green back turtles, or
giant medusæ with glassy discs and tentacles like
strings of beads.   Their riders were guiding them with
bridles of twisted sea weed, lashing them with their
rattan whips, blowing reed pipes and flageolets and
shooting at each other balls of clay from pith elder pop-
guns ; throwing nets over each others' heads or tossing
showers of water over each other from their urn shaped
tulips, trumpet lilies and pitcher plants, amid a perfect
revelry of fun, frolic and laughter which made the
woods ring.

In the centre of this merry circle floated a magnificent
Arcacea or pearl shell barge, drawn by a flock of snow
white swans, their delicate silken reins held by six
winged Auroras mounted on the prow, which was supported on the upraised wings of carved white falcons.
Along the gunwales of the barge stood rows of birds,
white and grey herons, scarlet flamingoes, crested
hoopoies, snow white ospreys, and other birds of gorgeous plumage unknown on Earth.   Above the Auroras
stood beautiful Horæ, or goddesses of the seasons,
crowned with chaplets and bearing cornucopias of
fruits, flowers and grain.   Behind these were the Graces
and Terpsichores, crowned with garlands and gracefully dancing to the sound of lutes.   Groups of Hesper-

ides holding golden apples in their hands, mingled with
the Muses, bearing myrtles, palms and roses. Behind
the birds stood rows of Euterpes, Eratos and Melpomenes, attired in white robes and playing delicious music
on harps, lyres and cytherns. High over the deck, the
upper leaf of the bivalve Arcacea hung like a great
canopy, its arched dome reflecting splendid prismatic
colors. On its summit, which was decorated with the
royal coat of arms of Mandal-Uttima, stood a magnificent white and grey eagle, looking calmly down with
his kingly eyes on the beautiful scene. As our chariot
drew near, the bands of Nereides and Naiads ceased
their sports and parted their ranks. The swans uttered
sweet notes of welcome as we drew alongside and
stepped on the deck. Passing through the ranks of the
Graces and Euterpes who ceased their music and dancing, we approached a splendid divan, hung with gauzy
curtains of amber and pearl, suspended from the beaks
of birds of paradise. On either hand stood a group of
beautiful young girls attired as Psyches, over their
heads floated a cloud of tiny humming birds, their fluttering wings resembling an aureole of rainbow hues.
As we drew near, the curtains parted and the living
vision of my dream appeared, a young girl of form and
countenance so transcendently lovely, of beauty almost
divine, she seemed an angel wafted from Paradise.

" My sister, the Princess Suhlamia," said the Prince.

As I knelt and kissed her hand which the haughtiest
monarch of Earth would have been proud to press, she
glanced at me from beneath the softly veiled lids of her
dark and magnificent eyes, while a glow of surprise and
pleasure mantled in her cheek as in a voice low and
sweet she bade me welcome.

It were difficult to describe the beauty of this young
Martian Princess by any æsthetic standards with which

we Terrestrians are familiar, for the Martian ideal
belongs to a superior order and is elevated on a higher
plane than ours. And this is all the more apparent
from the fact that, our usually accepted standards are
more or less fallacious, being founded upon erroneous
and often crude conceptions of the Beautiful in Nature
and Art. Many so called æsthetic writers have at-
tempted to formulate and classify what they call their
Ideals into standards corresponding to fanciful conceptions of their own, and designate these Ideals as the
spirituelle, the intellectual, the expressional and emotional, and arrange the physical beauty of mere form,
color, etc., into what they call the classical, passional,
voluptual, etc., this is particularly seen in the meretri-
cious French æsthetic school. To attempt the formula-
tion of rules or models of beauty or grace in human
beings is as futile as to lay down standards for horses,
cattle, birds, flowers, trees or landscapes, for, as the
beauties of the animal and vegetable kingdoms of
nature display an almost infinite variety, standards are
therefore impossible. The Ideals of all ages, races and
nations are different from each other. Those of the
ancient Assyrians and Babylonians are in striking contrast with those of the ancient Egyptians ; those in
turn from the Aryans, those from the Greeks and so on
to the Persians, Arabians, Romans, Teutons, Goths,
Celts and Franks. Every race and nation of to day
exhibit the same diversity and have each their own
standards or ideals of moral, mental and physical excellence and beauty, all of which keep pace with their progress in development, cultivation and refinement.

The Princess Suhlamia was rather above the middle
height ; her form exquisitely graceful and symmetrical,
and her features of that pre-eminently noble and spirituelle order rarely seen among the most highly favored

of Earth born womankind, and in this respect she
strikingly resembled her brother Altfoura. Her complexion was of the most delicate aureate hue, combined
with the soft, rich, creamy tint of the tropical magnolia.
Her luxuriant hair—which if unloosed, would have
flowed to the ground in great wavy masses—was a deep,
rich purple, verging on a glossy blackness, mingled
with a tinge of red gold, and shimmered with a sparkling lustre like the dust of sapphires ; her hands and
feet were small for her height and beautifully moulded.
Her eyes were magnificent, their color indescribable,
resembling that abysmal darkness seen in the fathomless gulfs of the celestial heavens. They were perfect
mirrors of her pure and noble soul, vividly displaying,
or softly veiling its deep and varied emotions. From
their depths emanated a resistless magnetism and her
glance now beamed with a gentle radiance and now
flashed with the fire of diamonds. These beauties of
form and feature combined with her refined and elegant
bearing, her sweet and ingenuous expression, together
with the irresistible fascination surrounding her, united
to form one of the most lovely creations among woman
kind. She was attired in a simple robe of pure white,
scarce concealing the exquisite outlines of her form and
without ornament save a little budding flower on her
breast.

John and the raven were now presented and received
graciously. The Princess placed a splendid medallion
around his neck and caressed the raven. It is needless
to add that the former was the proudest and happiest
of all Tanehoka war chiefs, and Commodore Jack the
proudest and happiest of all ravens on Mars.

We sat down and engaged in conversation while the
swans turned the Arcacea gracefully about and sailed
up the river accompanied by the bands of Nereides and

Naiads. The Princess displayed intellectual endowments of a high order, united with great elegance and
polish of manners, all of which were heightened by her
sweet amiability and charming sallies of wit.

The river narrowed as we advanced, the foliage of
the trees formed a complete archway overhead. The
mossy banks were thronged with groups of young girls
attired as Dryads, Oreads and Auloniads, nymphs of
woods, grottoes, trees and fountains. Sylvan shepherdesses and huntresses, armed with rustic crooks,
bows and arrows, and playing on pan-pipes, flutes and
flageolets. Others were dancing under the trees to the
sound of lutes, castanets and cymbals. The woods
resounded with their songs of welcome.

We now entered a beautiful little lake surrounded
with hills, woods and grassy meads. On its banks a
magnificent palatial villa of many colored marbles
appeared embowered among the trees. We drew up
and debarked on a broad marble platform, the barge
with the Princess and her companions, passing on to the
private entrance of the villa.

"This is the chateau of Athalton, the Grand Duke
Regnant," said Altfoura.

We were met by officers of the royal household and
escorted up a broad pathway through a grove of trees ;
the sward was covered with soft and delicate moss,
plants and flowers of all varieties of beautiful colors.
We entered a splendid portico which, with the villa,
was surrounded by lofty fluted columns of variegated
marbles ; the vestibule was paved in mosaic. We were
received by the grand master of ceremonies and his aids,
and escorted to an inner apartment, from which, after a
short time, we passed through a court into the grand audience hall, a magnificent rotunda surmounted by a lofty
dome of sky blue crystal, and surrounded with Gothic

arched windows of stained glass with panels of flamboyant tracery and paintings in fresco. A splendid ornamented gallery, supported on carved columns of different woods surrounded the hall, which was thronged with
crowds of both sexes comprising the élite of the realm,
forming a display of beauty and chivalry such as was
never seen in the grandest court receptions of Earth.
Strains of sweet music resounded as we passed through
the throngs and ascended an elevated daïs hung with
royal banners, together with the stars and stripes, which
had been brought from the Admiral's ship. We were
received by Athalton Zhangyal Thullivarrh, the Arko-
Basileus, or Grand Duke Regnant, a noble looking old
man of kingly bearing and venerable appearance. To
my surprise and pleasure the Princess now appeared,
attired in the robes of her royal rank and accompanied
by a suite of beautiful young ladies. We were presented to the assembled throng in accordance with the
Martian court ceremonial.

The reception concluded and the audience departed,
we retired to an inner apartment in company of the
Duke, Princess, and several distinguished guests, and
partook of a collation. We spent the remainder of the
day in the extensive grounds of the villa which, in
beauty of adornment, immeasurably surpassed the
most celebrated palatial surroundings in Europe. The
magnificent trees, foliage and flowers of gorgeous
hues ; the superb statuary and fountains of many
colored waters, filled me with astonishment and delight.
It seemed as if I were in an earthly paradise, or fairy
land. At the close of the day, after spending a few
hours with the royal family, we were escorted to our
apartments for the night.

The Doctor and I had been conversing together a
few moments. "I will now inform you," said he,

"concerning the Prince and Princess. Helion Zhang-yal Thullivarrh, surnamed the Just and Wise ; was the former Rajan-Indra, or Emperor of Mandal-Uttima, and the Rajan-ezza, or Queen, Amazelia, surnamed the Good and Beautiful, was his wife. Of this royal line which extends back many centuries, they were the noblest, wisest and best beloved that ever ruled this kingdom and were the parents of the Prince and Princess, who in their minds and persons are perfect counterparts of their father and mother. The Queen expired soon after giving birth to her daughter, and our beloved Helion died of a broken heart. His paternal uncle, Athalton, was appointed regent and he fulfills the duties of his station with eminent dignity and justice. He and the Grand Duchess Luzanda,—lately deceased,—having lost their only son and daughter in infancy, adopted the Prince and Princess as their own children—according to the custom of our nation, and no parent could lavish more tender affection on their off-spring, then the Duke on his royal wards. In a few weeks the Princess will have completed her eighteenth year and enters her majority, which will be celebrated by appropriate festivities. The Prince is now twenty ; on the following year he will reach his majority, the Duke will resign his regency, and Altfoura, who even at this youthful period gives full promise of being able to sustain the responsibilities of his royal station in a manner worthy of his father, will be crowned Emperor of Mandal-Uttima."

The Doctor now opened one of the windows over-looking the grounds of the villa.

"Come out and take a look at our moons," said he.

We stepped out on a balcony and I saw a beautiful little snow white moon hardly one twentieth the appar-

ent size of our own satellite, about half way up to the
zenith and sailing across the sky from east to west.

"That is our outer moon, Sudha Aryuna," said he.
"It is about twelve thousand five hundred miles from
us, and completes its orbital revolution,—about ninety
thousand miles,—in a little over thirty hours."

In a few moments another moon, twice the apparent
size of the first and of a deep blood red color, rose in
the west skirting low across the horizon, in a contrary
direction to the other. The rapidity of its motion surprised me.

"That is our inner moon, Sudha Rohanza. It is about
four thousand miles from our globe ; completes its orbital revolution, about thirty-six thousand miles, in a
little over seven hours, flying at the rate of over eighty
miles a minute. As it revolves around our globe nearly
four times a day we shall see it in the same position
again, before sunrise to-morrow.'

"Mars was never suspected to have a moon," said I.
"Although the planet had often been searched since the
invention of the telescope, by many distinguished
astronomers of our world. Your planet was called the
'Moonless Mars,' although from analogy, the existence
of a satellite might have been suspected. The honor of
this discovery is due to one of our distinguished
American astronomers."[1]

[1] Professor Asaph Hall of the U. S. Naval Observatory at
Washington, D. C., Aug. 11th, 1877. The Moons were named by
him " Deimos and Phobos " " Terror and Flight," the attendant
steeds of the Mythological God, Mars. Dean Swift describes
these moons in his " Gulliver's Travels," Voyage to Laputa, written nearly two hundred years ago. " They have likewise discovered two lesser stars, or satellites, which revolve about Mars,
whereof the innermost is distant from the centre of the primary
exactly three of his diameters and the outermost five. The for-

As the blood red Phobos swiftly traversed the southern horizon, it had a sinister and ominous look, as if
presaging some calamity, and I noticed that the Doctor's
countenance wore an expression of anxiety as we gazed
upon it.   Little did I dream of the tragic rôle that moon
would ere long play in the future destiny of Mars.

"Look yonder," said the Doctor, pointing to the
south west.   "Behold your World!   'Tis our evening
star.—How beautiful."

The tears came to my eyes as I gazed long and earnestly on my dear Mother Earth.   Calm, beautiful and
sweet she hung like a gem of purest ray serene in the
blue vault of heaven.   "O thou lovely Orb!" I murmured ; "thou holdest in thy bosom my home, kindred,
friends, and all that are dear to me.   Am I indeed forever separated from thee, and can only view thee from
afar, as thou sheddest thy nightly radiance o'er these
Martian skies?"

As these thoughts rose in my soul, they cast a gloom
of almost utter desolation o'er me.   I completely broke
down, and sobs impossible to restrain, burst from my
surcharged bosom as I threw myself on my couch.

mer revolves in the space of ten hours, the latter in twenty one
and a half; so that the squares of their periodic times are very
near in the same proportion with the cubes of their distance
from the centre of Mars, which evidently shows them to be gov-
erned by the same law of gravitation that influences the other
heavenly bodies."   Considering that the science of Astronomy
and the invention of the telescope were comparatively in their
infancy in Dean Swift's day, this is one of the most extraordinary guesses of modern times.

CHAPTER XXVIII.

THE MARTIAN NIAGARA.

"The thoughts are strange that crowd into my brain
  While I look upward to thee. It would seem
As if God poured thee from His hollow hand,
And hung His bow upon thine awful front,
And spoke in that loud voice, which seemed to him
Who dwelt in Patmos for his Saviour's sake,
' The sound of many waters;' and had bade
Thy flood to chronicle the ages back,
And notch His centuries in the eternal rocks."

Niagara.—BRAINARD.

During my sojourn at the villa, Altfoura and I took frequent excursions on horseback through the surrounding country. He possessed an extensive collection of fine blooded horses, which in beauty of form, spirit and speed, were wholly superior to the finest bred studs seen on Earth. The colors of some were similar to ours, but others were totally different, with bright and glossy coats the color of burnished gold, copper or dark blue, and *vice versa*, with manes and tails of purple, brilliant gold, or bright crimson. Their intelligence and docility, the result of careful and judicious breeding and training through many generations, were wonderful ; they required neither whip nor spur, being perfectly controlled by the voice of the rider. From early youth I was accounted a skillful horseman, and prided myself accordingly ; but I soon found myself quite overmatched by Altfoura, while the Princess surpassed us both in daring equestrian feats. I usually rode a bright bay, and as horses here, as well as on the terrestrial turfs are endowed with names,

that of mine,—by reason of certain fine points,—was
Atya Rohita. Altfoura preferred his favorite Turan-
iga-Krishna, a magnificent animal of dark purple with
golden mane and tail. Yavan-Arjuna, the favorite
steed of the Princess, was a mare of extraordinary
beauty and intelligence ; she implicitly obeyed the
slightest word, or gesture of her mistress. Her color
was white as snow, her mane and tail like rippling
mother of pearl. Her speed was amazing. In our con-
tests over the grassy plains not only would she out-
strip Atya and Turaniga, renowned as were their powers, but her wonderful leaps over lofty hedge rows,
stone walls and streams would have astonished the
most daring fox hunter or steeple chaser on the turfs
of Earth ; she absolutely seemed to fly like a bird.
When it is remembered that gravity is nearly two
thirds less on Mars than on Earth, and that, a horse
weighing a thousand pounds there, weighs not quite
four hundred here (according to the terrestrial scale) ;
also that the Martian atmosphere has less than half the
weight and density of Earth's, besides containing
nearly a double proportion of oxygen, it will not surprise my terrestrial friends to be informed that an
equine speed of a mile in two minutes is accounted
rather a snail's pace here, that Atya and Turaniga
have often covered thirty miles an hour and Yavan,
mounted by her mistress for a mile stretch, would turn
up her pretty nose in disdain at the idea of requiring
over forty seconds to accomplish it. What is called
the vital or pulmonary capacity, of the different classes
of the animal kingdom distinguished for powers of
speed or flight, is relatively much greater than among
those of Earth. So it is with the Martian races, their
chests are larger, deeper and more capacious, the
thoracic organs, lungs, heart and blood vessels are

larger and stronger than those of the Terrestrial races, while the configuration of all other parts of the anatomical and muscular systems, is cast in a much more compact and elegant mould. Let one of the Martian men, women, horses, eagles, lions, or any animal or bird, stand side by side with the finest selected specimens of Earth, as competitors for grace, elegance or beauty, the merest child would instantly award the palm to the former.

Our excursions were varied by occasional trips over the bay, in the Prince's yacht. Now and then a brilliant regatta was held, and sometimes a gay party would go out to sea mounted on Zeuglissa's back, and enjoy the playful sport of the Ocean Queen amid the rolling billows.

The natal day of the Princess' majority, for the celebration of which elaborate preparations had been made, was now at hand. In honor of the event there was to be a *fete champetre*, with other festivities, at the Duke's country seat on the banks of the lake Ambu-Cyama or "Green waters," a few hundred miles distant in the interior of the kingdom. In company of the ducal party and many distinguished guests we left the villa, embarked on several air ships and passed along the shores of the bay which were ornamented with highly cultivated gardens, vineyards, fine chateaux and villas, till we reached the broad and majestic Maha-nadi river which pours its waters into the bay. For many miles up stream it is occupied by great numbers of little islands, on which charming little cottages and pleasure gardens appear here and there, amid the luxuriant verdure. The channels between the islands are spanned by pretty bridges. Pleasure boats and gondolas with gay parties coursed over the waters. Youths and maidens were engaged in sports on the lawns or under the trees, with little children whose happy laughter mingled with the sounds of musical instruments. It was a perfect picture of the happy isles of Mirzah.

We passed up the river about two hundred miles and reached the base of a great mountain chain. Here a tributary river, the Giri-nadi flowing from the south west, pours into the Maha. We passed up this river which flows with great velocity. The banks are rugged and rocky, gradually increasing in height and the river flowing down a steeper declivity, rushes with tumultuous speed like the upper rapids of Niagara, while the precipices rise on either hand to enormous altitudes like the great cañons of the Colorado. After ascending many miles, the river's bed is level and the waters smooth. We coursed amid the deep gorges of the mountains for about a hundred miles and reached a station at the base of the precipices. Our party with a few of the guests debarked, while the Duke, Princess and suite with several of the cabinet officers continued their course up the river to the grounds of the chateau. We descended a flight of steps hewn out of the rock to a broad platform. Four richly caparisoned barges manned with crews lay in waiting ; we embarked and left the shore.

" We will now enter the great caverns of Nordoval, under the Brushanti Mountains," said the Prince, " where you will witness one of the grandest sub-montane displays on this planet."

We rounded a projecting promontory and entered a vast semi-circular amphitheatre nearly a third of a mile in diameter completely surrounded by tremendous precipices. In front and extending across it, rose the upright façade of an immense barrier of solid green and red rock, resembling the section of a lofty mountain split perpendicularly in twain. Its base is pierced

by three enormous tunnel shaped openings, nearly on
a line with each other, rising in great gothic arches
from three to four hundred feet high and forming the
giant portals of the sub-montane caverns, through which
the waters smoothly flow into the open amphitheatre.

As our barges glided under the great archways a
scene of unparalleled grandeur was displayed. The
whole interior of the mountain is hollowed out into a
series of stupendous caverns. Row upon row of pillars
and columns from fifty to a hundred feet in solid thickness, arise from four to six hundred feet high, supporting on their summits still loftier arches. Gigantic
stalactites hang from the arched roofs. Stalagmites,
pyramids, towers, minarets and colossal figures, resembling human beings and animals, arise from the waters ;
while strange and fantastic shapes, uncouth and terrible
forms loom up ghastly from the dark and deep recesses.

After pausing a while to view this wondrous scene,
the Prince ordered the caverns to be illuminated. This
was accomplished by men stationed along the rocky
platforms. From the vaulted arches hung suspended,
or floated slowly along, myriads of great globes, emitting variously colored and brilliant lights. The pillars
and columns were surrounded from base to summit with
spiral wreaths of flame. The arches glittered as if
spangled o'er with jewels. The stalactites, pyramids
and towers gleamed with sparkling effulgence and the
colossal images of human and animal forms, seemed
ready to spring into life and motion. The waters were
so pellucid and clear that even at the depth of fifty feet,
the sand, pebbles, and rocky bottom were plainly visible,
while their surface, reflecting the splendors from above,
resembled a vast crystalline mirror tinted with rainbow colors. At some places, the boat crews sang songs

which reverberated along the galleries with wonderful power and volume ; at others, a single word or shout would be re-echoed twenty times ; there was a famous acoustic cavern where a whisper could be distinctly heard from one boat to another, although separated an eighth of a mile apart. For many miles we rowed through the caverns and grottoes, then directed our course toward the outlet. The entire length of the cavern is seven miles. Finally we emerged through four great arched portals. As we passed out into open day, a vast aqueous amphitheatre of oblong shape, seven miles long by three miles broad, spread out before us.

"This is the famous intra-montane lake Ambu-cyama, hollowed out in the bosom of the mountains," said Altfoura.

A scene of unparalleled grandeur opens to view. The whole circumference of the lake is surrounded by stupendous precipices from six hundred to a thousand feet high. And now the united thunders of three great cataracts burst on the ear. On the right, about four miles distant, are two, the terminii of the Yokta-nadi river, a tributary to the Giri-nadi. The first issues from its narrow gorge and descends in five cascades. The waters, as they fall from one terrace to another, are torn into whirling masses of foam upon the sharp crags, and dashed with irresistible violence into the lake. This cataract is four hundred feet in height. About two miles beyond, the upright wall of the barrier is hollowed out from top to bottom in a semicircular gorge, straight as the shaft of a mine. Within this dark recess, which like some gigantic organ pipe, pours forth a deep and solemn tone, the waters fall steep down six hundred feet, in one long narrow sheet. From its apparently slow descent, graceful undulations and transparent envelope of snowy foam, it is called the " Wedding

Veil." From this point the precipices, sweeping around
to the left, arise in one solid wall, twelve hundred feet
high, forming the upright rampart of a great mountain
chain severed in twain, from which descends the great
cataract of Maha Solitambu. The waters of the Giri-
nadi, arising eight hundred miles distant, amid the Mali-
pondo mountains, which traverse the continent from
north to south, flow through the high table lands and
finally precipitate themselves into the lake, in one vast
unbroken sheet a mile wide, and a thousand feet high.

The aspect is inexpressibly sublime. Niagara, the
outlet of four great lakes, sinks into utter insignificance
in comparison with this mighty cataract which resembles a boundless sea falling from the skies. Its deep
and majestic roar reverberates among the surrounding
mountains, re-echoes amid the deep caverns, shakes the
adamantine walls and towering precipices ; while over
the weeping rocks, the clashing billows, and whirling
clouds of spray, so typical of life's conflicts and sufferings, a magnificent rainbow hangs, like a gorgeous
crown, emblem of that peace, happiness and glory,
which humanity, amid its struggles and sorrows, may
still hope to attain.

Nearly the whole circumference of the lake, except in
the vicinity of the cataracts and openings of the caverns,
is surrounded by broad, rocky platforms, skirting the
base of the precipices. We rowed directly across the
lake to the left of the cataract. The platforms were
crowded with people who greeted our arrival with
cheers. The barges moored up to the shore, our party
debarked and were received by a number of persons
attired in rich costumes and evidently of high rank.

The assembled throngs presented a brilliant appearance. The young people of both sexes were attired in
garments of gay colors. The display of richly deco-

rated uniforms, robes, mantles and plumes was like that of a gorgeous court reception. They surrounded us on all sides and even the presence of the Prince could not restrain their audible expressions of astonishment and curiosity at beholding a trio of denizens from the Earth. Many looked at me with awe as my stature towered above them all, and as the great Tanehoka war chief stalked majestically through the crowd with the Commodore proudly perched on his shoulder, bowing and kissing his claws right and left, young girls shrank back and little children took refuge behind their elders, evidently regarding them as a pair of genuine bugaboos from the nether world. The summits of the precipices in many places were festooned with all manner of flowering vines hanging down in long streamers and waving in the breeze. Innumerable little cascades and jets of water spouted from the crevices in the rocks, showering down in circular pools hollowed out in the platform. Flocks of birds of strange form and plumage flew over the lake diving for fish, the air resounding with their melodious cries ; pleasure boats, gondolas and barges, filled with gay parties, coursed over the waters in all directions. The facade of the precipices near the cataract was strait as a wall and over a thousand feet high. It was traversed with upright shafts cut deep in the solid rock from base to summit, in which elevators were swiftly ascending and descending, conveying crowds of people. We entered one and were quickly raised to the summit of the barrier.

CHAPTER XXIX.

THE FETE CHAMPETRE.

"There, St. John mingles with my friendly bowl,
The Feast of Reason and the Flow of Soul."
Horace, Satire.—POPE.

A charming rural scene was displayed. A broad and level plateau extended along the river's banks and ornamented with magnificent trees interspersed with bowers and open glades. Along the greensward were hundreds of tents and pavilions decorated with banners and occupied by the invited guests. We entered the Duke's *maison de campagne*, a beautiful chateau embowered amid a grove ; the ducal party had arrived a short time before. We retired to our apartments and having made our toilettes for the festival, passed out to the lawn where the guests were assembled. The Princess with her suite of beautiful young ladies were clad in rustic attire, as flower girls, nut and berry gatherers, dairy maids and shepherdesses. Prince Altfoura with his friends, as foresters, hunters, horsemen, farmer boys and fishermen.

The guests were attired in various rural or sylvan costumes. The dresses of some were composed of a beautiful vegetable lace or gauze, of exceedingly delicate texture and of various colors ; some wore girdles, necklaces and bracelets of delicate moss, leaves, capsules and seeds, scarfs and mantles woven from the fine tendrils of plants and grasses. The attire of the ladies presented a faërie like and beautiful appearance. The guests, numbering over two thousand persons,

comprised the highest dignitaries of the realm and
included the most distinguished representatives of the
three Martian races, the Arungas, Rohitas and Nilatas, belonging to the various kingdoms in friendly relations with the kingdom of Mandal-Uttima. We passed
through a long colonnade of trees whose foliage formed
a complete canopy overhead and entered a great circular amphitheatre floored with green and red moss, and
screened with silken awnings supported on rustic
pillars of wood.

We were greeted by a concert of feathered songsters.
Hundreds of birds of various species unknown on Earth,
assembled on a high platform under the trees, sang a
grand triumphal march. The melody was borne by
bands of white and grey colored birds in tones of wonderful sweetness and power. The voices of some were
like those of our nightingales, sky larks and thrushes.
Others resembled the tones of various orchestral instruments, violins, flutes, clarionettes, etc.; others like cor-
nets and French horns. The bass parts were sustained
by large grey colored birds resembling our loons and
wild geese, in deep and powerful tones like double-
basses and trombones. Some held drum sticks in their
claws beating drums ; others struck triangles and cymbals. In front stood the leader, a tall brown colored
bird resembling a stork, standing on one leg and waving a long white baton in his claw. They kept as good
time, and the phrasing and modulation was like that of
a well trained orchestra of human musicians. It certainly
was the most wonderful performance of its kind ever
witnessed by a denizen of Earth or any other planet.

"These birds," said the Doctor, "have been cultivated and trained in music for many generations until
their organs and abilities have attained the highest stage
of development."

The Duke now took my hand and drew me forward in full view of the guests.

"Dear friends," said he, "I take pleasure in presenting to you our esteemed guest, Lieutenant Hamilton, an officer in the Navy of the United States of America. He is the first inhabitant of Earth who has ever visited our World. I pray you extend to him all that kind consideration and courtesy which he, as a representative of the younger Earth born race, is entitled to receive."

I sustained the battery of two thousand pair of eyes as best I might, the assembled throngs greeting me in the Martian style. John and the raven were introduced by the Doctor and Prince. The Tanehoka war chief and Commodore Jack received the salutations with stately dignity, bowing to the right and left in a style worthy Beau Brummel in his palmy days.

Five long tables radiating from an elevated daïs, enabled the royal party and guests to view each other with ease. The *maitre des ceremonies* having arranged the guests in order according to their respective ranks, we sat down and the banquet began. Flocks of little amber colored birds flew down from the trees bearing in their beaks fragrant bouquets, and large white leaves on which were imprinted the *menu*, distributing them among the guests, while bands of young boys attired as Ganymedes, attended to the courses. The service was entirely rustic; the plates, dishes, centre pieces, etc., were composed of barks, vines and tendrils closely interwoven; the cups, goblets and flagons, composed of leaves, corollas and calyxes; the knives, forks and spoons of wood variously carved and ornamented. Every single article of the service was composed of vegetable materials, in all manner of unique and pretty designs.

As to the viands, had bounteous Nature as she displays her prodigal resources to us Terrestrians, been culled of her choicest products she could never have furnished half the delicacies and novelties here displayed. The " Dies festi " and " Epulæ," the " Canæ lautissimæ," and " Convivium sybariticum " of the Emperors and nobles in the days of old Rome's luxurious splendors. " *Les petits soupers* " of the old French monarchy, all sink into utter insignificance in comparison with the festival feasts of the Martians ; among the almost infinite variety of viands I recognized a few of Earth's productions, but none of the usual " stand bys " of rounds of beef, legs of mutton, haunches of venison, dressed ham, fowl, game, lobster, terrapin, etc., etc., so essential to our Terrestrial banquets, were visible.

" You miss your roast beef, etc., etc., doubtless ? ' remarked the Doctor.

Remembering that the last bit of meat I had tasted was on board my ship, I frankly confessed that I did and inquired if the inhabitants of Mars were vegetarians.

" The pure Martians who have kept their races distinct from admixture with each other, live exclusively on that diet. Many of the mixed races and nations occupying our southern hemisphere consume meats of all kinds and the pernicious effects are manifested among them," replied he.

I now informed the Doctor that, in the opinion of our Terrestrial physiologists, an exclusively vegetable diet tends to weaken the system by not affording sufficient nourishment to the tissues. That nearly all the civilized and enlightened nations of Earth lived on a mixed diet and consumed different varieties of meat. That the races and individuals who subsisted exclusively on a vegetable diet were inferior in bodily strength and mental vigor, were almost universally timid and slavish and that our wild races who subsist almost entirely on meat or game, were superior in physical strength and courage to the vegetable eating tribes.

"And they probably are correspondingly superior in evil passions, tyrannous dispositions, cruelty and brutality, not to speak of all kinds of constitutional taints, inflammations and other bodily and mental diseases. Is it not so?"

I was fain to acknowledge that, in respect to many of the meat eating inhabitants of Earth, this statement was not far from the truth.

"The same physiological law is manifested in the whole animal kingdom," said the doctor. "Contrast the superior strength, beauty of form and docility of disposition of the herbiverous animals adapted for the use of man, with the whole carnivorous tribes; their ferocity, treachery and utter destitution of kindly instincts. Not to speak of the reptiles, look at the whole ornithological kingdom, where will you find a single specimen of the carnivorous class of birds, that take kindly to man, or are susceptible of being tamed except by coercion, or can utter a single musical note. Listen to the nightingale, thrush, linnet, robin and the whole class of singing birds whose diet is purely vegetable, and contrast their beautiful tones with the harsh cries and discordant screams of the whole tribe of hawks, vultures, ospreys, cormorants, owls, etc."

I was compelled to acknowledge the truth of the Doctor's observation.

"Animal food has the inherent tendency to repress the development of the higher and nobler attributes of man, the moral sentiments and feelings, and it has the worse effect also, of stimulating and fostering the instincts and passions of our lower nature; you Terrestrians, in spite of your advancement in civilization, wealth, power and progress in science, will always have more or less discord, turmoil and warfare among your nations, societies and individuals—not to speak of poverty, vice and crime—as long as you devour meat. It will take several generations of total abstinence before you can disevolve your constitutional carnivorous inclinations. You may then hope to have peace and unity among your nations, and physical, mental and moral health and happiness among your societies and individuals."

Although it was hardly to be expected that I could entirely subscribe to the Doctor's view, being by birth and lineage a Terrestrial meat eater ; still, I felt compelled to acknowledge that, his statement embodied a great physiological truth, which it was to be hoped Terrestrians might in time be prepared to accept practically.

"Look around the board," said he. "Observe our guests. How do their physical appearance, forms, facial expressions, etc., compare with those of your flesh eating nations and races ?"

I was compelled to acknowledge that, while in respect to mere stature and bulk of frame, the Martian men were rather below the Terrestrial standard, yet in respect to exhuberant health, pure blood, buoyant spirits, beauty and symmetry of form and intellectuality of expression, they were fully equal to, and in many instances superior to, the finest specimens of physical manhood seen among the enlightened and cultivated races of Earth.

"And with respect to our Martian ladies also ; please give us your opinion, and do not permit it to be influenced by any sentiment of gallantry which gentlemen generally entertain toward the fair sex."

" I will endeavor to do so," I replied, " and view them simply from a physiological point of view. I frankly acknowledge that as regards beauty and symmetry of form and feature, as well as the higher charms of grace and expression, the Martian ladies are unsurpassed by the most highly favored of womankind among the inhabitants of Earth, and what is still more remarkable, they seem to combine the more pleasing characteristics of our different nationalities ; to wit, the amiability and gentleness of the Anglo-Saxon, the modesty and ingenuousness of the German, the voluptuousness of the Circassian, the fire and dash of the Greek, the mingled gravity and sweetness of the Spanish, the *languore delizioso* of the Italian, the *esprit* and vivacity of the French, and the high spirit, independence and refinement of the American."

" A thousand thanks for your admirably expressed compliment, and now I will inform you that not a single particle of meat of any kind has ever passed the lips of our guests nor those of their ancestors for remotest generations. We thoroughly detest meat as you would the reptilian and insect food of the lowest savages. Our blood is pure and untainted from the flesh of any living creature. Not a single life that God has given has ever yet been taken,—not a single drop of blood that He has warmed has ever been shed,—not a single frame that He has cunningly fashioned has ever yet been spread, a mutilated carcass on our tables, nor rolled as a sweet morsel under our tongues ; and what I say of our guests here, the same is true of three thousand million Martians."

A magnificent orchestra concealed among the trees discoursed charming and appropriate music at intervals, during the feast.

The appointments of the *cuisine* were the acme of

perfection. The Ganymedes sped swiftly over the sward, bringing on and removing the courses. Flocks of birds fluttered around, bearing in their beaks clusters of pods and capsules containing pleasant aromatic juices, oils and spices with which we flavored our viands. The flower bearing birds removed the bouquets already distributed, bringing new ones. Beautiful little humming birds hovered over the young girls, with buds, sprigs and sprays in their tiny beaks, fixing them in their hair, or to their bosoms, their swiftly fluttering wings resembling aureoles of rainbow colors. It were impossible to describe the dessert. The variety of delicacies was almost infinite. It seemed as if the gardens of the Hesperides and Elysian fields had been culled of their most luscious sweets and confections, and it is to be hoped that the juvenile darlings of Earth, hearing this tempting gustatory allusion, will not all clamor to be carried to Mars in a twenty million mile-per-minute Ethervolt car, next Thanksgiving or Christmas.

The feast drew near its close and the time for the toasts was at hand. A company of tall birds with long necks, and bills resembling storks, cranes, gosanders, and flamingoes, marched in line, bearing floral flagons, decanters and queer looking bottles containing sparkling liquors and set them before us. They were of all varieties of flavor and shade. The usual sentiments were offered with the appropriate responses. The health and prosperity of the nations of Earth, and particularly the United States of America, were drunk by the Duke, Prince and other dignitaries, to which I responded in as good terms as I could command. The Martians are brim full of wit, humor and vivacity, all of which are rendered the more piquant and agreeable by their high bred courtesy and refinement.

"What think you of our liquors?" the Doctor asked.

" The finest brands I ever tasted. The most epicurean
Terrestrian would go in ecstacies over them. Nothing
comparable is produced among the vineyards of Earth.
I fear, however, we shall soon become more than merry
over our generous libations."

" Have no fear. Our flowing flagons cheer, but do
not inebriate."

" Do you mean to say we are not drinking wine ?"

" They are the unfermented juices of rare plants dis-
tilled and rectified in the laboratory of Nature, and do
not contain a single drop of alcohol. They possess
exceedingly delicate and peculiar properties which have
a very kindly influence on the system. They relieve
bodily fatigue and increase physical and mental vigor.
They produce peculiar effects upon the different mental
faculties, the association of ideas is facilitated, the memory is sharpened, the judgment formed with greater
ease and accuracy, language becomes more fluent and
exact, imagination and fancy are stimulated to the highest degree, as manifested in the departments of poetry,
music, etc. Look around the board and witness the
influence of these liquors already. There is a company
of logicians elucidating some profound metaphysical
problem. There is a coterie of statesmen adjusting
some intricate question on international and state policy.
See those eminent members of the bar, they have had a
knotty legal problem before them for weeks ; they'll
solve it before they rise from the table. There is one
of our most distinguished mathematicians clearing up
an intricate calculation in fluxions ; there is one of our
great orators holding his listeners spell bound with a
brilliant forensic display. Yonder is one of our poets
entrancing his hearers with a fine extemporaneous
effusion, and one of our renowned musical composers

is jotting down on his tablets the theme of some new oratorio, symphony or concerto."

Several young ladies and gentlemen entertained the guests with dramatic recitals and songs which were received with applause.

"Come, Lieutenant," said the Prince, "please favor us with one of your Terrestrial songs."

"Your highness will please excuse me. I am no singer," I replied.

"No singer? Pardon me, Lieutenant, I have not forgotten your magnificent singing on the polar seas of your World, and I sincerely hope you will not refuse my friends this pleasure."

"A song from so distinguished a representative from a brother planet would greatly add to our festivities," said the Duke.

"Ladies and gentlemen," said the Doctor, rising, "our esteemed guest, Lieutenant Hamilton, will favor us with a song in his native language."

"A song!—a song!" ran around the board with a loud clapping of hands.

Feeling considerably abashed at the idea of posing in the rôle of a society warbler before this brilliant assembly, I was tempted to resort to the usual indispositional subterfuges so frequently affected by petted musical amateurs in our fashionable circles, and which are more often betrayals of vanity than otherwise, when a bright smile and winsome glance from the Princess inspired me with courage. I arose without more ado and dashed off into Tom Moore's famous drinking song.

"Fill the bumper fair,
Every drop we sprinkle
O'er the brow of care
Smooths away a wrinkle.

> Wit's electric flame
> Ne'er so swiftly passes,
> As when through the frame,
> It shoots from brimming glasses."

Immense applause rewarded my effort and the audience insisted upon my favoring them with others, of a still more convivial character, and the encores were vociferous. Several distinguished poets and musicians solicited the translations. I had previously quoted a few of the more grand and beautiful extracts from Shakespeare, Byron, Scott, Poe, Longfellow, etc., to my Martian friends and took pleasure in adding the sweet bard of Erin and one of our well known American song writers to the list. It was with feelings of great pride I reflected that I had been the humble instrument of introducing Earth's mighty bards to the world of Mars.

And now came an ornithological *opera comique*. The feathered songsters were dressed out in all varieties of stage costumes and arranged on the platform. There were kings and queens, princesses, belles and beaux, clowns, brigands, horned devils and imps. Other birds clad in fashionable attire, were assembled around as audience. The feathered songsters warbled, chirruped and trilled, in a style that would have done credit to high class Italian opera, while the audience expressed their approval, or disapproval, clapping their wings, piping out their little bravos and encores, or hissing and mewing cat-calls, after the style of high toned Parisian audiences. The performance was so irresistibly comical, as provoked shouts of laughter from the guests. Four beautiful snow white doves now appeared bearing in their beaks a veil of light gossamer, throwing off soft prismatic colors, then placing it over the brow of the Princess its falling folds enveloped her form like a halo, they were followed by flocks of birds scat-

tering oak leaves over the guests. This announced the
close of the feast and the guests arose from the tables.
The Princess, accompanied by her suite of maidens
passed around among them distributing to each a little
gold plate containing a salt cake, as a handsel or token
of friendship and memento of the festival.

And now came the finale. Hundreds of little children attired as fairies, sylphs, elfins, pixies, brownies
and all imaginable myths of Martian faërie land and
folk lore, rushed from the woods and bowers, accompanied by all the feathered songsters and stage actors,
assembling around the tables with loud shouts and
merry peals of laughter. They were waited on by the
Ganymedes, bouquet and fruit bearing birds, the storks
and flamingoes. The songsters, perched around or flit-
ting over the dishes, selecting the choicest delicacies,
drinking from the flower cups, standing on one leg and
wiping their beaks with their little napkins, while the
humming birds flitted in flocks over the tables picking
the tit-bits amid a perfect Babel of twitterings, pipings
and chirrupings. The Commodore, inspired by the
festive scene, marched with stately step to the highest
place on the royal daïs, glanced over the assembled
throngs, as if he were king of the feast, then with the
serenity of a superfine fashionable gourmand, deliberately appropriated the courses in regular order as they
were obsequiously presented by the storks and Ganymedes, politely declining, however, any such senti-
mental nonsense as button hole bouquets, cakes and
confectionery, but bestowing critical attention to the
sparkling potations in the goblets and bottles. This
concluded, he wiped his beak, bowed in stately style to
the faërie guests, descended from the daïs and mounted
to his accustomed station on his master's shoulder.

In the mean time the guests had assembled in the

pavilions on the glade. A deputation from the Nilatas now appeared with an invitation for the ducal party to visit their own festival held on the opposite side of the lake, in honor of the birthday of Princess Luzella, daughter of Oneigar Zhangyal Abdalon, Grand Duke Regnant of Raji-Vohandra, the kingdom of the Nilatas (corresponding to Madler's continent on our Maps of Mars) situated on the eastern hemisphere and separated from Galileo's continent by the great Tycho sea. This powerful nation of the blue complexioned race, numbering six hundred million inhabitants, was in close relations of amity with the kingdom of Mandal-Uttima, Duke Athalton and Oneigar being warm personal friends, and the Princesses Suhlamia and Luzella were bosom companions from childhood.

The Duke immediately accepted the invitation and our party, with several members of the cabinet and distinguished guests, descended the barriers, embarked in barges, rowed across the lake to the opposite side of the cataract and landed on the rocky platform skirting the precipices, and on which were erected splendid pavilions decorated with gorgeous banners. We were received by Oneigar, a noble looking old man of dark azure complexion, and his wife Thaloba, a lady of refined and highly aristocratic presence, descended from a long line of Nilata princesses and their daughter the Princess Luzella, a bewitchingly beautiful young girl of delicate hyacinthine complexion, brilliant dark eyes and radiant with smiles and dimples. They were attired in rich costumes somewhat resembling those worn by Oriental princesses of the old Persian and Arabian days of romance. Suhlamia and Luzella, who were of the same age, threw themselves in each others' arms, in the ardent and impulsive Martian mode.

"I esteem this visit of your highness a most distin-

guished honor," said Oneigar with a courtly salutation.

"But we looked for you, my old friend, the first amid
our festival, and were sadly disappointed. Come now,
what excuse can you conjure up?" replied Duke
Athalton.

"The azure hued Nilatas cannot presume to ascend
to the lofty eminence of the golden hued Arungas,"
replied Oneigar with polite deference.

"If the blue will not come to the yellow, why, then,
the yellow must go to the blue," replied Athalton.

"And the union will be bright green and may this
natal day of our beloved children be ever green and
fresh in our memories," said Thaloba, as she pinned a
beautiful emerald hued floral souvenir on Suhlamia's
bosom.

The ladies retired to the royal pavilions and in a short
time returned. The Princess was attired in a dress
similar to those of Thaloba and Luzella, but more rich
and elegant. A closely fitting jacket resembling burnished silver, amber tinted skirt embroidered in floral
and arabesque designs, a crimson mantle elaborately
decorated in pearl and silver, a jaunty turban of gold lace,
caught in the centre with a diamond spray, light blue
trousers resembling the old Persian mode, and gold embroidered slippers. This attire was so thoroughly in
keeping with her resplendent beauty as excited our admiration. The stately Oneigar relaxed his dignity, show-
ered compliments and with the air of a court gallant drew
near her side. Thaloba took the arm of Athalton. I had
the honor to escort the Princess Luzella. Altfoura, the
Doctor and John paired off with other royal ladies. We
entered an immense cavern, hollowed out in the rocks,
splendidly decorated and illumined with many colored
lights. The assembled throngs greeted us with enthusi-

astic cheers, mingled with strains of music and we were escorted to our stations. The appointments and decorations of the banquet were even more gorgeous than those of our own festival in accordance with the rich and Oriental fancy of the Nilatas. Congratulatory speeches were made in honor of the occasion, to which, Duke Athalton and suite made appropriate responses. Songs and recitals were given and toasts quaffed in brimming goblets circled the board. Along the platforms skirting the precipices crowds of people in gorgeous attire were witnessing all manner of sports and games. There were wrestling, boxing, foot racing and rowing matches in which the young men displayed their skill, agility and strength. There were jugglers, mountebanks and wizards, playing tricks and feats of legerdemain that would have confounded our most clever prestidigitateurs. There were exhibits and shows of all kinds ; giants, enormously fat and heavy folk, monstrosities from sea and land ; wax works and puppet shows, such as would make our Terrestrial juveniles weep for joy. There were trained animals, birds, reptiles, fishes and insects, performing the most wonderful feats. There were burlesque military displays, masquerades and fantastic dances ; such a carnival of fun, frolic and merry making never was seen and the Nilatas entered into it heart and soul.

It was now the hour for departure ; we bade adieu to our Nilata friends and passed to the platform. Several of Thaloba's maids of honor brought from the royal pavilion a magnificent casket and coffer containing articles of feminine apparel and ornaments, the sight of which would have made the proudest Terrestrial princesses and devotees of fashion perfectly crazy with astonishment and delight.

"Dearest Suhlamia," said the Duchess, "accept these

birthday gifts as mementoes of this joyful time and as an earnest of our love and esteem. Within the coffer are dresses especially designed for you by the most skilled *artistes* of our kingdom. Do me the honor to wear the one designated for the ball this evening, where we shall again greet you. Within the casket are jewels, family heirlooms, formerly worn on these occasions by the princesses of my race. For my sake wear them to-night, selecting from them what you deem appropriate for the occasion."

The boats now drew up and we embarked. The Princess with Luzella,—who was to spend the remainder of the day with her,—Altfoura and I, occupied one barge, Duke Athalton and suite, the Doctor and John, occupied the others. We rowed rapidly over the lake, and our barge which was in advance, having arrived nearly opposite the cataract, the Princess requested the oarsmen to approach nearer that we might obtain a fuller view. We drew so near, the spray fell over us in showers and the barge paused in its course, rocking on the billows.

CHAPTER XXX.

THE WHIRLPOOLS.

" The roar of waters !—from the headlong height,
    They rush and cleave the wave worn precipice ;
  The fall of waters ! rapid as the light,
    The flashing mass foams, shaking the abyss ;
    The hell of waters ! where they howl and hiss,
  And boil in endless torture."

Childe Harold, Canto iv.

The awful splendors of the mighty cataract were displayed in all their glory. A vast crystalline wall of

glittering emerald, seeming like the Miltonic battlements of heaven, rising from the waters to the skies.
Its foundations a roaring ocean of tumultuous billows,
whirling columns and vortices. Its summit crowned
with rolling vapors, amid which gleamed countless
rainbows. Its deep toned thunders resounding amid
the precipices and hollow caverns, almost overwhelmed
our souls with unutterable awe. With clasped hands
and heaving bosom, Suhlamia gazed upon the tremendous scene.

" O, thou mighty Maha-Solitambu !" she murmured,
in thrilling tones—" what grandeur !—what glory and
beauty are thine. Enthroned amid the deeps ;—veiled
in clouds ;—crowned with celestial halos,—thou art
indeed the symbol of Infinite majesty and power, and
thy dread thunders are as the voice of Him before
whose face the heavens tremble !"

" O Suhlamia !" murmured Luzella, clinging trembling to her companion, and hiding her face in her
bosom. " Thy great and noble soul can view with
calmness these awful glories, which overwhelm my
heart with terror."

The Princess now took out her tablets and pencils
and began to make a sketch of the scene. Having some
skill with the pencil I accompanied her with a sketch
of my own. I had occasionally noticed trunks and
branches of trees, swept down by the torrent above,
tossing around us here and there, amid the waves. The
sketches completed, we were comparing them and listening to the critical comments of Altfoura, when suddenly
Luzella uttered a piercing shriek, throwing her arms
around Suhlamia, as a large tree shot up under the gunwale, ripped the starboard oars short off in their locks,
crashed down, tore away the awning, and swept the

Princess out into the water. In an instant I dashed off coat and cap, and plunged in after her.

Stunned by the shock, she had sunk ; the next moment I caught a glimpse of her dress floating some distance ahead and with a few rapid strokes reached and drew her partly above water, while a glance at the boat showed Altfoura struggling in the arms of the crew who were holding him back from plunging in after us. The Princess soon recovered from the shock, regained her breath, flung off her turban and mantle, threw her supple form forward, and with rapid strokes swam towards the boat. Cautioning her against too great an outlay of strength, I kept close by her side for several minutes, then I saw that we were making no headway, but were drifting steadily backward toward the terrible line of whirlpools skirting the base of the cataract, while a glance ahead showed our boat helpless by reason of her broken gunwale, but the Duke's barge was hurrying to the rescue and boat after boat rowed swiftly towards us, while loud cries of terror and dismay burst from the assembled thousands on the shore.

The movements of waters under the influence of heavy gales, storms and cyclones are uniform and rythmical even amid their most tumultuous agitations ; but their movements at the bases of great cataracts seem no longer amenable to the laws of motion ; they are ungovernable, riotous, presenting fit symbols of the anarchies of revolutions, the turmoils of mobs and communes. The waters are in a state of amorphism. They seem to be stark mad, scourged into frightful insanities as if lashed by the whips of demons. Whirling clouds of spray conceal the pandemonium, where churned up surges, pyramids of spume, vortices and whirlpools are raging ; the victim who is caught here perishes at once, and his body revolves like Ixion bound to his wheel, until by chance it is thrown out from the whirls. Beyond these, lies the battle ground of chopped up billows and surges, jumbled pell mell together; there is something fantastical in their uncouth and drunken flounderings; whoever falls here is speedily suffocated. On the outskirts of this chaos extends a broad area of undulations, swells, see saw movements and tangled cross currents in which the expertest swimmer is utterly bewildered and from which he cannot extricate himself.

We were now tossed to and fro on the angry surges. The most powerful efforts barely kept us above water and we should have speedily perished but that we were thrown upon the broad surface of a revolving eddy where we were able to get breath.

"Courage!" cried the Princess, sweeping her long hair back from her brows. "I see the boats!" A dozen or more, headed by the Duke's barge were pulling towards us with all their might. "If we can keep in the centre of this eddy till the boats reach us—" said I, "we are safe—" but it required an incessant struggle to accomplish this and to my inexpressible dismay I saw that my brave companion was losing strength. I drew her near my side, directing her to lay her head upon my shoulder and grasp my garments in her teeth. She obeyed my directions and for a short period we were able to keep our position, but at last were gradually drawn from the eddy, and looking back I saw to my horror that we were rapidly being swept towards one of the swift overtow currents running directly to the whirlpools at the foot of the cataract, where it was lost in clouds of spray. The Princess saw at a glance the terrible danger.

"Leave me; leave me to my fate," she cried. "O, Frederick, why did you imperil your life for mine?"

"Never will I leave you!" I exclaimed. "Courage!"

—and we sprang forward to regain the centre of the eddy in vain. The current seized us with o'er-mastering grasp and hurried us toward the cataract whose thundering roar rang like a death knell in our ears, mingled with the despairing cries of the boats' crews as they vainly strove to stem the raging waves. I glanced at the barge and saw the Duke standing in the prow, wringing his hands and with features convulsed with agony, while my faithful John far in advance, stripped to the waist, with a rope clenched in his teeth was swimming toward us,—followed by Altfoura, who had broken loose from his crew.

One glance at the hell of waters around us,—one glance at the mighty sea descending from the sky;—and Sunlamia with a calm and sweet resignation, raised her lovely eyes, and clasping her hands, breathed one short prayer. The next moment, clasped in each others' arms,—amid darkness and the roar of commingled thunders we were hurried to our doom.

. . . .

Suddenly a terrific scream rent the air! My arm was seized in an iron grasp and I was dragged up with irresistible power from the waters. My lapsing senses enabled me dimly to discover the enormous head and fiery eyes of a gigantic bird whose talons clutched my form like hooks of steel, while high in air his broad expanded wings flapped amid the rolling vapors. It seemed as if we were seized by some terrible demon of the waters, and I sank into an insensibility as deep as hers whose inanimate form I unconsciously strained to my breast.

. . . .

When I recovered consciousness I was lying on a cot in a tent under the grove.

"Thank God!—he breathes," whispered a voice. Altfoura was bending over me. "Dear, dear friend," he fervently murmured, pressing my hand.

"The Princess,—Suhlamia!" I exclaimed. The next moment the clouds in my brain cleared away ; I felt as if awakened from a frightful dream, the memory of which still lingered.

"The Princess was unharmed ; is safe and quietly reposing in her pavilion," said Dr. Hamival.

"Thank God!" I fervently ejaculated ; then after a moment—

"My faithful John ?"

"Hi! hi!" exclaimed a familiar voice. "Me feelee so muchee proud happy to see dear Cap'n Fred gettee all right again," and John bent over me, his honest face all in a glow.

"The brave fellow seized a rope in his teeth and sprang from the Duke's barge to rescue you," said the Doctor. "He swam far ahead of the barge, but was beaten back again and again, and finally rescued with difficulty by the boats."

"My dear and faithful John," said I, "how can I ever sufficiently thank you ?"

"By no speakee any more 'bout it."

"Who rescued the Princess ?" I asked.

"You ; yourself," replied Altfoura, "Suhlamia owes her life to you."

"No ; I remember an enormous bird."

"It was Leuca—the Princess' favorite eagle," said the Doctor.

"The grasp of her talons seemed to crush the very life out of me."

"She was compelled to clasp you with tremendous power, as she dove down and dragged you,—holding the Princess in your arms,—from the billows. That terrible, but saving clasp, was the cause of your prolonged insensibility."

In a short time I arose and resumed my attire. Duke Athalton paid me a visit, expressing his gratitude in the warmest terms. Then came a message from the Princess inquiring after my health and announcing that she would be happy to see me, soon as I felt able to visit her.

"I accept the Princess' invitation, immediately," said I.

"Why this haste ?—you are not strong enough ;—wait a while," said the Doctor.

"I'll go at once."

Altfoura and I left the tent and passed over the sward to the royal pavilion which was decorated with the standard and crest of Mandal-Uttima. At the portal stood several ladies of rank and beautiful girls of the Princess' suite ; their countenances were wreathed with smiles. The curtains were raised and we entered the pavilion. The atmosphere was laden with the sweet fragrance of roses. On a divan festooned with rich hangings reclined the Princess. Her matchless form, lovely countenance and almost angelic expression, seemed like a vision of heavenly beauty. The Princess Luzella was by her side. Suhlamia rose from the divan as we advanced, glancing upon me with her resplendent eyes which shone like twin stars at night, while on either lid hung a tear, glittering like a dew drop under the sun's ray.

"Lieutenant Hamilton," said she in trembling accents, "at the risk of your life, you rescued my brother from imminent death and you have now saved my own. I owe you a debt of gratitude which I never can repay."

"Dear and honored Princess," I replied, "speak not of it, I implore you."

Suhlamia extended her beautiful arms, bare almost to the shoulder, toward me and a sweet smile irradiated her countenance.

"Come hither, my friend," she murmured ;—my feelings were too deep for utterance ;—I trembled as I drew near that royal couch, knelt and kissed her hand.

Suhlamia bent forward and laid her hand almost caressingly on my head ;—her warm and delicious breath fanned my cheek ;—I raised my face to hers ;—one ravishing glance from her resplendent eyes met my ardent gaze ;—one bright smile that thrilled my soul with ineffable joy, a faint blush mantled in her cheek,—she kissed my brow and softly murmured—

"Dear Frederick ;—'tis the seal of our friendship."

"My dear," said Luzella, who was standing with the Prince near a vase of exotics, "don't you think these flowers rather becoming to my hair ?"

"Very becoming indeed," replied the Princess calmly.

"I shall wear them at the ball to-morrow evening. Prince, I select you for my partner," said the Hebe glancing at him coquettishly.

The Prince joyfully accepted the honor.

"And shall I not have the pleasure, Lieutenant Hamilton, to select you as my partner for the dance ?" asked the Princess quietly.

The Lieutenant bowed his acceptance.

CHAPTER XXXI.

THE BALL.

> . . . "had gather'd then
> Her Beauty and her Chivalry; and bright
> The lamps shone o'er fair women and brave men;
> A thousand hearts beat happily; and when
> Music arose with its voluptuous swell,
> Soft eyes look'd love to eyes which spake again,
> And all went merry as a marriage bell."
>
> *Childe Harold*, Canto iii.

On the following day the festivities, which had been temporarily suspended, were resumed. The Princess had quite recovered from the shock and received the congratulations of her friends. The rôle I had played was the theme of éclat. The Duke and Prince, notwithstanding my remonstrances, had determined to make my part in the drama a subject of ovation, and I was compelled to sustain the ordeal of a court reception. This concluded, we prepared to witness the races and entered the grounds a short distance from the villa. It was a great circular amphitheatre three miles in circumference, surrounded with commodious stands hung with awnings and seating many thousand spectators. Two hundred racers entered the field, mounted, not by professional jockeys,—that profession being quite unknown in Martian equestrianism,—but generally by their owners, young men and ladies, the majority of whom were of high rank. Altfoura's favorite Krishna was ridden by one of his friends. Yavan-Aryuna, the snow white steed of the Princess, was mounted by Luzella, who was second only to her in equestrian skill.

The first courses were led by the young men; the speed of the horses was tremendous, but in every heat Krishna distanced all competitors. The second was led by the equestriennes attired in appropriate costumes and although many of the racers surpassed their previous records, Yavan-Aryuna was victorious. To my surprise, the most important elements in racing business, in our Terrestrial point of view, were wanting on this occasion; to wit, betting books, stakes, pool peddlers, piles of money, etc. Such a thing as betting on the speed of a horse, is quite unknown among Martian equestrians; in which respect they would of course, be regarded as quite behind the times by our Terrestrial sporting circles and their races as very stupid and uninteresting affairs.

The races closed with a grand cavalcade. A thousand young ladies and men were mounted on splendidly caparisoned steeds. In this the Princess and Altfoura joined. She was attired in a superb riding habit, the gift of Thaloba, royal purple velvet embroidered with gold, and hat to correspond. The pageant was magnificent. They swept around the arena in solid phalanxes, every horse head to head in accurate lines. The Princess Suhlamia and Luzella with their coteries of young maidens, all on snow white steeds, leading the van.

The preparations for the ball had been arranged on a scale of elaborate magnificence and many of the crowned heads of the Martian kingdoms who were to honor the festival with their presence, were arriving with their suites in fleets of air ships and chariots, some from countries far distant, and were escorted to the royal pavilions and apartments of the château assigned them.

The grand *salle de bal* of the villa, was an immense elliptical amphitheatrum and capable of accommodating several thousand guests. Its magnificence and beauty almost defy description.

Its walls consist of triple rows of lofty columns of different colored marbles sweeping around the whole circumference, and supporting on their capitals a splendidly carved entablature from which ascends a vast dome of sky blue crystal. Between the columns were flowering trees, plants and ferns, amid whose luxuriant foliage gleamed marble statues and fountains of all imaginable forms and colors upspringing from the mouths of carved dolphins and sun fishes, and falling in glittering showers in marble lavers. The floor of the arena was paved in mosaic, and surrounded by a broad platform elevated one step above it, and on which were rows of seats and divans for the guests. The vast concavum of the dome, the cornices of the entablature and capitals of the columns were draped with gorgeous banners and festoons of flowers. At regular intervals among the columns were open portals, decorated with flowering vines and hung with curtains. They were the entrances for the guests and communicated through leafy colonnades with the private pavilions surrounding the amphitheatrum. Seven of these portals, loftier and more richly decorated than the others, were surmounted with the royal coats of arms and emblazoned standards of the seven Martian Kings and Dukes Royal. The amphitheatrum was brilliantly illumined with countless globes of many colored lights, gleaming amid the gorgeous draperies of the dome.

As we entered, a panorama of wondrous beauty and splendor was displayed. The surrounding platform was occupied by thousands of elegantly attired ladies and gentlemen comprising the élite of the different races of the Martian kingdoms, and all along the brilliant circle, the glittering sheen of superb toilettes min-

gled with the flashing coruscations of countless gems
was like a vast and gorgeous rainbow brought down
from the skies.

Amid the cheerful strains of pastoral music from a
concealed orchestra, throngs of little children attired as
Cupids, Psyches and Floras, issued from the leafy portals, singing songs of welcome, flinging showers of dewy
odors from their gauzy wings, and strewing the platforms with flowers from their cornucopias. Following
these came bands of Euterpes and Melpomenes playing
on harps, lutes and cytherns ; their full and melodious
voices mingling with the songs of the children, while
throngs of fairies, peris, elves and Terpsichores,
assembled in the arena, mingled in the bewildering
mazes of fantastic and beautiful dances. 'Twas like a
scene from fairy-land.

And now the loud fanfare of trumpets, the roll of
drums and clash of cymbals resounded through the hall.
The flower bearers, singers and dancers flitted back
among the trees and fountains. The veils of the seven
royal portals were raised, and the beauty and chivalry
of seven mighty Martian kingdoms poured into the
arena, in streams of dazzling splendor. The magnificence of the scene was truly beyond description. The
array of gorgeous robes, decorations, the glittering arms
and uniforms, the jewelled helmets and coronets, the
flashing crowns and tiaras, was like the superb Miltonic
picture of the marshalled celestial hosts along the battlements of heaven. The grand national anthem of
Mandal-Uttima, rolled in mighty waves of harmony
through the amphitheatrum. As the royal suites
marched in solid phalanxes over the arena, the national
anthem of each kingdom was played, the national character of each being expressed in the different themes.
Some were cheerful and joyous ; others were stately

and majestic ; the strains of some were pathetic and mournful, while others resounded with a wild, barbaric, and even savage clangor. No such martial music was ever heard on Earth. It was like the mighty and resistless tread of innumerable armies. The grand *entrée* concluded, they assembled on the platform under their respective portals, receiving the salutations of the guests, while the music sank to soft and delicate measures mingling with the subdued hum of conversation.

Beneath the portals crowned with the royal crest and standards of Mandal-Uttima, the Princess Suhlamia stood leaning on the arm of Duke Athalton, with Luzella, Thaloba and Altfoura in his splendid uniform, by her side. She was surrounded by the court ladies and maidens of her suite, cabinet officers, nobles, peers and distinguished personages of both sexes, all in magnificent costumes. Duke Oneigar, his royal officers and suite were gathered under the adjoining portals crowned with the coat of arms and standards of Raji-Vohandra.

A description of a ball, or reception, its appointments, decorations, etc., with no description of dresses to match, might justly be regarded by many of our fashionable dames, with whom that subject is of such vital importance, as a very crude and unfinished sort of affair, like the play of Hamlet with the part of Hamlet left out, but had a posse of our fashionable society reporters, whose business 'tis to observe and chronicle the petticoat department of our *haut ton*, been present on this occasion, aided by the most skilled corps of fashionable female milliners and upholsterers, yclept *modistes*, whose sceptres sway so many million female hearts ;— they would have been utterly overwhelmed by the magnitude of the task, and the *modistes* themselves would probably have gone insane over what they could

not comprehend, much less describe. The toilettes of
the princesses, court ladies, etc., of the different kingdoms were composed of materials unknown on Earth,
immeasurably surpassing in elegance and beauty any
thing of the kind seen in our most splendid court receptions or *recherche* aristocratic crushes. What we Terrestrians designate as style, mode, or fashion in dress,
is quite unknown among Martians ; neither is there any
word, nor figure of speech to express the idea, if any
such idea lurks in the Martian feminine mind. The
attires of each and all are in keeping with their race,
station, occupation, age, peculiarity of personal appearance, etc., of which latter, the varieties being almost
infinite, permit an equal variety in dress and adornment, in accordance with the fancies of the individual,
all of which, are regulated by perfect taste and elegance ; hence the Martian female heart is quite ignorant of those manifold anxieties and perplexities, and
quite innocent of those heart burnings, mutual envys
and jealousies which, in affairs of dress, as well as of
love, hold such omnipotent sway over countless millions
of our Terrestrial feminine hearts.

The Princess Suhlamia was attired in what might be
described as a close-fitting princess dress, *decollette* and
en train, showing the exquisite outlines of her form. It
was of nameless hue ; faintly luminous, almost phosphorescent, which at every movement or flicker of light,
threw off the most beautiful play of delicate prismatic
tints, like the irridescence of opals, or mother of pearl.
The outer dress was a perfectly transparent crystalline
gossamer, or illusion, of delicate hyacinthine hue, decorated on the borders with what seemed gauzy butterfly
wings, and every part of it, flashed like the rays of the
morning sun on new fallen snow. It enveloped her
form like an ethereal cloud, resembling those celestial

nebulæ amid whose shadowy depths gleam galaxies of stars. She wore no ornaments save the royal insignia of her rank ; one solitaire gem, whose resplendent lustre rivalled Arcturus as it gleams o'er the midnight skies of Arabia. Her whole appearance was so ethereal and beautiful as elicited expressions of wonder and admiration. In the meantime bands of fairies, peris and Cupids were passing among the guests distributing the programmes of the dances imprinted on little ivory tablets in letters of gold and azure.

Conspicuous among the royal portals on the opposite side of the arena towered the lofty standards and decorations of Prince Diavojahr, heir apparent of the great kingdom of Sundora-Luzion, the most wealthy, powerful and populous of the seven Martian monarchies and comprising the greater part of the south eastern hemisphere. His suite numbered a thousand of the highest nobles and dignitaries of his realm, and amid the loud blare of trumpets, the roll of drums and clash of cymbals, they marched in gorgeous array across the arena. The brow of Prince Altfoura darkened, he beckoned to the lord high chamberlain in whom was vested the arrangement of the festivities, and that nobleman stepped quickly forward.

" How is this, my Lord of Montobar ?" he whispered. " The Prince Diavojahr here ? His royal highness was not invited."

" Can it be possible ? I crave your Highness' pardon," replied his lordship. " I knew not of it—having been informed that he was on the way hither with his suite, I directed his pavilions and portals to be prepared accordingly."

" There is some mistake here ;" replied the Prince ; " but there's no time for explanation ; and although his visit is an intrusion, we will extend to him all due honor, out of courtesy to his unfortunate father, his majesty Probitos Hautozan."

The suite now deployed in front of the portals of Mandal-Uttima and gave the customary imperial salute. The Oriental gorgeousness of their costumes, the glitter of their arms and decorations were like streams of mingled jewels and gold.

A man of tall stature, clad in magnificent dress decorated with royal insignia, advanced from the throng. He was apparently about thirty five years of age. His bearing was haughty, his countenance handsome, but marked with dissipation ; its expression was sinister, displaying arrogance, duplicity and cruelty. He approached the Grand Duke with a sweeping quasi-obsequious salutation, to which he and the Prince responded with suave, yet stately dignity.

" Prince Diavojahr Hautozan," said Altfoura. " Peace be unto you. Permit me to present to your royal highness our honored guest from Earth, my esteemed friend, Lieutenant Hamilton."

His royal highness measured me from head to foot with a right royal stare, and deigned to bestow a condescending nod of recognition. As they did not quite overwhelm me, and as I did not feel disposed to toady to royalty on Mars, any more than on Earth, I returned them both with compound interest, as I fancy any officer in Uncle Sam's Navy would have done. He now approached the Princess and after a somewhat high flown shower of compliments, in which obsequious obeisances, seductive glances, wreathed smiles and handsome teeth were conspicuously mingled.

" Will the bright and glorious star of Mandal-Uttima deign to accept the escort of her humble adorer ?" offering his royal arm.

" Excuse me, Prince," replied Suhlamia with the

politest of smiles. " I have already accepted Lieutenant Hamilton, as my escort,—shall do myself the honor to accept that of your highness, later on."

Had Prince Diavojahr possessed the eye of a basilisk, the furtive and malignant glance he cast on me, would have turned me into stone, but with a still sweeter smile and bow, he approached the Princess Luzella with the same royal request.

" Excuse me, your highness," replied the Hebe, radiant with smiles and dimples, " but I prefer the escort of Prince Altfoura."

" Which I am proud to accept," said he, taking Luzella's arm. " So our royal cousin(1) must seek a partner from among the many princely beauties here assembled,"—bowing almost to the ground.

A dark and sinister glance shot from the eyes of Prince Diavojahr, as with a profound obeisance he retired with his suite and mingled among the royal throngs of the adjoining platforms.

The declination on the part of the two Princesses to accept the inaugural escort of Prince Diavojahr, heir apparent to the throne of the most powerful of Martian kingdoms, created a profound sensation among the surrounding circles, but there was no time for comment. The joyous strains of the orchestra resounded through the amphitheatre. The brilliant suites of the seven kingdoms and throngs of guests, descended from the platforms, assembled on the floor of the arena and the dances began. They were at first of a stately and ceremonious character somewhat resembling our old style minuet and quadrille ; gradually, however, they changed to livelier measures, until the whole arena presented a most brilliant display of beautiful and

(1) Martian kings and princes are accustomed to address each other by this title.

graceful Terpsichorean evolutions. It were perhaps needless to say that I deeply appreciated the special honor conferred upon me by the Princess Suhlamia. Nothing could equal the exquisite grace with which she glided through the mazes of the dance. Hers was indeed the very poetry of motion. With her lovely form, angelic countenance and resplendent eyes, she seemed like a spirit of air. Her attire gracefully floated around her like the wreathing mists encircling the fountains of Helicon, kissed by the sun's rays and—

> . . . " her feet
> Gleamed whiter than the mountain sleet;
> Ere from the cloud that gave them birth,
> They fell and caught one stain of Earth."

CHAPTER XXXII.

MUTTERING THUNDER.

> "But hush! Hark! A deep sound strikes like a rising knell.
> Did ye not hear it? No; 'twas but the wind,
> Or the car rattling o'er the stony street;
> On with the dance. Let joy be unconfined;
> No sleep till morn, when Youth and Pleasure meet
> To chase the glowing Hours with flying feet,
> But hark!—that heavy sound breaks in once more,
> As if the clouds its echo would repeat."
>
> *Childe Harold*, Canto iii.

The night was waning. The giddy whirl of excitement and pleasure was at its height. Bright eyes beamed, and rosy cheeks glowed, as the brilliant throngs, thrilled with an almost intoxicating joy, mingled in graceful evolutions to the soft and voluptuous waves of music that floated on the fragrant and delicious air. Suddenly amid one of the pauses, the sound as of a rushing wind, rising, swelling and dying away in mournful tones, swept over the great dome.

"A storm is gathering," said Duke Athalton.

"A different storm from what you ween," said Duke Oneigar, holding up his hand in warning. "Hark!"

In a few moments a murmuring sound like distant thunder arose, swelling to a deep and solemn peal, then died away in faint reverberations. The guests looked around in astonishment, gazing at each other in silence.

"Well do I know the import of that sound," said Oneigar, in a low tone to Athalton.

"What mean you, my friend?" he asked.

"We shall soon see."

The master of ceremonies with his aids, now advanced hurriedly through the throngs, his countenance expressing anxiety, and in a low tone to the Duke—

"His highness, Prince Diavojahr, has suddenly departed with his suite."

"Can it be possible!" exclaimed the Duke. "Without bidding adieu to the Prince and Princess of Mandal-Uttima?"

"'Twas the wings of his air ships, like the sound of a rushing wind we heard over the dome," said Oneigar.

"Really, our royal cousin has taken our sister's declination of his escort in high dudgeon," said Altfoura with a laugh. "His highness is evidently blessed with a peevish and testy temper."

"He has committed an act of princely discourtesy to our kingdom, and our persons," said Duke Athalton.

"It's a piece of outrageous insolence!" said Thaloba with indignation.

"Quite in keeping, however, with his well known character and disposition," said Duke Oneigar.

Polath Zhangyal Hugovan, emperor of the kingdom of Machival-Purantos,(1) containing a population of five hundred million Arungas, now came forward in company with Prince Harovian Zhangyal Audresar, heir apparent to the kingdom of Rohita-Savoyal,(2) containing eight hundred million Rohitas.(3) Polath had been an old friend of King Helion, Altfoura's father. Prince Harovian was a bosom friend of Altfoura's. The Duke briefly informed them of the occurrence.

"I think I will have to send one of my little court pages to this Prince Diavojahr, to teach him a few lessons in etiquette," said the young and handsome Prince Harovian.

"Etiquette?" exclaimed King Polath. "My dear Prince, he has committed a most reprehensible act, and subjected himself to severe condemnation."

"And I have been the innocent cause of this most unfortunate misunderstanding, which has thrown a dark cloud upon this bright and happy day," exclaimed Suhlamia, her eyes filling with tears.

"Nay; nay; Suhlamia. Take it not so to heart," Altfoura replied.

"Dear brother, why should Prince Diavojahr have taken such deep offence because I extended a simple act of courtesy which I was only too proud to bestow, on our honored guest, to whom we owe our lives? I told the Prince I would accept his escort later, as I told

(1) Corresponding to Herschel's continent on our Martian maps.

(2) Corresponding to part of Newton's continent.

(3) The red race.

others of our royal guests who had preceded him in their requests, and all courteously yielded to the regulation, and why not he? Does he assume that his remote relationship to our family, confers upon him a prior right? Ah, me, I fear that my act, innocent of any design to slight him or what he may deem his royal prerogative, may embroil us in unfriendly relations with his kingdom, disturb the peace of our own country and those of our friends, and bring sorrow and tribulation on us all," and Suhlamia threw herself weeping on his breast.

"Dearest Sister," he replied, " you have no cause for self reproach. Prince Diavojahr, in his relations with us, can claim no royal prerogative whatever." Then turning to the Duke, " What says my honored father to this?"

"Your view, my dear son, meets with my entire approval," Athalton replied. " Yet 'twere well, perhaps, to ascertain the sentiments of our friends on it." Then beckoning to the lord high chamberlain who stood by with his aids :—

"Call our friends hither," said he.

In a few moments, the kings, princes, nobles and cabinet officers of five great kingdoms assembled under the portals of Mandal-Uttima.

"Cousins," said Athalton, " was it obligatory on our beloved Princess to extend the highest honor of our festival to Prince Diavojahr in virtue of any royal prerogatives he may assume?"

"No such obligation was predicated of the Princess," replied Oneigar, Polath and Harovian, with emphasis.

" Does Prince Diavojahr's remote relationship to our royal house, entitle him the assumption of any prerogatives with respect to us?"

"It does not," they replied.

"Thanks, cousins, for this expression of your sentiments. We feel truly grateful that our friends coincide
with us on this point."

The two Kings, Sharitol and Gautovas, each representing a kingdom of over seven hundred million Martians, were conferring with their cabinet officers and
nobles near by.

"Will your Majesties kindly favor us with your views
also?" asked the Duke.

King Sharitol stepped forward from the throng.

"Hail to our royal cousins of Mandal-Uttima !" said
he. "Ye fully know that the kingdom of Sundora-
Luzion is the most populous, wealthy and powerful of
all our monarchies. They are also a proud and haughty
race, quick to resent any slight they may conceive
thrown on what they regard their rights and privileges
as a nation. Therefore our cousins will permit us to
say that, while we entertain the highest esteem and
affection for our royal hostess, the Princess Suhlamia,
still, for the maintenance of friendly relations, we opine
that, the Princess should have waived her private feelings and sentiments on this occasion, and should, in
accordance with the accepted usages of court etiquette,
have extended the high honor of her festival to Prince
Diavojahr, the heir apparent of our greatest monarchy,
numbering three thousand million Martians."

"Your Majesty lays much stress and unction on the
wealth, power and population of this great kingdom of
Sundora-Luzion," said Duke Oneigar sarcastically.
"They are unworthy the name of race, being a nation
of mongrels,—Arungas, Rohitas and Nilatas, inextric-
ably mixed together. As a nation, they are morally
corrupt, and we, pure blooded Nilatas, thoroughly
detest them."

"Furthermore, our royal cousin Sharitol," said King

Polath, "you seem quite oblivious of the fact that, in the veins of this Prince, whose prerogatives you dwell upon, and in the veins of this nation of mongrels upon whose wealth and power you expatiate, runs the bad blood of those corrupt and depraved Plutonian races who fled to our planet six thousand years ago, whom our ancestors received with such kind hospitality, and who repaid them for it by seducing and corrupting so many millions of our hitherto pure Martian races."

The two kings shrugged their shoulders, unable to deny the truth of their royal cousin's statement.

"And you, proud monarchs," exclaimed Thaloba in accents of scorn. "You uphold this Prince, who you well know has no regard for truth, honor, or virtue."

Sharitol and Gautovas fell back before the intense indignation that blazed from Thaloba's eyes.

"Worse than that," quietly remarked Prince Harovian, "this Diavojahr is a scoundrel and villain of the worst sort, and a liar and cheat in the bargain."

"Ho! there, Sir Prince," angrily exclaimed King Gautovas, stepping quickly forward. "I deny your assertion. Retract your words, sir, at once. Prince Diavojahr is my friend."

"Indeed! then, I wish your majesty joy of his friendship and sincerely hope you will derive much pleasure and profit thereby. But as for retracting my words, all I have to say is that, I am prepared to sustain them in each and every particular, at whatever time and place your royal majesty may be pleased to designate," replied the Prince significantly touching his sword.

Altfoura alone excepted, Harovian Audresar was the gayest, handsomest and most gallant Prince among all the seven monarchies of Mars. He was a *preux chevalier* of the first water. He and Altfoura might find their Earthly prototypes in the gallant Marquis de Cinq-Mars of Richelieu's days, and that admirable pattern of knightly chivalry, Pierre de Bayard, of whom even his enemies were compelled to acknowledge, he was "*Le chevelier sans peur, et sans reproche.*" The proud and haughty Gautovas was a brave warrior and withal of quick, though generous temper. Galled at being defied by the young Prince, he uttered a fierce exclamation, dashed his hand on his sword and sprang forward. Harovian smiled, raised his glove, the next instant would have flung it in his face.

"For Heaven's sake! Gentlemen," exclaimed Suhlamia, rushing in between them. "Add not to the gloom that has fallen on this happy day. Add not, I implore you, to my deep sorrow, by this unseemly quarrel," and Suhlamia, the tears streaming from her lovely eyes, looked the picture of grief and despair. Harovian and Gautovas with true knightly gallantry, instantly bent their knees, kissed her hand, and implored her pardon, which she as instantly granted, smiling like an angel through her tears.

"My noble cousins, if ye cannot be friends, at least be not enemies."

"Most noble and beautiful Princess," they replied; "your royal behest shall be obeyed. We swear it on our sacred honors, and more than all, on this lovely hand."

"Cousins Sharitol and Gautovas," said Altfoura, "with all due respect and honor to your royal dignities and persons, permit me to say that, the views you have advanced with regard to the course taken by our honored sister have no weight with the kingdom of Mandal-Uttima, nor with me. I fully endorse her act and will sustain it, if need be, at my sword's point."

The perfect calmness and self possession of the Prince impressed the whole circle.

"Furthermore," he continued, "I will now inform you that his highness was not even invited to our festival."

"Not invited?" exclaimed all in astonishment.

"No," replied he.

Had a bomb shell fallen in the circle, the surprise could scarce have been greater. The act seemed one, such as could never have taken place except between kingdoms in open enmity with each other.

"Some of our officious friends," continued he, "who had enjoyed the luxurious suppers of Prince Diavojahr; and in this respect I acknowledge him a liberal host—"

"It's always well to give the devil his due, you know," interrupted Prince Harovian. "For one who repudiates his debts and wears his morals as loosely as he wears his dressing gown, his royal highness is a capital getter up of midnight revels, saturnalias and other questionable entertainments."

"Thought proper to affix his name to the list of invitations. I submitted the same to her grace, the Duchess, who, as you know, is our acknowledged censor in such matters," continued Altfoura.

"And in the exercise of my prerogative, I took my pen, and drew a long black line through the imposing title of his royal highness, Prince Diavojahr Hautozan," said her grace, looking calmly around.

Kings Sharitol and Gautovas with their suites, nobles and cabinet officers, looked perfectly astonished at what they conceived to be a most unheard of exhibition of feminine audacity toward the heir apparent of Sundora-Luzion.

"All honor to the hand that did it," said King Polath and Prince Harovian, as they gallantly kissed the Duchess' hand.

"Although we cannot altogether endorse the act of

our cousin Thaloba," said Sharitol and Gautovas, "still, we acknowledge that, her grace possesses remarkable courage and independence."

"Thanks, for the compliment," replied she, "then you'll admit that we poor weak women can sometimes be almost as brave as you men."

"And often far more so, dear Duchess," replied the two kings, bowing.

"Thanks, Cousins, for your compliment to our sex. Now would you, mighty monarchs, brave as you are, have dared to show your faces at this festival if I had seen fit to erase your names from the list of invitations?"

"Certainly not; we should have bowed in humble submission to the irrevocable fiat of your grace."

"Your friend Diavojahr is a far braver man than you."

"Dear Duchess, you are very complimentary," said King Gautovas, bowing profoundly.

"And I hope you appreciate it. Your royal friend intruded himself here without leave, and assumed the right to the high honor of leading the dance with our honored hostess. Really, gentlemen, you'll confess that, it required either the courage of a lion, or the impudence of a fox, to do that. Now which was it?"

As the question involved a rather unpleasant admission on their part, the two monarchs manifested no little embarrassment, and finally confessed their inability to decide.

"O, we all know his royal highness is gifted with a prodigious amount of impudence," said Prince Harovian.

"And that is only surpassed by his stupendous vanity," said Thaloba.

"One of the cardinal virtues of your sex, my dear

Duchess," said King Sharitol, glad of the opportunity
to retort on her.

"And how is it in yours, dear Cousin ?" queried the
Duchess with a twinkle in her eye.

" Always regarded as a petty weakness, if not a glaring fault, dear Duchess."

" Which you, dignified monarchs, never own to,"
replied the Duchess with a merry laugh. " When you
wish to make an impression on us susceptible women,
and show off your fine points, you carefully select your
finest attires, anxiously consult your looking glasses,
turning yourselves this way and that, to be sure that your
royal persons and costumes are in satisfactorily attractive order ; but that's not vanity, of course not. As for
this Diavojahr, he is merely the gayest peacock of you
all, with his showy plumage."

Their majesties winced under the Duchess' rather
left handed compliment.

" What a darling little coxcomb his highness is, with
his bows and smiles, sweet compliments and finery,"
murmured Luzella. " He evidently flattered himself
that Suhlamia and I were dying to receive his atten-
tions."

" And how delightfully you snubbed him before his
whole suite," said Prince Harovian. " Really, dear
little cousin, it was positively killing."

" As I would snub any man, were he twenty times a
Prince, who stared so haughtily as he did, at our honored guest, to whom we all owe such a debt of gratitude," replied Luzella.

Again that roll of thunder burst over the dome, followed by a loud explosion.

" Your majesties ;—friends,—witness ye this insult to
our kingdom," said the Duke, sternly.

" And to you, Oneigar ;—to you, cousins, Polath and

Harovian," Thaloba cried. "To you, Kings Sharitol and Gautovas ;—to our honored guests here assembled ; —but above all, to our beloved hostess, the Princess Suhlamia, is this insult flung by that royal scoundrel, Diavojahr."

"The insolent ruffian !—the dastardly dog !" exclaimed Altfoura with a furious expression. "By heaven !—I'll follow him to his palace ;—I'll drag him to his knees before his whole court ;—I'll—"

"Nay !—Nay !—" Suhlamia cried, throwing her arms around him. "The wretch is beneath your notice."

"Leave him to me, my friend," said Harovian quietly, laying his hand on Altfoura's shoulder. "This is my affair ;—you shall not stir."

"This outrage demands immediate satisfaction," said the Duke, then calling the Lord High Chamberlain, who came forward—

"My Lord of Montobar, communicate at once with the court of Sundora-Luzion ; make known to his majesty, King Probitos, the insult of his son against our kingdom and royal persons. Announce to him that, the Duke of Mandal-Uttima demands full and complete satisfaction for the same."

"And please convey to Prince Diavojahr the compliments of Prince Harovian, and say that, unless his royal highness makes a full and humble apology to the Princess Suhlamia, and the Grand Duke Athalton for this insult, I, Prince Harovian, toss my glove in his face, and if he refuses to fight, I will do myself the pleasure of laying a horsewhip over his serene shoulders wherever I find him."

The Lord High Chamberlain bowed and departed on his errand, while King Sharitol and Gautovas, with their cabinet officers and suites, gazed with profound astonishment on the nonchalant Prince, as he gaily chatted with Luzella.

Fortunately, this scene was unnoticed by the other guests amid the hum of conversation, and after a pause, the seductive strains of the waltz arose.

"Come, Gentlemen," gaily interrupted Altfoura, "let's defer this discussion to a more opportune season. Mirth and Pleasure now rule the hour, and we must obey."

"Your royal highnesses will please take your positions for the waltz ;" called out the *maitre des ceremonies.*

"And your partners, also ;" said Luzella, with an arch look at Prince Harovian, who flew to her side.

"Cousin Gautovas," said Suhlamia with her brightest smile, "permit me to select your majesty for my partner."

The haughty warrior monarch gallantly acknowledged his high appreciation of the honor, sprang to her side, and took her arm with the air of a knightly courtier.

"Cousin Sharitol ;" said Thaloba somewhat condescendingly, "has your royal majesty any partner in view at present ?"

"Had I a score, dear Duchess, I would instantly decline them all for the honor and pleasure you now deign to confer on me," advancing to her side.

Throngs of beautiful young ladies of high rank were absolutely dying for Prince Altfoura's escort, but he disarmed all envy, by gallantly leading off the oldest and plainest of the Court ladies present, universally beloved, by her own sex, for her great amiability and kindness of heart.

The voluptuous strains of the waltz now rolled through the hall. The brilliant throngs gathered in the arena, and a magnificent panorama of beauteous forms, lovely faces, glowing cheeks and flashing eyes appeared, floating as it were, on a sea of gorgeous rainbow colors, amid waves of delicious harmony.

" Hark !" whispered Oneigar, raising his hand.

Once again those muttering thunders rose, vibrating on the air ; then died away.

"Thank heaven !" murmured Athalton, glancing o'er the arena. " Those joyous ones hear not that ominous sound."

Yes ; little did those gay and happy throngs dream that, the sound of the rushing wind, erstwhile moaning o'er the crystal dome, and the deep roll of thunder echoing from afar, was but the prelude to the rising curtain of a dark and terrible drama, whose unfolding would shake the Martian World from pole to pole, and drench her fair fields in blood.

CHAPTER XXXIII.

THE PLUTO-MARTIANS.

" Ill fares the land, to hastening ills a prey,
　Where wealth accumulates, and men decay ;
　Princes and lords may flourish or may fade :
　A breath can make them, as a breath has made ;
　Ye friends to truth, ye statesmen, who survey
　The rich man's joys increase, the poor's decay,
　'Tis yours to judge how wide the limits stand
　Between a splendid and a happy land."
　　　　　　　　Deserted Village.—GOLDSMITH.

On the following morning the crowned heads of six Martian kingdoms with their cabinet officers and suites, assembled in the audience room of the château. The action of Prince Diavojahr in coming to the festival without invitation ;—in presuming to the highest honor of inaugurating the evening's festivities as escort of the Princess,—which had been accorded to another ;—by taking offence at her declination and that of the Princess Luzella ;—by departing without paying his respects to the Prince, Princess and Grand Duke of Mandal-Uttima, and above all, by exhibiting his petty resentment in firing the artillery of his air ships over the grounds of the château ;—were denounced, not only as a gross violation of the established rules of court etiquette, but as a flagrant insult to the kingdom and court of Mandal-Uttima, also to the royal guests assembled and requiring a full and ample apology from the court of Sundora-Luzion. It was also conceded that the refusal of such satisfaction would necessarily involve the disturbance of all friendly relations existing between the two kingdoms and eventuate in the recall of their respective *corps diplomatiques*, with all the unpleasant consequences resulting therefrom and even place the two kingdoms in an attitude of hostility toward each other. King Polath, Duke Oneigar and Prince Harovian declared that, the refusal of ample satisfaction on the part of King Probitos would be a sufficient *casus belli* and demand an instant appeal to arms on the part of the powers of Mandal-Uttima. Kings Sharitol and Gautovas dissented from this extreme view and actuated by private and prudential reasons of their own, decided to remain neutral in the event of any hostile demonstrations arising between the two kingdoms. The appearance of the portals decorated with the royal crest and standards of Sundora-Luzion, among those of the other courts in the amphitheatrum, was explained by Lord Montobar who had charge of the evening's festivities

By some oversight, his lordship was not informed that
the name of Prince Diavojahr had been stricken from
the list,—and having received notice late in the day
that the Prince and suite were *en route* and would be
present, he had prepared the pavilions and portals
accordingly,—that the sudden appearance of the Prince
and suite on the scene was a surprise to the Grand Duke
and Prince Altfoura, who nevertheless received them
with the same honor they had extended to the other
royal guests.

King Polath and Duke Oneigar advanced from their
suites and drew near the side of Athalton.

" Cousins of Mandal-Uttima ;" said they, " whatever
action you take in this affair, rest assured shall receive
our firm and united support."

" Thanks ; dear friends ;" replied Athalton and Altfoura, and they joined hands.

" Cousins ;" said Kings Sharitol and Gautovas, " we
sincerely hope this unfortunate affair, which we so
greatly deplore, may not eventuate in any unfriendly
relations between yourselves and the kingdom of Sundora-Luzion."

" That depends entirely on the course taken by his
majesty, King Probitos, with reference to my demand,"
replied Duke Athalton, gravely.

" And still more upon the course of his royal highness with reference to my own request," said Prince
Harovian, with a determined expression. " Your
majesties will please bear in mind that this part of the
affair is in my hands alone. If this princely scoundrel
refuses to make, or attempts to evade, the apology I
demand, I'll challenge him. If he declines, I'll post
him everywhere for a coward and poltroon and I'll lash
the hound with my horsewhip till he begs for mercy,

wherever I find him, and any man who interferes, I'll run him through with my rapier."

So saying, the Prince bowed sweepingly to the assembled kings, nobles and officers, and his countenance was wreathed in a winning smile. It was well known of this gay and gallant chevalier that he was a man not to be trifled or interfered with, in anything he said or did. Altfoura alone excepted, he was the expertest swordsman on Mars ; and his smile was most sweet, exactly in proportion as he was most dangerous. Martian gentlemen, generally, though jealous in honor, are not sudden and quick in quarrel. They are rather of that Hamlet quality,—

> " Rightly to be great,
> Is not to stir without great argument ;
> But greatly to find quarrel in a straw,
> Where honor's at the stake."

Neither do they resort to the shield of the law for protection from, or redress of personal affronts or injuries. It may perhaps please some of our Terrestrial carpet knights and fashionable bloods to know that, *le code d'honneur* is in full flower among the royal and aristocratic circles of our martial brother planet, and affronts calling for personal redress, are adjusted, not by law courts, nor the cold blooded trigger and bullet, but by that time honored weapon whose nice manipulation requires coolness of nerve, agility of movement, suppleness of wrist and quickness of eye, and which was regarded in our by gone days, not only as an elegant accomplishment, but as an essential branch of the education of a gentleman.

The conference having closed, Dr. Hamival took me aside.

" I will now inform you," said he, " concerning the

kingdom of Sundora-Luzion and its relations with ours. Just before the destruction of the Planet Luzio-Avani Dhramza, or the 'Great Shining One,' sometimes called Pluto, which took place about six thousand years ago and of which Asterion and Hartilion, have already informed you,—many of the royal and noble families, having been forewarned of the coming catastrophe, fled hither in Ethervolt fleets. Many were lost on the passage ; the survivors landed on our south pole and were received with great kindness and hospitality by the early Martian races dwelling on the southern hemisphere. Being a far older race than ours, and much farther advanced in knowledge of all kinds, they taught our races many useful arts and inventions. Physically, they were a magnificent race, great of stature and of remarkable personal beauty, as is seen in our renowned Leviathan tamer, Hartilion and his brother Benoidath, who are lineally descended from one of the most distinguished Plutonian kings ; but the majority of the others were morally corrupt and utterly godless. They formed marriage alliances with many of our races and as time passed on, increased greatly in numbers and power, made war on the surrounding nations, extended their conquests, reducing to their sway or absorbing the other races. They are now a great nation of mongrels numbering over three thousand millions and holding the balance of power in the southern hemisphere— except in the lands immediately surrounding the south pole, which belong to our kingdom. Their wealth and power are enormous, their character is overbearing and aggressive, and although we and our brother kingdoms endeavor to keep on quasi-friendly relations with them to avoid the unpleasant consequences of open rupture, still, we have been compelled to forbid any of their people from entering our dominions except under special

regulations. We pure Martians regard inter-marriages
of our different races with abhorrence. Such alliances
are contrary to the laws of God and Nature and produce
great deterioration of the original stock and dreadful degeneracy of offspring.([1]) The royal ancestors of
Hartilion and others who kept themselves pure and
intact from the corruptions of their Plutonian brethren,
refusing to form these unlawful alliances, were cruelly
persecuted and slaughtered by the more powerful mongrel races and were driven to take refuge with us.
Even the few that are left are fast passing away.

" Many years ago, one of the Princesses of our royal
house eloped, and married the son of one of those
Pluto-Martian Emperors. The foolish act of this fro-
ward Princess was a source of great mortification and
sorrow to our kingdom. From her has descended,
through a line of crowned heads, the present Emperor,
Probitos Hautozan, a weak monarch, mentally and physically, but possessing many good qualities. He and his
son Prince Diavojahr are the only representatives of the
male branch of that family closely related to the house
of Thullivarrh, of which the only survivors are the
grand Duke, Altfoura and Suhlamia. Duke Athalton is
childless. Should our beloved Prince and Princess die
without offspring, according to the laws of our kingdom, our throne and sceptre would fall to Probitos, or

([1]) Dr. Hamival's statement involves a great physiological
truth. The laws of heredity are inexorable. The moral, mental and physical degeneracy of the greater part of our semi-
civilized and barbarous races is due to these admixtures. It is
also seen in our own country, in Mexico, and in parts of South
America, in the mongrels of indian and negro, white, indian and
negro, as is shown in our half-breeds, mulattoes, quadroons, etc.
This, of course, does not apply to the alliances of different
nationalities of the same race.

Prince Diavojahr, or his eldest lawful male descendant, but Diavojahr is so universally detested by our people, that any attempt on his part to assume sway over us, would inaugurate a revolution. He is deeply in love with the Princess Suhlamia, has solicited her hand in marriage and is ardently pressing his suit, but with what chance of success you may easily imagine, for she would throw herself into the raging sea, sooner than join her hand with his."

"It strikes me," said I, "he has thoroughly killed what little chance he may ever have had, by his insolent act. We Terrestrians would call his royal highness a consummate fool."

"It seems to be the general impression that, if she refuses to accept his offer—which she certainly will—he will endeavor to induce his father to enforce his suit by an appeal to arms, and if he can bring him over to his views, the tocsin of war may sound in our kingdom before this year is out."

CHAPTER XXXIV.

THE GIANT EAGLES.

" Bird of the broad and sweeping wing,
　　Thy home is high in heaven ;
　Where the wild storms their banners fling,
　　And the tempest clouds are driven."
　　　　　　　　　The Eagle.—PERCIVAL.

The air ships and chariots of the guests, to the number of several hundreds, manned with their officers and crews were mounted on platforms in the glades near the château.   The kings, princes and royal suites, with the assembled throngs, left the pavilions and made ready for departure to their respective kingdoms and places of abode. Bidding adieu to the Grand Duke, Prince and Princess, they embarked on their fleets. It was a grand and beautiful sight to see these ships and chariots decorated with their royal insignia and banners, rising gracefully from the green lawns like flocks of birds on their migrations, their shining hulls and glossy wings glittering under the bright sunlight with various colors. Some sailed majestically over the landscape like eagles ; some flew around in great circles like falcons ;—others like sky larks, swiftly ascending in lofty spirals, till they were lost in the fleecy clouds.

While the ducal party were preparing for their departure, Altfoura and I walked out on the lawn in front of the château. A young man of dark red complexion and piercing black eyes came forward, and greeted the Prince. He was clad in a dark green suit, belt and cap ; his name was Zar Ronizal, the keeper of the royal eagles.

" I will now introduce to you the little chicken that pulled you and Suhlamia out of the water," said Altfoura.

Ronizal blew a shrill whistle from his silver pipe and an enormous eagle flew from the foliage of the trees and alighted on the sward before us. I confess I was not a little startled as I stood in the presence of this formidable bird whose aspect and dimensions called to mind the fabled roc of the Arabian Nights.

" Come hither, Madame Leuca," said the Prince holding out his hand. The eagle approached and bent her head to receive his caress. She was full nine feet in stature, her plumage a rich lavender color mottled with dark brown shades, her breast from the throat down was snow white ; her wings and tail were edged with bands of golden yellow ; her beak dark blue and her feet armed with long, steel colored talons. Her eyes were hazel, their expression soft and gentle ; a long tuft of crimson feathers ornamented her head, her wings when expanded, measured thirty-six feet from tip to tip. Altfoura requested Ronizal to relate the incidents of the rescue.

"I was in a cleft of the rocks on yonder peak, a thousand feet above the lake and a mile from the cataract with Ombrion and Leuca, who were building their eyrie there, when I heard the cries of the people and saw the red flag, signal of danger, floating from the Duke's barge, announcing that some one had fallen overboard. The next instant, Leuca, whose keen sight had discovered her beloved mistress in the water, sprang from the rocks and flew like an arrow from the bow. I instantly mounted Ombrion and followed her. I never knew her to fly so swiftly before. She made that distance of a mile in less than twenty seconds. I had to lie flat down on Ombrion's back and clasp his neck with all my strength to prevent being blown off as he followed close behind her. Reaching the cataract, Leuca swooped down, sailing over the raging waves in great circles, with her eyes fixed below. Sometimes she disappeared amid the clouds of spray. No human eye could have seen, nor human hand rescued you from that hell of waters. Finally she caught a glimpse of you and dove down like a rifle ball, seized you with her beak, dragged you almost from under the foot of the cataract and clutching your body with her talons, carried you, holding the insensible Princess in your arms, to the boats, flying round them till you were safely landed on shore."

The Princess now came forward with two of her maids. Leuca uttered low cries of pleasure at sight of her beloved mistress; crouching on the ground, fluttering her wings. The Princess caressed her, and taking from a casket a gold chain and medal, carved in commemoration of her rescue, bound it round Leuca's neck, while a maid presented a basket of bonbons with which the Princess fed the bird who ate them with great gusto.

"Here comes Ombrion," said Ronizal.

A loud flapping of wings was heard and another gigantic eagle of still greater dimensions, came flying over the lake toward us and alighted near Leuca's side.

"Come hither, Ombrion," said Altfoura, and the eagle stepped forward, bending low his royal crest for his master's caress. As he stood upright, Ombrion was twelve feet in stature ; his plumage iron grey, his wings and tail edged with dark green, a tuft of jet black feathers tipped with white surmounted his head like a plumed coronet. His large dark eyes shaded by heavy brows, had a majestic and commanding expression. His enormous and hooked beak was black, and his talons a foot long. One blow from his claw or one stroke of his beak could have crushed the ribs or split the skull of a lion.

"Stretch out your wings," said Altfoura.

Ombrion rose to his full height, expanding his mighty pinions like the sails of a great ship. They measured nearly fifty feet from tip to tip.

The intelligence and docility of these formidable birds were extraordinary. They understood and obeyed the slightest word or gesture of command from their masters and their instinct in rescuing persons from drowning was superior to that possessed by any of the canine tribe. Ronizal informed me that their usual speed when mounted, was from sixty to seventy miles per hour and they could easily make eight hundred miles per day with occasional rests. When urged, they

could fly over a hundred miles per hour ; for short distances still higher rates. Ombrion had often flown
twenty five miles in ten minutes, and Leuca could cover
two miles within forty five seconds.

"Come, Princess," said Altfoura, "let's take a trip
over the lake and show Lieutenant Hamilton the mettle
of our feathered steeds."

The Princess assented and Ronizal put the eagles in
harness ; this consisted of a light saddle, with stirrups
and holding straps securely fastened around the body
behind the shoulders and wings. We advanced to the
brink of the precipice, the Princess mounted Leuca, and
Altfoura, Ombrion. Feeling rather nervous over this
somewhat bold adventure, I could not refrain from
manifesting it.

"Do not entertain the slightest apprehension," said
the Princess. "There is no danger. I have often
enjoyed these trips, and feel even more secure with
Leuca, than when mounted on Yavan-Aryuna."

"Do you not use bridles ?" I asked.

"What ! bridle our royal birds ?" said Altfoura.
"No indeed ; you will see how they will obey the
slightest word or gesture of their masters."

Leuca now turned her head around, bending her soft
dark eyes on her mistress with an almost human expression of affection, while the Princess caressed her.

"Are you all ready ?" asked Altfoura.

"Yes ; and in haste to be gone," Suhlamia replied,
her beautiful features all aglow with the anticipated
pleasure.

Altfoura gave the signal, the eagles spread their wings,
arose majestically in the air and launched out over the
abyss. For a moment my heart seemed to cease its
beating as, standing on the verge of this awful precipice,
a thousand feet steep down, the thunders of the cataract

resounding through the rocky amphitheatre, I watched
their flight. In a few moments they crossed the lake
and paused on the summit of a lofty precipice ; then
they coursed to and fro over the waters with an easy
and graceful motion. The facility with which the
Princess and Prince guided their feathered steeds was
marvellous. Amid their swift circlings, sudden detours,
down swoopings and uprisings, they held their seats
firmly as if on a rock.

Suddenly like arrows from the bow they flew toward
the cataract, rushed through the wreathing mists, and
appeared hovering above the verge, majestically sailing
to and fro with a scarcely perceptible motion of their
wings, then poised high o'er the awful gulf like Tell's
eagle.

> " O'er the abyss, his broad expanded wings
> Lay calm and motionless upon the air,
> As if he floated there without their aid,
> By the sole act of his unlorded will,
> That buoyed him proudly up."

All at once they swooped down to the base of the
cataract, plunging amid the columns of foam and
whirling spray. The sight was appalling. For an
instant I caught a glimpse of Suhlamia amid the awful
chaos. She seemed to have lost control over Leuca
and swayed to and fro as if reeling,—falling.

" Heaven save her !" I involuntarily exclaimed, covering my face with my hands. In a few moments they
emerged, sweeping round and round in great spirals ;
ascending higher and still higher even to the fleecy
clouds, until they were lost from view. The next
moment, down they plunged from those awful altitudes
like meteors, then gracefully lighted on the grassy
sward. The Princess and Prince dismounted, while
the eagles shook their dripping plumage amid the

branches of the trees. The countenances of Altfoura and Suhlamia were animated with excitement and pleasure. Altfoura stepped aside to confer with Ronizal.

" I sincerely hope your highnesses enjoyed your trip from sea to sky and from clouds to earth again," said I.

"O, it was glorious !" exclaimed Suhlamia with enthusiasm. " That grand and majestic roar ;—that chaos of billows and foam ;—those whirling columns of spray amid which we dashed to and fro ;—that flight amid the clouds, which, as we rose far above them, gleamed under the bright sun like a vast aërial ocean of rainbow waves, whose crests were crowned with millions of glittering jewels."

As I looked upon her glowing countenance, radiant with almost celestial beauty, she seemed like a superior being whose dauntless heart and exalted soul, transcended the highest ideal of mortals.

" I marked the spot where you rescued me yesterday," said she with a pleasant smile. " And I threw a jewel there as a memento."

" You lost control over Leuca, did you not ?"

" For an instant only. We had approached a little too near the falling columns of water ; that was all."

" You seemed as if on the very verge of falling into the raging abyss."

" Really, Lieutenant, you compliment me highly on my skill as an equestrienne," replied she with a merry laugh.

"But if you had fallen ?" said I, feeling my cheeks growing pale.

"Admitting it possible that I could have been so awkward ; Leuca would have rescued me instantly."

" O, Suhlamia," I fervently exclaimed, " how could you, for the sake of a brief pleasure, risk such awful

danger? I would not again endure the anguish I suffered when I beheld that sight, not for the wealth of
kingdoms. No, not if I could add years of untold
happiness to my allotted span of life."

For an instant Suhlamia shuddered,—grew pale,—
then with a fleeting glance of her lovely eyes, and in
tones of deepest feeling—

"And I have caused you this pain," she murmured.
"O, how thoughtless I have been. Dearest friend,—
forgive me ;—I implore you."

The tears came to her eyes as she struggled with her
emotions.

Altfoura now joined us and we returned to the
chateau.

On the following morning the Duke announced our
departure to the royal palace in the city of Elfrezulah,
the capital of the kingdom, situated about six hundred
miles distant in the interior of the continent on the
Lake Ambu-bhasanta, or "Shining Water." In company with Oneigar, Thaloba, the Princess Luzella,
Prince Harovian and several distinguished guests, we
left the chateau, embarked on the royal air ships and
chariots, passed over the Ambu-cyama lake and moun-
tainous regions of the Giri-nadi River, and reaching the
plains, crossed two of the great linear cities traversing
the continent from east to west. Sometimes we advanced at moderate speed in order to view the charming scenery, at others we flew at the rate of two hundred miles per hour. Finally reaching a great mountain
chain we ascended to its summit, and the beautiful lake
of the "Shining Water," spread before us.

On the opposite shore appeared the magnificent City
of Elfrezulah, its domes, towers and temples glittering under the sun like burnished silver and gold. We
flew across the lake, reached the City, alighted in the

royal grounds and entered the palace of the Grand
Duke.

The following day in company with Prince Altfoura
and Harovian, we took a tour over this great city, compared with which not only do the proudest capitals of
Europe sink into utter insignificance, but which, in its
superlative grandeur and beauty, might be an earthly
pattern of the mansions of the blest.

CHAPTER XXXV.

ELFREZULAH.

> " Fabric it seemed of diamond, and of gold ;
>   With alabaster domes and silver spires,
>   And blazing terrace upon terrace, high
>   Uplifted.   Here, serene pavilions bright,
>   In avenues disposed ; there, towers begirt
>   With battlements that on their restless fronts
>   Bore stars."
>
> *The Excursion.*—WORDSWORTH.

Elfrezulah, the capital city of Mandal-Uttima, is
situated in the central part of the continent on a lofty
plateau, bounded on either side by mountain chains,
running north and south.   The city lies on the eastern
shore of lake Ambu-bhasanta, or " Shining Water,"
which is about a hundred miles long by thirty wide
and pours into the Havita-nadi river, so named from the
dark green color of its waters and which empties into the
great Tycho sea, two hundred miles distant.   The city,
in its ground plan, is a quadrangle ; fifty miles square
and is divided into a hundred departments, each nearly

five miles square. Each department is subdivided into
two hundred squares. Of these, one half are domicil-
iary, occupied by private. residences, the others are
parks. Their arrangement is alternate ; first a domicil-
iary square ; second, a park, and so on ; hence each
square is bounded on its four sides by a park. The
squares are occupied by the residences of the citizens.
The parks by public buildings, and are beautifully
ornamented with trees, fountains and statuary. The
architecture of the private residences presents a pleasing variety. Their grounds are laid out on an ample
scale, and separated from each other by shrubbery or.
hedge rows. The dwellings are large and commodious ;
their adornments, tasteful and beautiful. They are
generally built of granite or marble of different colors,
are from two to three stories in height, surrounded by
balconies and surmounted by domes, turrets, etc., of
various styles. In the centre of each department is a
circular artificial lake a quarter of a mile in diameter.

The city is adorned with palaces, temples, towers, etc.,
whose magnificence defies description. Four great
avenues, a thousand feet wide, and radiating from the
grand centre, traverse the city at right angles. Twenty
lesser avenues also traverse the city at right angles,
separating the departments from each other. The
squares are separated by streets. The pavement
resembles dark green glass, is hard as flint and smooth
as a floor. The centre of the city,—which is elevated
above the environs, is occupied by an artificial, circular
lake, six miles in circumference, called the Ambu-bharu,
or "lake of the Golden Water," from the brilliant color
of its surface, reflected from the bright yellow hue of
the rocks and sand with which the bottom is overlaid.
It is supplied by underground aqueducts from the distant mountain streams. On a great esplanade in the

centre, is a vast and magnificent temple. The surroundings of the lake are of surpassing splendor. Fifty fountains equi-distant from each other, occupy its circumference, each four hundred feet high and divided into terraces of different colors, similar to the great fountain at the entrance of Gulomezal bay. Between the fountains are rows of colossal statues, single and in groups, of marbles, bronzes and brilliant metals. Sweeping around the lake are broad *plazas* paved in mosaic, colonnades, monoliths and towers, their pedestals carved with symbolical figures. Beyond these are rows of magnificent palaces, temples, public buildings and floral gardens. The avenues are occupied in the centre by canals supplied with water from the lake and spanned by handsome bridges ; the borders are edged with mossy banks, platforms of green and white marble, and rows of trees whose branches interlacing, form archways of foliage. On either side are palatial residences, theatres, opera houses, museums, art galleries, etc.; all in splendid architectural style. The avenues and streets are thronged with all kinds of wheeled equipages propelled by electro motors, conveying the occupants to and fro with great speed. Countless air ships and chariots fly overhead, ascending from or descending to the streets and residences in all directions. The canals are thronged with pleasure boats, gondolas, etc., propelled by electro motors, sails or oars, as suits the tastes of the occupants. The city is surrounded by a great boulevard paved with dark green rock and adorned with rows of trees ; beyond this are pleasure parks, gardens, etc., stretching out many miles into the surrounding country.

The manufactories, wholesale trading establishments, markets, etc., occupy quarters beyond the city limits. On the lake side of the city are great numbers of docks,

piers, warehouses, etc. The merchant marine of Elfrezulah is immense ; thousands of ships traverse the
oceans, and 'sail up the Havita-nadi river and lake.
The population of the city is about ten millions, comprising the *élite* of the kingdom. The Raja-vich-
anda, or royal palace of the Adhi-raja Sam-tanasya, or
race of the Thullivarrh Kings occupied by the Grand
Duke, Prince and Princess, is situated on the great
pláza surrounding the lake Ambu-bharu. Its grounds
are half a mile square. The palace is a quadrangle
four hundred feet square, built of marble white as
snow. It is surmounted by domes, minarets, and towers,
and surrounded with lofty porticoes, supported on fluted
columns. In order to relieve the too dazzling effect of
the white marble, others of different colors, are
employed in the architectural details. The bases and
shafts of the columns are wound spirally with flowing
vines and tendrils, carved in marbles corresponding
to the colors of nature ; the capitals with their
foliations and lilies, so perfectly resemble the living
plants as to deceive the eye. The arches between the
columns resemble the Moorish or Saracenic, as seen
in the palace of the Alhambra, though far more beautiful, and are engraved with emblematical figures and
flamboyant tracery. The architrave of the entablature
is sky blue, the frieze of light rose color, the cornice is
of a bright golden hue. The effect of these different
varieties of color offsetting the white marble of the
palace is exceedingly beautiful. The interior apartments are decorated in various styles. The walls and
ceilings are inlaid with agate, lapis lazuli, malachite,
etc., or adorned·with paintings in fresco representing
landscapes, sea, lake and mountain views ; the apartments are floored and panelled with woods of different
colors. The central court is ornamented with trees,

flowering shrubs and statuary. In the centre is a great circular basin of bright green marble, embellished with carved water-nymphs, dolphins and sun-fishes, from which upsprings a lofty fountain arranged in terraces of different colors ; in other parts of the court are smaller fountains of liquid crystal spouting in all manner of bewildering forms.

The grand banquet hall, where State banquets are given by the Duke, is a marvel of splendor. It is elliptical in shape, and capable of seating eight hundred guests. Its architectural details and ornaments are magnificent. The windows are of variously colored crystals ; the walls adorned with splendid paintings in fresco. A gallery runs around the circumference of the hall twenty feet above the floor, its entablature of colored marbles, with carvings in alto-relievo. It is surmounted by a lofty dome of sky blue crystal, supported on the uplifted wings of carved eagles. The gallery is supported by rows of caryatides, figures of beautiful girls and young men of the three different races, upholding it on their upraised hands. Around the pedestals on which they stand, are images of swans, aquatic birds, tritons and dolphins, the latter pouring from their mouths streams of variously colored and sparkling waters, falling in marble basins, while between the caryatides are sea and wood nymphs, dryads, bearing vases, urns and cornucopias filled with all manner of beautiful plants and flowers. In another part of the palace is an immense ball room. It would be superfluous to describe its splendid appointments and decorations. It is also surmounted by a dome, and its walls hung with great crystalline mirrors, by which the perspective is increased to an almost boundless extent. The extensive grounds surrounding the palace are filled with all varieties of trees, fragrant and flowering plants, superb statuary, fountains of all varieties, some arranged in terraces ; some shooting up in lofty columns or spreading out in broad showering sheets ; others resemble fans, whorals, spirals and intricate network ; others, great bubbling masses of foam of all the colors of the rainbow. The trees are occupied by different varieties of birds of beautiful plumage, whose songs fill the air with melody. It would be impossible adequately to describe one half the charms and beauties of this Martian Paradise.

One day, in company with Prince Altfoura and a party of friends, we embarked in four swift air ships for an extended tour around the northern hemisphere. We visited nearly all the places of interest in the kingdom of Mandal-Uttima and continued our trip over the five great continents and principal islands on this part of the Martian world and some of the lands lying in the southern hemisphere, the kingdom of Sundora-Luzion excepted. We visited the several kingdoms, capitals and principal cities, receiving distinguished courtesies from the Kings, Princes, royal dignitaries and people of the various dominions. Magnificent court receptions were held in honor of Prince Altfoura, his guests and suite, the splendors of which wholly surpassed any thing of the kind ever seen among the proudest monarchies of Earth. The tour occupied several weeks, and we returned to the palace of the Grand Duke.

CHAPTER XXXVI.

WONDERS OF MARS.

" I rather would entreat thy company,
To see the wonders of the world abroad."
Two Gentlemen of Verona, Act I., Sc. i.

The name of Mars in the Martian language is Arios
Vizulojah. Since the destruction of the great Planet
Luzio Avani Dhramza, or Pluto, it is the oldest inhabited planet in our system. Its inhabitants are called
Vizulojah Samtonarz ; they are the oldest, most highly
cultivated and developed of human beings. They consist of three different races distinguished from each
other by their physical appearance, complexion and
mental endowments. The first and superior, are the
Arungas, or yellow race ; second, the Rohitas, or red
race ; third the Nilatas, or blue race. The complexions of these races are not sharply pronounced, but all
varieties of the original foundation color are shown in
many pleasing tints and shades ; that of the Arungas
from the most delicate magnolia or aureate hue, to
amber, bright yellow, or deep bronze ; of the Rohitas,
from a light carnation to dark red, or mahogany ; of
the Nilatas from a delicate cerulean, or hyacinthine, to
bright azure, or sapphire. The physical organization
of the Arungas is far more delicate than ours ; their
forms are graceful and symmetrical. The Rohitas are
more muscularly developed and the Nilatas more robust.
The chests of all the races are relatively larger and
deeper than ours ; the diminished density of the atmosphere, compared with that of Earth, requiring deeper

respiration. Their average stature is less than ours ; a man six feet high is rarely seen except among the Pluto-Martians ; their muscular strength is also much less than that of Terrestrians, but their agility and powers of endurance are superior. They seem endowed with a much greater degree of what is termed nerve force. John, who is the fleetest runner I ever saw, is outstripped by a Martian boy of sixteen ; in their foot races they seem almost to fly over the ground. Their heads are more symmetrically and largely developed than ours ; those of the Arungas markedly so, showing greatly increased brain volume, the result of ages of development and cultivation of the mental powers. Their countenances are generally noble and handsome, their expression pleasing and ingenuous, often surpassing our highest types of manly beauty. Such a phenomenon as a villainous, mean, crafty, sensual, ferocious, or brutal physiognomy (except among some of the Pluto-Martians) is unknown here ; there are no dwarfs, misshapen or deformed persons. The lineal descendants of the pure Plutonian races (of which a few are still left,— Hartilion and Benoidath being remarkably fine specimens) are physically the most magnificent and beautiful of all human beings. Their stature is gigantic ; their bodily conformation perfect, and their muscular strength immense. That of Hartilion is almost superhuman ; being equal to fifty of our strongest Terrestrial men.

The hair of the Arungas is soft and fine, generally of a deep purple, and in the females often shaded with a rich golden hue ; that of the Rohitas is dark blue, or black ; of the Nilatas, bright or dark red. As the Martians advance in years, the hair becomes silvery, or snow white like ours, but the more sad features of old age, so often seen with us,—wrinkles, baldness, dimness

of sight, loss of teeth, weak piping voice, and the usual
accompaniments of decrepitude, are never manifest.
The eye of the Martian patriarch is as bright, the voice
as strong, the limbs as active, almost as in middle life ;
the only manifest evidences of age are deeper lines in
the brow, and more thoughtful and introspective expression of countenance.

The forms and features of the females are exceedingly graceful and beautiful, in many of the Arungas
far surpassing the highest types among our most highly
favored races. Their voices are sweet and melodious,
the manners of both sexes are models of good breeding
and politeness, and the pleasing amenities of social life
are strictly observed. All possess those greatest of all
human blessings, sound minds and bodies, vigorous
health and buoyant spirits, purchased by strict observance of the laws of health. The engrossing cares and
anxieties involved in the pursuits of ambition, wealth
and station, the daily toil, drudgery and struggle for
the necessities of life, the ignorance, poverty and
crime, so prevalent on our Earth, are unknown on
Mars. With a beautiful nature blooming every where,
every bodily need and healthful appetite supplied, with
the mental and physical powers cultivated and enlarged
to their highest development and possessing the most
extensive field for the cultivation and gratification of
the loftier aspirations of the soul,—human life on this
delectable planet is almost a realization of Paradisaical
happiness.

The age of Mars, although greater than that of
Earth, is far less than the estimates of many Terrestrial astonomers and scientists who have assigned to it
periods of many millions of years. Such estimates are
purely speculative and founded upon more or less
hypothetical data. Like our own planet it has passed

through its successive geological epochs and prehistoric times. The chronology of the Martian races—not like that of ours, which, reaching beyond the dim twilight of history is lost in the darkness of tradition—extends more than sixteen thousand years beyond that of our Adamic race. It begins with the creation of the Arunga, or superior race, the Rohitas and Nilatas having been created many centuries before. At the period when our (so called) primeval ancestors, whose fossil remains and stone implements are found side by side with the bones of the mammoth, cave bear and woolly rhinoceros, extinct ages ago, who knew not the use of fire, clothed themselves with the skins of beasts, had no language, and lived in under ground burrows or caves —the Martians had, long before, reached almost to the summit of their civilization.

This remarkable planet abounds in wonders of which we Terrestrians have no conception and which it would be impossible to describe, simply because there are no words in our language to express objects and phenomena that do not exist in our world. There are wonders in the earth, air, seas and skies of Mars which would startle and confound all our scientists. While the geological aspects of all habitable planets are similar at corresponding periods of their evolution and development, those of Mars are quite different from those of Earth ; this is the result of great age. Time works great and important changes, not only on the surface of a planet, but also throughout its solidified crust and deep interiors ; geological stratas become more dense as the planet cools and contracts, and the long continued effect of pressure effaces more or less the sharp distinctive lines existing between them, and gradually merges them as it were, into each other.

Could any of our Geologists, Mineralogists, Botanists

or Zoölogists be transported to this planet, they would be utterly astonished at the aspect of Martian Nature as displayed in her three kingdoms, for while the planet has all the productions belonging to earth, it abounds in others wholly unknown or undreamed of in our world. Trees, plants, flowers, animals, birds, reptiles, fishes and insects, metals, minerals, salts, earths, of which we have no conception and the variety is almost infinite. There are rocks, minerals and marbles of all varieties and colors ; there are metals possessing properties wholly unknown to us and of purple, blue, crimson, snow white and jet black colors. In the floral kingdom, everything seems more refined, delicate, brilliant and beautiful. The varieties of cereals, vegetables, fruits, etc., are numberless and far surpass in nutritive properties and lusciousness, anything of the kind growing on our planet. This Martian world is in fact, an immense garden, under the highest cultivation that Martian science as applied to agriculture can produce. Could a thousandth part of these products be transported to our world, every man, woman and child could luxuriate in feasts unknown on the tables of our monarchs and millionaires.

In addition to the great undulatory forces of light, heat, electricity and magnetism, there are also other wonderful forces of which we have no conception. The interiors of the planet furnish inexhaustible supplies of these forces, drawn from their profound and flaming depths and utilized in many ways.

In all those sciences which appertain to the great elements, powers and phenomena of Nature ; as well also in all mechanical and useful arts, Martians are thousands of years in advance of us. They seem almost to have brought the whole domain of Nature under their control and compelled her mighty powers to do their bidding. Volumes could hardly describe the achievements in this field which this wonderful people have accomplished. In the department of internal improvements alone, triumphs have been effected which would astonish us.

Our astronomers will be surprised to learn that, the present aspect of the planet's surface as seen through our telescopes,—the peculiar arrangement of continents, oceans, lands and seas, bays, peninsulas, etc., with many other strange and apparently inexplicable appearances, —are for the most part wholly artificial, and for purposes heretofore described. All these great improvements are accomplished by gigantic and powerful machinery, compared with which the strongest mechanisms of our world are but as children's toys. Could our civil and military engineers witness the enormous scale on which internal improvements are conducted, they would be overwhelmed with amazement. Rocks like our famous Gibraltar, levelled, and their fragments cast into the ocean depths within a single fortnight. Roads cut straight through mountain ranges ; immense precipices like those of our Alps or Rockies, levelled ; submontane and underground tunnels, compared with which our Mont Cenis or St. Gothard seem as mere burrows,—canals, compared with which our Suez is a mere rivulet,—ravines and gulfs filled up,—artificial lakes excavated,—coast lines laid out along the shores of continents, thousands of miles long and scores wide, —great mountain chains levelled off into cultivated plateaus, fields and gardens. Volumes could scarce describe a hundredth part of the improvements long ago inaugurated and still going on in this wonderful planet.

The art of working in metal and stone is brought almost to perfection. The Martian metallurgists possess the science of manipulating and altering the atomic

and molecular structure of metals and minerals, and
endowing them with new properties and forces. Could
our practical and scientific workers in metals, etc., walk
into some of these great foundries, they would see
glass, quartz and crystal converted into a liquid state
and flowing like water. Artificial, glacial, or crystal
fountains, in all varieties of form, color and dimensions,
are made and distributed as ornaments in numberless
parks and gardens. Metals, minerals, rocks, etc., of
every kind, are rendered plastic like clay, or liquid.
Think of dipping one's hand into reservoirs of cool
liquid, or plastic iron, gold, silver, copper, granite, marble, limestone ; handling and moulding them like clay or
pouring out like quicksilver. All these wonderful processes are produced not by heat, but by transmitting
through the solid substances a few flashes of a peculiar
undulatory force unknown on Earth. They are run
into moulds or fashioned into the desired forms and
then by transmitting a few flashes of a different force,
instantly solidified into any degree of hardness, toughness or elasticity required. All buildings of stone or
structures of metal, are made in this way and Martian
iron, steel, granite, etc., submitted to these processes,
are from fifty to a hundred times harder, stronger
and more durable than any thing of the kind we can
produce.

Immense structures, thousands of feet high, compared
with which the Eiffel Tower or Washington Monument
seem but as children's toys, are erected in various
parts of the continents and poles. They are surmounted
by powerful magnetic engines which attract air ships
from distances of hundreds of miles with a speed fifty
times swifter than any railroad train.

Our electric light and gas companies would be
astounded at the magnificence and splendor of the Mar-

tian modes of artificial illumination, by which not only houses and streets, but great tracts of country are lighted at night. 'Tis like sunlight, uniformly diffused and with no deep shadows like those produced by our electric lights. Walk into the apartments of any house or public building in the evening ; a little globe of crystalline material hangs from the ceiling diffusing a bright, yet soft and pleasing radiance all over the room. Touch one of these globes with the hand, it is perfectly cool. The phenomenon of light is caused by vibrations of the luminiferous ether pervading all space. The great fountain of light is the Sun. These little globes are like miniature suns and they simply set the luminiferous ether in the room vibrating. They receive their supplies of illumining power from the great Tamoioz reservoirs, described further on.

The great coal beds, with which all habitable planets are supplied from the partial decompositions of vast primeval forests flourishing in the geological ages, were exhausted on Mars thousands of years ago. The resources of Nature, however, are immense, and when in the lapse of time any of her great products are used up, the ingenuity of man finds, or manufactures others, which fully supply the need. The Martians draw from the deep interiors of their planet all the forces required for the production of what we call heat, and utilize them accordingly. These forces are collected, concentrated and stored in machines and engines for use as occasion requires. To give an idea of the immense heat producing power that can be evolved for purposes of assault or destruction, from a military point of view, could a score of these terrible calorific engines be ranged against the Capitol at Washington, Brooklyn Bridge, or St. Paul's Cathedral in London, the streams of fire hurled upon those structures would not only melt, but reduce them to slag and scoriæ within two hours. This force is employed on the most stupendous scale to disperse storms, by means of air ships, scattering, vaporizing or crushing them with overwhelming power. Could a hundred or two of these ships, manned with their tempest destroying artillery, be transported to Earth during our winter season, they could destroy the severest ocean storm, or blizzard raging over our western prairies, melting the showers of snow, sleet or hail, converting them into vapor, over hundreds of square miles of territory, within twenty four hours. When any of the great winter snow storms come tearing down from the poles of Mars over the plains in the temperate zones, they are attacked and dissipated by fleets of the aërial flying artillery.

The art of producing rain falls, when needed over dry sections of country during the heats of summer, has been known thousands of years. Showers of rain covering hundreds of square miles can be called up any time. The means employed are quite different from our crude and noisy processes. Look up at the sky toward the close of a hot sultry day, when the flowers hang their drooping heads, and the leaves of plants and trees almost curl up for want of moisture, when animals and birds seek the shade, and the very insects cease to hum. Low down in the horizon appear long lines of the Weather air ships ; following in their wake come dense masses of rain charged clouds gathered from the vapors that ascend from the numerous oceans, seas and inland lakes. Conducted by the ships, the cloud masses cover the sky. At a given signal they are condensed, the showers fall gently, with no thunder and lightning, refreshing the thirsty earth.

Our photographers would open their eyes could they witness the Martian mode of photography ; photopin-

gery is the better word, for the productions are genuine
sun paintings, showing all the colors, light, shade, etc.,
to the very life. The mode is so simple and expedi-
tious, every man, woman and child can be his or her own
photopinger. Families are provided with any number
of prepared plates, which resemble mirrors, from the
common hand glass up to any size required. All one
needs is, to step into a tolerably well lighted room, or
out doors in good sun light ; hold the mirror up to the
face and the reflection is instantly and indelibly
imprinted on it. If any member of your family, from
the baby upward, happens to get a fit of the sulks or
ill temper, hold your little mirror up, and the dear one's
expression is fixed for all time. The varying moods
expressed on the human countenance are often thus
portrayed and hung up on the walls of apartments as
pleasant reminders. The moral effect of this " holding
the mirror up to nature," is apparent. It greatly tends
to keep people in a show of good humor, at least. Our
Terrestrial rogues would probably steer clear of these
tell tale mirrors. All natural objects, landscapes por-
traits, etc., are taken this way. The art of painting
in colors is almost entirely confined to ideal subjects
and the finest specimens of our Terrestrial artists are no
more to be compared with those of the Martian schools,
than the daubs of a sign painter are to the works of
Raphael, Correggio, or Michael Angelo.

Travelling here is a delightful luxury, which the
poorest workman owns and which our earthly aristocrats and millionaires would be proud to possess.
Aërial vehicles are of all sizes, styles, appointments and
decorations ; from the great government ship to the
infant's nursery car, according to the taste and fancy
of builder and owner. Some resemble eagles, swans,
doves ; others are more fantastical ; like fishes, horses,

dragons, bats, butterflies, bees, etc., and the imitations
of these creatures are to the life.

If you are a well to do Martian citizen, you have your
aërial family chariot, or private car ; your wife, sons,
daughters, have their own private cars, and you can
possess as large an establishment in this line as your
fancy dictates or bank account allows. Whenever your
family wish to take a trip, a business call, or a round of
social visits, you touch a bell, your car floats out from
its little house in your grounds, manned with driver and
footman—if your social position requires these necessary
essentials—is wafted to the front entrance or embowered balcony of your mansion, where it hangs motionless, with gently moving wings. You take your seat
on the elegant chair or divan, screened if you like with
silken awnings. You, or your driver touches a key, the
wings expand, you are wafted along the streets, or
over the house tops to your destination, your car slowly
descends and you step out ; or if through the country,
you float over the grassy meads, fields, magnificent gardens, skimming over lakes, rivers, forests and hills,
with an easy and graceful motion, no sound save the
pleasing rustling of the light glittering wings. What
an inestimable blessing ! No noise, rattle and roar of
wheels and machinery, clatter of hoofs, hissing of steam,
whistles, bells, gongs, buzzing and howl of trolleys and
cables, no collisions, runaways, capsizings, smash ups ;
no mud, dust and all the other nuisances inseparably
connected with our Terrestrial modes of travel. If the
sun shines too hot or rain threatens, you touch a key
and the silken or water proof awnings are spread over
you. If a storm comes up, you can descend to the
ground, or unfold your storm wings and sail on in spite
of it. You can vary your speed from five to ten, or
fifty, or two hundred miles per hour. Can ascend in the

air, above storm belts amid the regions of calm, or if your vehicle is provided for it, can skim over the surfaces of lakes or descend and swim in the depths of the seas.

On pleasant summer evenings, countless chariots with gay throngs on their pleasure excursions course through the air beneath the light of the moons and stars that gleam in these beautiful skies, with songs and strains of music. Oft at midnight have I heard floating on the fragrant and balmy breezes, sad and sweet sounds calling to mind the romanza of Maritana.

> "I hear it again ; 'tis the harp in the air !
> Tho' none knew its minstrel, or how it came there ;
>   It telleth of days that are faded and gone ;
>   It tells of the brave, the lovely and fair.
>   You'll hear it at night, when the moon shineth bright ;
>   You'll hear it at dawn, in the grey twilight.
>   List, pilgrim, list,—'tis the harp in the air !"

During this period of the Martian summer, which corresponded to the early part of August on our planet, Mars was in opposition to the Sun, Earth being on a line between it and the luminary, and only about thirty five million miles distant. Our Terrestrial astronomers will be surprised to learn that, the Martian astronomers were exchanging telescopic compliments with them at this time. While the telescopes of the observatories of Earth were directed toward this ruddy planet, those of Mars were also levelled at Mother Terra ; but observations are not as satisfactory at these periods as when she is in quadrature, because, like our planet Venus with respect to us, she is nearly swallowed up in the overpowering solar light, except for short periods at dawn and sunset. The Martian telescopes immeasurably surpass ours in magnitude, space penetrating power, and clearness of delineation ; their powers are from one to five hundred thousand. As to size, they range from one to six hundred feet long, and with object glasses from five to sixty, or more, feet in diameter. What would not our astronomers give to possess a Martian equatorial, which would bring our Moon within the distance of half a mile to the naked eye ; Mars, in opposition, within seventy miles, the Sun within less than two hundred miles, and the other planets and all the fixed stars, constellations, galaxies and nebulæ, in the same proportion ? How immensely our science of Astronomy would be enlarged.

One evening we visited the Royal Observatory situated on the loftiest peak of the Baraponto Mountains, three hundred miles distant from the city. The views of Earth we obtained were splendid, notwithstanding the great depth and density of its atmosphere as compared with that of Mars. The views of the other planets, also the Sun and fixed stars taken at other times, are so magnificent, and display so many wonders wholly unknown to our science of Astronomy, the full description would require a separate treatise.

Perhaps the most wonderful of all works on Mars are the great Tamoioz reservoirs. They are immense circular, shallow basins, or rather lakes, constructed of a peculiar adamantine igneous rock, and from ten, to a hundred or more miles in circumference, erected in certain parts of the continents, and on the summits of lofty mountains. They are filled to the brim with a peculiar metallo-crystalline substance in a semi-fluid state and possessing extraordinary properties. It is generally admitted in our science of Solar Physics that, the appearance of an unusual number of Sun spots is more or less intimately connected with the outbursts of Solar storms, and certain electric and magnetic phenomena manifested on our planet. Our science has not yet attained precise knowledge of this subject which is still involved in mystery. The Martians have long since mastered it and found that certain highly important forces, beyond those of a mere electrical or magnetic character, are poured out from those black and awful abysses in the solar photosphere,—many of which are large enough to engulf a score of worlds like ours at once. To explain the nature and power of these stupendous and mysterious forces, of which we Terrestrians are yet so ignorant, would require the construction of a new scientific nomenclature and a voluminous treatise. The office of the Tamoioz reservoirs is to attract and retain these forces as they emanate from the luminary, and they are applied to the production of many great and important purposes. They supply, through conducting channels, nearly all the artificial light required on the planet. The immense supplies that are stored up during the long Martian summer (twice the length of ours) are used for effecting changes in the meteorological and climacteric states of the atmosphere, in various parts of the temperate zones. Air and wind currents are regulated ; temperatures altered ; the extremes of cold and heat modified over vast portions of the continents and islands. In fact, a very great part of the climates on this planet are adjusted to certain required standards by means of these reservoirs. They are sometimes called " Weather regulators."

They are also applied to certain mechanical and other important uses on an immense scale, and which we Terrestrians, in the present comparatively crude state of our physical science could not comprehend, and were our people to witness them unprepared, they would certainly be greatly alarmed and probably pronounce them supernatural. By night, the surfaces of these reservoirs throw off a brilliant light in the far distant space, and some of the larger ones erected on the mountain tops, constitute the so called mysterious bright spots visible through our telescopes, which some astronomers have supposed to be snow clad peaks, and other enthusiastic observers have fancied were for the purpose of communicating signals to us Terrestrians.

When the denizens of one World can make flying trips and communicate in *propriæ personæ* with the denizens of another, they will not resort to interplanetary signals, thrown from thirty five to two hundred and forty million miles distant, for the purpose.

Telegraphy is brought to perfection and leaves nothing farther to be desired. Messages are transmitted through the aërial magnetic currents which run between the poles, or the electric currents that traverse the earthy crust in all directions. No wires or other mediæ are employed. The instruments are of exceedingly delicate yet simple construction ; one is called the Opsiferon or voice bearer. Persons situated on any part of the planet, land or sea, no matter how far distant from each other, can converse together as if seated side by side.

There is another and still more wonderful art called Eidolifery, or image transmitting ; the instrument is called the Eidoliferon ; it consists of a simple mirror of highly polished metal, and of any size required. Seated in your office or parlor, conversing with your friend, hundreds or thousands of miles away, through your Opsiferon, you can bring his image right before you on your Eidoliferon as plainly as if he was seated by your side. You can bring any scene or event that is taking place at any distance in the same way. Millions of *tête-à-têtes* are going on between husbands and wives

parents and children, friends and acquaintance absent
from each other, all over Mars, continually.   Nearly all
correspondence, news, etc., is carried on in this way.   The
saving of time, pens, ink, paper, P. O. stamps, worry and
delay, are incalculable.   If some of our sharp corpora-
tions could get hold of these machines, the whole U. S.
Postal service would collapse, the P. O. Dept. would shut
up shop, and the Presidential Cabinet be minus one of
its most important officers.

I was sojourning a few days with Dr. Hamival at his
elegant villa a hundred miles from the city.   It was
our intention to return in the evening and visit the
royal theatre and Odéon in company with the Prince
and ducal party ; but a severe rain storm coming on and
our air ship needing repairs, prevented our return.   As
evening drew near we took supper and adjourned to the
Doctor's library, a commodious apartment elegantly
furnished and filled with choice works on general literature, science and art.   In an alcove on one side of the
room was the Opsiferon, mounted on a small table ;
close to it was a small concave disc of bright metal
about six inches in diameter.

"I will now communicate with the Prince at the
palace and announce to him that we shall be unable to
accept his invitation for this evening," said he, touching a
key ; the next instant the bell sounded, the Doctor being
seated in his chair and in his ordinary tone of voice,
expressed his regrets ; in a few moments the reply of the
Prince sounded from the Opsiferon as if he himself were
seated beside us.   The evening advanced and the clock
struck eight.

"We will now witness the theatrical performance,"
said the Doctor.

"What !" I exclaimed, "witness a play going on a
hundred miles distant ?"

"Certainly, and with far more comfort than if we were there. The house will be crowded, and the buzz of conversation and waving of fans between the acts is intolerable to me. I never attend theatres or concerts unless by special invitation. We will now enter the Eidoliferon room."

We passed into another apartment. In a large alcove on one side of the room and protected by a low balustrade, was a mirror about twenty feet long by ten feet high ; attached to it was a large Opsiferon disc about three feet in diameter ; the Doctor touched a key and spoke—

"Notify the theatrical manager to adjust his reflecting mirror and lenses so that we can witness the performance."

We drew our chairs up to the balustrade ; the Doctor touched another key and the mirror was brightly illumined. In a few moments the interior of a magnificent theatre,—auditorium, orchestra chairs, balcony, boxes, stage, actors and a brilliant audience,—were flashed out on the mirror. The scene was like one of enchantment.

"How is this wonderful visual effect produced ?" I asked.

"By under-ground tubes running from the theatre here. They are provided throughout their whole length with magnifying lenses and mirrors of perfect adaptation and great power, by means of which an absolutely perfect picture is thrown on the mirror. All places of amusement are provided with tubes and mirrors communicating with private residences all over the city and country. The theatre can accommodate an audience of ten thousand ; but probably half a million people are witnessing the play on their private Eidoliferons."

The Prince, Princess and ducal party were seated in their private boxes. It seemed as if we could almost converse with them face to face.

" We will now hear the play," said the Doctor, touching another key.

The next moment the voices of the actors and actresses, in their soliloquies and dialogues, issued from the Opsiferon. It seemed as if we were seated in front of the stage listening to the performance. At the close of the second act, the ducal party left the theatre.

" They are going to the Royal Odéon, where a grand orchestral symphony is given, which we will also hear," said the Doctor, touching the key and the theatrical picture disappeared from the mirror.

A few moments passed and the interior of the vast Odéon was flashed out on the mirror. Its decorations were magnificent. The audience consisted of over thirty thousand persons. On the stage were assembled a thousand musicians, who, having finished the first two movements, were preparing for the third, when the ducal party entered. The audience rose in salutation, then resumed their seats ; the conductor raised his baton and the grand music of the orchestra, more than a hundred miles away, poured through the opsiferon in all its sweetness, volume and power ; the phrasing, light and shade, the piano, crescendo and forte, most exquisitely rendered. It seemed as if the musicians were playing right before us. The general effect was even more pleasing, for the music seemed to issue from the opsiferon in one solid, coherent mass. We listened to the conclusion and the picture disappeared from the mirror.

Among the many remarkable natural productions, are the Ambhu Juvenas, or Healing Waters ; and certain plants and flowers possessing extraordinary medicinal qualities. They are found on a few small islands in the Vodraga Ocean, in the equatorial regions of the western hemisphere. The islands are owned by the government of Mandal-Uttima, under control of the Grand Duke; the waters and plants being in great demand by other kingdoms are a source of much revenue to the government. The islands are under strict guard, no persons from other kingdoms being allowed access except by special permission of the government. One of these islands is called the Magic Isle, and on it is a fountain which, from its remarkable properties, is called the Fountain of Youth. It arises from deep subterranean springs, where it is subject to intense heat and the action of certain magnetic metals, and powerful electric currents. When drank, it stimulates all the vital functions to an extraordinary degree, and imparts new strength and vigor to the bodily organs.

The Doctor explained to me the uses of the medicinal plants and waters in curing disease. The Martians are free from those dreadful constitutional taints and inherited diseases, which have for ages past, and still afflict so many millions of our Terrestrial races. Insanity, consumption, scrofula, cancer and other destructive and multiform cachexias do not exist. Martians thoroughly understand the avoidable causes of disease and act accordingly. The so called germ theory,— a favorite one with our medical faculty nowadays, is but the alphabet of a comprehensive and exact science thoroughly understood here and which we may hope to attain in the course of a few more centuries of scientific investigation.

The dreadful epidemics from which we suffer, the choleras, yellow and typhus fevers, grippes; and the scar-latinas, diptherias, whooping coughs, measles, etc., which afflict our tender juveniles, find no congenial germ soil on Mars ; but as humanity is the same, whatever planet may happen to be its birth and dwelling place, diseases which arise from climacteric vicissitudes, unavoidable accidents, exposures to the elements, etc., will, of course, continue to afflict human races through all time. Vast multitudes of mongrel Pluto-Martians inhabiting the great continent of Sundora-Luzion, suffer many maladies resulting from their immoral and dissolute lives, and the diseases they bring upon themselves are of the most terrible character and unknown in our world.

We passed into the conservatory and the Doctor showed me several of the plants. They were of peculiar appearance and odor. Their medicinal properties reside wholly in the fragrance or perfume emanating from their flowers or leaves, which, being inhaled by the sick patient are absorbed into the blood through the pulmonary air cells and act in that way. Their effect is remarkable in quickly curing, or aborting many diseases when applied at the proper time. I had often seen a violent attack of headache or neuralgia, cut short in a few moments, merely by inhaling the perfume of a pretty bouquet ; and a fever, or inflammation of an internal organ, or a disorder of function, cured in a few hours or days, according to the progress the disease had made in the system, by inhaling odors of properly selected flowers. Our Terrestrial medical faculty would be astonished at the simplicity of Martian Therapeutics. All our complicated medical prescriptions, with the whole farrago of so called tonics, anti-malarials, mercurials, opiates, hypnotics, alteratives, cathartics, expectorants, bromides, hypodermics, etc , etc., with which we poor Terrestrians wage so desperate and often fruitless a combat against hydra-headed disease, are unknown here, for Martian medical and surgical science is as far in advance of ours, as ours is beyond that of barbarous tribes. It penetrates and explores the secret recesses of the human frame and with a skill unknown in our medical world, discovers the germs of diseases and destroys them immediately ; consequently such a phenomenon as a patent medicine factory, a proprietary establishment, or drug shop, is unknown on this planet, and our spiritualistic disease discoverers, magnetic healers, prayer and faith curers, if transported here, would have to take up some other trade for a livelihood.

"I will now show you some water from the Fountain of Youth," said the Doctor. A servant set a few bottles on the table and filled glasses. The liquid was a bright topaz color, and foamed like sparkling champagne. I drank of it ; the taste was pleasant ; in a few moments I began to experience a peculiar and pleasurable sensation permeating every fibre of my frame, quite different, however, from that produced by any kind of wine, or other alcoholic stimulant, and it was followed by a sensation of greatly increased vigor and elasticity of mind and body.

"Many millions of our people, when they find their powers begin to decline, partake of this water, and it restores to them almost youthful strength and vigor," said the Doctor.

"This is truly a wonderful water and almost seems to realize the Elixir of Life, in search of which our ancient alchemists spent their lives and toiled in vain," I replied. "Can it restore primeval youth to the silver locks and tottering limbs of age ;—can it prolong human life beyond the allotted term of three score years and ten ?"

"It cannot restore youth, but it can prolong life by

imparting to the system increased power to ward off and resist the assaults of disease and the infirmities incident to old age ; but the man must strictly obey the laws of his physical and mental being. It must also be partaken of rarely ; too frequent indulgence in its use has the tendency to shorten life by producing over stimulation of the vital functions. I will show you a sample of its wonderful life giving and stimulating powers. Here is a withered rose "—taking one from a flower vase—" its bloom and fragrance are gone, it is apparently dead. I immerse it in the water ; notice the result."

The Doctor poured a quantity of the water into a bowl. I dropped the flower in it ; within thirty minutes the shrunken leaves, corolla and stamens expanded, resumed their usual color and I withdrew it from the bowl, perfectly restored to its pristine bloom and fragrance.

"I will now show you another pretty experiment. Here are the spawn of small fish "—and the Doctor dipped from an aquarium near by a few spoonsful of spawn and threw them in the bowl. " In natural process of time this spawn should hatch out in about three days from now, as they are quite near incubating. Here also are some seeds of plants ; they should sprout out in about the same time. Note how rapidly the process takes place in this water," and the Doctor threw the seeds in the bowl.

We sat up late, watching the process. In about two hours the seeds cracked open and the delicate little sprouts appeared. In another hour the spawn eggs opened and hundreds of tiny little fish were swimming vigorously about in the water. I could scarce believe my eyes as I gazed on this astonishing

phenomenon.   It looked like the work of ancient Egyptian Magic.

The next morning we returned to the palace, and the
Prince and I made arrangements to take a trip to the
Magic Isle and Fountain of Youth, on the following
day.

***

CHAPTER XXXVII.

THE FOUNTAIN OF YOUTH.

" My youth then restore me.   Life let me enjoy ;
My youth with its pleasures, that never can cloy."

Faust.—GOETHE.

Altfoura proposed to make the trip to the islands on
the great eagles.   The idea of taking a journey of six
hundred miles on feathered steeds was novel and I
accepted.   Having taken occasional excursions on them
with the Prince, I had become quite an adept in Eagle
riding.   One morning we attired for the trip, fastened
a pair of aerostats and gyrals to our shoulders in case
of accident.   Ronizal saddled the eagles.   Altfoura
mounted Ombrion and I, Leuca, they spread their
mighty pinions, we rose from the ground and flew over
the city and surrounding country at moderate speed in
order to view the charming scenery.

During the journey, Altfoura, in the exuberance of
his spirits indulged in various gymnastic pranks, standing upright in his saddle ; turning somersaults, hanging by an arm or leg around Ombrion's neck.   His
audacious daring made me shudder, we were elevated
a thousand feet in the air, all at once to my horror he

sprang from the saddle, falling two hundred feet; I fully expected to see him dashed to pieces on the ground; when the crystal globe of his aerostat began to emit showers of electric sparks; his fall was gradually checked, and he hung motionless in the air. Ombrion swooped down like a meteor and hovering beneath with expanded wings, Altfoura remounted and flew to my side.

"Altfoura," said I; "don't indulge in these feats; they are too terrible to witness."

"There is no danger, I assure you."

"Suppose your aerostat had got out of order; you would have been dashed to pieces."

"Not so; Ombrion would have dove down and caught me ere I reached the ground. He can dive swifter than a body can fall. Now I'll show you; I'll jump off without my aerostat, get a hundred feet start, call my bird, and you'll see how quickly he'll catch me. I have done it often."

"No!—For Heaven's sake, no!" I exclaimed.

By noon we had made four hundred miles and reached the base of a mountain range, ascended the rising slope; passing over deep gorges, ravines, cliffs and finally reached the summit. The view was magnificent; great mountain peaks from fifteen to twenty thousand feet high, capped with snow. In the valleys and along the mountain slopes were great forest trees, some varieties common to our World, mingled with species unknown there; many were of immense size, from three to four hundred feet high, with trunks fifteen to thirty feet in diameter and crowned with vast canopies of foliage. We now dismounted and tethered the eagles; sat down on the grass and took refreshments, giving them an occasional morsel. Birds began to assemble around; eagles, vultures, ospreys, hawks and other predatory

birds, manifesting the greatest awe in the presence of
our feathered steeds. Ombrion and Leuca regarding
them benignantly as a pair of game cocks would a
brood of chickens.

After a short rest we remounted, flew down the mountain slope, and directing our course due south, swiftly
passed over the country, reached the southern sea-
shore of the continent and alighted on the sandy beach.
Before us stretched the great Vodraga Ocean, which
is about twenty five hundred miles long, by five, to eight
hundred, wide.   It is subject to violent storms, cyclones
and tidal waves such as are sometimes seen in our
Caribbean Sea, and Indian Ocean.   On the opposite
side, across the equator, lies the great continent of
Sundora-Luzion.   The day was bright, and unusually
warm, and although there was little or no breeze, the
tide swept along the shores with great power and speed,
and the waves rolled high.   This is caused by the
powerful tidal action of Mars' two moons, whose orbits
lie nearly in the plane of the planet's equator.

We took a short rest, then put out over the Ocean.
After a flight of two hundred miles, a group of small
islands appeared in the distant horizon.   They were
evidently of volcanic origin ; resembled the peaks of a
submerged mountain chain like the Azores, or the Poly-
nesian clusters of our Pacific.   We approached one of
the larger, which was several miles long, and environed
by a great coral reef against which the waves dashed
tumultuously.   Its shores consisted of lofty precipices
of red and yellow rock alternating with sandy beaches.
We flew over these and entered the interior country
which was covered with dense forests and swamps,
teeming with a rank and luxuriant vegetation.   Several
miles distant was a great volcano in full action, spouting columns of flame and smoke.   Its thunderings and

explosions resounded over the sea. Amid the rocks were boiling springs and geysers throwing up great columns of water mingled with clouds of steam, and sulphurous vapors. The atmosphere had a peculiar hazy and yellowish appearance as if permeated with volcanic dust. The heat was like that of the tropics. Birds of strange and uncouth form flitted among the trees, uttering discordant cries. Insects of all kinds buzzed through the air, while the dank morasses and jungles resounded with the snortings and bellowings of huge monsters and reptiles such as are unknown on our Earth.

"This is the Dushan Illeos, or 'Magic Isle,'" said Altfoura.

"Its whole physical appearance, its flora and fauna seem to present a perfect picture of the Reptilian age of Earth's later geological epochs, long before the creation of Terrestrial Man," said I.

"It is one of our Zoölogical and botanical gardens," replied Altfoura. "Its physical features are quite adapted to the maintenance of these forms of vegetable and animal life. The seeds of the plants and young of nearly all the monsters and reptiles of these forests and swamps were brought by Asterion's ancestor from the planet Venus many years ago. They have greatly increased in numbers. We allow the latter to propagate and utilize them for studies in prehistoric natural history. When we take our journey to Venus, which I look forward to as soon as Asterion returns from his trip to the Asteroids, we shall have a splendid field for study in this direction, and plenty of fine sport."

We now entered an open glade surrounded with trees. In the centre stood a lofty hillock of red rock surmounted by a circular platform on which stood a great urn shaped basin of dark blue marble. It was

filled to the brim with a bright aureate colored water,
which bubbling over, streamed down the sides of the
basin, and ran in a little rivulet toward the woods.
Near by was a commodious house of red stone.

"This is the famous 'Fountain of Youth,'" said
Altfoura.

We dismounted from the eagles and permitted them
to roam around in search of food of which the forests
and jungles abounded in plenty ; then walked to the
house where we were greeted by Pedro, the keeper of
the Fountain, a sturdy and honest old Nilatian, with
his two sons, who had charge of the medicinal flower
gardens. Pedro took his key, ascended the hillock and
opening the valves of the basin, an immense column of
water, resembling liquid gold, spouted up, falling back
like showers of glittering gems. It was boiling hot ;
we filled our cups and after cooling, drank of it. The
effect was almost magical ; in a few moments we were
entirely relieved from the fatigue of the journey and
experienced a feeling of greatly increased strength and
vigor. At the foot of the hillock was an iron door.
Pedro opened it, we took lighted torches and descending a long spiral stair-case of stone, reached a great
vaulted cavern. It was pervaded with a peculiar
electric aura, which produced a tingling sensation in
our faces and hands and made our hair almost stand on
end. In the centre of the cavern was a deep and dark
abyss, from which ascended clouds of steam, and the
sound of boiling waters was heard from below.

"The Waters of the Fountain," said Pedro, "issue
from deep volcanic reservoirs, where they are subjected
to intense heat and the action of the electric and
chemical forces of rare metals and minerals."

Leaving the cavern we visited the gardens of the
medicinal plants ; Pedro, who was learned in this

department of botany, gave us interesting descriptions of their wonderful healing properties. The day declining, we took quarters in his house for the night, and next morning remounting the eagles, continued our journey over the island. In a few hours we reached a small and picturesque lake, surrounded by precipices, forests and mossy glades. We dismounted, tethered the eagles, and taking seats under the trees, Altfoura took out his tablets and began to make a sketch of the scene. Suddenly, Ombrion uttered a loud scream of rage and struggled to break loose from his bonds; the scream was answered by a loud and discordant cry from above.

"Look! look!" said Altfoura, pointing upward.

A gigantic winged reptile was flying overhead. It was twenty feet long and covered with black scales. Its neck was like a serpent's; its head and jaws like an alligator's, and armed with sharp teeth. Its wings were shaped like those of a bat, with long hooks. Its hind legs were like those of a stork, with long curved talons. Its forked tail waved to and fro like a whip lash. As the hideous creature flapped its wings, its eyes blazing like coals of fire, it resembled one of the flying dragons of ancient fable.

"What is that horrible monster?" I asked.

"It is a Gnakrip-Tihogos, or Alligator bat," replied Altfoura.

"It resembles the pictorial illustrations of our Pterodactyles," said I, "a species of flying reptile that flourished during the early geological ages of our planet and whose fossil remains, in company with those of other reptiles, are found in various parts of the Earth.[1]

[1] Pterodactyles, flying reptiles that flourished in the swamps and shallow lakes in the ancient geological epochs. Their fossil

"A number of these reptiles were brought from
Venus many years ago when they were young, by Asterion's ancestor and placed in our Zoölogical Gardens on
some of the islands. We allow them to propagate in
limited numbers to illustrate our studies in ancient
natural history. The gardens are surrounded by high
and strong walls to keep them from straying out, for
many of these monsters are dangerous. This fellow
has evidently broken loose from his enclosure, and is
on a voyage of discovery."

The flying monster was followed by several others
uttering harsh grunts and roars. Ombrion and Leuca
seemed transported with rage as they glanced upward, snapping their beaks and struggling in their
bonds.

"Here come three big fellows," said Altfoura.

The giant reptiles now loomed over us ; they were
much larger than the others. Their wings stretching
full forty feet. Their jaws could take in the body of a
man ; the loud flapping of their wings sounded like the
sails of wind-mills.

"Our birds are impatient for battle," said Altfoura ;
"I will let them loose."

"They are no match for those huge reptiles," I
replied. "One snap of their jaws could crush them
instantly."

"You shall see how the eagles will serve them out,"
said he, beginning to unloosen the tethers. In the
mean time the reptiles had flown over a lofty rock and
disappeared from view.

remains have been found in various parts of Europe, whose
wings stretch from ten to fifteen feet. In Kansas and Colorado
they have been found of gigantic size, with wings stretching from
twenty to forty feet. See Dana's Geology ; Guyot's "Earth and
Man ;" U. S. Geological Survey, West of 100th meridian.

In a few moments loud cries of alarm were heard ; we rushed down to the beach, ran around the rock and saw a small boat, manned by a single oarsman, pulling swiftly toward the shore. In the stern was crouched a young woman screaming with terror ; over her stood a tall and powerfully built man desperately defending himself and companions from the flying monsters who were swiftly pursuing the boat, wheeling to and fro over the occupants, trying to seize them with their jaws or talons, while the man was vainly striving to beat them off with his oar.

" Good God !" exclaimed Altfoura. " They will be devoured by the monsters."

We quickly unloosed the eagles and snatching up broken branches of a tree, ran to the beach. The boat reached shore and the occupants sprang out as we rushed forward to aid them. With loud screams of rage Ombrion and Leuca dashed toward the reptiles who flew forward to meet them, twisting their long snaky necks in all directions, snapping their jaws and uttering horrible roars. The eagles circled high above them for a moment, then Ombrion suddenly swooped down on the largest and grasped its neck with his powerful talons. The monster fought desperately with its hooked wings and claws in vain. Ombrion's talons clutched deep into its windpipe ; the reptile opened its bloody mouth, thrust out its tongue, its eyes seemed bursting from their sockets ;—until finally strangled, Ombrion let go and the hideous body fell with a crash on the ground. In the mean time, Leuca had not been so fortunate in her attack on the other monster, which had managed to seize her foot in its jaws. Leuca plied repeated blows with her beak on the skull of her antagonist in vain. Finally with two well directed strokes, she pecked out both eyes, but the blinded

monster still held on.   Ombrion flew to her assistance ;
clutched the reptile's neck in his talons, and speedily
strangled him.   In the mean time Altfoura and I
killed the third monster with our clubs, and aided by
the stranger and his oarsman, we succeeded in beating
off three more reptiles who had joined in the assault,
and they fled over the lake with loud screams.   The
stranger was a tall, fine looking elderly gentleman with
a jolly, good natured countenance and richly dressed.
The lady was bewitchingly handsome, with winsome
eyes and fascinating manners.

"Your Royal Highness," said the stranger with a
courtly salutation, " I am Lord Chumivant of Hautozan,
cousin to His Highness Prince Diavojahr of Sundora-
Luzion,—but not over proud of the relationship I beg
to assure you.   Permit me to introduce my newly wedded wife, Lady Chumivant, formerly Elfine Joyemal, the
distinguished *Comedienne* of our Theatre Royal.   You
have saved our lives, Prince of Mandal-Uttima, and
we owe you and your friend, a corresponding debt of
gratitude."

" Speak not of it, I beg you," courteously replied the
Prince.   " I am only too happy to have rendered your
lordship this service, the more so as it gives me the
very great pleasure of meeting in the person of Lady
Chumivant, so distinguished an ornament of the Martian comic drama ;" and Altfoura gallantly kissed her
ladyship's fair hand.   Lady Chumivant replied to the
Prince's compliment in terms winning and graceful,
showing that she was thoroughly *au fait* in court
etiquette.   Altfoura then introduced me.

"I am truly delighted to meet you, Lieutenant,"
replied her ladyship.   " Your great courage and gallantry in saving the lives of His Royal Highness and
the Princess Suhlamia, who is the most lovely and

charming of womankind, are the theme of all praise.
Oft have I gazed at even tide on your world, our beauteous Evening Star. Oft have I longed to behold one of
the inhabitants of that world—"

"Particularly of the masculine gender, my dear—"
interrupted his Lordship with a twinkle in his eye.

"Certainly," she replied with a merry laugh and
bewitching glance at me; "really, Lieutenant, if your
Terrestrial gentlemen are all so brave and handsome, I
fear we susceptible Martian ladies would quickly lose
our hearts, should we meet them."

"Ahem!" retorted his lordship, "I am quite sure the
Terrestrial ladies are paragons of grace and beauty, and
I shall solicit his highness to take me with him on his
next trip to that planet, and you may be quite sure, my
dear, I'll take my heart along with me also;" whereat
the young bride administered a no very gentle reproof
on her gallant spouse's ear.

Lord Chumivant informed us that he was on his
bridal trip, taking a short tour over the islands with a
party of friends in air ships; he and his wife were rowing
over the lake in their little boat when the Alligator bats,
escaping from their enclosure, attacked them.

In a short time a handsome air chariot manned with
its crew came flying over the lake and descended to the
shore. With many courteous expressions of gratitude,
my Lord and Lady made their adieus, embarked on their
chariot and flew swiftly on their homeward way.

"His Lordship is a good natured, jolly, easy going
sort of fellow, rather wild in his bachelor days, but
truthful and honorable; altogether different from his
rascally cousin, Prince Diavojahr;" remarked Altfoura.
"His young bride, Elfine, is one of the most renowned
Comediennes of their kingdom, highly esteemed and

deservedly so ; her character is above reproach, and she will make him a good wife."

We remounted the eagles, continued our trip over the island, spent the night in Pedro's house and early next morning wended our flight homeward to the Palace of the Grand Duke.

Little did I dream that, this chance meeting with Lord and Lady Chumivant would be the means of gaining me friends in an hour of fearful peril, and of rescuing one who was dearer to me than life itself from a fate worse than death.

On the following morning Duke Athalton, Oneigar and King Polath were assembled in the Council Chamber of the palace and Lord Montobar announced that he had delivered the Duke's message to King Probitos, but that Prince Diavojahr was not to be found.

" Humph !" muttered Oneigar. " His Highness is evidently hiding somewhere."

One of the gentlemen of the chamber now announced the arrival of Colonel Armatoff, special messenger from the court of Sundora-Luzion.

" Admit His Grace," said Duke Athalton.

Colonel Armatoff, with several officers of his suite, entered the room. He was a man of middle age, bright bronze complexion, showing his pure Arunga lineage unmixed with Pluto-Martian blood, and one of the highest peers of his realm. He was an officer in the royal life guards of the King ; his air and bearing were dignified and soldierly. Athalton and Oneigar greeted him with great cordiality ; he was also an old friend of King Polath.

" I have the honor to be the bearer of this communication from His Royal Majesty, and the Minister of State, to your Highness," presenting a letter sealed with the coat of arms of Sundora-Luzion, to Duke Athalton, who opened and read it.

" To His Grace, Athalton. Grand Duke Regnant of Mandal-Uttima, and their Royal Highnesses, the Prince Altfoura and the Princess Suhlamia, of the Royal House of Thullivarrh, greeting,—

" The Minister of State has the honor to convey the salutations of His Royal Majesty Probitos, of the Kingdom of Sundora-Luzion, to his Grace, the Grand Duke Regnant and their Highnesses, the Prince and Princess of Mandal-Uttima, together with his sincere regrets that, His Royal Highness, Prince Diavojahr, should have so far forgotten the honors and courtesies due to His Grace, the Grand Duke Athalton and their Royal Highnesses, on the night of the festival, etc., etc., and begs the acceptance, on the part of the Grand Duke and their Royal Highnesses, the sincere apologies of His Royal Majesty, in behalf of His Royal Highness, Prince Diavojahr.

" With sentiments of the most distinguished consideration to His Grace, the Grand Duke Regnant and their Royal Highnesses, the Prince and Princess of Mandal-Uttima, the Minister of State has the honor to be, etc., etc.

" ELIFF XURIOTH JOVANDEUS."

At this moment Prince Harovian entered ; the Duke handed him the letter ;—then to Col. Armatoff—

"This apology is perfectly satisfactory, Your Grace ;"
—then to Lord Montobar,—" please convey to His Majesty, King Probitos, and to His Excellency, the Minister of State, the sincere thanks and high considerations of Duke Athalton of Mandal-Uttima."

Lord Montobar sat down to write ; Prince Harovian

stepped forward, and with a courtly salutation to Colonel Armatoff—

"My Lord Duke," said he, "as you are aware, my rank, and the intimate relations of friendship existing between my own, and the kingdom of Mandal-Uttima, entitle me to say that, while this apology on the part of His Majesty is highly honorable, it does not satisfy me. I have already demanded an apology from the original offender, and cannot accept one from His Majesty in lieu thereof."

"I regret being compelled to announce to Your Highness,"—replied the Duke, "that, diligent search has been instituted to find Prince Diavojahr, but his whereabouts are unknown."

"Pooh !"—exclaimed the Prince scornfully, "your Grace will not have far to search. Send out a posse of your Court pages. I'll warrant they'll find him skulking behind the petticoats of his Court beauties."

The Duke shrugged his shoulders.

"The coward and sneak. I'll not stoop to cross swords with him,—'twould disgrace my steel If I ever come across him outside his kingdom, I'll lash him with my horse trainer's whip till he begs for mercy."

The Duke, brave soldier as he was, fell back before the fiery impetuosity of the Prince.

"Diavojahr's act is universally denounced by the whole rank and file of our army, and the royal life guards of which I am sorry to say, he holds by courtesy, the rank of Colonel," replied he. "The only excuse we can make for his conduct is that, he must have been intoxicated at the time."

"Which he generally is, except when engaged in something worse," remarked Duke Oneigar.

"Were any Prince or Officer in my kingdom to perpetrate such an act, whether drunk or sober, he would

be cashiered and disgraced from the ranks instanter,"
said King Polath.

" I have the honor to convey a communication from
the Minister of State to Lieutenant Hamilton," continued
Col. Armatoff, presenting me a letter which I opened
and read.

" The compliments of the Minister of State of Sundora-Luzion to Lieut. Hamilton of the United States of
America, situated on the Planet Earth, and requests
the pleasure of his company at dinner on the — day
of — at 7 o'c. P. M."

I glanced at the Duke inquiringly.

" Accept by all means," said he. " You will find His
Excellency an accomplished gentleman, and a charming host."

" To which it gives me great pleasure to certify, and
I hope to have the pleasure of meeting Lieutenant
Hamilton on that occasion," said the Colonel.

The Lieutenant's acceptance was drawn up and dis-
patched together with the letter of Duke Athalton to
the Minister of State by Lord Montobar, who had
received a similar invitation. As the dinner was set
for the next day, Colonel Armatoff and suite accepted
the Duke's invitation to remain over night, and we
would start on the following morning in their air-ship
for that kingdom. Toward the close of the day, Dr.
Hamival took me aside.

" I will now give you information concerning the
Minister of State, whose invitation you have received,
and I can assure you, it is a distinguished honor.

" Eliff Xurioth Jovandeus is the most remarkable man
of the age ; of giant intellect and wonderful gifts ; the
greatest of Martian statesmen and the power behind

the throne. On his accession to the Premiership, the kingdom of Sundora-Luzion was in a state of anarchy and almost dissolution ; but by his consummate ability, tact and force of will, he has unearthed every dark plot and secret conspiracy, and conciliated or crushed every enemy arrayed against him. He has done more to establish the prosperity, wealth and power of his kingdom, than any monarch, or minister of state that ever preceded him. He wields his power with an iron hand and his influence is felt and acknowledged in every kingdom in our World. He is descended from one of the most renowned Plutonian kings and is eminently worthy of his noble lineage. Personally he is of commanding stature and dignified presence, yet his manners are exceedingly winning ; he possesses a personal magnetism few can resist, and reads the character of every one who enters his presence almost at a glance. He cares nothing for honors, wealth, nor the objects that usually engage the ambitious desires of men."

" For a Prince and Statesman occupying so high a position ;" said I, " this is certainly extraordinary. I doubt much whether in the courts or kingdoms of Earth, such an instance of indifference to worldly renown could be found."

" He accepts titles merely as the insignia of his official position. Of pure life and upright character, he despises the allurements of beauty, the ostentatious displays, frivolous amusements and pleasures of royal courts."

" This is certainly still more remarkable, and could not be affirmed of any royal or aristocratic individual on my Planet."

" He wields a most extraordinary influence over the minds and actions of his fellow men. The strongest intellects yield to his indomitable will. He also possesses astonishing powers over many of the elements and forces of Nature, which in their manifestations are almost miraculous. Some of our over-scrupulous theologians, who know little or nothing of natural or occult science, darkly hint that he is in league with Satanic powers, but from whatever source he derives them, he wields them for good. The Court, royal and fashionable circles of Sundora-Luzion,—with a few exceptions,—are given up to the gratification of pleasure, luxury and ostentation. This corruption has infected a great part of the Pluto-Martian population. Eliff is the only safeguard of the realm ; he stands between the oppressions of the nobles and the rights of the people who love him. The great mass of the royal aristocracy hate him, yet stand in dread of his power. The unfortunate Emperor Probitos, a good, but feeble monarch and who is now in his last illness, clings to his Minister, for he knows, full well, that Eliff alone can save his kingdom from ruin."

"I greatly desire to meet this remarkable man," I replied.

On the following morning I donned my naval uniform and accompanied by Lord Montobar and Duke Armatoff, we embarked on his air ship for our journey to the great City of Xerione, the Capital of Sundora-Luzion, which is about fifteen hundred miles distant. We swiftly flew over the city and continent of Mandal-Uttima, crossed Vodraga Ocean and entered the kingdom of Sundora. The country is under the highest cultivation, abounding in beautiful landscapes, lakes, mountain ranges and linear cities. Toward afternoon we reached an immense plain traversed by a broad and beautiful river resembling our Hudson, but larger and more picturesque. On its southern shore stood the Capital City

of Xerione, which in the grandeur of its dimensions
and splendors of adornment, in many respects surpasses
the beautiful Elfrezulah. It is the largest of the
Martian Capitals, covers an area of six thousand square
miles and contains a population of twenty millions,
comprising the royal family, and the *élite* of the Pluto-
Martian nobility and aristocracy. Passing rapidly over
its splendid avenues, palaces and magnificent buildings,
—whose domes and towers glittered under the rays of
the setting sun, we reached the Palace of the Minister
of State in the eastern quarter of the City,—a grand
and massive structure of dark gray marble. Its grounds
were embellished with magnificent trees, flowering
plants and ornamented with fountains and statuary.
The air ship descended to its platform on the glade.
We were escorted by officers of the household through
a lofty portico to an ante-chamber, thence into the
reception room and were received by the Minister of
State.

------◆------

CHAPTER XXXVIII.

THE MINISTER OF STATE.

> " I was born
> " Beneath the aspect of a bright-eyed star,
> And my triumphant adamant of soul
> Is but the fix'd persuasion of success."
> *Richelieu*, Act III., Sc. i.

Eliff Xurioth Jovandeus was a man whose appearance would have elicited universal attention among
the proudest imperial courts or most distinguished
legislative assemblies on Earth. Of tall stature, ma-

jestic presence and stately bearing, he might have
found his earthly counterpart in Constantine the Great,
Charlemagne le Grand, or Harold, the last of the
Saxon Kings. His head was like that of the Capitolean Jove, its raven locks, streaked with iron grey,
descending in leonine masses to his shoulders. His
forehead was Websterian in its intellectual massive-
ness. His countenance, cast in the grand and beautiful
Plutonian mould, showing perfect self poise, inflexible
resolution and an iron will, yet softened with an
expression of great kindliness and benevolence. His
eyes were large, and gleamed beneath their dark o'er
hanging brows like glittering steel ; their expression,
imperious and commanding, yet at times softened with
a gentle and winsome look. His complexion was like
the hue of ancient Corinthian bronze. His voice was
deep, powerful and resonant as the tone of an organ.
The air of immense and irresistible power surrounding
him, impressed me with a feeling almost of awe, but
his charming courtesy of manner, winning gentleness,
and almost magnetic attraction, at once awakened my
confidence and esteem.

"Lieutenant Hamilton," said he, warmly pressing
my hand, " I cannot express to you the pleasure I feel
in meeting a representative of our nearest brother
World, younger in years, but larger in its youthful
growth than ours. Oft have I gazed at even tide on
your World, our bright and beauteous evening star,
and in fancy's dreams have pictured its great races,
nations and kingdoms ; their daily lives, their hopes
and joys, struggles, aspirations and final destinies. All
honor to that brave planetary navigator, whose brilliant
genius has converted those interplanetary magnetic
streams into great highways, uniting distant worlds,
o'er which his chariot flies on wings swifter than light.

Proudly do we Martians hail this glorious union of brother Worlds. May they never be dissevered, but united in still closer and firmer fraternal bonds throughout all time. Proudly do we hail this first advent of an inhabitant of our brother Earth to our World of Mars. Highly do we appreciate this distinguished honor, and applaud the courage and daring you have exhibited in traversing these awful abysses of Space, this infinite ethereal Ocean, within whose depths Stars, Suns and Planets roll."

I replied to Eliff's courtly salutation in terms as polite as I could command. After a short conversation, the invited guests arrived, to whom I was introduced. They comprised members of the Royal Cabinet, Naval and Military officers of high rank, scientists and members of the learned professions. All were of the pure Plutonian, or Arungan and Rohitan races ; no representatives of the Pluto-Martian race being present. Our party numbered twenty, including Lord Montobar and Duke Armatoff. The master of ceremonies announced the hour for dinner, the great doors of the *salon* were opened and escorted by the host we entered the splendid dining hall.

The banquet was magnificent, the *menu* everything that could be desired. New and charming surprises appeared on every hand. Our great Webster once said that a well appointed dinner was the climax of civilization ; and certainly this quiet little repast of twenty covers was the *chef d'œuvre* of royal Martian elegance and refinement. The Minister of State was the most delightful of hosts. I was surrounded by a galaxy of intellects bright as diamonds, deep as the seas and clear as the pellucid Martian skies. It was wonderful to see with what ease and precision every topic touched upon, however profound and intricate, was unravelled of per-

plexities and cleared of obscurities. Philosophy, law,
politics, ethics, literature, poetry, art, music and the
drama, were discussed with marvellous thorough-
ness, and embellished with brilliant flashes of wit and
repartee. There were no tiresome platitudes, senseless
chit-chat, or society gossip, but swift and brilliant
thought, embellished by felicitous illustration and
happy anecdote ruled the hour, and the feast of reason
and flow of soul that ran around that board was like
the outpour of glittering streams of mental jewels
flashed from brains whose cells were mines of intellectual wealth and gardens of beauty.

At the request of Eliff I briefly described our World.
Its physical and geographical divisions, great continents and oceans, its nations, races and kingdoms, its
various forms of religion and government. I described
the power, wealth, progress and wonderful achievements of the dominant white race, and wound up with
an enthusiastic eulogium on my native land, the greatest and happiest Republic on the face of the Terrestrial
globe, to all of which my audience listened with absorbing interest, expressing their astonishment that a world
so much younger than theirs could have attained such
great progress within the short space of six thousand
years.

"Your world is yet very young;" said Eliff;—"still
in its adolescence. Your race is growing to early and
vigorous manhood. A great and glorious future is
before you. Our World and race have passed their
prime and are on the decline. You have scarce
unfolded the spring flower of promise, and the fruit is
yet to come. We are in the sere and yellow leaf, like
the old oak whose strong arms have weathered the
storms of many centuries, now, alas! our leaves and
branches fall one by one, and we witness the infancy

and rise of your young world with mingled pride, joy
and sorrow. Such is the destiny of all the Worlds in
the Universe. Such is their rise, progress, culmination
and downfall. The same fate that awaits our World in
the not far distant future, awaits yours."

" Heaven grant that untold ages may yet roll on,
ere that dark day dawns on Mars or Earth," I replied.

" Amen," said he. " Yet that hour will surely come,
when your descendants will witness the destruction of
this Martian World as our ancestors witnessed the
doom of that great and glorious planet Pluto, six thous-
and years ago, and whose Asteroidal fragments now
revolve around the Solar luminary. As the ages pass
on, the planet Venus, now in its infancy, and inhabited
only by the lower forms of animal and vegetable life,
will become the abode of the Venusian man, who, in
his turn, will pass through the successive stages of
development and progress, and at last witness the final
downfall of your World, which will but prefigure the
destruction of his own, and all the Worlds of our system, yet to be inhabited."

The banquet concluded, the guests departed and we
retired to our apartments. The next day we took a
trip with Eliff and a few friends in his air chariot over
the city and surrounding country, visiting many places
of interest with which this remarkable kingdom and
planet abounds. Toward the close of the day, Lord
Montobar having gone to visit one of the Cabinet
officers, I spent the evening with Eliff in his private
apartments. In the course of our conversation, I asked
how long he had held the premiership of the realm.

" Fifty years ago," he replied, " I was placed in this
arduous and responsible office by the present Emperor's
father."

" Fifty years !" I exclaimed.

" You will perhaps hardly believe me, when I inform you that I am in my eightieth year."

I was astonished ; Eliff looked like a man in the prime of life, about forty five.

" Our Plutonian race are very long lived, and retain their bodily and mental powers to the last. After reaching our prime we seldom show the marks of advancing years. Such a phenomenon as a decrepit old Martian or Plutonian of pure blood was never seen. The secret is that, for generations past, our ancestors have strictly obeyed the laws of mental and physical hygiene. If no accident happens to me I shall probably survive to a hundred, then fall like the frost stricken autumn leaf. 'Tis my ardent desire, that my life may be prolonged till I see this kingdom raised to that elevation of moral excellence, which has been the one great and absorbing object of my life, to achieve."

I begged Eliff to give me a short sketch of his career as premier.

" My ancestors, though poor and humble, were of royal Plutonian blood and fulfilled their duties to their Pluto-Martian masters with honesty and fidelity. When I was appointed to the premiership of this kingdom, I found it in a frightful state of confusion, discord and lawlessness. The King was helpless, the nobles were immersed in pleasure and luxury, lawless and oppressive. The people were practically slaves, crushed beneath the heel of cruel tyrants. Science and art were dead. Commerce and trade languished to their lowest ebb. I felt appalled at the magnitude of the task imposed upon me, nor can I describe the fearful conflicts and revolutions through which this kingdom passed for nearly half a century. I stood between a haughty and lawless nobility and a down trodden people. I was compelled to wield my power with an iron hand ; success finally crowned my efforts ; I restored order, checked the oppressions of the nobles ; gave new life to commerce and trade, confirmed harmonious relations with surrounding nations, established justice and obedience to law, fostered and gave new impetus to education, science and art, and I have raised this great kingdom to its present station of power, prosperity, wealth and grandeur, among the nations. I have the confidence and love of the people and of my King ; but the nobles hate me, because I have curtailed their unjust emoluments, and checked their oppressions. My enemies call me ambitious, unscrupulous, tyrannical. So I am, and ever shall be, where justice, truth, virtue, the peace and prosperity of a people are at stake. There are times when one has to fight the devil with his own weapons. When you are threatened by open and secret enemies, you must circumvent treachery with counter-craft ; you must overwhelm cruelty and oppression with crushing power, and scourge vice and crime with an unsparing hand. My conscience approves my acts, and I am content to await the verdict of posterity. Much yet remains to be done for this kingdom. The unfortunate King Probitos is in his last illness ; in the event of his death, Diavojahr will be King. The career of this prince has been a source of great anxiety and grief to his father. He has no regard for truth, honor nor virtue, is thoroughly corrupt and demoralized, his disposition is deceitful, treacherous and cruel, and he takes no pleasure in any thing save the gratification of his animal appetites and propensities. When he assumes the sceptre I have every reason to fear the worst for this kingdom. He will give loose reins to his evil inclinations and wicked ambition, surround himself with councellors and advisers as corrupt as himself,

and whom he can bend to his will ; his dissolute conduct and example will produce great demoralization of
manners, he will foment hostilities with surrounding
nations and plunge this kingdom into war and bloodshed, which must inevitably end in its final dissolution.
Heaven grant I may not live to see that dark and
dreadful day."

We now entered an inner apartment. In the course
of conversation I informed Eliff of what I had heard
concerning the power he was said to possess over the
elements and forces of Nature, and although the subject
was rather a delicate one to touch upon, still, I made
bold to do it, and informed him I had been told that,
certain theologians had explained it on the assumption that, he was in league with the powers of darkness,
in other words, of Satan.

Eliff broke into a merry peal of laughter.

" O, yes, I've heard it often. It's quite amusing. If I
sought notoriety in that direction I might be disposed
to compliment my theological friends for their efforts
in my behalf. It is only one of the many evidences,
however, of the inherent tendency to superstition, still
lingering, and sometimes ludicrously apparent, even in
highly cultivated minds ; whenever they happen to
see phenomena they cannot explain by natural causes
or laws, they call it supernatural, and attribute it either
to celestial or infernal influence, and as I am not quite
holy enough to claim the former, my theological friends
assume the latter. Well, let them hold to that opinion
if it suits their fancy ; it's of little consequence to me.
'Tis true, I do possess certain powers or influences over
a few of Nature's workings, her laws and forces, to a
degree beyond that possessed by any other man in the
kingdom. These powers may be termed superhuman,
but it does not therefore follow that they are supernat-

ural, or need be relegated to the domains of the celestial or infernal. Whatever this power is, that I possess, its nature or laws, I know not. It cannot be explained on any theory of electricity, magnetism or what you would call spiritualism or theosophy, electro-biology, odylic force, nor by any such *diablerie* as witch-craft, black art, or any mumbo-jumbo jugglery. In the exercise of it, I simply *will* to do ;—in other words, I *will* to have the act accomplished, and it is done. You may be quite sure I never employ this power but for good ; were I bad enough to misuse it for selfish or evil purposes I should soon be deprived of it as I would deserve to be. I sometimes exhibit striking manifestations of it to impress the ignorant, or overawe my enemies with wholesome fear. During my long and arduous struggles to save this kingdom from anarchy and dissolution, I frequently brought it into play ; detected many a dark plot and crushed many a conspiracy and outbreak against law and order. I have the ability also to delegate a few of my powers to my tried and faithful subordinates, reserving the more striking manifestations of them to my own hands for occasions of great moment. Would you like to witness a few exhibitions of the phenomenon ?"

" It would give me great pleasure to witness them," I replied.

Eliff touched a bell and an officer of the household entered.

" Where is Thaumatour ?" he asked.

" In the tower, Your Excellency, consulting the genethliatic tables, the astralodic and crystallogenic instruments," replied the officer.

" Announce to him that I desire his presence."

The officer bowed and retired.

" You will now meet an extraordinary man ;" said

Eliff. "His name is Thaumatour. He is dumb, and communicates with me by signs."

We were seated at a table in the centre of the room.

* * *

CHAPTER XXXIX.

THE MAGICIAN.

Mephis.—" If it so please thee, I'm at thy command;
Only on this condition, understand
That, worthily thy leisure to beguile,
I here may exercise my arts awhile."
Faust.—GOETHE.

The door opened and a man glided into the room whose appearance was so formidable I involuntarily rose from my chair and drew back. His entrance was noiseless, almost like that of a spirit. He advanced in front of Eliff, made a profound obeisance and drawing himself up to the full height of his gigantic stature, stood with folded arms before him. He was nearly eight feet tall. His meagre frame and long, attenuated limbs were like those of a living skeleton. He seemed an osseous automaton, strung with sinews and tendons of steel. He was clad from head to foot in scarlet, covered with leopard-like spots and fitting close to the skin. A short purple mantle with tiger-like stripes hung jauntily over his shoulder, a red skull cap on his head, surmounted with a long, stiff, green feather. With his sharp bony visage,—hawk nose,—lofty forehead corrugated with wrinkles,—livid complexion, cavernous mouth and glittering teeth,—his stealthy step and serpentine movements, he was a perfect realization of the ideal Mephistopheles, as he is faintly represented on the dramatic stage. Could Goethe, Marlowe, or Gounod, have seen this formidable personage, they would have drawn a far grander conception of that incarnated infernal divinity than the one they have represented ;—the sneering, mocking sophistical devil who restored the decrepid Faust to his youth at the price of his soul ;—who hob-a-nobbed with German soldiers in beer cellars, drawing different brands of wine from gimlet holes bored in the table ;—who conjured up visions of the Grecian Helen ;—who connived at Faust's seduction of poor Margaret and the slaughter of her gallant brother ; —who played the buffoon with witches, imps and goblins, tramping over the ghost and *wehr* wolf haunted Hartz mountains with his soul bought victim, whirling in the witch revels of Walpurgis night ;—who galloped on the demon horses of darkness, past the gibbets of murderers, amid the wailings of sheeted ghosts and the dreadful vision of Margaret, with the red line around her neck, back to the dungeon of the living and ruined Margaret, her poor surcharged brain wandering in the illusions and horrors of madness ;—and all winding up with the triumphant apotheoses of one unfortunate victim and the everlasting damnation of the other, amid laughing demons and infernal flames. But the most extraordinary features about Thaumatour, were his eyes ; they were positively diabolical. They shone beneath his black, shaggy brows with the cold glitter of the Python amid the jungles of Africa. As this formidable being stood motionless, rigid as the Sphynx, with his stony, Gorgon like glare, he was a perfect realization of Beelzebub, hot from Pandemonium.

"Lieutenant Hamilton," said Eliff rising from his chair, "I take pleasure in introducing to you Thaumatour Zaron Rajindra, one of my most tried, faithful and attached friends, who would lay down his life for me. Then turning to him,—" Thaumatour, this gentleman is an inhabitant of Earth ;—the guest of the kingdom of Mandal-Uttima and esteemed friend of Prince Altfoura ;—he has honored us with a visit ;—bid him welcome."

Instantly, the whole satanic aspect of this terrible man changed,—his eyes beamed with an open and honest expression, his countenance became almost beautiful in its look of kindliness and sincerity,—the transformation was so sudden as almost took away my breath,—he advanced with a courtly gesture and winning smile,—the grasp of his finely shaped hand was warm and hearty. We spent a short time in conversation, conducted on the part of Thaumatour through signs, which were interpreted by Eliff.

" Thaumatour,"—said he. " Our guest has expressed a desire to witness an exhibition of your remarkable powers in occult science. Suppose you favor us with a materialization of the invisible atoms, molecules and elements of matter, making them appear in solid, tangible forms, for instance,—as in a handsome collation service."

Thaumatour bowed, rose from his chair, went to a closet, brought out a metallic box, or casket, opened and took from it a long slender rod of blue colored metal, tipped on the end with a small globe of glittering crystal ; then drew from his breast an immense chrysolite, suspended by an amber chain around his neck,—the gem was large as an egg, and glittered with the resplendent hues of the rainbow ; he rapidly rubbed the tip of his wand with the gem several seconds, and the crystal globe began to emit brilliant magnetic halos, then replacing the chrysolite in his

bosom, he glided around the room, waving his wand to
and fro over his head. Soon a faint misty vapor
appeared floating in the air. We drew our chairs to a
distance ; waving his wand hither and thither, he
guided and collected the vapor in a more dense, cloud
like mass, over the table, where it rested, undulating
like an immense bubble of semi-globular form. Soon
it began to glimmer with a faintly luminous golden
hue, mingled with streaks of silver, bronze and alabaster white. The phenomenon was so wonderful and
beautiful as excited my profound astonishment and
admiration.

" This ethereal nebula which he has collected and
condensed from the atmosphere of this room," said
Eliff, " contains all the atoms, molecules and elements,
—metallic or mineral—of the various substances he will
now make appear before us. The solidification and
shaping of these elements in separate tangible forms
puts his powers to a severe test."

Thaumatour laid down his wand and took another
from the box, its handle resembling a rod of glittering
steel, its extremity tipped with a spear pointed head of
an unknown metal ; he rubbed it with the chrysolite
and in a few seconds it glowed with a brilliant light;
and emitted showers of electric sparks.

He now drew himself up to his full stature,—his
countenance became rigid and stern,—his eyes assumed a fierce and commanding expression,—he looked
like some incarnated spirit of immense and concentrated power, about to grapple with dark and mysterious forces. Grasping his flaming wand and whirling
it around his head he smote the cloud in all directions,
—every stroke resounding like the report of a pistol.
The nebula seemed writhing in agony, as if in the
throes of parturition, and suddenly there appeared

upon the table,—one by one, and miraculously evolved from that floating chaos,—fruit dishes of gold, silver and bronze, vases of alabaster and Parian marble, of elegant forms and splendid carving ; plates and goblets of rare china or porcelain ; and fine cut decanters of pure crystal. The phenomenon was so tremendous, so appalling, I involuntarily sprang from my chair and drew back. The remnant of the cloud vanished in air, the Magician laid down his wand, quietly folded his arms, looking as nonchalant as if he had merely tossed off a simple feat of legerdemain.([1])

" Examine the service and pronounce upon it," said Eliff.

I stepped forward, almost trembling, and examined the pieces one by one.

" These gold, silver and bronze dishes," said I, " are perfectly genuine ; their purity and carving are marvellous. The marbles, alabasters, porcelains and crystals are the finest I ever saw. No such beautiful productions are to be found among the most celebrated jewelry or *bric-à-brac* establishments on Earth."

" How does this part of the performance strike you ?" asked Eliff.

" I am forcibly struck with the fact that our friend is the swiftest manufacturer of elegant table ware and beautiful ornaments, I ever had the pleasure to meet, and what is equally surprising, he appears to have created them out of nothing."

Thaumatour bowed his appreciation of the compliment.

" Now, Thaumatour, order up your refreshments," said Eliff. The Magician took up his blue wand and again applying the chrysolite to its head, walked around the

[1] See " Occult World," by Sinnet. Pages 67 and 75, *et al*, or analogous creations.

room waving it to and fro. Soon another nebulous cloud gradually evolved itself from the air and settled over the table. It gleamed with a variety of colors, blue, green, yellow, crimson and white, undulating and intermingling with each other.

"This nebula," said Eliff, "contains all the different organic and chemical elements of the various refreshments he will now set before you."

Thaumatour laid down his fiery javelin, carefully drew from the casket a long, slender, willowy bough, tipped on the end with what seemed a small cluster of leaves and buds. It looked fresh and green as if just plucked from the tree. He gently stroked the buds and leaves with the chrysolite, then waved the bough to and fro through the cloud, and one by one, different varieties of fruits appeared in the dishes, and different species of flowers in the vases ; then dipping the end of the bough in a bowl of water near by, he sprinkled the cloud, and different varieties of wines appeared in the decanters. As the remnants of the nebula floated away, the Magician glanced at us with an interrogatory look as much as to say,—"Well, gentlemen, how does the dessert please you ?"

"Come, Lieutenant," said Eliff, "let's partake of the refreshing collation, Thaumatour has so generously provided for us."

We drew our chairs up to the table and it was with feelings of awe, almost of terror, that I ventured to place to my lips fruits grown by no process of Nature,— cultivated by no mortal hand, but evolved as by miracle, from the unsubstantial air.

"Are any of these fruits indigenous to your Terrestrial orchards ?" he asked.

"These apples are equal to our best Spitz-bergens or Baldwins ;—these pears are like our finest Bartletts, and these plums remind me of our good green gages," I replied.

" And the flowers ?"

I drew the vases before me,—the flowers were of wondrous beauty and as I inhaled their delicious fragrance it almost seemed as if they had been newly plucked by spirit hands from the bowers of Paradise.

" These are genuine roses, lilies and violets, exactly like those of our earthly gardens, though far superior in hue and perfume," I replied.

" Favor us with your verdict on the wines," said he, as Thaumatour filled glasses from the decanters.

As I raised the glasses to my lips, one by one, it seemed as if I were tasting materialized nectars from the tables of the gods.

" They remind me of our choicest brands of Oporto, Monte Christo and Champagne, though immensely superior in all respects," I replied.

We drank each others' good healths all around. Thaumatour smacking his lips, and nodding his head like an upright liquor manufacturer who could honestly avouch the unadulterated purity of his distillations.

" As variety is the spice of the festive board as well as many other enjoyments of life," said Eliff, " suppose we have a little change in the menu ?"

" With pleasure ;" I replied, wondering what new wonder would come next.

" Have you any choice as to what you would like ?"

" I leave the selection to Thaumatour," I replied.

" Thaumatour, will you kindly favor us with a variation in the collation ?" said Eliff.

The Magician laid down his bough and drew from the casket a long, three pronged Fuscina apparently of brass. It resembled the trident of the sea god Neptune ; he then rubbed the prongs with the chrysolite several seconds.

"He will now transmute these fruits, flowers and liquors into other varieties," said Eliff. "This task is more difficult than the preceding, for it involves total changes in the molecular and chemical relations of the elements contained in these substances."

Thaumatour's countenance now changed to a stern and commanding expression, his eyes blazed with a terrible light,—every muscle, nerve and sinew seemed strung up to the highest tension, as if preparing to grapple with organic forces even more potent than those encountered before. Waving aloft his trident, he brought it down with swift strokes, one by one, over the fruits, flowers and liquors ;—every blow resounding with loud and sharp reports ;—the table trembled beneath the electric discharges which shot like flashes of lightning from the prongs of his terrible weapon. This mighty magician looked like some powerful Afrit of the abyss, beneath whose sceptre the elements and forces of Nature were yielding reluctant submission, and right before my eyes, the apples, pears, plums, roses, lilies, violets and wines, were changed into other varieties. It seemed as if I were looking at the swiftly changing pictures of a magic lantern.

"Come, Lieutenant ;" said Eliff, "we must compliment Thaumatour, by partaking of his frugiferous transmutations."

It was several minutes before I could quite recover my composure at this stupendous exhibition of *diablerie*. Finally, summoning courage, I drew my chair up to the table and we proceeded to discuss the new *menu en régle*.

"Kindly favor us with your opinion," said Eliff.

"These oranges," said I, "are equal to our finest

Indian river Floridas. These peaches are quite up to our best Jerseys, and the grapes remind me of our choicest Californias."

"And the flowers?"

"These honeysuckles, buttercups and daisies are exactly like those I've often plucked in my native fields."

"And the liquors?"

Thaumatour now filled several glasses from the decanters.

"I beg your Excellency's pardon; but having had the pleasure of drinking your good health in such delicious wines, 'twould be nothing less than an insult to jolly Bacchus, were I to wind up with this cold tea, lemonade and water gruel."

"Really, Thaumatour," said Eliff, glancing at the glasses, "you appear to have become a teetotaller; your change of sentiment on the temperance question is as rapid as your change of nutriment."

Thaumatour shrugged his shoulders with a grim smile, and pointed to the wall on the opposite side of the room.

"O, I see. You don't wish to throw temptation in the way of your corps of waiters, a very proper precaution in view of their bibulous proclivities; I fear they will be sadly disappointed,—you may as well call the frisky little rascals up to clear the cloth. The Lieutenant and I propose to have a quiet chat about philosophy and other subjects we know nothing about."

Thaumatour stepped across the room to the wall,— tapped thrice with his wand, and without the slightest apparent separation of the wall, out walked a dozen or more little creatures, about a foot high, looking like the dwarfs, trolls and pixies of our fairy tales. They had jolly round faces,—twinkling eyes, hawk, or snub noses,—round, fat, little bellies and spindle shanks, knock kneed, or bow legged. They were attired in motley costumes, and tall peaked hats. At a signal from Thaumatour they performed a dwarf dance, which was so irresistibly impish and comical, we were almost convulsed with laughter. They then hopped on the table and proceeded to regale themselves with the refreshments, which they did with great gusto ; they inspected the glasses and decanters, evidently expecting something nice and cheerful, but turned up their noses emphatically at the cold tea and water gruel, and seemed dreadfully disappointed. Then at a sign from Thaumatour, they selected button-hole bouquets from the flowers, pinned them to their bosoms, shouldered the empty dishes, vases, etc.,—flung the contents of the decanters into a bowl, clambered down the table legs,—marched in single file to the wall, within which they all disappeared, like the unsubstantial pageant of a dream.

"How do Thaumatour's exhibitions compare with those of your Terrestrial magicians ?" asked Eliff.

I confessed that, could the most renowned sorcerers of old Egypt or India have witnessed a tenth part of these wonders, they would have given up the ghost in despair and our distinguished Frikell, de Kolta, Houdin and Herrmann would consign their whole *diablerie* paraphernalia to the flames, and take to Punch and Judy shows for a livelihood.

"These are only a few of his more pleasing exhibitions. On great occasions he can display the most tremendous manifestations of the occult art," said he. Thaumatour rose to take his departure ; as Eliff and I expressed our thanks for the delightful entertainment, he took my hand, closely examined the lines of the palm, then looked earnestly in my face,—his wonderful eyes seeming to read me through and through.

"Thaumatour is a clever soothsayer," said Eliff, "and will tell your fortune, if you like."

"I confess I am not altogether exempt from the natural curiosity of mortals to pry into the book of fate," I replied.

"Give him the date of your birth,—he will then ascertain what star was in the ascendant on your planet at the time."

"Aug 20th, 1866, Terrestrial time, the date of the proclamation of the President of the United States of America, declaring that the War for the Union was at an end. On that glorious day, all the Stars of the American Flag were in the ascendant, and all the sons of Liberty and Union shouted for joy."

"Truly, a splendid galaxy to be born under, and a glorious day to be born in," said Eliff,—"a man ought to be proud of such a natal day."

"So I am,—proud of it as of our glorious Fourth of July."

"But I'm surprised to hear you had a war in your great Republic."

"Sorry to say,—a family quarrel,—will sometimes spring up in the best regulated families, you know ;— pretty tough fight on both sides ; lasted four years ;— but it's all over, and we are a more closely united band of brothers than ever, and pay strict obedience and loyalty to Uncle Sam."

"And 'tis to be hoped you'll always remain so."

"You may be quite sure of that," I replied.

Thaumatour went to the closet, took out a celestial globe on which were depicted the constellations, stars and planets of the heavens ; drew from his pocket a small book printed with cabalistic characters and geometrical symbols, studied the globe and book for several moments, drawing up a rapid calculation on his tablet, conversed with Eliff a few moments by signs, then shaking me warmly by the hand left the room.

" He has calculated the horoscope of your fortune for a short time to come," said Eliff.

" And as I am the interested party, Your Excellency will please communicate the same to me," I replied.

" You have met with many surprising adventures during your brief sojourn on this planet."

" As people expect to meet, who take trips to ' other worlds than ours.' "

" More surprising ones await you."

" I hope they will be of a stirring character."

" You will enjoy a lively adventure with a royal personage in which your temper and your steel will be tested."

" My steel was tested at the U. S. Govt. sword factory. My temper is generally of a quiet character, but if tested too far, may become rather testy."

" You will be in danger of death, but just in the nick of time you will receive an ardent declaration of love from a beautiful Princess."

" This is a surprise, indeed !   Death and Love meeting together ;—the arrival of Love on the scene is quite opportune ;—they will probably have a fight over me,— Love will conquer, for Love is stronger than Death."

" There will be an elopement."

" How delightfully romantic."

" A flight over the sea."

" Splendid !   Magnificent !—' Come o'er the sea, maiden, with me.   Mine, through sunshine, storm and snows.   Seasons may roll, but the true soul burns the same where'er it goes.'—Go ahead."

" But, she's no maiden."

" Great Scott !"

"She's a married woman."

"Angels and Ministers of grace, defend us !"

"You will encounter—"

"O, I know what's coming, exactly,—you needn't say."

"What ?"

"Injured husband,—pistols,—coffee,—damages,—"

"But Thaumatour didn't say that."

"It's bound to come, any how,—surer than fate,—in spite of Thaumatour or any other fortune teller."

"Well, what do you propose to do about it ?"

"When does this thrillingly amatory and sanguinary tragedy begin,—date specified ?"

"This evening."

"Short notice. However, I will endeavor to be in readiness to meet, like a brave man, whatever fate has in store for me."

To while away the interim, we discoursed on various subjects appertaining to occult philosophy,—the natural and spiritual world,—the mysterious laws and forces prevailing in those worlds,—the relations existing between mind and matter.

"Did it ever occur to you," said Eliff, "that what we call the laws of Nature are but the manifest workings of Spiritual Beings ?"

I replied that, the hypothesis was a favorite one with many highly cultivated minds in our world ;—was a reaction against gross materialism ;—was not denied by many scientific men and was also the foundation of many charming and beautiful poetical conceptions.

"The time will come," continued he, "when gross materialism will be swept away, and your world will be awakened to the true philosophy of the close relations existing between the material and spiritual world. Every kingdom and department of Nature is under the control of Spiritual intelligences of different ranks and stations. All the phenomena of life, birth, growth and nourishment ; every seed that germinates, every flower that blooms and every plant that bears fruit, are under the direct control of these invisible beings. In short, all the wondrous and varied phenomena of Nature are under the government of myriads of Spiritual intelligences. The powers they wield are various in degree and manifestation. Some are kindly, pleasing and attractive,—others are unfriendly and inimical to man. Some are gigantic and terrible in their manifestations ; others are almost of a satanic or infernal character,—permitted so to be, in order to fulfill the mysterious designs of the Almighty. Over many of these Spiritual intelligences I have control and I can cause them to appear in forms visible to the bodily eye. I will now bring before you some of the more pleasing of these beings who have charge over the flowery kingdom of Nature."

———————◆———————

CHAPTER XL.

SPIRITS OF FLOWERS.

" These our actors,
As I foretold you, were all spirits, and
Are melted into air, into thin air."
Tempest, Act. IV., Sc. i.

Eliff touched a bell ; an attendant entered and drew a round table of black marble in front of a lofty alcove on one side of the room, screened with falling *portières* of purple velvet, then placed four alabaster flower vases carved with emblematical figures on the table and poured water in each.

"The floral kingdom," said Eliff, "is divided into many different departments, all having different orders of spiritual beings presiding over them. I will exhibit to you the spirits of any species of flowers you may desire."

As roses, lilies, violets and chrysanthemums are generally regarded by the inhabitants of our world as among the most beautiful, I selected them. The attendant went into the garden and brought four large bouquets of these flowers freshly culled, arranged them carefully in the vases and left the room. Eliff opened a closet and drew out two large veils of finely woven crystal ; they were soft and flexible as gossamer, and perfectly transparent.

"These veils will protect us from the powerful aura which emanates from the spirits when they appear," said he. "This aura is neither electrical nor magnetic, and cannot be described. It produces on those not accustomed to it, extraordinary effects upon the brain and nervous system, a species of intoxication almost amounting to delirium, often lasting many hours, and ending in a profound lethargy accompanied by beautiful and sometimes fantastical visions. Many persons on awakening from them often remain several days oblivious to all surroundings and seeming to be wholly absorbed in the recollection of them. It is not altogether safe for every one to witness these scenes, and too frequent repetition of them produces injurious effects upon the bodily health."

Eliff unlocked a cabinet of inlaid woods, and withdrew four golden censers, embossed with symbolical emblems, filled them with aromatic herbs, placed them on the table in front of the flowers and kindled them ; then extinguished the lights. We moved some distance from the table and put on the veils, which enveloped us from head to foot. The room was immersed in darkness, save where the moonlight, glimmering through the windows, cast its feeble rays on the floor ; the smoke of the burning censers slowly ascended to the ceiling and hung in clouds over the table, almost concealing the flowers and diffusing its aromatic perfume through the room.

"I will now call up the spirits who have charge over this department of the floral kingdom," said Eliff, "and they will appear in their natural forms, not tangible, but plainly visible to the eye, and you will also hear their voices." He then extended his hands, and enunciated in deep and solemn tones, the words of incantation in an unknown tongue.

Soft and sweet strains of music, like the tones of Æolian harps sounding from afar, now arose faintly vibrating on the air. 'Twas like the music sometimes heard in dreams and which never greets the waking ear. As it swelled in waves of ravishing harmony and died away in trembling vibrations, with it were mingled as it were, the voices of Seraphs, joyfully singing amid the flowery portals of Paradise,—

"Spirits are we, singing in glee,
　'Mid the depths of our flow'ry home ;
In the summer night on our wings of light,
　'Mid fragrant bowers we roam.

"The dew we sip from the lily's lip,
　And nectar sweet from the rose ;
Ambrosia new from the violets blue,
　And drink where the tulip grows.

"In the silver glance of the moon we dance,
　On the banks of rippling streams ;
'Neath the poppy's head we lay our bed,
　And sleep in the land of dreams."

The song ceased, but the music still gently vibrated in faint undulations, like the dying echoes of the harp of Maritana.

"Spirits of the Floral World," said Eliff in low and thrilling tones, "ye, who have charge over these beauteous flowers. Your Master calls. Appear, clothed in your airy forms to mortal eyes."

And now rich perfumes, as from the rose gardens of Arabia in the blooming time, filled the air, and from the corollas of the flowers, shadows arose, like the nebulæ that gleam in the midnight skies. Slowly unfolding amid the smoke of the burning censers, they wreathed into dim outlines, like spectral phantoms floating in mid air. Soon they gradually assumed shapes of wondrous beauty, female forms, like the Peris hovering near the golden gates. The Spirit of the rose glowing with the hues of the ruby ;—that of the lily, sparkling like the snow on the mountain peak ;—of the chrysanthemum, flashing with the lustre of virgin gold ; —of the violet, like the hyacinthine tints of the Martian skies. And now they shone in forms of exquisite loveliness such as never yet met mortal eye ;—the beauteous curves of rounded limbs ;—the rippling waves of lustrous hair ;—the flashing of star like eyes, and smiles from rosy lips that angels might long to press, while a halo of almost celestial glory gleamed over all.

Spell bound I gazed upon this beautiful vision, as if the slightest breath might waft it forever from view.

"'Tis enough," whispered Eliff,—"they cannot long remain,"—then spoke a few words in the unknown tongue. The music ceased,—the spirit forms faded away and the smoke of the censers melted in air. We removed our veils, replaced the censers in the cabinet, and the lights were lit. The roses, lilies, violets and

chrysanthemums were withered,—their hue and fragrance departed.

"The tender life;—the beauteous hue and sweet
perfume of every flower that blooms and dies, form, in
the spirit realm, the garments of those innocent and
lovely beings," said Eliff,—"yet these are but spirits of
the lower plane, although belonging to one of the most
pleasing departments of Nature."

"And with what forms and hues are the spirits of
higher orders clothed?" I asked.

"Of such loveliness that, mortal eye once gazing on
them would never care to look on mortal forms again,
and the soul would be filled with an inexpressible long-
ing to join them forever in their abode of happiness."

"And those of the Angelical Orders, and Human
Spirits?" I asked.

"Visions of those who dwell in Celestial bliss are
never granted to mortals. Of those who dwell in the
Spiritual realms, many are of such pre-eminent grandeur
and majesty as would overwhelm the most courageous
soul with awe; others are of a beauty so ineffable, as
language cannot describe nor the imagination conceive."

"How is it with those human beings, who depart this
life with the stains of sin upon their souls, unatoned
for?"

"Confined to that sad place of ordeal, the prison house
of purgation, till the crimes done in their state of nature
are burnt and purged away, their aspect of sorrow and
suffering,—their agonizing struggles to reach the realms
of light and joy, would draw tears from the hardest
heart. Yet one consolation is granted them,—the
heavenly boon of Hope, that, though their period of tribulation may be prolonged through many ages, 'twill end
at last, in their release, and in the enjoyment of peace and
happiness. 'Tis a sad reflection that, to not a few of us

mortals who are so careless as to their final salvation, this is the only path to heaven."

"And the souls of lost and damned ones,—if such there be, and the infernal hosts of Satan ?"

"The former, whose consciences in this mortal life were seared ;—lost to all good, confirmed in all evil and at eternal enmity against God,—language cannot express, nor imagination conceive the dreadful punishments and torments to which they are subjected, alleviated at times with infernal joys. Their aspect is direful and revolting. As to the Infernals, they are consigned to the realms of 'Outer Darkness,' and subjected to tortures ineffable. Hell is within them, as well as without. Their appearance,—which is the reflex of their interiors,—is so indescribably hideous, as would almost freeze the soul with horror. The forms of some, are frightful admixtures of the human and bestial, or reptilian. On occasions of great moment, the power is granted me to evoke even the most tremendous of these demons from their infernal kingdom and compel them to do my bidding. It requires almost superhuman courage and resolution to face them, and rarely is the mortal found, however intrepid his soul may be, who can sustain the fearful vision."

CHAPTER XLI.

PRINCE DIAVOJAHR.

> " The King becoming graces,
> As justice, verity, temperance, stableness,
> Bounty, perseverance, mercy, lowliness,
> Devotion, patience, courage, fortitude,
> I have no relish of them ; but abound
> In the division of each several crime,
> Acting it in many ways."
>
> *Macbeth*, Act. IV., Sc. iii.

At this moment an officer entered, announcing the arrival of Prince Diavojahr and suite, requesting an immediate interview with the Minister, and Eliff left the room. In a few moments a clamor of voices was heard from the audience hall evidently in angry dispute, amid which the voice of the Minister was heard in stern and commanding tones. In a few moments he returned ; his countenance wore an expression of displeasure.

" This spendthrift Prince," said he, " squanders vast sums annually in riotous living and gambling. His conduct has been a source of great grief and anxiety to his unfortunate father, who has nearly impoverished his own private resources in paying his debts. None of the Prince's companions will lend him a single garnuta nor go his security, for they are as deeply in debt as he. He has borrowed large sums from the money lenders who are pressing their claims and threaten to levy on his palace and landed estates to satisfy their demands. He is urging me to issue an order to the Lord High Treasurer of the Exchequer that his debts be paid out of the Royal Treasury, which I have refused, until a special meeting of the cabinet is called to consider the question, and I doubt if they accede to his request."

"In some of the kingdoms of our Terrestrial World," said I, "we have a few specimens of these royal spend-thrifts who live only for pleasure and give their parents no little trouble in this respect. But their subjects seem quite willing to be taxed for their support and pay obsequious court to them ; and I am sorry to say not a few of our snobbish Americans, who adore titles and ape foreign manners, court introductions to them, esteeming it one of the highest of earthly honors. Some of our fashionable females, also, who happen to be blessed with large bank accounts bestowed on them by their rich papas, or deceased husbands, are perfectly crazy to form matrimonial alliances with these titled peacocks, in order that they may be able to hold their heads a little higher than their sisters, and be addressed as—' Your Grace '—' Your Ladyship,'—' Madame la Comtesse,'—' Madame la Baronne,' etc., purchasing their titles with gold, their petty vanity and ostentation, —the ruling sentiment of their lives,—being gratified."

"I shall satisfy a few of these more pressing claims out of my own private means, although I hardly expect to receive any thanks for it from this ungrateful Prince," and he drew up his check on his private banker for a large amount payable to Diavojahr's order. I ventured the remark that, I feared he erred on the side of generosity, in thus contributing to the indulgences of a royal squanderer.

"Perhaps so, but I do it for the sake of peace in the royal household, and to save our unfortunate king the repetition of many a painful scene through which he has passed," then rising from his chair—" Come with me and see the sort of company this Prince keeps, and you may judge what is in store for this unhappy kingdom when he assumes the throne."

We entered the reception room which communicated by open doors and windows with the garden of the palace. Prince Diavojahr with a dozen of his suite were assembled around a table partaking liberally of the refreshments and wines served by the attendants of the Minister's household. I took the opportunity to observe this specimen of royalty more closely. He was of tall stature and athletic form ; his rather handsome countenance was stamped with the indelible impress of evil passions, duplicity and cruelty ; his eyes were furtive and treacherous ; his bearing haughty, arrogant and disdainful. His companions were dukes, lords, barons, etc., many of Pluto-Martian descent ; some were young and handsome, but their expressions were dissolute and their countenances showed the effects of dissipation. The rest were made up of royal weaklings and fops of effeminate appearance and manners. They were attired in rich and elegant costumes glittering with orders and decorations ; they wore the keen and deadly Martian rapier and other weapons, ready to draw on the slightest provocation. They had evidently returned from a prolonged pleasure excursion, their voices were loud and boisterous, their laughter flippant and they were amusing themselves with coarse anecdote, ribald jest and *double entendre*. Most of them looked extremely *blasé*, and indulged the fashionably languid drawl so popular among certain swell aristocratic circles. Eliff advanced and presented the check to the Prince.

"I hope this will relieve your Highness from temporary embarrassment," said he. The Prince took it with an air as if he were conferring a high favor on the Minister and glanced at it carelessly.

"Thanks;—we appreciate the kindness of your Excellency," then passed it to a foppishly attired nobleman at his side,—" Duke,—attend to this little matter for us."

The Prince always used the plural number when speaking of his royal self. Duke Dandyprat, who was his cousin, received it gingerly with the tips of his fingers.

" Deah me!—Couldn't youah Excellency have made it a little highah figah ?"

"The amount must satisfy His Highness' creditors for the present," replied the Minister with a slightly perceptible sneer.

" But, weally, we must quiet these beastly money lendahs. Excessively na-a-asty to be obliged to come in contact with 'em, da-a-awn't you kna-a-aw !"

" It is to be regretted that your Grace is under the painful necessity of so doing. Still we can hardly do without them, sometimes."

" O, ya-a-as,"—remarked Sir Julius Jacknapes,— " we'll admit the fact ;—but bless me soul !—vewy distwessing, nevahtheless ; the vulgah unappweciative swine ;—no souls above gold garnutas and cent. per cent. Isn't that so, me la-awds ?"

" Me la-awds " loudly applauded Sir Julius' profound and original observation.

" Beg pa-a awdon," squeaked a weakling at his elbow. " By the way,—er—er—what's the figah ?"

" Fifty thousand garnutas," replied a keen, sharp nosed personage, evidently the Prince's agent or man of business, putting the check complacently in his pocket book.

The amount was equal to $1,000,000 U. S. currency.

" A-a-a-wfully nice," chirruped the weakling.

"Vewy,—vewy cha-a-awming;" warbled a darling little dude.

"Demmed handsome,—must say,"—puffed Baron Biborax, whose obese abdomen, dropsical legs and red nose would have astonished Jack Falstaff. "Egad! me lawds, we must drink his Excellency's noble health."

"O,—of—*hic*-co-o-ahse, mus' pay ouah complimens— *hic*,—to noble Ministah of—*hic*, Sta-a-a ;—*hic* ;"—grunted Sir Gregory Gluttonog, Earl Eatemall and Count Crapulence, a highly presentable trio of Pluto-Martian prize hogs, who looked as if they had been fed on pork chops, brandy cherries and devilled crabs.

The noble health was liberally guzzled all around, to which Eliff briefly responded, then taking my arm he drew me forward.

"Your Royal Highness and my lords of Sundora-Luzion. I take pleasure in introducing my honored guest, Lieutenant Hamilton, an inhabitant of the planet Earth and a citizen of its greatest Republic,—the United States of America," and I bowed to the royal party.

The Prince slowly and methodically affixed his monocle to his left eye, screwing up the brow, nose and mouth on that side and letting down the corresponding features on the other, to hold this important optical instrument in position, and favored me with a long and leisurely stare, sufficiently vacant, quite *comme il faut* and strictly in accordance with the accepted aristocratic mode prevailing in full flower among certain fashionable circles, and deliberately turned his back on me. Duke Dandyprat, who often acted as spokesman for His Highness, raised his optical, stared at me *à la mode*, then drawled :—

"Egad !—have heahd of the individual befoah ;—pwehaps we 'ave seen him somewheah,—but—er—er—bless me soul ! ca-a-awn't pwecisely remembah."

The fops, dudes and weaklings, followed suit, favoring me with their optical observations and audible comments on my personal appearance, etc., as if I were some circus, or dime museum freak, trotted out for their especial amusement. Eliff restrained his resentment at the insolent boorishness of the crowd ; for my own part, I was only waiting an opportunity to pull their royal noses all around.

" I propose the health of the planet Earth, and the United States of America," said Eliff, and the attendants filled glasses.

"O, ya-as," drawled the Duke,—"ouah evening sta-ah. Weally quite pwetty,—da-awn't kn-a-aw much about it. Inhabitants dweadful bahbawians, we are told."

The lordlings laughed consumedly at the Duke's sally, the toast was drunk, I briefly responded, Eliff, being my only listener, the lordlings chatting among themselves. Eliff now proposed the health of Mandal-Uttima, which was drunk only by about one third of the party.

" Here's health to Duke Athalton and Prince Altfoura," said I, drawing a bow at a venture.

"Who offers that toast ?" sneered His Royal Highness, wheeling about and staring loftily around.

" My guest, Lieutenant Hamilton," Eliff replied.

" Quite out of place,"—and His Highness wheeled back again.

The heir apparent always assumed his royal prerogative of proposing, accepting, or refusing any toast he saw fit, regardless of any body else and expressing his pleasure or displeasure accordingly.

" Bless me soul !—Ca-a-awn't think of it ;—vewy impwopah, indeed," echoed the crowd.

Duke Sybarite, one of the most dissolute peers of the realm, the Prince's favorite boon companion and with a face like a satyr, rapped loudly on the table.

"Here's success to the suit of our gallant Prince for the hand of Her Royal Highness, the Princess of Mandal-Uttima."

The toast was drunk with immense enthusiasm. The Minister and I never raised our glasses.

"Your Excellency does not join in the toast," said the Prince, glancing haughtily at the Minister and threateningly at me.

"Your Highness is fully aware of my objections to this proposed union for official reasons, which I am not at liberty to communicate.   Furthermore, it's quite evident that your efforts in that direction will not meet with the success you anticipate."

"Ah, indeed.—Will your Excellency condescend to give your reasons for your highly valuable opinion in the matter ?"

"For the simple fact that, you have made no apology to Duke Athalton nor Prince Altfoura for your conduct at the Princess' festival."

"Apology !—Does your Excellency intend this as an insult ?" he haughtily queried,

"I intend no insult to the Heir Apparent to the throne of Sundora-Luzion," replied the Minister gravely. "Your royal father and I, deemed it not only an act of courtesy, but our duty, to apologize for you."

"Hah !—Then my royal father played the fool, and you have been guilty of a contemptible act of servility. I advise you to keep yourself to your ministerial trade, and not meddle with affairs that don't belong to you."

The eyes of Eliff flashed fire at this brutal insult, and for a moment it looked as if he would crush the royal

ruffian with an avalanche of wrath, but he simply
bowed and smiled. The lords stood gaping with astonishment at the Prince and Minister. At this moment
Colonel Armatoff and Lord Montobar entered, the
former hurriedly announced to Eliff that a messenger
from the King had arrived requesting an immediate
audience and the Minister left the room. Lord Montobar approached the Prince.

" I have the honor to bear a message from His Highness, Prince Harovian of Audresar, Heir Apparent to
the kingdom of Rohita Savoyal," presenting the letter.

The Prince opened it and burst into a loud laugh.

" By Jupiter !—A challenge from that puppy, Harovian ;—only think of it,—unless I apologize,—pretty
good ;—must say,—" passing it to his suite.

Their lordships laughed boisterously, passing it
around. The Prince snatched it, tore it in two, and
handed it to one of the attendants.

" Here, fellow, pass that paper to yon messenger and
tell him to carry it back to the puppy who sent it."

The man hesitated, Colonel Armatoff stepped forward.

" Your Royal Highness will pardon me, but you are
subjecting the honored guest of our Minister of State
to a shameful humiliation."

"Colonel Armatoff," shouted Diavojahr, "none of
your sage remarks here,—request yon go-between
messenger to tell that rascal Harovian I toss his challenge back in his face."

" Prince Diavojahr, I am your equal in military rank,
though not in royal station, and I positively refuse to
convey any such message to Lord Montobar,"—replied
he sternly.

Lord Montobar's eyes flashed fire,—anticipating an
instant explosion, I stepped forward and in a low tone,—

"Gentlemen, let us leave the scene of these insults," —and arm in arm we left the room, and passed through the open doors into the garden which was brilliantly illuminated.

"Good God!" exclaimed the Colonel,—"this Prince seems destitute of common decency. I am truly grieved, my Lord, that you should have been subjected to such a dastardly insult."

"His insults cannot touch me. I expected nothing better,"—replied he ; "but I am at a loss to know what course to pursue with respect to Prince Harovian's ultimatum."

"Your age and position exempt you from that ungracious affair," replied the Colonel,—"there's no telling what he might not do. He would certainly insult you brutally, and although you are the guest of our Minister, might order your arrest on the ground of insult to his royal dignity."

"Leave that to me," said I,—"I will deliver Prince Harovian's ultimatum on the first opportunity."

CHAPTER XLII.

THE DUEL.

"Why, I will fight with him upon this theme,
Until my eyelids will no longer wag."
Hamlet, Act V., Sc. i.

We were walking under the luxuriant foliage. At a distance, the granite tower of Thaumatour loomed above the trees ; a dim light glimmered through the casement ; voices were heard announcing the arrival of the royal party in the garden ; footsteps rapidly approached ; some one touched me on the shoulder. I turned, and Prince Diavojahr stood before me, his features distorted with passion.

" A word with you," said he.

" I am at Your Highness' leisure," I replied.

" You refused the toast offered by Duke Sybarite."

" And you refused the toast offered by me."

" As Prince of the blood royal, I have the right to refuse any toast I please."

" As a citizen of the United States of America I have the same right."

" Your refusal was an insult."

" You may take it as you please."

" I demand an instant apology."

" And I refuse."

" What.—Do you dare—?"

" You have refused to apologize for your insult to my honored host, Duke Athalton, and my friend, Prince Altfoura, and the Princess of Mandal-Uttima thoroughly despises you."

Lord Montobar stood appalled. Diavojahr grew almost black in the face, for an instant was speechless with rage,—then hissed out,—

" Hah !—This to me ? You despicable adventurer,— hanger on of that Court,—"

" Certainly ;—right to your face ;—and I now announce the ultimatum of Prince Harovian that, he'll not stoop to cross swords with you, but will post you for a coward and poltroon, and horsewhip you wherever he can lay hands on you, which castigation would be eminently appropriate to your case, and give me much pleasure to witness."

With a roar more like that of a wild beast than a human being, he struck me a blow in the face, drew his rapier and rushed on me. I sprang back, whipped out my sword and for the first time in the history of this planetary system, the clash of steel resounded between denizens of different worlds. The nobles rushed forward, several with drawn weapons, evidently bent on attacking me.

"Stand back, my lords," exclaimed Colonel Armatoff sternly, and drawing his rapier. "The insult and blow have passed,—His Royal Highness and Lieutenant Hamilton stand on equal ground ;—I'll allow no interference here."

As the Colonel was an acknowledged authority on all matters appertaining to the code of honor and, furthermore, as he was known to be one of the most formidable swordsmen in the army, their lordships evidently concluded that discretion was the better part of valor and drew back ; besides, it was evident that the majority rather wished the threatened combat to go on. After the first clash, the Prince and I lowered our weapons and stepped back several paces. The nobles approached and whispered to him ; he nodded acquiescence ; one of them, who might have found his Terrestrial counterpart in Sir Lucius O'Trigger, and who rejoiced in the title of Captain Swaggerchop, stepped toward me, with a toss of his head.

"His Highness consents to waive his royal prerogative of refusing passage at arms with a foreigner and inferior, and condescends to give Lieutenant,—'What's his-name,'—full satisfaction."

"Lieutenant Hamilton has heard the oration of Captain 'What-d'ye-call-him ?' and consents to give His Highness, ditto," I replied.

It was evident that the Prince was desirous of displaying his courage and accomplishments before his friends and showing them how easily he could lay out the despicable adventurer.

"Hah! I shall take pleasure in giving this pet of Mandal-Uttima a few lessons in fence and cool his blood a little."

The lords expressed immense satisfaction at the prospect of a little blood letting; the preliminaries were quickly arranged,—the Prince chose Captain Swaggerchop as his second,—Colonel Armatoff politely offered his services to me, which I thankfully accepted. The Prince and I were about the same height and in that respect the chances seemed about equal; his rapier, —a magnificent weapon,—was a little longer than my naval sword and lighter in weight, but I waived the difference; we threw off our coats, a handkerchief was bound around the wrist and this most graceful, elegant, and in all respects most satisfactory mode of adjusting personal grievances was begun. The Martian style of fence is quite different from ours and its various movements of *avance, longe, recouvrir, feinte, engages*, etc., puzzled me. My antagonist was an expert swordsman, had few superiors among the *maitres des armes* in his kingdom and handled his rapier with consummate skill; for some time I confined myself to the defensive, parrying his thrusts and studying his mode of attack. To my surprise and perplexity, the blade of his rapier was elastic as whalebone and flexible as rubber, and had a trick of coiling around my own, and creeping up over the handle in a very serpentine fashion and wounding me in the wrist. Twice I received its insidious thrust on the arm. Once I succeeded in getting inside his guard and planting a powerful stroke on his breast, which made him stagger, but to my astonishment, instead of wounding him, as I fully expected, my blade bounded back as if it had struck a rock;

this was a great mystery to me. I now determined on another mode of tactics in which I had been regarded as rather expert, namely, disarming. It is a dangerous manœuvre, requiring more than usual skill and strength, and unless accomplished neatly and expeditiously, renders the assailant liable to be run through by his antagonist. Parrying a fierce *longe*, I sprang forward, locked my hilt in his and with a swift motion, twisted it out of his hand and hurled it to a distance ; —the Prince turned pale,—threw up his hands,— wheeled about and retreated.

"Ho ! there, Your Royal Highness," shouted Colonel Armatoff. "Shall I have the pleasure of announcing to your regiment that, you acknowledge yourself conquered ?"

"By no means !" said I, lowering my sword. "Captain Swaggerchop will have the kindness to restore the rapier to His Highness."

The lords stared at me with open mouthed stupefaction. Such an act of courtesy on the part of a victor at the sword, being unheard of in the kingdom. Swaggerchop picked up the rapier and handed it to the Prince who received it trembling.

"Splendidly done, Lieutenant," said Colonel Armatoff to me.

"This is the first time His Highness was ever disarmed," murmured the lords.

"Pooh !" said I. "Any ensign in our Navy can do that."

Diavojahr's face grew dark with rage and as Swaggerchop adjusted the handkerchief to his wrist more securely,—

"The fellow has a wrist of iron," muttered he, with a fierce oath.

It was evident the Prince and lords were much impressed and somewhat alarmed at my manœuvre ; a prolonged whispering took place, during which, as they closely surrounded him, he seemed to be adjusting something around his waist, under his dress, Col. Armatoff became impatient.

"Is Your Royal Highness in readiness?" asked he.

The lords stepped back.

"Be on your guard ; when you touch him, let fly," —whispered Swaggerchop, with a meaning look.

Diavojahr answered with an equally meaning glance, then poising his weapon, advanced with a triumphant look to meet my assault. He was now more wary, so was I,—the mutual *engages* were given and recieved with great caution ; but in spite of all I could do, that snaky rapier would crawl up my sword, wounding my wrist ; it seemed to be endowed with an infernal life ; every stroke was like an electric shock, almost paralyzing my arm, and whenever I planted a stroke on him, my sword's point failed to penetrate. I got three powerful thrusts on his breast which would have run any man through, but although my weapon staggered him, it flew back as from a shield of iron. The combat now became furious. The loud clash and rattle of the swords resounded among the trees. I was growing weak from loss of blood and my arm was becoming paralyzed. My antagonist saw it, and a smile of malignant triumph wreathed his lips. I knew full well that my heart's blood would soon dye the green sward. Collecting all my remaining strength, I rushed with fierce onslaught, driving him back step by step. Suddenly his look turned from me and became fixed on some object over my head ;—an expression of terror came over his face ;—I beat up his weapon,—sprang forward,—grasped his sword arm in my left hand, and with a powerful exertion of strength hurled him to the ground ;—he grew ghastly pale ;—his eyes dilated as if some fearful vision had opened before him ;—he gave a smothered cry and sank insensible. I glanced around, and in the window of Thaumatour's tower appeared what seemed the spirit form of a beautiful young woman, clothed in the cerements of the tomb ; her countenance expressing the depths of anguish and despair ;—with dishevelled hair and colorless lips,—her eyes, glittering with the fires of madness, were fixed on the prostrate Prince, while down her pallid cheeks streamed tears of unutterable sorrow. For an instant only, this inexpressibly sad vision gleamed before my eyes, then disappeared ;—the point of my sword hung over my antagonist's breast ;—the throng rushed forward with drawn weapons.

"Stand back," sternly commanded Colonel Armatoff. "By the gods ! whoever interferes, I'll run him through. The life of His Highness is forfeit,—he must purchase it by full and ample apology to his antagonist ;—'tis the law of the code ;—I am sole arbiter here ;—advance a single point, and the best of you shall breathe his last."

The lords fell back,—suddenly a cry was heard and a beautiful child, the very image of that sad vision, rushed from the trees,—her long wavy hair streaming in the wind,—fell on her knees before the prostrate man, clasped her arms around his neck, kissed him, then raising her innocent face to mine, her eyes filled with tears and in touching tones.

"Please,—O, please do not hurt my dear papa."

I flung down my sword, and took the little one in my arms.

"The Princess Allezona," whispered all, bowing with marked respect and removing their hats.

The young Princess threw her arms around my neck and kissed me on both cheeks.

" O, you are so good,—you would not hurt my dear papa?—now, please promise;—poor little Allie will love you so dearly."

I caressed the child, giving my faithful promise;—two elderly court ladies came quickly forward and bore her away, weeping and holding out her arms imploringly to the prostrate man. Suddenly a gigantic and meagre figure clad in sombre black, glided from the trees and pushed through the throng. It was Thaumatour. Stooping over the insensible Prince he tore open the waistcoat and under garments, disclosing to our astonished gaze a complete suit of chain armor, sword and bullet proof, investing his body; while around his waist was a belt containing a small, but powerful electric battery and communicating by a flexible wire along the arm and hand, directly to the blade of the rapier.

The paralyzing strokes I had received from the weapon of my antagonist were explained.

" The Devil !—" muttered several.

" Bless me soul !—who ev-a-a-ah heahd of such a thing ?" queried the swells.

" Vewy, — vewy hextro-o-ornary," chirruped the dudes.

" We-e-ally ; it ca-a-awn't be possible," squeaked the weaklings.

"Col. Armatoff," stammered Captain Swaggerchop,— " we hope—er,—you'll not—suspect that any of us had —er,—any knowledge of—er,—"

" Pooh !"—sneered the Colonel with unutterable contempt.

" Me La-a-wd Do-o-ok,—" dawdled His Grace of Dandyprat, " we 'ope youah Gwace will pwemit us to say in be-e-a-alf of ouah Royal cousin,—"

" Bosh !" thundered the Duke.

Thaumatour strode amid the throng,—stooped his

colossal stature, peering into their faces one by one
with a look that Mephistopheles would have envied,
uttering peculiar sounds, whether sneers, laughs, or
applause, none could interpret ; they fell back as if
Beelzebub himself was among them, then thrusting a
scrap of paper in my hand, he strode swiftly to his tower.

I looked around,—Eliff stood by my side ; with a
glance almost of pity on the prostrate man, and of
haughty contempt on the lords, who looked as if they
scarce knew where to hide their heads, he took my arm
and accompanied by Lord Montobar and Duke Armatoff we entered the salon, while the Prince rose from
the ground shaking with impotent rage ; his companions
clustered around him and all hurriedly left the grounds.
Eliff called an attendant who applied a healing lotion
to my wounds, which fortunately were only flesh deep,
and skillfully bound them up. Duke Armatoff now
rose to bid us adieu. I expressed my sincere thanks
for his courteous kindness to me.

"Don't speak of it, my dear sir, I beg of you," he
replied. " I shall be only too happy to render you any
service in my power. I only regret, however, that you
had not met a foeman worthy your steel,"—then turning to the Minister,—

"I have decided to resign my commission in the
army, and I beg your Excellency's immediate acceptance."

"But, my dear Colonel—"

"It is totally incompatible with my feelings of honor
to remain any longer in the ranks with that royal
catiff," replied he, indignantly. " The *esprit du corps*
of the army is tarnished, stained, while that coward
remains there."

"I appreciate your feelings, but I cannot accept the
resignation of one of our most distinguished officers,

who has won such laurels and high renown on the field. You are too highly appreciated and your services too valuable to our kingdom," replied Eliff, warmly pressing his hand.

"Well, then, I shall have to desert, and you'll have to hang me—that is,—provided you can catch me," replied the Colonel with a grim smile and merry twinkle in his eye, as he left the room.

The attendants departed. Lord Montobar bade us good night and retired to his apartment. Eliff and I were left alone ; I looked at the paper Thaumatour had given me,—

"My very clever, but somewhat unsophisticated young Terrestrial friend ; Lieutenant of the U. S. N. You are a right good fellow and a gallant fighter, but you are no match for H. R. H. Diavo,—with his coat of mail and battery,—one of his cheap tricks, and you would not have had a ghost of a chance against him, had I not favored him with a ghostly vision which rather took the pluck out of him. It's lucky for you, his rapier was not poisoned also. In the hurry of the affair he forgot that essential part of the business. Take my advice, and get out of this part of the Martian world at once and stand not on the order of your going. A word to the wise is sufficient.

"THAUMATOUR."

"P. S. How stands the fortune telling business up to date ?"

"Thaumatour's prediction has come true to the letter, so far," said Eliff: "You have had the lively adventure ; the temper of your sword and disposition has been tested, and you have had a pretty close call at Diavo-jahr's snaky rapier."

"But my honor has come out all right, so far,—" I replied.

"Perhaps that test will come by and by."

"That's true ;—he advises me to get out of this kingdom,—what shall I do ? I should be very loth to deprive myself of your Excellency's hospitality on any such imputation."

"And I should equally regret to lose the company of my honored guest."

"But there s the love affair,—elopement,—a married woman,— injured husband,— pistols,— all bound to come.—Great Scott ! It strikes me the sooner I get out of this kingdom, the better."

"But that will not break the spell,—" replied Eliff,— "they're all bound to come, wherever you are."

"In that case, I would rather take my chances among my friends, than here."

At this moment two elderly female attendants entered with little Allezona. She ran to the Minister with a cry of delight ; he took her in his arms and caressed her, then presented her to me. The poor child had entirely forgotten the event in which she had taken part. It was evident the faculty of memory was wanting, or undeveloped. She was a beautiful child of ten years ; well grown and of exceedingly affectionate disposition ; but her intellect seemed weak and the expression of her countenance was of deep sadness, as if some great shock of terror or grief had fallen upon her in early childhood, and left its lasting impress on her mind. For a while she amused us with her childish prattle, then affectionately kissing Eliff, bade us good night and departed with the attendants.

"That dear little one is the only being left for me to love and cherish," said he in a sad voice,—"she is the child of my only daughter, who was the pride and joy of my home. Like a pure and innocent flower was she, one of the most lovely and accomplished of woman kind, the idol of my heart, whom I guarded with jealous care. Secluded within the privacy of our home, she knew nothing of the world. By accident she met Prince Diavojahr, and long ere I dreamed of it, she had given her innocent heart into his keeping. Their meeting was by stealth, and he had employed all his arts of persuasion and cunning in which he is well skilled. My knowledge of this came too late,—her love was irrevocably fixed,—they were united in marriage,—he treated her most cruelly,—broke her heart and drove her to madness and death. This poor little one, the fruit of that union, has inherited the innocent, confiding and sensitive nature of her mother, but her mind is clouded with the same deep melancholy and she is often visited by the same dreadful terrors and illusions that closed the last years of her unfortunate mother's life. The unnatural father cares nothing for his child and you can imagine how I feel toward him who has blighted two innocent lives,—"and the Minister bowed his head almost overcome with grief.

'Twas the portrait of this wronged and suffering Princess,—now in her grave,—Thaumatour had taken from his Master's apartment,—placed in his window, and illumined with a bright light,—which struck terror, if not remorse, to Diavojahr's heart.

CHAPTER XLIII.

THE ARREST.

"Seize on the ruffian,—bind him—gag him,—
Off to the Bastile!"

Richelieu, Act III., Sc. iv.

The next morning Lord Montobar and I bade adieu to the Minister, who requested us to convey his respectful greetings to the Grand Duke, Prince and Princess of Mandal-Uttima; mounted his air ship under command of Captain Troyan, flew over the city and continent of Sundora, and by noon had crossed nearly midway Vodraga Ocean when a large government air ship was seen swiftly approaching from the south. She fired a gun, the signal for us to lay to, and we paused. In a few moments she drew alongside and several Pluto-Martian officers, clad in uniform, stepped on our deck. One, evidently the chief, addressed Capt. Troyan,—

"I am Capt. Noriox of the royal police. I have orders for the arrest of Lord Montobar and one Lieut. Hamilton—" presenting a paper to Troyan, who handed it to his lordship,—

"Arrest !—" exclaimed he, " really, sir, what does this mean ?"

"I exceedingly regret the duty imposed on me," replied Capt. Noriox, bowing politely, " but my orders are imperative."

" Orders ? From whom ?"

" The Grand Marshal of the kingdom."

" And for what ?"

" On the complaint of His Royal Highness, Prince Diavojahr."

" And what may be His Highness' grievance ?"

" I know not, Your Lordship."

" Probably because I disarmed him in the sword encounter, and laid him on the grass," said I.

" It's a pity you didn't run him through, then and there," replied Lord Montobar.

" So I would, if it had not been for his concealed armor,—electric battery,—and the intercession of his unfortunate child."

Captain Noriox and officers shrugged their shoulders.

" This arrest is a high handed outrage on the part of your catiff Prince !" exclaimed Lord Montobar.

" And this is the private ship of His Excellency, the Minister of State," said Captain Troyan. " You have no right to board her except by his permission. Had I sufficient force I should resist you."

" And within ten minutes we should have been over the sea-board line, and within the jurisdiction of Mandal-Uttima,' said Lord Montobar, " and you would have boarded us at your peril."

" I exceedingly regret the occurrence," replied Noriox, " but the orders of the Grand Marshal admit of no delay. Your Lordship and Lieutenant Hamilton must go aboard my ship. Captain Troyan and officers are not included in this order."

" I shall appeal to His Majesty, King Probitos, against this outrage," replied Montobar.

We got aboard,—both ships wheeled about, sped swiftly back, and by evening we reached the city.

" Capt. Troyan," said Montobar, " you will immediately report this to the Minister, and request him to despatch the news to Duke Athalton at once."

The ships parted company. Troyan's to the Minister's palace, and ours to the north quarter of the city and landed in the grounds of the great castle of Petrovon, where prisoners of State are incarcerated prior to trial. We were escorted through the great bronze doors to the reception room of the keeper, Capt. Noriox showed his order and we were conducted by the guards to separate apartments for the night.

The next morning one of the principal advocates of the Imperial Law Court, accompanied by two junior barristers entered my apartment. He was an elderly gentleman of courteous manners, and one of the most eminent members of the bar. Proceeding at once to business, he informed me that, I was charged with high treason and conspiracy against the royal dignity and felonious assault against the royal person of His Highness, Prince Diavojahr, the penalty of which, on conviction, was death, and that Lord Montobar was charged with complicity in the same. I was thunderstruck at the high handed audacity of the charge.

"As for the charge of treason," I replied, "I am a free born citizen of the United States of America and owe allegiance to no kingdom or monarch on this planet or any other. As to the charge of assault, I deny it. Prince Diavojahr grossly insulted me, and drew his rapier on me. I defended myself as was my right. You may call it a duel if you please. He accepted it. Lord Montobar, Col. Armatoff and the nobles witnessed it, and will give their testimony to the fact. My friends of Mandal-Uttima will call this kingdom to strict account for this outrage on their guest, and Lord Montobar."

"This is a very serious matter, Lieutenant," replied he,—"His Highness swears directly to the contrary ; that you gave the insult and made the assault on him."

"He is a liar and a coward."

" I beg of you not to express your private opinion ; it might seriously compromise your case. You shall have the full benefit of counsel and if you will accept my services, I shall be happy to render you all the assistance in my power."

I accepted the advocate's offer with thanks and the junior barristers took my deposition.

" I was not aware that, there were any statutes against duelling in your kingdom and had every reason to believe that, the affair between His Highness and myself was a fair duel," said I.

" According to our laws, duels between persons of equal rank and station are allowed, but not between those of different ranks."

" Then those of superior rank are privileged to insult or assault their inferiors with impunity ?"

" The assaulted have legal redress ; but for any one of inferior rank to draw weapons, under any provocation whatever, against a person of royal blood or station, is a penal offence."

" The bulls and the bears seem to have it all their own way in your kingdom. If my Ox happens to gore your Bull, I am held responsible, but if your Bull gores my Ox, nobody is responsible," and I related the fable of the countryman and the lawyer, and the wolf and the lamb, at which my advocate and the juniors laughed heartily. He then informed me that, being a foreigner, as well as a prisoner, I would not be permitted to testify in my own behalf ; neither would Lord Montobar, being under arrest for complicity and also a foreigner. I replied that, in my opinion, the legal code of his kingdom with reference to the prerogatives of royalty, and the rights of foreigners, presented a highly inviting field for the cultivation of Nihilism, and I expressed my astonishment that the Minister of State or the royal council could for a moment tolerate such in-justice.

"Eliff has rectified many an outrageous wrong in our kingdom and has fought this one for many years; but it has been established by royal precedent for centuries, and seems impregnable against his efforts," replied the advocate. Business concluded, he and the barristers departed.

The next day Lord Montobar and I were conducted to the Palace of Justice in the east quarter of the city, and taken to one of the private Court rooms. The Court Judges,—Prosecuting Attorneys,—my own and Lord Montobar's counsel,—Duke Armatoff,—several members of the Minister's household and the nobles of Diavojahr's suite being present; the Prince himself not present, his royal prerogatives granting him exemption, but he was represented by counsel. His sworn deposition was read by the government prosecutor, the witnesses were examined, the testimony of the Minister's household was ruled out. Duke Armatoff swore positively to the first assault of the Prince upon me, but his testimony was also ruled out on the ground that, he had acted as my second and it was intimated that, he had rendered himself liable to a heavy fine for so doing; all the royal swells, fops, dudes and weaklings, grunted, puffed, warbled, chirruped and squeaked their testimony on their solemn oaths and sacred honors that, the "was-cally bahbawian" had made the first assault on the person of His Royal Highness,—"Vewy, vewy, dwead-ful,"—and when asked by my advocate about the coat of mail and electric battery,—"Bless me soul!—A most outwageous slandah!—Nevah heahd of such a thing befoah," and in spite of their well known reputa-tion for untruthfulness and the fact that it was pretty well understood they had been coached by the Prince, their testimony outweighed all. Full indictments were made out against me for treasonable assault, and Lord Montobar as bearer of a challenge against His Highness and we were remanded back for trial.

In the mean time the news was flashed through every Martian kingdom and created the greatest excitement and solicitude. Duke Athalton despatched a special embassy to the Sundora court demanding our release, or at least, a change of venue, on the ground that, being a foreigner and owing no allegiance to any Martian kingdom, the charge of treason could not be sustained against me. Appeals came thick and fast from King Polath, Prince Harovian and Duke Oneigar for justice, or that I be allowed counsel from other kingdoms, but all were denied. On the tenth day the court convened for trial in the grand hall of the Palace of Justice. The crown judges,—twelve in number, clad in their official robes, the prosecuting attorneys, counsel for the defence, and officers of the law, were assembled. The hall was crowded with the *élite* of Pluto-Martian royalty and aristocracy, representatives of the learned professions and throngs of spectators. Such an event as a denizen of one World being tried for treason and felonious assault, in the law courts of another World rolling in the abysmal depths of Space a hundred million miles off,—was hardly to be seen once in a life time, and worth going many miles to see.

The trial lasted three days. My advocate and his colleagues, aided by several distinguished members of the bar, made strenuous appeals in my behalf and the royal halls rang with torrents of Martian eloquence, such as the House of Lords in the days of Pitt, Fox, Sheridan and Burke, and the Senate of the United States, in the palmy days of Adams, Clay, Calhoun and Webster, would have adjourned *sine die*, to listen unto, could they have conveniently travelled there,—and even Demosthenes and Cicero would have gladly jumped out of their graves to hear. The Minister of State threw the whole power of his thrilling eloquence into the contest. He scored His Royal Highness most unmercifully for his unprincely conduct and his touching allusions to the coat of mail and electric battery, so necessary to guard that precious life from the assaults of Terrestrial adventurers and cranks, elicited shouts of laughter. He flung the lordlings under the legal harrow, showing up their dissolute lives and flagrant conduct, hurling on their heads such a tempest of overwhelming invective and withering scorn, as made every man and woman, judges, lawyers, officers, cover their faces in very shame. In the mean time the royal swells were reclining on their downy divans in the royal gallery, discussing their delicacies and sipping their wines, whispering soft sentiment into the ears of their frivolous court beauties, who, —attired in their gaudy attires—were sucking sweetmeats and languidly gazing on the grand scene as if it were gotten up for their special amusement. The lords enjoyed the entertainment hugely, and spread themselves accordingly, staring around through their opticals, nodding, smiling and applauding *comme il faut.* "Bless me soul !—'Pon me honah !—Ouah noble Ministah's eloquence is weally vewy, vewy, chawming. Demned fine,—must say."

Loose as Pluto-Martian justice is in many respects, there is one feature about it that might be well for some of our Terrestrial courts to cogitate upon, and that is, with reference to the benevolent interest and protection we Terrestrians are often inclined to throw around our unfortunate and afflicted Giteaus, wife and mistress murderers, and husband and lover murderesses, in the w y of insanity investigations. It would have been the worst possible policy for my advocate to have called insanity experts in my case, to make their investigations into the moral, emotional and intellectual status of my brain cells. The line of demarcation between demoralized wits, and demoralized morals or emotions, is pretty plainly drawn on this planet ; so much so, in fact, that the so-called insanity dodge is a highly dangerous manœuvre for any prisoner to undertake, for on the very first exhibition of it, he is regarded as a bigger devil than ever, and strung up all the quicker ; the courts are saved the infliction of the learned theories of insanity experts on jumbled up neurotics, melancholics, katytonics, morals, emotionals, intellectuals, confusionals and responsibles, which rarely agree in any case. The public is relieved of much suspense, and mawkish sentimentality on behalf of the prisoner, (principally feminine) is nipped in the bud.

Our case went by the board, just as we expected. The jury, a set of stupid, gormandizing royal old swine,—principally occupied in snoring through the trial,—blinked their bleared eyes and grunted out their verdict of guilty in the first degree, without shifting their adiposities in their chairs. The crown judges sentenced Lord Montobar to pay a heavy fine for insulting His Royal Highness by conveying a challenge to him from a foreign Prince, and I was sentenced to death, whereat the lords applauded in genuine kid gloved style. Their honors very benevolently recommended me to appeal to the mercy of the crown. But as every body knew that King Probitos was in his last illness and unable to write or speak, the audience shrugged their shoulders at this little bit of pleasantry on the part of their honors. The trial concluded, I expressed my sincere thanks to my counsel for their efforts in my behalf. Eliff drew me aside and whispered,

"This atrocious sentence shall not be carried out,—I'll see to that. You have friends here, and will receive help when you least expect it," then spoke a few words to Lord Montobar, who smiled and pressed his hand. His Lordship bade me adieu and was conducted back to the castle.

I was taken to the prison of Ironak, a massive and funereal building of black granite, where prisoners of State are incarcerated prior to execution. I was delivered to the jailer and his turnkeys, and escorted through the dark and gloomy halls to my cell. There was a rattling of keys,—a crash of bolts and bars,—I was thrust in,—the door was locked, and I was left to my reflections.

CHAPTER XLIV.

THE CONDEMNED CELL.

" A prison in a house of care,
　　A place where none can thrive ;
A touchstone true to try a friend,
　　A grave for men alive.
Sometimes a place of right,
　　Sometimes a place of wrong,
Sometimes a place of rogues and thieves
　　And honest men among."

Inscription on the Old Prison of Edinburgh.

"Heigho !"—said I to myself. " Here's food for reflection. Life is full of surprises where'er our lot may be cast, and on whatever World we may happen to be.

Were it not so, twould hardly be worth being born
and living. My trip to this Planet has abounded in
pleasing incident and exciting adventure. It begins
with a voyage to the South Pole of my mother Earth
where I discover an open polar sea, and wave the Stars
and Stripes over its rolling billows. Then comes an
ice berg prison from which I am fired out amid blazing
and bomb bursting ice bergs ;—I kill a twenty foot shark
with an ice pick,—meet a blind professional mind reader
who overhauls my brain cells while I am sound asleep
and extracts their linguistic furniture within forty eight
hours ;—I travel on an Ethervolt car through empty
space at the rate of a hundred miles, to twenty million
miles per minute ;—reach a spot where I lose all my
weight avoirdupois ;—perform a death dance in chaos
and encounter more things in heaven and earth than
are dreamt of in Hamlet's philosophy, or any body's
philosophy ;—ride on an air ship that defies the lightning,—on the back of a genuine Leviathan and on a big
Eagle's back.—I see the Stars and Stripes float in the
skies, and hear the Star Spangled Banner played by
the military bands of this other World.—I drink from
the fountain of Youth,—fight Alligator bats,—eat and
drink refreshments created from thin air,—see and
hear genuine singing flowery spirits ;—get my fortune
told and here it comes exactly as predicted, a duel, and
danger of death according to programme ;—the love
affair comes next,—elopement with a married woman,—
flight,—injured husband,—pistols,—bound to come,
sure as fate. By Jupiter ! a pretty pickle I've got
myself in by accepting a foreign Minister's invitation
to dinner,—no, it's not I, but my fate, dinner or no
dinner, and fate is the sole arbiter of human affairs.
What's to be done in my case ? 'Tis said that fortune
favors the bold. Well, I'll put on a bold face and face

my fortune, perhaps she'll smile on me. In the mean time I would give fifty dollars this minute, provided I had it, if the old Commodore were only here to enliven me with his,—'Cheer up, me brave boy;—never say die;—all ri'—Cock-a-doodledoo.'"

I now proceeded to take a survey of my prison cell. It was commodious; blue stone walls, floor and ceiling,— somewhat suggestive of the blues,—there was a rug, cot, table, two chairs and toilette stand,—two heavily barred windows on one side of the room admitted plenty of air and light, with a cheerful display of prison cells all around the area. On the opposite side was a single barred window screened with a curtain and apparently communicating with another cell. Toward afternoon my jailer entered, accompanied by his two turnkeys. He was an old Pluto-Martian of grim, but honest aspect, his name Hardigoth, and a man of few words. The turnkeys were big burly fellows with coarse, ruffianly faces. They brought me a suit of prison clothes, I put them on, and hung my uniform on the wall. They removed my valuables, among which was one I prized more highly than all, a handkerchief presented to me by the Princess Suhlamia, with her initials worked by her own fair hand. They permitted me to retain my watch. Night coming on, a light was lit in the corridor;—its rays shone through the barred transom over the door and I retired to my cot.

The days passed on. I was allowed no communication with the outer world and to all my queries the jailer was mute. I was alternately buoyed up with hope from the promise of the Minister, and sunk in the depths of gloom. One day I thought I detected a glance of pity in the eye of my stern and impassive jailer.

"Many a prisoner of State has languished out his life in these dungeons," said he.

" I haven't the slightest doubt of it," I replied. " By the way,—Hardigoth, it's rather tedious here,—can't you give me something to read, to while away the time ?"

" You want something cheerful and lively ?" he asked.

" It would be quite acceptable."

The next day he sent me a package of books; I opened them with joyful expectation, there were several,—the principal subjects,—" Meditations in a Dungeon,"—" Reflections of a Prisoner on the Eve of Execution,"—" Natural History of Death,"—" Is Life Worth Living ;"—How to Cheat the Hangman ;—Lawfulness of Suicide,"—" The Easiest Way to Shuffle Off This Mortal Coil," etc.

" How do you like your books ?" he asked, on his next visit.

" Exceedingly cheerful and entertaining class of literature," I replied. " Eminently appropriate to the occasion, calculated to drive away dull care, inspire perfect contentment and peace of mind."

" Our prisoners of State generally have such enjoyable times all their lives, before they get here, our Governor thinks it best to turn their thoughts in more serious directions, so they may be led to reflect on the dark side of life," said he with a grim smile.

" It is a good thing for man to see and experience a little of both sides," I replied. " It teaches him the vanity of human affairs, generally."

" You are right, and confinement in a death cell, or a long and painful illness are about the best things to prepare a man for translation to a better world. They tend, more than anything else to inculcate humility, resignation and other modes of self preparation, which if a man avails himself of them, will put him in tolerably respectable trim for the journey, but if he refuses those wholesome teachings, his journey will probably be in another direction."

I agreed that my jailer's philosophy was, in the main, correct.

" 'Tis not that the gallows is a passport to heaven," continued he,—" but it is sometimes one of the necessary means of preparation for the journey. Between you and me, Lieutenant, it's my humble opinion that people who live in ease, luxury and enjoyment here, and pass away comfortably in their beds, will have rather a hard time of it on that journey to where they flatter themselves they're going,—even if they ever get there."

I was compelled to admit that, Hardigoth's view was not far from the truth and that many of those who have such easy and comfortable times here, may find out, somewhat to their disappointment, that " Jordan am a hard road to travel."

One evening he entered my cell, and with an air of mystery, whispered,—

" A lady has called to see you."

" Who is she ?"

" I know not,—she has a permit from the Minister of State, to the Governor."

" Admit her."

He opened the door, a lady entered, closely veiled and clad in a long mantilla ; Hardigoth departed. She advanced quickly as I rose, threw off her disguise and stood before me, a young and beautiful woman,—her countenance was pale, and her eyes suffused with tears, then in trembling accents,—

" Forgive me, I pray you, this perhaps unseemly intrusion, but 'tis my sincere desire to serve you. I am the Duchess Allessandra, widow of the late Duke Basileos, one of the highest peers of this realm. I have long known of you and 'twas my earnest desire to see one whose courage and gallantry were the theme of praise from all. In company with the daughter of King Sharitol, with whom this kingdom is in amity,— I saw you at the festival of the Princess Suhlamia,—" her voice fell as she struggled to conceal her emotions,—

" O, scorn me not, I implore you, when I confess that from that hour, my heart was irrevocably yours. Associated as I have been from early youth with this court,—familiar with royal splendors,—surrounded by throngs of admirers who obey my slightest wish and would joyfully lay their hearts and fortunes at my feet, —their devotion finds no response. I am cold, haughty and indifferent to all,—despising flattery and adulation. You are the only one who ever awakened the sentiment of love in my proud heart. Day after day have I, in deepest sorrow, watched you unseen, through all the horrible injustice of that trial, and when the dreadful sentence was pronounced, my very soul was crushed in its own agony. You are in the hands of a merciless and bloody tyrant who stops at nothing to accomplish his atrocious designs. Aye,—a murderer,—whose hands are now reeking with the blood of my young and innocent brother, slain in a duel with the wretch who impugned his sister's honor, and was protected from my brother's vengeful steel by his armor,—"

" God in heaven !" I exclaimed,—" is it possible ? Had I known that, not even the pitiful pleading of his innocent daughter would have saved the ruffian from my sword."

For several moments she was almost overcome with emotion, then resumed,

" King Probitos and the Minister of State were devoted friends of my honored father, who ranked highest among the royal peers of this realm. Were the

King able, he would instantly revoke this atrocious sentence, but his mind now wanders in the delirium of his last illness. Diavojahr is now Regent and wields supreme power ;—he is inimical to the Minister and refuses all his appeals ;" then whispering in my ear,—

"Listen,—Eliff and I have determined on your rescue ;—our plans are secretly arranged ;—the next dark and stormy night will be the signal. A thousand of my retainers,—brave and faithful men, trained warriors, masked, will descend in air ships on these grounds, —will surround this prison,—the guards captured,—if the governor refuses to deliver the keys, the doors will be broken down ;—you will be taken to my palace,—the only safe place of refuge and concealed from all possible search until you can be safely conveyed to Mandal-Uttima."

At this moment the door opened and a female attendant closely veiled, entered.

"O, my lady,—" she hurriedly whispered,—"we must be gone ;—the governor fears to permit a longer interview,—if this should be known to the Regent,—" then quickly departed, closing the door.

"But if this plan should fail ?" I replied,—"your safety,—the Minister's,—the lives of your brave men ;— Diavojahr's vengeance,—"

"Eliff incurs no danger,—I alone take the hazard ;— the peril is mine, and as God in heaven hears me, gladly would I die to save you,—you, 'who are all the world to me :'—Farewell !"

The dauntless soul of this beautiful woman shone in her eyes as they glanced into mine, and a crimson blush mantled in her cheek as I knelt and kissed her hand.

"Farewell," she murmured,— "till we meet again," —replaced her veil and quickly departed from the cell.

"Now by the arrows of Cupid and the girdle of

Venus !" said I to myself, as hurriedly pacing around my cell, I strove to collect my scattered faculties. " This bloody drama is progressing with a vengeance ;—first act over ;—second act,—declaration of love, come and gone. Truly can I say with Macbeth, ' Two truths are told as happy prologues to the swelling act of the imperial theme.' The plot thickens,—what next ?—the elopement,—and I have got to face the irate husband. 'Tis my fate, and as Macbeth says, ' I must embrace the fate of that dark hour.'—I must screw my courage to the sticking place, and say with Hamlet,—'My fate cries out and makes each petty artery in this body as hardy as'—well, as every fellow's arteries ought to be, who undertakes to run away with another fellow's better half. But, hold,—I'm running ahead of my horse. This Duchess can't be the one ;—she's a widow and a magnificently beautiful one also ;—rank, power, wealth, everything. She would grace a throne, and what's better, loves me devotedly ;—but the married one will soon put in her superfluous presence on the stage, with fate to back her. What's to be done ? I have it,—Julius Cæsar says, ' Men, at some time, are masters of their fate.' Tennyson says, ' Man is man, and master of his fate,' and Lucifer says, ' What I will is fate.' All right, I'm ready, and when that designing worser half puts in her appearance I'll hold on to these prison bars like grim death and smile on her like Lucifer. But hold. Who knows what irresistible enticements, what arts, what persuasions, that sinful female may employ to seduce me ? The Oriental legend says that, Satan first yielded to the sinful enticements of a celestial beauty ;—any how, according to Milton, he had Sin for a partner in the form of a lovely creature half female and half serpent. The great progenitor of my race yielded to female persuasions,—King Solomon ditto,—and many a strong and wise man since. The devil's most irresistible temptations lie in lovely woman's eyes and smiles ;—I may yield and fall, as many a better man has fallen. Perhaps the best thing a fellow can do under such distressing circumstances is to kill himself ;—he saves his honor thereby and Cato says,—' It's better to die ten thousand deaths than wound my honor ;' quite an array of deaths it must be confessed, and it's very hard to make up one's mind which style to select. I'll confer with these essays on 'The Lawfulness of Suicide,' and 'The Easiest Way to Shuffle Off This Mortal Coil,'" so taking up the books I threw myself on my cot, plunged in *medias res ;*—read myself to sleep, while delightful visions of elopements, —pistols,—coffee,—knives,—halters and poisons, floated amid my dreams.

CHAPTER XLV.

LIFE OR DEATH.

> " I have already
> The bitter taste of death upon my lips;
> I feel the pressure of the heavy weight;
> But if a word could save me, and that word
> Were not the Truth ; nay, if it did but swerve
> A hair's breadth from the Truth, I would not say it."
> *Longfellow Christus,* Pt. iii.

The days passed on, during which I patiently awaited the hour of my rescue. The day of my execution was not made known to me. Prisoners of State never knew the hour of their doom. To a man of feeling this suspense is worse than death. During the Reign of Terror in France, the prisoners of La Force and the *Conciergérie* in. Paris, were daily conducted to the great hall, where the death list for the day, made out by the Assembly, was read off to them by the jailer or *gens d'armes*, and the standing joke being, "Come out and hear the *Evening Gazette ;*" the doors of their cells were chalk marked for the next morning. During those bloody days (which ended on the 9th Thermidor, 1794) when the Legislative Assembly declared the rights of man and swept away all nobility, peerage, hereditary distinctions, feudal *régime* and titles ;—when Republicans, Girondists and " the Mountain " sat facing each other in the great hall ;—when " Liberty, Equality, Fraternity, or Death " were the watch words ;—when every body addressed each other by the title of Citizen, or Citizeness ; when all the men wore the red Jacobin caps and fashion in female attire, for a wonder, ceased to sway the Parisian female heart.

In those days when the black shadow of the Guillotine enveloped all Paris,—when the " Terrible Five," sat in their judgment seats, judges, jurors, prosecutors, wearing their bloody hued caps,—when those mighty Autocrats of the Commune, Robespierre, Danton and Marat, —wielded their sceptres of life or death, and the streets of Paris, at midnight resounded with the crash of musketry, the roll of drums, the thunder of cannon, and the howls of the mob, " Death to the Aristocrats ;" —when tumbrils cushioned with straw, were the equipages of a Monarch and his Queen, nobles, court gallants, royal dames, scholars, scientists, poets, delicate ladies, fops, painted Jezebels, poor seamstresses, beggars, thieves and cut-throats, all alike,—all on one common level on the ride to death ;—those death carts at break of day slowly rumbling between ranks of bayonets

amid the howls and oaths of mobs, up to Saint Antoine,
up to the maw of the insatiate axe, whose measured
strokes spouted out royal and plebeian blood together on
the sawdust, and whirled their gory heads pellmell in
the basket. These bloody tragedies closed the downfall of a corrupt and effete monarchy, ninety and nine
years ago. Little did I dream that the downfall of an
infinitely mightier monarchy,—an infinitely more magnificent, beautiful, gay and luxurious capital,—compared
with which, Paris is but a village suburb,—would ere
long close, with far more awful scenes, on this Martian
world.

One night I was awakened by the deep tolling of a
bell. I sprang from my cot,—'twas the hour of execution. I looked from the bars of my window and in the
area far below, I saw one poor condemned prisoner, led
by the masked guards with torches, to the death room.

Day after day I patiently awaited the downfall of
this Pluto-Martian Bastile and my exit from the ruins.
I ardently hoped the weather might prove propitious,
and that Jupiter Pluvius would o'erspread the skies of
night with his dark cloud mantle and pour down his
most copious showers, embellished with liberal displays of thunder and lightning to celebrate the event.
The weather was quite warm, I oft scanned the skies
in search of any passing cloud that might hold the bow
of promise for me. I oft consulted my jailer as to bar-
ometrical affairs, high, low and average, but old Hardigoth reposed more faith in the indications furnished by
his joints, than by any weather glass, or weather bureau
probability predictions.

" My rheumatics are all right, and of course we're
having a dry spell. When my joints begin to stiffen
up, or growl, we'll have rain, surely."

I mentally hoped that the rheumatical weather indications might manifest themselves without serious inconvenience to the joints of my jailer.

One evening after taking a two hours' pull at my "constitutional," as Dickens calls it, jumping and thrashing around my cell after the style of the famous Baron Trench in his Prussian dungeon, to keep my joints limber and my muscles from getting stiff, I threw myself on my cot and began to read " Reflections in a Dungeon ;" suddenly a voice broke the silence,—

" You appear to be highly interested in your book."

I glanced around, and behind the bars of the adjoining cell, sat His Royal Highness, peering at me through his monocle, with his usual arrogant stare and sneering smile.

" O, yes,—" I replied with a leisurely yawn,—" enjoying and criticizing 'this excellent work on Ethics and Moral Philosophy, including a treatise on ' The Natural History of the Devil.' It describes Devils of all classes, species and varieties, moral, intellectual and physical, royal, noble, political and fashionable ;—Devils in the Church, the World and Society. According to the writer, who, being a Pluto-Martian, is of course quite competent to handle the subject, the horned and hoofed gentry swarm everywhere all around and within us, like flies around and inside a molasses cask. There must be something very attractive in this kingdom, to draw such immense emigrations from the bottomless pit. Furthermore, this Satanic essayist says,—and I quite agree with him on this point, it's always best to give the devil his due ; that, after all, he is a very much maligned personage, never quite so bad as he is painted, also, that; not a few very fair seeming, and eminently respectable individuals and ornaments of society, can quite take the shine out of him in his own tricks, circumvent him in his own game, and beat him in a bargain any day, which means, of course, whipping the devil around the stump. But in this chapter, ' On the conduct of Princes,' he makes the most outrageous charges I ever heard of. He accuses them of an utter want of truth, sincerity, honor and virtue. He says they are frivolous, mean, immoral dissolute, cruel, tyrannical, etc. Really, what sort of Princes has he come in contact, or associated with ? All the Princes in the World I come from, are without exception, perfect models of truth, honor and virtue, particularly the latter, and patterns of chivalry besides. Really, this writer is a most awful slanderer. Why don't you burn his books, cut off his right hand and banish him to Misery land for life ?"([1])

" I am not here to discuss morality and virtue," said he with a sneer.

" Of course not, I hadn't the slightest idea you were ; such subjects are too trivial and commonplace to engage the attention of Pluto-Martian Princes, whose boon companions are pimps, gamblers and swell-loafers."

" Another of your insults and I'll order the turnkeys to beat you with their bludgeons," replied he, his face distorted with rage.

" Go ahead ;—you and your turnkeys are a well-matched trio ; you look like old hands at the business."

He looked mad enough to bite my head off, but finally controlled himself. It was evident he was bent on getting something out of me that bludgeons would have interfered with.

" I have condescended to confer with you on business of the greatest importance to yourself."

" Really ; your condescension does me immense honor ; but why don't you come inside ? You'll certainly get your death of cold at that window. I heard

([1]) One of the islands on our Martian maps.

you took ill from your faint turn on the grass the other
day. You should take better care of your precious
health. I sincerely hope this proposed conference will
not quite exhaust your intellectual abilities. This
writer says that all intellectual exertions are highly
injurious to Princes, lordly aristocrats and swell fashionables, and whenever they are compelled to go
through so exhausting an ordeal, they should take frequent hypodermic injections of Cerebrine, extracted
from the brains of peacocks and turkey gobblers to
prevent brain fag. Whenever they have to fight with
anybody, they should take injections of Cardine,
extracted from the hearts of mice, to keep their
courage up. Whenever they get agitated, indisposed,
or out of sorts any way, they should be carefully
swathed in cotton batting, put to bed, medical special-
ists summoned, nurses, consulting doctors, all ready
for any serious complications that may arise ;—prayers
should be said in all the churches, half hour bulletins
should be issued, all about their heroic battle for life,
etc., to soothe the flustiferous anxiety and alarm that
agitates royaldom and flunkeydom, until the darlings
are medically pronounced out of danger and able to
take an airing."

I would have given five dollars for a good snap
photograph of His Royal Highness' face at this speech :
—it looked so much like the devil with the toothache.
For several seconds he could not speak from sheer
fury, finally he hissed out,—

"Your life or death hangs on the touch of my
finger."

"That's what our old Roman emperors used to say
about their thumbs, when they turned them up, or
down, in the gladiatorial shows. You seem to be a
sort of Martian Nero."

His Highness evidently did not quite comprehend the flattering compliment, and continued,

"Listen to what I have to say, prisoner, and make no comments."

"All right, I'll keep my comments till you've had your say;—provided it's not too tedious, otherwise I may take a nap in the mean time."

"As you are doubtless aware, I have formally dèmanded the hand of the Princess of Mandal-Uttima in marriage. My kinship to her family gives me a prior claim beyond that of any Prince, or person of royal blood, in this or any other kingdom. It is rumored that the Princess entertains toward you—" here his physiognomy expressed the most intense disdain,—"sentiments more tender than those of mere friendship and esteem. I have good reason to believe it to be true and consider it the only present obstacle to her acceptance of my hand and the consummation of my marriage with her. If she were convinced that you entertained no other sentiments than those of mere esteem or friendship for her, she would naturally feel piqued, as any woman would, and her very natural pride, awakened by your indifference, would prompt her to accept a matrimonial alliance with the Prince Regent of the most wealthy and powerful of Martian kingdoms."

"Your twaddle is getting tiresome," said I, yawning. "What are you driving at?"

"The question of your life or death."

"Already settled by your venal court, your perjured witnesses and your hireling jury."

"Your life will be spared on one condition."

"Name it."

"As follows. You will write a letter, signed with your signature to the Grand Duke and Prince of Mandal-Uttima, stating that, if the Princess Suhlamia will accept the hand of His Royal Highness, the Prince Regent of Sundora-Luzion, in marriage and sign the contract for the same in the presence of duly authorized witnesses, His Royal Highness will pardon and restore you to liberty. Furthermore, that you will marry a lady of high rank and great beauty in this kingdom, who entertains a devoted attachment for you, which is fully reciprocated by yourself. You will also state that, you have heard with deep regret the rumors afloat respecting the Princess Suhlamia's feelings toward yourself, and that, for your own part, you never did and never could, entertain toward her any other sentiments than respect and esteem ; also, after your marriage, you will become a resident of this kingdom and His Royal Highness will bestow upon you a peerage, great wealth and honors."

" Who is the lady ?"

" Her Grace, the Duchess Allessandra."

I could not refrain an involuntary start, but he did not perceive it.

" One of the most beautiful and accomplished ladies in this kingdom. Of high rank and immense wealth,—your marriage will be one of the most brilliant ;—you will possess a lovely bride,—a peerage—"

" And if I refuse your conditions ?"

" Your death follows."

" Then let it come. Sooner than stain my honor ;—sooner than utter so base a falsehood to further your infamous scheme,—I would die."

" Do you see these letters ?" holding up several which the marshal had permitted me to write during the trial, to my friends in Mandal-Uttima. " They never reached their destination, you see, they are opened."

"So you add the trade of a mail robber to your other honorable pursuits."

"They have all been examined by one of my most clever experts. Your handwriting and signature thoroughly studied and copied, so accurately that you yourself could hardly detect the copy from the originals," he replied with a cool smile.

"Forger also. What an ornament you would be among the select society at our Sing Sing!"

"How would you like to have my proposal, you so scornfully rejected, written out by my expert, signed with your copied signature and sent to your friends;— how do you fancy the Princess Suhlamia would-."

I sprang from the cot almost overwhelmed with horror.

"Wretch!—Coward!—Murderer!—Wearing coats of mail to protect your vile body, and electric batteries to paralyze your antagonists. I spared your worthless life at the intercession of your child, whose heartbroken mother you drove to madness and death. Sooner than allow my life to be purchased by your villainous plot;—sooner than see the hand of the Princess Suhlamia touched by so foul and loathsome a reptile as you, I'll dash my brains out against these walls."

"Ha! ha! ha!" he laughed,—"ravings of a lover deprived of his mistress. I'll have you chained,—I'll have my proposal all written out in your handwriting and signature, and sent to your friends; my expert shall write love letters in your handwriting and signature, addressed by you to the Duchess Allessandra, brim full of passionate love and devotion. I have in my possession letters from the Duchess. My expert shall master her handwriting, and write love letters, exactly in her style,—most ardent, gushing, filled with

undying love and devotion,—you understand, addressed
to you. Do you see this locket?"—holding up a beautiful miniature of the Duchess, set with brilliants,—
"I'll have this locket you have so ardently longed for,
you understand, enclosed in her letter to you. All
this sweet correspondence and mementoes, intercepted,
you understand, and placed in my hands. Do you see
this handkerchief?" holding up the one given me by
the Princess,—" I'll have my expert write a letter from
you to the Princess Suhlamia, expressing your regrets
that you can no longer keep her little memento and
therefore return it to her;—the handkerchief shall be
enclosed in that letter and all shall be despatched to
the Princess. Ha! ha! Fool! Are you so ignorant
of womankind as not to know that hell hath no fury
like a woman scorned? She'll despise you from the
bottom of her heart;—she'll accept my proposal at
once, and—"

" Out of my sight,—dog!—" I exclaimed,—"here;
—study the 'Natural History of the Devil,' if you
have brains enough to comprehend your teacher,—see
if you can't get up a better trick,"—and I hurled the
book full in his face. It flew strait through the bars
and struck him square on the nose; I was pleased to
see the blood spout.—" And here's a strong argument
on ' Ethics and Moral Philosophy,' "—hurling another
book,—" perhaps you'll profit by it."

The philosophical argument was heavier than the
Devil's tricks, and almost knocked him flat.

" Ho! there,"—sputtering and bawling through his
bloody handkerchief,—" Jagivoc !—Bolak !—Torinox !
The villain has assaulted me. Chain him, beat him
black and blue !"

There was a rattling of keys and drawing of bolts,

the door was flung open and three turnkeys, burly, villainous looking fellows, armed with manacles and bludgeons, rushed at me. I jumped up,—hit one fellow a kick in the stomach that doubled him up,—snatched his club,—dodged the other fellow's blow, —hit him a whack on the skull that knocked him flat, —hit the third fellow a clip on the jaw that sent him staggering out,—pitched the senseless ones out after him,—jerked the keys out of the door, slammed and locked it on the inside and strode to my cot.

"Good !" said I to myself. "This is a regular variety performance. The elopement was to come next to the love declaration, but Thaumatour has arranged a pleasant interlude without letting me know it beforehand. The Prince, it seems, was to be booked, and the turnkeys polished off, as a lively little by play between acts. Hope I'll have a few more of the same sort ; they make the play all the more spicy."

I glanced at the window ;—the Prince had disappeared. I felt quite disappointed.

"Gone to be treated for a sudden attack of epistaxis," said I. "Hope the rest of the performance will open shortly."

There was a shuffling of feet outside and a rattling of keys.

"Open the door," ordered several voices. I strode to the portal, club in hand.

"Private meeting of the club," said I, "executive session, terms of admission to outsiders are, knock down and drag out."

"Unlock it, or we'll break the door open," vociferated several voices.

"And the club will break your heads open."

There was a council of war for a few moments.

" He's a terrible fighter," muttered one.

" Ordinarily peaceable,—but when he's on the war path ;—look out," replied the club.

" He kicked Jagivoc's breath out of him," muttered another.

" He knocked three of Torinox's teeth out," growled one.

" Ready to knock several more out, and settle the dentist's bill in the bargain," replied the club.

" Bolak will have to be sent to the hospital with a broken head," whispered another.

" Can supply the doctors with a few more cases of the same sort."

" Lieutenant," said a voice.

" Is that you, Hardigoth ?"

" Yes,—open the door,—I pledge you my word, you shall not be harmed."

I turned the key, Hardigoth entered with a dozen guards, manacles in hand.

" Stand back in the hall, men," ordered he, and the guards departed.

" Lieutenant," said he, " I hate to do this thing, but I must obey the governor's orders."

Without a word I held out my hands ; he locked the manacles on my wrist and the gyves on my ankles connected with chains ; locked an iron hoop around my waist, connected with a chain to a heavy iron ring and staple in the stone floor near my cot ; the chain allowed me about six feet tramping room.

" It's His Royal Highness' orders to keep you chained day and night," said he.

" All right," said I.

> " Oft in the stilly night,
> While slumber's chains do bind me,

> Fond mem'ry 'll bring to light,
> The iron chains around me."

"It's a d—d shame, any how," muttered he.
"Not a bit, my dear Hardigoth."

> "Honor and shame from no condition rise ;
> Act well your part, there all the honor lies."

"The Prince, turnkeys and prisoner, acted their parts in the performance pretty well, didn't they?"

"First class,—it was a right lively little play, but you didn't finish up your part of the performance, as you ought to have done."

"What was that ?"

"Killed the big villain," whispering in my ear,—"I only wish you had finished him on the spot, with something heavier than the Devil's history, but the Devil is so sure of him, he's in no hurry for him. I am sorry for you from the bottom of my heart. You are a brave and gallant fellow, and it's a pity to see you cut off in your prime. I have led many a brave man from these cells to the scaffold of the executioner, but before I'll consent to lead you there, I'll throw up my office and fly this kingdom, which is as good as death, for if they catch me, as they probably will, it's solitary confinement for life." The tears stood in the old man's eyes as wringing my hand, he departed from the cell.

.　　.　　.　　.　　.　　.　　.

Time passed unheeded, as with my face bowed upon my hands, the full horror of my situation now came o'er me. Suddenly a letter thrown through the transom, fell fluttering to the floor. I picked it up, opened and read,—

" Copy of Article 19, Section 7, appertaining to criminals under sentence of death.—From Criminal Statutes
of the kingdom of Sundora-Luzion."

" Be it enacted that, assaults by condemned prisoners upon persons of royal dignity and station, with
intent to inflict bodily harm or injury, are adjudged to
the 4th Degree of High Treason and are punishable
with death by crucifixion, or burning, or both,—the selection of which is submitted to the discretion of the
royal person, or persons, so assaulted."

For a moment my blood turned cold ;—appended to
the article was the following note.

" His Royal Highness' compliments to Lieutenant
Hamilton, and has condescended to favor him with a
picture of this mode of execution above described and
which is now being performed in the death room on a
prisoner of State, convicted of the above offence. His
Royal Highness sincerely hopes that Lieutenant Hamilton may derive much pleasure from the same."

The note was in Diavojahr's hand writing.

Suddenly a bright light as from an immense mirror
gleamed through the bars of the inner cell, and there,
on the opposite wall was the figure of a naked man,
stretched on an iron cross and writhing in the agonies
of crucifixion, the gouts of blood dripping from the
nailed hands and feet. Beneath, was an open brazier
of flaming coals and the roasted flesh was shrivelling on
the limbs ;—horrible green adders were clinging around
his loins,—themselves tormented with the heat, and
sticking their fangs deep in the trembling flesh,—a vul-
ture was perched on the victim's head, whetting his beak
to peck the eyes out. The dying man turned his face
towards me,—his eyes upon me,—God in Heaven !—

That look !—with a cry of inexpressible horror I threw myself on the cot.

.   .   .   .

I do believe my good angel carried up my soul felt prayer to the Throne of Mercy, for with that vision of horror glaring in my face, I sank in a dreamless sleep and in the moment of my last lingering consciousness, methought a voice whispered softly in my ear—the voice of one far away—

" Courage.—Hope ;—trust in God."

———————◆———————

CHAPTER XLVI.

TOMMY TOPSAIL.

" Swiftly may the bark go
   O'er the sea foam :
Briskly may the breeze blow
   My sailor laddie home."

Old Song.

Seven long, weary days and nights I passed with that dreadful vision ever present in my mind. I had given up all hope of rescue. The cruelty of my captor did not descend to petty annoyances ; he knew full well they would pass unheeded, rightly deeming the contemplation of my horrible fate a sufficient torture. Hardigoth made his usual visits, always alone, the turnkeys were kept away from my cell. His words were few, often he never spoke ; knowing full well he could bring no hope nor consolation. I sometimes tried to school myself with the philosophical reflections of the old Greek and

Roman stoics, on death ; but was compelled to acknowledge, with Rochefoucauld that, while philosophy easily
triumphs over past and future evils, present evils
always triumph over philosophy. Sometimes I felt
inspired with that Byronic, but none the less gallant
courage, which can make even the most timid soul
sing—

> "There's a sigh to those who love me,
>   And a smile to those who hate;
> And whatever sky's above me,
>   Here's a heart for every fate."

But I soon found that, while any brave man can face
danger with courage, and contemplate the violent and
painful termination of his mortal career with fortitude
and manly resignation, still, the only balm to hurt
minds, when suffering "the slings and arrows of outrageous fortune," and waiting the approach of death,
it's to be found in that true Christian Philosophy which
is alone the anchor to the soul.

One night I was awakened by a gentle touch on my
shoulder. I glanced around ; by the feeble ray of the
prison lamp shining in the corridor, I saw a figure
bending over me and a voice whispered my name.

"Who's there ?" I exclaimed.

"Hush !" whispered the voice. "'Tis I, Lady Chumivant,—Elfine that was."

I sprang from the cot in astonishment ;—a tall form
was standing in the gloom near the door.

"Who is that man ?"

"Speak low,"—replied she, placing her finger on my
lip. "'Tis my husband, Lord Chumivant.—We have
come to release you from this prison."

I clasped her hand in astonishment and gratitude.

Lord Chumivant came forward. I could not distinguish his features in the dim light, but recognized his voice. He shook me warmly by the hand.

"Lieutenant Hamilton," said he with fervor, "my wife and I can never forget the great service you and Prince Altfoura rendered us on the Magic Isle. Had it not been for you and your brave eagles, those infernal alligator bats would surely have made a dinner off this newly wedded pair in the midst of their honeymoon, a not very pleasant winding up of our bridal trip. We wish now to return the compliment ; my little wife has got up a plan, into which I enter heart and soul, for your release, and I assure you she never yet failed in anything she undertook. We'll have you out of this dungeon in less than sixty minutes in spite of my sweet coz Diavojahr and all his turnkeys. The precious rascal ! It's a pity you had not smashed him effectually with that solid and forcible treatise on Ethics and Moral Philosophy."

"The cowardly wretch," exclaimed Lady Chumivant with indignation. "His insult and attack upon you, Lieutenant, at the Minister's Palace ; his coat of mail and electric battery ;—the farce of your trial and condemnation. Except among his own favorites and his corrupt court, he is universally despised by every one in his kingdom."

"And now," continued Lord Chumivant, "time presses and what is to be done, must be quickly. You've heard the news ?"

"No," I replied.

"Our good and long suffering King is dead,—Diavojahr is at the palace ; he is now virtually emperor and wields supreme power ; his coronation will take place immediately after the obsequies of his father. He is known to be inimical to our Minister Eliff, who will resign,—he will dismiss the cabinet and appoint his own favorites."

" Heaven help this unfortunate kingdom," said I.

" And so say I ; under Eliff's power all went well ; he stood between the haughty and tyrannous nobility and an oppressed people, but now the outlook is terrible. Diavojahr is one of the most vicious, depraved and cruel of men. Under his *régime* and that of his licentious court, universal corruption of manners will prevail, increased taxation, misrule and tyranny will hold sway, rebellion and bloodshed will arise, which will end, either in his dethronement, or the destruction of the kingdom.

I briefly related Diavojahr's plot to secure the hand of the Princess Suhlamia by means of the forged proposal, letters, etc.; my interview with the Duchess Allessandra, without alluding to her confession, nor her plan to effect my rescue.

" Her Grace occupies an eminent station in the ranks of our nobility," said he, " she is one of the most noble hearted and generous, as well as most beautiful woman in our kingdom. She and Diavojahr's late wife were devoted friends, exchanged miniatures, letters, etc. That's the way he obtained her's. She has done everything in her power to secure your release, and had the King survived, would have effected it. By Diavojahr's orders, the death watch was kept on you in the adjoining cell and her visit was immediately reported to him, but he has gained nothing by it, as the watch could not hear your conversation ; she is his sworn enemy, and he stands in fear of her influence ; many of the more powerful and better class of our nobility, are enlisted on her side."

I breathed freely ;—the plot to secure my release was not discovered.

"Our plan is all arranged ; my rank and kinship to Diavojahr give me the privilege to visit condemned prisoners. Hardigoth is under great obligations to me. I once saved his life from Diavojahr's violence and secured his appointment here. He will help me at the risk of his life,—has given me the keys and will be conveniently absent until the proper time. The death watch has been dismissed for the night. My wife and I gave a little banquet to the guards and turnkeys this evening and plied the latter liberally with wine, dosed with a sleeping potion."

"I'll take a peep at them," said she, then stepped to the door, looked out and tripped back.

"The potion has worked admirably ; they are sound asleep."

"And as it would hardly be deemed proper for Lady Chumivant to visit condemned prisoners in *propria personæ*, in order to carry out our plan, she has assumed disguise and appears as my young sailor nephew, a scape-grace of a Midshipman just returned from a long sea voyage," and he turned up the light.

My Lady Chumivant threw off her cloak and to my astonishment was completely transformed into a hand-some sailor lad, a jaunty cap cocked one side her pretty head, covered with its glossy black curls, swaggering up to me in regular sailor style, her eyes dancing with fun.

"How are ye, shipmate ? Glad to see ye, my heartie. Shiver my jib, but you're a right trim looking chap. I'll introduce myself,—my name is Tommy Topsail ;— I'm a Middy and a regular out and outer. This old chap is my Uncle Chummy. D'ye understand ?"

"Perfectly," I replied.

"All right, Lieutenant. We are to get up a little serio-comedy entitled,—' How to Get Out of Jail,—in

one act, and with four *dramatis personæ*. Lord Chumi·
vant assumes the character of Lieutenant Hamilton ; the
Lieutenant assumes that of his Lordship ; I assume that
of his nephew, Tommy Topsail.   When we get outside
and appear before the audience, I'll prompt you what to
say ; you must play your *rôle* and I'll play mine.   You
must call me Tommy, and I'll call you Uncle Chummy,
Governor, or old fogy, as occasion requires."

"We will now dress for the performance," said his
Lordship.

"And as we have but one dressing room in common,
modesty dictates that I close my eyes to this part of the
performance ; in the mean time I request you gentlemen
to hurry up and get through with the toilette business
soon as possible," and throwing her cloak over her
head she took a seat in the corner.   His Lordship drew
out a key, unlocked my manacles, hoop and chains ; we
quickly changed costumes, he putting on my prison
suit, and I, his rich dress ; as we were about the same
size and height, the exchanges fitted tolerably well.

"All's ready, Tommy," said his Lordship.   "Bring
on your beautifiers."

Tommy drew from the pocket of his cloak a little box
of paints, brushes, bottle of hair dye and a wig of black
hair, then with the skill of an artist, painted my face,
neck and hands in genuine Pluto-Martian colors, dyed
my eyebrows and moustaches black, put the wig on my
head, completely concealing the prison cut of my hair,
then,—

"Smash my dead lights ! if I haven't got a twin pair
of Uncle Chummys here !"

I looked at myself in the glass and was compelled to
admit that I was twin No. 2.   Tommy now painted his
Lordship's countenance in the Lieutenant's colors and

dyed his hair, moustaches and eyebrows a rich chest-
nut.

"Capital!" said he. "I am transformed into the
Lieutenant; now clap on the irons and tie me to the
cot."

We put on the manacles and fastened him hand and
foot to the cot, with a rope she had brought.

"Now the gag, so I can't call for help."

Tommy tied a handkerchief over his mouth, then
rolled up my uniform in a bundle, threw on his sailor's
hat and cloak. I donned his lordship's hat and boots.

"Come here, Scamp," said she, and a diminutive, but
exceedingly frisky, specimen of a Pluto-Martian terrier,
capered out from the corner. His appearance would
have excited immense enthusiasm among our fair
fashionables who affect such pets. His grey hair was
upright and stiff as wire, his abbreviated caudal append-
age was like a spike and had only two movements, up
and down; his ears were cropped *comme il faut ;* he could
jump like a kangaroo, run backwards, sidewise or forwards with equal facility, and his diabolical physiognomy, would have made any Terrestrial bull terrier,
skye, pug, or poodle, expire in convulsions of horror.

"Now, you Scamp," said she, shaking her finger at
him, "when your cue comes, be sure you don't make
mistakes; if you do, look out !"

"Yep! Yep! Yep!" the Scamp replied, evidently
fully comprehending the importance of the *rôle*
assigned him.

"Scamp's part in the play is a highly prominent one,"
said she.

"Come, be off," puffed Lord Chumivant through the
gag.

"All right, Chummy," said she, kissing him on the

cheek and taking the keys, "it's a regular elopement, you understand."

The prediction of Thaumatour was fulfilled.

"What !" I exclaimed, "an elopement ! I don't exactly understand this performance. What's his lordship going to do about it ?" and dim visions of the pistols, coffee, etc., began to float around.

" Pooh !" he puffed through the gag. " Can't you see ? I lay quiet here till the jailer comes in to-morrow morning. You and I have had a fight. You knocked me down on the first round, made me change clothes, painted and dyed me, and eloped with my wife to parts unknown. The hue and cry will be raised, Diavojahr will fully sympathize with the wronged and injured husband, order up the police air ships, and scour the kingdom. In the meantime you'll be safe with your friends in Mandal-Uttima. When all's over, as my wife can't come back here, of course I'll go there, if they'll receive me."

" Come, by all means," I replied, warmly pressing his hand. " The Duke and Prince will never forget this noble act of yourself and lady."

" Be off, quick !" he replied. " Farewell, little wife, till we meet again."

Lady Chumivant kissed and embraced her lord affectionately ; pinned on the lapel of his coat a paper which she had just written, put the bundle under her arm, called Scamp, we passed out and locked the door ; on the paper was written :

" DEAREST HUZZY-BUNDY :—Your darling wife has concluded to try conclusions with the U. S. Lieutenant, who enters heart and soul in the eloping business. Variety is the spice of love, as well as of life. You are at liberty to try another matrimonial experiment.

Regards to dear cousin Diavojahr ; tell him I wish him
joy of his matrimonial speculation. Remind him also
that, there's many a slip between the cup and the lip
and the best laid schemes of mice and men gang aft
aglee."

" P. S.   Think tenderly of me, Chummy, as ' One who
loved not wisely, but too well ;' and you can sing
' Thou art gone from my gaze, like a beautiful dream,'
or ' Fly away, pretty moth,' as you please. Meanwhile
I'll sing ' Farewell ; farewell, and if forever ; still forever, fare thee well.'

> " Your loving wife (that was),
>
> > " ELFIE."

CHAPTER XLVII.

AMATEUR THEATRICALS.

> " All the world's a stage,
> And all the men and women merely players ;
> They have their exits and their entrances."
> *As You Like it*, Act II., Sc. 7.

" Actors, supes, walkers, scene shifters, take your
positions ; mind your cues ; the curtain's up, highly
critical and appreciative audience ; play opens, ' How
to Get Out of Jail,' act first, scene first," ordered
Tommy Topsail as we stalked into the hall, the mighty
Scamp leading the van.

Four turnkeys, in their chairs, were snoring in concert. We passed through the corridors receiving the
silent salutations of the guards. By Tommy's instruc-

tions I imitated the voice and swagger of his lordship.
We reached the great entrance hall which was brightly
lighted, and here the serio-comedy began. It was
filled with prison guards and officers, many of whom
were acquainted with his lordship. They were discussing the events of the day, the death of the King, prospect of a new cabinet, the assault of the prisoner on
the Prince and turnkeys, and it was generally conceded
that the Terrestrial barbarian was the most terrible
specimen of a miscellaneous fighter ever seen or heard
of. As we neared the throng, my brave little companion showed herself equal to the *rôle* she had assumed
and sustained it with immense *éclat*. She threw in her
sailor boy swagger, shaking hands with them all
around.

"Hello there ! You Cops, how are ye ? Split my
tops'l, but you're a solemn looking crew. Been to a
funeral ? Afore I'd be a jail bird's cop, I'd be the
bird. Howsomever, 'every man to his trade ;' as the
hangman says, 'Some folks have to be pulled into this
world and some pulled out, and somebody has to do the
job for 'em ; one trade is good as another.' I'm a sailor
boy ; Tommy Topsail's my name and a tip-top Middy
in the bargain. Nevvy to Lord Chumivant here. Uncle
Chummy, I calls him, for short ; tired of horse tack
and sea biscuit aboard ship. The old Cap,—blast his
eyes ! wouldn't give me a furlough, so I kicked up a row,
knocked the boatswain into a cocked hat, smashed the
coxswain's head lights, pitched the cook down the hold,
stuffed the cabin boy in the stove pipe, jumped overboard, swam ten miles and here I am. Have took
Uncle Chummy under my wing, been around your
corporation boarding house here, seen all the chaps
you're going to string up to the yard arm. We're on a
first class lark, don't you see ? Bound to paint this

town red as a boiled lobster afore morning,—blast me eyes if we aren't." Then putting his arms akimbo he dashed off into a tip-top sailor's hornpipe, singing at the top of his voice,—

> " I'm here, or there, a jolly dog,
> My land to see, I'm all agog ;
> To kiss the girls whene'er I can,
> Or fight the foreign midshipman.

> " When I'm ashore I heave the log,
> To sing, or dance or drink the grog ;
> To kiss or fight where'er I can,
> For I'm a jovial midshipman.

> " A frisky, airy midshipman,
> I'll sing or dance, or tip the can,
> I'll kiss the girls where'er I can,
> For I'm a jovial midshipman."

The song was received with immense applause. Tommy then dashed off into such a whirlwind of cancanesque pirouettes, leaps, millwheel involutions and acrobatic evolutions as would have made the whole *corps de ballet* of the French *théâtre comique* expire with envy and despair. Officers and guards shook their sides with roars of laughter. We leisurely sauntered toward the great doors of the prison. Suddenly three enormous and ferocious dogs, bigger than any Russian bear hounds or great Danes I ever saw, barred our exit. Their keen scent had detected the smell of my cast off prison dress and uniform. One of them had often accompanied the jailer on his visits to my cell, recognized me at once, and manifested his decided disapproval of the *rôle* I was playing. He drew his cropped ears back, showing his ugly fangs and utterings angry growls, while his companions snuffled

and snorted around my legs like blood hounds of the
old slave hunting days.

"Blast these infernal brutes!" exclaimed Tommy.
"Hello, here. Scamp.—Rats! Rats! Rats!"

Scamp took his cue and the way he marched into the
ratting business was a terror. It was not rodents he
was after, but canines. "Yowp! yowp! yowp!" was
the battle cry. He jumped and skipped, danced and
whirled, forwards, backwards, sideways, and all other
ways; yelling and snarling like a genuine little hell
hound, his physiognomy corkscrewed up into a diabolical conglomeration of teeth, eyes, ears, and wrinkles,
as would have frightened Beelzebub himself. He bit,
snapped and nipped the tails, noses and toes of the
astounded brutes at such a terrible rate they turned
tail and beat a hasty retreat, amid roars of laughter
from the guards, and we passed on, the mighty Scamp
receiving the enthusiastic cheers of the crowd. The
officers with obsequious obeisance, opened the great
prison doors, and Hardigoth met us at the threshold,—

"My dear Lord Chumivant," queried he in a tone of
deep commiseration, "pray inform me, what is the
spiritual condition of our unfortunate prisoner?"

"My dear Hardigoth," I replied, "he appears to be
in a highly resigned state of mind;—indeed quite cheerful, and anxious to take his final departure to other
scenes than these."

"I am truly delighted to hear it," Hardigoth replied,
bowing very low, looking very solemn, and winking
slily at me with his left eye. I returned the salutation
with due solemnity, and Tommy winked at him with
his right eye. Hardigoth entered and the doors were
shut.

We swiftly passed the portico, descended the granite
steps and paused on the green sward. Behind us tow-

ered the massive prison walls, the night breeze rustled
amid the trees, and the glittering stars shone bright.
Elfine blew a low whistle and a man stepped out from
the foliage.

"Captain Navikoff?" said she.

A stout built and honest looking old Pluto-Martian
officer clad in uniform, came forward.

"Your ladyship's chariot is in waiting," said he.

We passed through the trees to an open glade where
the chariot was in readiness with its crew. Elfine took
Scamp in her arms ; we ascended the deck, wrapped
ourselves in our cloaks and took seat upon the divan.

"Home," said she, "and quickly."

The chariot rose above the trees, flew swiftly over
the city to his lordship's *château* several miles distant,
and descended to the grounds in a grove. We dismounted and entered a pretty little pavilion embowered
with flowers and near which a fountain was playing.

"Captain," said she, "get the air ship in readiness
immediately. His lordship is on an important mission
to the Capital of Mandal-Uttima."

"How long will it take to reach there ?" I asked, with
my cloak muffled around my face and imitating the
voice of Lord Chumivant.

"It's fifteen hundred miles distant, your Lordship. If
the wind is fair we can reach it by 9 o'c. to-morrow
morning ;" replied the captain.

The clock from the tower of the *château* now chimed
the midnight hour.

"Spare no speed," said I.   "I have an audience with
Duke Athalton in relation to the prisoner."

"In my humble opinion, your lordship, he has been
very unfairly treated."

"Yes, but it will surprise many to know that he is
out."

" Is it possible? I'm glad to hear that, Prince Dia-vojahr's heart has opened at last."

"As to his heart, I cannot vouch, but as to his prison doors, I can."

" Yep! Yep! Yep!" resounded from Elfine's cloak, corroborating my statement, and as the Captain left to get the ship ready, the Scamp stuck his beautiful head out and winked one eye at me.

"O, you sweet, precious, lovely darling!" exclaimed Elfine gushingly, kissing the dear little ferrety eyes and dear little cold nose.

I frankly confess this was the first time in my life that I ever looked with any complacency upon the feminine caresses so often bestowed upon these pets, but I was compelled to admit that, this canine specimen, had hon-estly earned the meed of praise and was certainly the greatest of all scamps.

The glittering domes and turrets of the *château* shone under the bright moonlight.

"Yonder is my happy home," said Elfine ; " I have arranged all the rooms so prettily. I wish you could see them. My lord is good and kind to me,—my house-hold are honest and faithful ; they all love me, and we are so happy there, and now I must leave them all per-haps forever, for I can never return here again," and she burst into tears.

" Rest assured, my dear lady," I replied, " that in the kingdom where we go, you and your husband will meet warm friends and you shall have a new and beautiful home."

A pretty snow white pigeon fluttered down from the trees, and softly cooing, lit on her shoulder.

" 'Tis my dear Columba," she murmured, holding it to her bosom, then plucking a few flowers. " These are the only mementoes I can take with me !"

Captain Navikoff now came forward.

"The ship is in readiness," said he.

Elfine wafted a kiss to the glittering towers of the *château*, and in tones of deep sadness,—

"Dear, dear home ; where I have passed so many happy hours. Farewell, I shall never see thee more."

We hurried from the pavilion and mounted the ship. The crew were at their posts, the signal was given and she rose in graceful circles to an immense height in the air ; we descended to the cabin ; Captain Navikoff took his bearings ; the ship unfurled her mighty wings and flew to the north with the speed of the whirlwind.

"Out of the tiger's den at last ; and you are free. Thank God !" murmured Elfine, as with a faint sigh she sank upon the divan. Her nerves had given way under the terrible strain, and as her beautiful face was upturned to mine, her dark fringed lashes shading her pale cheek, the curls of rich glossy hair flowing down her neck, 'twas with feelings of deepest gratitude that I pressed my lips to the brow of the brave little lady who had sacrificed her home and risked her life for me.[1]

[1] In this kingdom, the punishment of those who connive at the escape of prisoners of State is frightful; they are condemned to death under terrible tortures.

CHAPTER XLVIII.

THE ELOPEMENT.

"You shall hear I am run away :—know it before the report
come. If there be breadth enough in the world, I will hold a
long distance."   *All's Well*, Act III., Sc. i.

By the grey of morning we had made eight hundred
miles ; had crossed Sundora continent and were coursing over Vodraga ocean whose waves rolled high. The
equatorial group of islands came in view, on reaching
which we should be within the sea-board jurisdiction of
Mandal-Uttima. The machinery being somewhat out
of order from the high speed, we descended to a quiet
little cove on the shore of a small uninhabited island
for repairs, which delayed us two hours. We then
resumed our journey. The sun was rising in the east,
shedding his glories of light and color over the sea ;
Elfine, who was seated near one of the cabin windows,
suddenly uttered an exclamation. I hastened to her
side.

"Look !—Look !—" said she.

I looked through the spy-glass. Far to the south,
and just rising above the horizon, a long line of air
ships appeared flying to and fro, over the waters in
various directions.

"They are the government air cruisers," she hurriedly
whispered, "the swiftest ships in the kingdom and
manned with government officers ; our flight has been
discovered ; they will arrest us. Great God ! what is
to be done ?"

I glanced through the bow-window and recognized

the Magic Isle among the group ahead.   It was fifty miles distant.

"If we can reach that island," I replied, " we are safe. Pedro will conceal us.   Are the Captain and crew of this ship to be trusted ?"

"They are honest, faithful and devotedly attached to my lord and me."

"Call the Captain, and draw the window curtains ; it's daylight and he may recognize that I am not the genuine Lord Chumivant."

Elfine drew the curtains ; I muffled my face in the cloak and threw myself on the divan.   Captain Navikoff entered.

"I have just discovered the government cruisers," said he, " they are after us, probably with some import- ant message for your Lordship."

"Yes ;" I replied, "and a different sort of message from what you fancy.   The fact is, I've had the bad luck to incur the displeasure of my royal cousin.   He is blessed with a very uncertain temper and I thought best to make myself previously and conspicuously scarce till it blows over and he gets in good humor, and the devil only knows when that will be.   My sweet coz is after me with a sharp stick and if those infernal cruisers overhaul us, off go your heads, for complicity in this lit- tle elopement.   Now, Captain, will you stand by me ?"

"Through thick and thin ;" he replied with a hearty grasp of the hand.

"Call the boys," said I.

The crew entered the cabin.   I told my story, and they swore by all that was holy, " they'd face Old Nick himself for his lordship ;—d—n their eyes if they wouldn't."   The cruisers were now rapidly approach- ing, having discovered us.

"Captain," said I, " fly to the Magic Isle, swift as you

can ; if we reach it in time, we can hide the ship in the jungles."

"All right," he replied, then to the crew, "fly low, and the cruisers can't see us so easily."

The ship descended and sped over the crests of the high rolling waves like a sea skimmer, the spray whirling around us in showers. In half an hour we reached the island, flew over the long coral reefs and rugged precipices, coursed over the forests and swamps, passed by the great volcano spouting its columns of flame and smoke amid clouds of sulphurous vapors. Reaching the interior we cautiously lowered the ship in a deep jungle, filled with tall weeds and grass, which concealed her from view. We dismounted and pushed our way through the underbrush till we emerged into the open glade. In the centre stood the fountain of youth, its spouting columns and falling showers glittering like gold under the morning sun. To my great joy, I saw Pedro and his sons working in the garden ; telling the Captain and crew to remain behind, I took Elfine's hand and followed by Scamp, we hurried across the glade toward them ; Pedro discovered us.

"Hello ! boys, here comes the cousin of that devil Diavojahr,—his crew are somewhere around, call up the dogs."

The boys whistled and four huge dogs, bigger and fiercer than even the prison hounds, rushed out from behind the house, bow-wowing and ramping as only such canines can.

"Yowp ! Yowp ! Yowp !" remarked Scamp, rushing forward like a small cyclone with a tornado attachment. The monsters paused, lowered their noses and their tails began to wag dubiously.

"Good morning, Pedro," said I, "how are you ?

You had better call off your big towzers, unless you
want Scamp to eat them up."

"Yep!" emphatically replied the Scamp, who had
not yet taken breakfast, and his jaws opened like a
small sized bear trap.

"Clear out o' here, you kin to the devil's own," roared
Pedro.

"O, I'm in no hurry to go, my venerable friend;
have come to make you an early morning call; besides
I'm not the kin you refer to."

Pedro joyfully recognized me; I told the whole story
and introduced my lady Chumivant, alias Tommy.

"Heigho! an elopement. Really, Lieutenant, I had
no idea you were such a gay Lothario. However, all's
fair in love, as well as war," said he.

"It was I who took the initiative;" said my lady.

"O, I see. A woman's rights movement."

"Certainly, we ladies generally take the lead in all
charitable and benevolent enterprises."

The cruises were swiftly approaching.

"Now for a game of hide and seek," said he. "Quick.
Call your Captain and crew."

Captain Navikoff and the men came out from the
trees, we hurried to the house. Pedro lit a lamp, we
descended to the cellar, its walls and floors were composed of granite slabs. He went to a corner, put his
finger through a little hole in the floor, pressed a concealed spring and one of the great slabs in the wall
slowly revolved on its hinges like a door, disclosing a
dark vault. We entered, Pedro lit a small taper hanging from the ceiling, the vault was filled with casks
arranged in tiers.

"This is the private vault where our choicest collec-
tions of the healing waters are stored for shipment to
the palace," said he. "You are safe here; keep quiet,

utter no sound till I release you," then taking the lamp he passed out and closed the rocky door.

As good luck would have it, Scamp was accidentally left outside. After scratching and whining at the door for a while, he squatted down quietly in front of it.

In a few moments three of the cruisers reached the island and landed on the glade. The officers debarked. The deputy marshal called Pedro, who was working in the garden with his sons ; they laid down their tools and came forward.

" Hello !—Old man. Have you seen any air ship around here ?"

" No ;" he replied, which was the fact.

" One was seen flying over the waves, and disappeared among these trees a little while ago."

" Never saw her,—trees pretty thick around here,— perhaps she got smashed. Who are you ? What are you after ?"

" Government officers from Sundora. I am the chief ; we are in search of an escaped prisoner,—broke jail."

" He must be a pretty cunning old fox to get outside one of your prisons."

" And that is not the worst of it,—he's run off with a nobleman's better half in the bargain."

" Whew !—Worser half, I should say. Happy riddance. I should think his lordship would dance on his head for joy. I didn't know you had such queer goings on in your kingdom. When you catch the precious pair, pack 'em off to Storm land and when they get tired of each other they can storm away to their heart's content."

" We must search this island."

" Have you a permit from my government ?"

" No,—had no time to get one."

" Then you're trespassing here, you've no right.

" But I'll take it nevertheless."

"O, yes, that's the style with you Pluto-Martians; might makes right. Go ahead,—hope you'll find 'em, —they're probably billing and cooing in the bushes," and Pedro resumed his grubbing.

The marshal gave his orders ; the officers dispersed in all directions, diligently searching the neighboring woods, swamps, etc. Other ships came up and their crews were detailed to other parts of the island among the forests, jungles and precipices.

"Better advise your boys to steer clear of the volcano, unless they wish to be smothered in sulphur or toasted in lava," suggested Pedro.

"We must search your house," said the marshal.

"All right,—shall be most happy to aid you,—welcome to my humble domicile," and Pedro led the way. Every where and every thing was searched, high and low, rooms, cupboards, trunks, beds. 'Twas like the hunt of Don Alfonso after Don Juan, but the gay Lothario failed to materialize. They finally descended to the cellar and began pounding on the walls with hammers to discover any concealed opening ; suddenly a tremendous blow sounded on the stone door, Scamp began to scratch and whine, the marshal recognized him.

"The devil !" he exclaimed. "Why, that's the whelp that belongs to the woman who ran off with the prisoner. I've seen him often, he's the ugliest cur in our kingdom."

"Yep !" ejaculated Scamp corroboratively.

"How did he ever get here ?"

"Perhaps she dropped him from the air ship you saw flying over the trees," replied Pedro.

"Then they must be around here somewheres."

Our hearts stood in our mouths. It is needless to add that I mentally anathematized that cursed terrier from the bottom of my heart.

" Squee !—Squee !—Squee !" squeaked Tommy Topsail in exact imitation of a rat.

" O, it's rats he's after ;" yawned Pedro.

" Yep ! yep ! yep !" replied Scamp.

" Rats ! Rats !"—bawled Pedro, clapping his hands.
" Sick 'em, sick 'em, you little devil."

" Squee ! Squee !"—echoed from behind the door.
At this moment one of the big dogs, aroused by his
master's voice, came tearing down the cellar.

" Yowp ! Yowp ! Yowp !" vociferated Scamp, flying
strait at him.

" Bow—wow—wow !   Bow ! wow ! wow !"—thundered the big fellow in tones that almost lifted the
house off its foundations.

" Hark !" said Pedro, clapping his hand to his ear.
" Didn't you hear the rat squeak ?"

" Squeak !" growled the officer.   " Good God ! sir.
The bark of your dog is enough to wake the dead and
make the grave stones howl !   Come, boys, let's get out
of here.   I'm not on a rat hunt," and the whole party
lumbered up the staircase.

We drew a long breath of relief.

" Lieutenant," whispered Elfine in my ear, " you'll
admit that rats are sometimes useful."

" They are at a premium, on this occasion, at all
events," I replied.

" Officer," queried Pedro as they passed out from the
house, " who is the fellow you say broke jail and ran
off with a nobleman's wife ?"

" A terrible white barbarian from the planet Earth,"
he replied.

" He must be pretty hard up for a wife to come all
the way here after one.   Women must be scarce on
that planet."

" Perhaps he has had the mitten so often that he

wants to try his luck on other planetary feminine productions, or perhaps he's an escaped bigamist,—who
knows ?" replied the marshal.

" Perhaps he's a chronic destroyer of domestic bliss,"
remarked Pedro.

" Why didn't he go to Venus ? The women are all
Venuses, and pretty free and easy, too, I'm told," said
the marshal.

" Or to Mercury ; the women are slippery as quicksilver there ; run off whenever they can get a chance,"
said Pedro.

After several hours, the searching party returned
covered with dust, mud, clothes torn, faces and hands
scratched with thorns and brambles, bitten and stung
by insects. They dolefully recounted their hairbreadth
escapes from the monsters and reptiles of the swamps,
the bats and feathered Gorgons of the caverns and
forests. They had searched everywhere with a patience
and persistence that would have aroused the admiration of the Russian Nihilist detectives, the Paris police,
Pinkerton boys, Scotland Yard deacons and the U. S.
Secret Service combined ; but the great mistake they
made, was, they overdid the business, searched every
place but the right place. The marshal swore at them
roundly, called them a set of asses and ordered them to
go over the ground again, and that was all the satisfaction they got.

In the mean time as the hours dragged wearily on,
we were in a state of mind better imagined than described. Late in the afternoon the searching parties
returned completely fagged out and disgruntled.
Other cruisers coming up, the marshal ordered them
off to search the other islands, and announced his
intention to remain over night. Pedro treated him and
his party courteously, offering them draughts of the

healing water, which, combined with the wine they had drunk, made them quite merry. He dilated largely on the wonders and beauties of the cavern beneath the fountain, and they expressed a desire to visit them, so he unlocked the great door, and the whole party, headed by Pedro's eldest son torch in hand, descended the staircase. Pedro quietly closed and locked the door.

"Good!" chuckled he, "safely stowed; run, my boy, and let the other prisoners out."

The boy ran to the house, rushed down the cellar, turned the key and let us out.

"Where are the police?" whispered Tommy.

"Pap's got 'em locked up in the steam box," giggled the lad. "Goin' for to cook 'em."

We rushed up the staircase to the glade.

"Caged," said Pedro with a grin.

We all congratulated him on his wonderful *finesse*, and Tommy celebrated the event with a vigorous hornpipe.

"Haste! Go and get your air ship," said Pedro, and the Captain and crew ran to the jungle. We sauntered over the glade for a while; finally a loud pounding and smothered voices were heard behind the iron door.

"Now, we'll have some fun," said Pedro.

"Hello! there, old fellow;" bawled the marshal.

"Well, gentlemen;" replied Pedro, "what do you wish?"

"Let us out."

"Have you seen all you wish to see?"

"Seen? Who the devil can see any thing in this hole, the torch gone out.—Open the door."

"That's what I'm trying to do," twisting the key in all directions but the right one.

"What's the matter with the door?" bawled the marshal.

"It won't open ;—stuck fast ;"—tugging at the key.

"What the devil did you shut it for?"

"Have to shut it to keep the rats from running out ; the cavern is full of 'em," replied Pedro's boy.

"I've turned on the steam a little," whispered Pedro.

"But your son?" queried Elfine.

"O, he's used to it."

"Confound you ; why don't you open this infernal door?" roared the marshal, "we're getting steamed alive here."

"The electricity is beginning to fly around. Our hair is standing on end,"—cried several.

"Steam baths and electricity cure all the ills flesh is heir to," enunciated Pedro. "You'll come out new men."

"Open ;—open,—for God's sake!" roared the whole crowd, *una voce*.

"Shall have to break it down, 'twill take an hour, perhaps, to do it. You'll have to stand it out as best you can."

"But we shall all be boiled or electrocuted to death," groaned the crowd.

"Pap ; shall I get the hammers and wedges?" queried the young one.

"Yes, sonny, but you needn't be in a hurry about it."

The hammers and wedges were finally brought and Pedro and son began to pound at the door like a pair of professional safe burglars.

The air ship now came sailing over the trees and lighted on the sward.

"Get aboard and be off," said Pedro. "You've got six hundred miles to travel. It's now 5 o'c. and if you

make good speed you'll get to the palace in time for a
late supper. I'll go on with my hydropathic and elec-
tropathic treatment, till you get well out of sight, then
I'll turn the key the right way, and let 'em out."

We hurried aboard ; the ship rose from the sward,
spread her wings and flew over the forests and precipices toward the sea. I retired to the rear cabin ; by
the aid of a chemical wash, removed my disguise and
resumed my uniform, and as it was not prudent to
appear before the Captain and crew in *propria personæ*
at present, I entered an alcove, while my lady took her
seat near a window in the forward cabin.

CHAPTER XLIX.

RIDE FOR LIFE.

" Word was brought to the Danish King,
            (Hurry !)
    That the love of his heart lay suffering,
    And pined for the comfort his voice would bring ;.
        (O, ride as though you were flying !)"
        King of Denmark's Ride.—CAROLINE NORTON.

Swifter than arrow from the Tartar's bow, or eagle
mounted on the winged gales, we flew over Vodraga
ocean and the southern part of Mandal-Uttima. By 7
o'c. we had flown five hundred miles, and were skirting
one of the great mountain ranges traversing the continent, their snow clad peaks glittering like polished
marble. The day was declining and the evening shades
drew near. The sky became overcast with clouds
announcing a gathering storm. Captain Navikoff,
stationed at the dome, called out,—

" Air ship ahead !"

I looked out and saw a government cruiser approaching at full speed.

"Lay to, and hail her," said I.

We drew up and fired the signal gun ; in a few moments she drew along side ; her Captain raised the bow window and called out,—

"Where from ?"

"Sundora-Luzion," replied Navikoff.

"Whither bound ?"

"Elfrezulah,—palace of the Grand Duke."

"We are direct from there, bound to Rohita-Savoyal, with an important message from His Royal Highness, Prince Harovian."

"What news ?"

"Have you not heard ?"

"No."

"The news is terrible."

I sprang to the cabin window,—breathless.

"You are aware that Prince Diavojahr, who is now Regent, holds the guest of our kingdom, Lieut. Hamilton, under sentence of death. Every possible effort has been made by our own, and other kingdoms to save his life. Immense ransoms have been tendered and our government has offered to cede all her possessions in the southern hemisphere, including the equatorial islands and lands around the south pole, to the Sundora government, to secure the prisoner's release ; but Diavojahr demands, in addition to these immense concessions, the hand of the Princess Suhlamia in marriage. He has already sent his Ambassador to the palace, with the marriage contract and final ultimatum, under instructions that, if the Princess accepts his proposal he will pardon the prisoner. Further conditions are that, she will immediately depart, accompanied by two government ships for Fatol island,—the neutral ground between the two kingdoms. Two ships from his kingdom will meet her there and the formal exchange will be made, the Princess to be conveyed to Diavojahr's palace, the prisoner to go wherever he desires. No other ship from either of the two kingdoms, nor any other, to be allowed within five hundred miles of the island. If the Princess refuses this offer, the prisoner's death follows. A declaration of war on the part of our kingdom would only hasten the execution. Diavojahr has the game in his own hands and defies our kingdom. The Ambassador is now at the palace with the marriage contract, the letters of the prisoner and intercepted correspondence between him and the Duchess Allessandra. Diavojahr has allowed her only twenty four hours to make her final decision and the time for it expires at 8 o'c. this evening. It is believed she will accept, to save the prisoner from the fate awaiting him. The whole court is plunged in grief, the sufferings of our beloved Princess are heart-rending, she is enduring the tortures of a living death," and the cruiser wheeled about and sped on its way.

With a gasp of agony that seemed to tear my very soul from its mortal tenement,—amid which rang the thrilling shriek of Elfine, I sank senseless to the floor.

"Haste! O, haste!—For the love of God!" she cried. "To the palace. Unless we reach it in time, the Princess will sign the accursed contract ;—will depart to the island expecting to meet Lieutenant Hamilton ; Diavojahr's cruisers will be there, in force, concealed ; she will fall into his hands. God in Heaven! Let not that demon triumph."

Captain Navikoff shouted to the crew, the ship wheeled about and sped over the mountain with the rush of the unchained hurricane.

When I recovered consciousness, I was lying on the divan. Elfine was bending over me ; the Captain stood by my side.

"Lieutenant," said he, "my lady has told me all ; I am with you heart and soul ;—be sure of that."

I could only reply with a grasp of his hand.

"We are making strait for Elfrezulah ; our brave little ship is doing her best ; she is flying right in the teeth of a gale our stoutest cruiser would hardly dare face."

The tumultuous surging of the ship showed that she was tearing through the air at terrific speed ; she careened from side to side, like a falcon winging his flight on the edge of a storm.

"What's the hour ?" asked Elfine.

"Half past seven," replied the Captain.

"How far have we flown ?"

"Fifty miles."

"You are within fifty miles of Elfrezulah," said I. "Can you make it on time ?"

"Yes ; unless the storm increases."

I threw open the window ;—the gale shrieked through the cabin,—flashes of lightning flew across the sky illumining the dark clouds as they were swept onward in tumultuous masses ;—this gathering tempest seemed but the faint shadow of that which was overwhelming my soul,—the roar of waves was now heard ;—the man in the dome called out,—

"We are nearing a great lake."

"'Tis the Ambhu-Cyama, or Shining Water," said I. "Thirty miles across ; on the opposite shore lies Elfrezulah."

The ship sped onward ; in a few moments the man called out,—

"We are right over the lake."

" We will soon reach the palace ;" said Elfine.

The palace ;—dreadful thought ! What scenes might now be enacted there,—what grief, dismay and despair ? The haughty demands of the bloody tyrant—from whose fangs I had just escaped,—now offered for her acceptance ; the forged letters, his atrocious plot to secure her hand as the price of my life and liberty ; perhaps even now accepted, or, if not, the hour for her final decision swiftly approaching. It seemed as if my brain would give way as I pictured the anguish that might now be crushing that noble and gentle heart. The billows that raged like a hell below, seemed but to image the hell that was raging in my soul.—" God in Heaven !" I cried, " save ! O, save her that awful fate ;—then would I gladly die."

" O, trust in Him," said Elfine, placing her hand on my throbbing brow. " He will not suffer iniquity thus to triumph. I know it ;—feel it ;—again do I say to thee.—Courage.—Hope.—Trust in God."

CHAPTER L.

THE CYCLONE.

Lord of the winds, I feel thee nigh;
I know thy breath in the burning sky.
And I wait, with a thrill in every vein,
For the coming of the hurricane !"
The Hurricane.—BRYANT.

The blackness of midnight rapidly enshrouded sea and sky. A low, sad and mournful tone now rose on the murky air ; 'twas like the wail of a lost spirit wan-

dering amid darkness and desolation, now rising and
swelling, now dying away in ominous silence. Once
again it rose in deep and sonorous vibrations like the
tones of a vast organ, louder and still louder, higher and
still higher, till it swelled in one mighty and brazen
blast, like the clangor of a gigantic trumpet, blown by
the demon of the tempest.

"'Tis the Cyclone!" shouted the Captain. "Quick,
—shoot the ship above the storm belt!"

A loud rattle of the machinery,—the prow was directed
upwards and she ascended in great spirals almost to the
region of calm. The cloud masses in which we were
immersed slowly drifted to the east. Suddenly a blinding flash of lightning that seemed to split the firmament, shot from horizon to zenith, and a thunder peal
shook like an earthquake. It was the signal of the
Storm King.

"Look!—Look!—" exclaimed Elfine, pointing below.

Down in the heavy cloud bank on the horizon a great
ragged hole appeared scooped out in the blackness,
from which issued a long, slender stream of whitish
vapor like that from the escape pipe of a steamer.
Slowly creeping like a serpent from its den, it stole
stealthily over the waters, crushing the waves down
flat beneath its resistless march and enormous pressure.
The whole watery expanse along its track was converted
into a seething mass of foam. Suddenly it straitened
itself out, shooting its apex forward like the point of a
spear ; the rear of its shaft expanded in the shape of a
gigantic fan or the tail of a comet, twisting and coiling
in all directions, while from its depths flew balls of fire,
livid lightnings, hissings and explosions. The aërial
monster now sped over the waters with the rush and
roar of a thousand railroad trains ; the whole surface of
the lake was utterly blotted out ; the surrounding air

and clouds were being rapidly sucked down in the vortex beneath, and it required an incessant struggle to prevent the ship from being drawn into the whirl. Language cannot describe the horrors of the scene. The mad chaos below was like Milton's picture of the surges of hell ; cascades of lightnings ripped and tore it in every direction, disclosing dark abysses, fathomless gulfs, and all manner of horrible shapes and forms. The cyclone now curved around toward the shore ; by this time we had nearly crossed the lake.

" Lights of the city ahead !" shouted the man at the dome.

" Make strait for it," replied the Captain.

The cross wind in which we were immersed was bearing us away in a contrary direction, while the tornado was swiftly approaching the city. The lights of the palace now came in view. I pointed it out to the Captain.

The clock now struck eight. It was the hour for the Princess' final decision ;—the sound smote like a knell on my ear.

" Captain," said I, " we must fly to the palace immediately."

" It will be impossible, except by passing directly through the cyclone. Our ship would be torn to pieces ; we must wait here till it blows over."

" How long ?"

" Perhaps ten minutes ;—perhaps half an hour :—no one can tell ; besides there's the tempest that follows in its wake, almost as fatal as the cyclone itself."

" 'Twill be too late !" exclaimed Elfine. " All will be over,—the Princess—"

" Yes, too late !" I cried. " Perhaps e'en now it may be too late. Haste ! Lose not a moment ! 'Tis the hour for life or death, to her,—to me. Fly to the palace instantly !"

"I'll risk it ;" replied the Captain, "though death and destruction lie before me." Then calling to the crew, they entered the cabin ;—he explained all.

" Will you take the risk, boys ?"

" Aye, aye," they heartily responded. " 'Tis our business to face death. To die, if need be, in the line of duty."

" Then let us say our farewells all around ; for we may never meet again this side the grave."

We silently clasped hands. That grasp was firm and steady as a rock. Though many an eye was moistened, not a single cheek paled, not a nerve quivered ; every countenance displayed unflinching courage and determination ;—some even smiled ; the farewells over,

" Every man to his post ;" ordered the Captain, and the crew took their stations.

" Fold mid-ship and aft storm wings. Withdraw fore wings up to their tips, to steady her ;—shorten and double fold the rudder ; link extra chains and put two men at the wheel."

In a few moments the order was accomplished.

" Are you all ready ?" he shouted.

" Aye, aye ;—"

"Shoot the ship strait down through the eye of the cyclone, and if Almighty God helps her to clear it, make for the palace."

" Aye,—aye,—Captain."

Elfine sank to her knees in silent prayer.

Like an eagle swooping from her eyrie, down plunged the ship into the tornado ; the impetus of her rush alone saving her from being capsized. We were instantly immersed in Egyptian darkness,—tossed and whirled

amid thunderings and explosions, sheets of fire and
flashes of lightnings. The convulsions of the tornado
reached the heavens ; sky, billows, clouds and foam
were one furious chaos—mingled with whistlings,
shrieks and howls, like wild beasts or demons in torture ; and high above all, rose the dreadful roaring of
the sea as if lashed by the whips of fiends.

And now the sound of crashing branches and
uprooted trunks announced that the aërial monster was
tearing its way through the groaning forest. Soon
came the splitting of timbers, off torn roofs and crash
of falling walls ; the tornado was cutting its path
through the city.

The steersmen tugged at the wheel. The next
moment we were tossed like a leaf out of the vortex ;
there was a violent concussion and our trembling ship
was thrown to the ground. We sprang from the windows unhurt, sank to our knees on the sward and
breathed our prayers of thanksgiving to Him who
" maketh the clouds His chariot, and rideth upon the
wings of the wind."

We were in the midst of a grove in the grounds of
the ducal palace. The cyclone was speeding away on
its path of destruction. The storm in its wake was
howling through the trees and the rain fell in torrents.
In front towered the marble walls of the palace.
Leaving the Captain and crew to look after the ship I
took Elfine by the hand, we passed rapidly through the
grounds and ascended the steps of the balcony surrounding the palace. I looked through the lattice.
The grand *salon* was brilliantly illumined and thronged
with dignitaries of high rank, officers, court ladies and
members of the royal household. In the centre was a
large table. On one side were grouped Duke Athalton,
King Polath, Prince Harovian and Duke Oneigar,

their countenances expressing intense solicitude and anxiety. Altfoura was seated, his head bowed upon his hands. On the other side, stood a man of stern and impassive countenance, attired in the robes of his official rank ; he held in his hand a roll of vellum stamped with royal seals ; near by stood several members of his suite.

"That is Lord Vendicar, Royal Ambassador and special *envoyé* of Prince Diavojahr," whispered Elfine.

The Ambassador now spoke. The windows being partly open, his words could be distinctly heard—

"Princes, Peers and Dignitaries of Mandal-Uttima ; I beg to assure your Royal Highnesses, and all assembled, that never, in the whole course of my official career, have I been sent on a mission so utterly repugnant to my feelings, to my convictions of honor and justice as this. The whole course of His Highness, Prince Diavojahr, although viewed as strictly legal by our government, is universally condemned by our people. Nevertheless I must fulfill my duty, however painful it may be. The hour now approaches for the decision of Her Royal Highness, and this contract, accredited with the seal of Sundora-Luzion, awaits her signature."

The Ambassador unrolled the vellum and placed it on the table. The great doors of the *salon* rolled open, and the herald at arms announced—

"Her Royal Highness, Suhlamia Angelion, Princess of Mandal-Uttima."

My heart almost ceased its beating,—I clung to the lattice—Elfine drew near my side.

Nothing could exceed the stately dignity and solemnity of this royal court ceremonial. Princes, Dukes, Nobles, Cabinet officers, the Ambassador and his suite, arose as if awaiting the approach of Imperial Majesty. All stood motionless ; the silence was profound.

CHAPTER LI.

SAVED.

" There's not an hour of day or silent night,
    But in my thoughts and dreams I am with thee;
    There's not a wind but whispers of thy name ;
    There's not a flow'r that blooms beneath the moon,
    But in its fragrance tells a tale of thee."

ANON.

Suhlamia entered the *salon* with Luzella, Thaloba, and the royal ladies of her suite, the countenances of the latter expressing bitter sorrow. She was attired in a simple robe of white. Her beautiful hair flowing in glittering waves of purple and gold to the ground. Pale as the lilies that bend their drooping heads o'er the holy sepulchre in its hour of desolation, she seemed a bride attired for the tomb, and as her starry eyes were raised heavenward, a sweet and holy calm resting on her brow, it seemed as if her pure spirit was ready to wing its flight to realms of celestial bliss.

" O, what a vision of heavenly loveliness !" murmured Elfine through her tears.

Suhlamia paused and saluted the assembled throng with a sweet smile of recognition. Lord Vendicar had never before seen the Princess ; his negotiations having been conducted through the Grand Duke and Prince Altfoura. As she stood before him, his wonder and admiration of her perfect beauty, and loveliness of soul, that seemed almost to envelope her form like a halo, overcame his stately dignity, and with a profound obeisance he never yet bestowed on the highest dignitary of any Martian kingdom, this haughty Ambassador addressed her in tones trembling with emotion.

"Most noble Princess, I implore you, pardon me the ungracious and painful duty I am called upon to fulfill. When this commission was placed upon me by the Prince Regent of my kingdom, had I known then what I know now, I should have refused its acceptance, but having advanced thus far, my only course is to bring it to as speedy a termination as possible. The moment has come for your final decision, your signature to this contract saves the life, and restores to liberty, the prisoner now under sentence of death."

"My Lord of Vendicar,"—replied Suhlamia in tones of winning gentleness, "you have no pardon to ask of me. Your honorable sentiments command my respect, your generous expressions claim my thanks." She extended her hand, he sank to his knee and pressed it respectfully to his lips.

At this moment an officer entered.

"A despatch from His Royal Highness, Prince Diavojahr, to the Ambassador ;"—said he, handing the message to Lord Vendicar who opened and glanced o'er it.

"God in Heaven ! Can it be possible !"—exclaimed he, sinking into his chair and covering his face with his hands—the despatch fell to the floor.

"What tidings have you received, my Lord ?" asked the Duke.

"I cannot announce them,"—replied he in a faint voice.

"Read the despatch, officer ;" said the Duke.

The officer picked it up and with pale and trembling lips, read—

"Lord Vendicar will announce to the Grand Duke and Prince of Mandal-Uttima that, unless the Princess Suhlamia immediately signs the contract and departs at once to Fatol Island, where the exchange is to be made, the prisoner will die by crucifixion and burning within twelve hours.   DIAVOJAHR."

"He evidently has the idea that, we are still in his kingdom and hopes to find us," whispered Elfine. "'Tis his last desperate stake to consummate his villainous plot."

A universal burst of horror filled the room ;—sobs and cries from the women, frightful curses and imprecations from the men on the demon whose hellish cruelty and revenge bade defiance to God and man. Suhlamia grew deadly pale—trembled—a faint cry escaped her lips,—then advancing from the throng she waved her hand as if entreating silence, and in tones of perfect calmness,—

"Dear friends, listen to my words ; Lieutenant Hamilton, our esteemed and honored guest, who saved my own and my brother's life, is now in the hands of a bloodthirsty and merciless tyrant, and there is no other way by which he can be rescued from a cruel and ignominious death, except by my acceptance of the conditions presented to me. That intercepted correspondence purporting to have been written by him, was never penned by his hand nor by his sanction. He is incapable of such an act. They are forgeries of that base wretch, to further his scheme. I will not speak of the struggle,—the more than mortal anguish through which I have passed ; but now, since I have made the final decision, peace has come to me. When he returns safe to you,—as I may never see his face again,"—her voice faltered, for a moment she trembled, then raising her eyes to heaven as if imploring strength ;—"tell him that, I believe God will accept this sacrifice which I offer in the spirit of holy resignation, tell him of my deep gratitude, tell him that I joy to make this sacrifice for his sake, and that the last prayer I breathe shall be for him !"—then turning to the Ambassador,—

" My Lord, I have accepted the conditions, and will now sign the contract."

The witnesses advanced, the Ambassador placed the paper before her, then in accordance with the usual court formula, spoke,—

" If there be any in this assembly, who can call Almighty God to witness that, he has just cause of hindrance or impediment to this procedure, let him now speak, or forever hold his peace."

A dead silence fell over all, as they stood with bowed heads.

Suhlamia approached the table,—suppressed sobs murmured through the room. Altfoura, Luzella, Thaloba, sank to their knees before her, weeping, imploring ; she gently, but firmly, waved them aside, drew near the table, seized the pen, for a moment trembled ; her bosom heaved, her countenance grew white as marble, then raising her eyes upward, while the tear drops that hung there, shone like diamonds under the sun's ray,—

" I will pass the fiery ordeal !" she cried. " I will embrace my doom ! O, Merciful Heaven ! support me in this hour, and on him now far away, whom I ne'er shall see again, shed the light of happier stars lost ever more to me."

Scarce had the words left her lips, when a flash of lightning o'erspread the heavens with a hellish glare ; an awful thunder peal shook the palace to its foundations. I tore open the shutter and sprang into the room.

" Hold !" —I cried—" the voice of God in thunder, lightning and tempest now speaks, and forbids this sacrifice."

I rushed to the table,—seized the contract, the letters,
—tore them to pieces, and flung them at the feet of the
Ambassador.

" Tell that royal wretch,—that bloodthirsty and
cowardly tyrant who sent you here with his contracts
and forgeries that, the devils he serves would hide
their heads in very shame at his foul plot, and ere it
could be consummated, the avenging gods would crush
him and his throne with their thunderbolts !"

Shouts of astonishment and delight rang through the
salon. Suhlamia stood as if in the presence of one
risen from the dead,—a faint cry of joy trembled on
her lips,—I sprang forward,—" O, Frederick !" she
faintly murmured, and sank insensible into my arms.
Altfoura, Luzella and Thaloba sprang to my side,—we
bore her to a little boudoir and laid her on the divan,
—the curtains were closed—I knelt by her side—in a
few moments she revived and turned her lovely eyes
to mine.

" O, Suhlamia !" I murmured in impassioned accents,
—" my life—my love,—thou knowest full well, gladly
would I have died a thousand deaths to save thy dear
heart one single pang of sorrow—"

" O, Frederick !" she whispered,—" kind heaven
has listened to the prayers I hourly breathed for thee ;
but had fate decreed that I should never see thee more,
and had I met the tyrant who sought your life, the
instant thou wert freed from his power, ere his
hand had touched mine,—this dagger—" drawing the
weapon from her bosom—" would have shed my heart's
blood."

I clasped her in my arms ; with a look full of tender
love, and a smile that thrilled my soul,—

" Dear,—dear Frederick—" she softly murmured as I
pressed her to my throbbing heart.

CHAPTER LII.

ASTERION'S JOURNEY TO THE ASTEROIDS.

> " Long were to tell
> What I have done, what suffer'd, with what pain
> Voyag'd th' unreal, vast unbounded deep
> Of horrible confusion ;   .   .   .
> Toil'd out my uncouth passage, forc'd to ride
> Th' intractable abyss, plunged in the womb
> Of unoriginal Night and Chaos wild."
>
> *Paradise Lost*, Book X.

The astonishment and delight of my friends were better imagined than described. I hastened to bring in my brave rescuers and they were greeted with acclamations of joy. Elfine was at first, overwhelmed with confusion, but the Princess received her with open arms. Peace and happiness now ruled the hour, and when all were assembled at the joyous feast which followed, my Lady Chumivant related the amusing incidents of the rescue, the palace rang with applause and mirth. On the following day the royal Ambassador departed with his suite. This distinguished nobleman had been deeply impressed by the Princess' beauty and loveliness of character, the scenes that had transpired, and the courtesies he had received from all, and he was so shocked at Diavojahr's villainous plots he determined to resign his office and dissolve his connection with the court. On the third day, Lord Montobar, accompanied by Lord Chumivant and my old jailer Hardigoth, arrived at the palace. They gave an animated description of Diavojahr's rage at the escape of his prisoner and the failure of his plot. The Grand

Duke and Altfoura bestowed distinguished courtesies on Lord Chumivant and Hardigoth, in which my lady also received her full share from the Princess.

The same night, the equatorial regions were visited by a meteoric shower of great severity.   It was described by those who witnessed it as one of the heaviest that had been known for many years. The meteorites were of enormous size, surpassing any before seen.   Fortunately no lives were lost, the great bulk of the shower having fallen into the ocean.   The occurrence of the downfall at this season of the year was so unusual it excited great interest among astronomers and scientists.   The moons, Rohanza and Aryuna, which were on that side of the planet at the time, seemed to have received the full force of the shower, for they were completely enveloped by the cloud of meteorites.

The next morning Altfoura rushed into the reception room from the private telegraph office of the palace, his countenance glowing with excitement and delight.

" News !" he cried,—" news from Asterion !" handing a despatch to the Duke.

As a long time had elapsed since Asterion's departure, all had felt great anxiety and solicitude for his safety.   The terrible dangers of the journey were well known.   Some had even given him up for lost.   The Duke read the message.

" South Pole.   Ethervolt Station.   No. 4, 10 o'c. A. M.
" To His Highness Athalton Thullivarrh, Grand Duke Regnant of Mandal-Uttima, greeting :—I have the honor to announce that, I have this moment returned from my tour of inspection among the Asteroids.   Have news of the highest importance to communicate to Your Highness and the Astronomer Royal ; shall immediately embark on the fleetest air ship.   If

no unforeseen delays prevent, shall reach the palace at
8 o'c. p. m.

"I have the honor to be, etc.,

"ASTERION."

"We have looked forward to the results of this journey with great interest," said the Duke.

Despatches were sent to several kingdoms, and as
evening drew near, the grand *salon* of the palace was
thronged with a brilliant assembly, representing the
royalty, wealth and learning of Mars. The Grand
Duke and officers of the household, King Polath, Prince
Harovian and Duke Oneigar with their suites, the
Astronomer royal, Solaris, and several of his colleagues,
members of the Royal Academy of Sciences and professors of the Royal College, members of scientific and
learned societies, Military and Naval Officers, and distinguished representatives of the bench and bar ; con-
stituting a display which would have commanded the
profound respect and admiration of any International
Congress on this Terrestrial globe.

Precisely at 8 o'c. the doors were opened and Asterion, escorted by the Princes Altfoura and Harovian,
and accompanied by Vidyuna and Bhuras, entered the
salon. Every eye was fixed on these intrepid interplanetary voyagers. Asterion looked pale and care-
worn. An expression of deep anxiety appeared on his
countenance, whose lineaments displayed the highest
order of intellect and courage. His eyes shone with a
light as if from the radiant orbs amid which he roamed.
His *spirituelle* presence, lofty air and bearing, were
almost a realization of Milton's Ithuriel, as he landed on
Earth from his flight through the Celestial Spheres. His
reception was a grand ovation. Tumultuous applause
rang through the *salon.* It was a spontaneous outburst

of homage to Science and the man who represented it in its highest and noblest department, Astronomy. Science represents one form of Divine truth as displayed in the material world. The voice of Science is as the voice of God, and 'tis meet that royalty, wealth and power should yield obeisance and submission to that mighty voice which unfolds and elucidates the mysterious laws that govern the Universe of Worlds. Compared with this magnificent ovation, how utterly trivial and insignificant appear all the pompous ceremonials of courts, and the ostentatious displays of wealth and fashion, which absorb the thoughts and aspirations of millions of Earth's gay and frivolous throngs.

It was with difficulty the Princess succeeded in extricating Asterion and his companions from the enthusiastic felicitations of the assembly. Order being restored, they ascended the platform and after a brief expression of thanks for the honors bestowed, Asterion addressed the assembly as follows :

" Dear friends, I have the honor to announce to you that I have returned from that vast zone of Asteroids lying between our planet and Jupiter and sweeping in an orbit of nearly sixteen hundred million miles circuit around the sun ; and which was once occupied by the planet Luzio-Avani Dhramza, or the ' Great Shining One,' now called Pluto, the fragments of which constitute this Asteroidal belt,—a revolving desert of ruins, sad mementoes of departed grandeur and glory. All the planets of our system, as you well know, are united in one paternal bond to their great original parent, the Sun, by the power of his attraction. They are also united in one common bond of brotherhood by the great Cosmo-magnetic currents emanating from their poles and flying from planet to planet with a speed far outstripping that of electricity or light. It is by means of these currents we are enabled to wing our flight through the realms of Space from one World to another. These Interplanetary journeys are attended with great difficulty and danger. Ceaseless vigilance is required to keep our Ethervolt car within the narrow boundaries of these streams, and follow their great curves produced by the orbital motions of the planets. We are also liable to encounter the great belts of Meteorites which traverse the orbits of many of our planets, and hurl their terrible cannonade in all directions around us. All these, together with other vicissitudes and dangers, not necessary to mention, render these journeys full of peril.

"In this trip we took the track of the great Martio-Jovian magnetic current running between our planet and Jupiter, about three hundred and fifty million miles distant. Reaching the inner ring of the Asteroidal belt we paused awhile to examine Medusa, the nearest planetoid, then traversed its entire breadth, over two hundred million miles to Thule, the most remote; making trips here and there in various directions along the belt, and what I have discovered, confirms the results of my former observations. Some of the larger Planetoids, from one to three hundred miles in diameter, shine with different colored light, others are surrounded by atmospheres,[1] the presence of which it is impossible to explain otherwise than that, they are fragments of the original Plutonian atmosphere still clinging to them after the explosion. The lesser asteroids and still smaller fragments, of which there are countless millions, quite too small to be discovered by our telescopes, are composed of the same mineral and metallic

[1] These are well known facts discovered by astronomical observations on the Planetoids.

materials, with the exception of a few unknown elements, of which all planets are made. They all show the evidences of fusion, plainly indicating the intense heat to which they were subjected at the planet's explosion. I have brought some specimens of fragments which I shall be happy to present to the Astronomical Society."

Vidyuna and Bhuras now opened a chest and drew out a number of specimens, which were passed around and examined with great interest by the learned Scientists and Astronomers.

"They resemble in all respects the specimens of Aërolites which fall on our planet during our meteoric showers," said several geologists.

"I have long been of the opinion that many of our meteoric showers are stray offshoots which have wandered away from the Asteroidal belt," remarked the Astronomer Royal.

"Isolated meteoric streams and clouds float along various portions of the Interplanetary space, filled with countless millions of these smaller fragments," said Asterion.

"Perhaps one of the conservative offices of our comets, which sweep through these vast realms, may be to gather up these deserters and restore them to their Asteroidal ranks again," remarked one professor.

"I am rather inclined to the opinion that, these lively celestial coryphées, whisking their gauzy skirts around the Interplanetary stage, are scattering these fragments around among our planets as mementoes to remind them of their lost brother," remarked another.

"The whole Asteroidal Zone is filled with vast clouds of mineral and metallic dust, ground to powder by the force of the explosion," continued Asterion, "the particles are continually clashing against, and uniting with each other, the smaller with the larger, and these are continually increasing in size and joining in their turn with others."

"Which gives us every reason to expect that, in time they will all unite and roll up together, forming a new planet," said Astronomer Solaris.

"Hardly a new one;" remarked one of his colleagues. "Like the Phœnix rising from his ashes, it would be the same old Pluto, *redivivus*."

"Having been purified by fire, we may hope the new Pluto will be rather a better specimen than the old original," remarked another.

"And let us hope that the spirits of the departed Plutonians, may again be reunited to their mortal bodies, to begin life over again under more favorable auspices," said a disciple of the re-incarnation theory.

"And also be permitted to retain a lively recollection of the tragic winding up of their sinful career, which may teach them a wholesome moral lesson,—for experience is a dear school, but fools will learn in no other— and induce them to lead better lives," suggested a disciple of the spiritual progression theory.

"And if this remarkable event should happen to take place in our day," said Altfoura, "I propose that we take the new planet under our especial supervision and discarding the old name of Pluto, which Lieutenant Hamilton informs me is the cognomen of the Terrestrio-mythological monarch of hell,—we christen it by the name of our distinguished Interplanetary navigator, Asterion."

The Prince's suggestion was received with applause. Asterion expressed his thanks for the compliment and resumed,

"As we traversed the Zone, while the armies of

revolving Asteroids were flying swiftly past us, we were beset with dangers on every side. Continual watchfulness alone saved us from destruction. Days and nights were passed without sleep. In many parts of this Asteroidal chaos the great Cosmic and Molecular forces are displayed on a scale of terrible grandeur. Millions of the larger Asteroids, and many of the Planetoids, heated by the energy of the chemical action going on in their interiors, and the impact of smaller masses, are revolving globes of red hot metal and mineral. Vast fields of smaller masses, mingled with clouds of meteoric dust and covering millions of miles in extent, are like boundless oceans of flame, o'er which sheets of Cosmic lightning cast a lurid glare.[1] Tornadoes,—compared with which, the cyclones that sweep along the fiery cloud belts of Jupiter are as gentle breezes,—rage and tear through this horrible chaos with indescribable fury. Should any of our planets encounter these flaming deserts, all animal and vegetable life would be instantly consumed, oceans dissipated in vapor, and the planet converted into a molten globe. On our return passage we encountered one of these tempests. Fortunately we were on its outer edge, else we should have met with instant destruction. We took refuge on the lee side of a cooled Asteroid nearly two hundred miles in diameter. It was a mass of igneous rock and metal. We succeeded in anchoring our car to it, and were swept several million miles out of our course, the Asteroid screened us from the awful cannonade of meteors pouring around us in tempests of fire. Finally we came to an open space, cut loose the anchor, put our Cosmic motor to its fullest powers and

[1] Sudden flashes of Cosmic light are not unfrequently seen in those parts of the heavens occupied by the Asteroidal Zone.

dashed through the inner circumference of the belt into the free planetary space."

Tumultuous applause rang through the *salon* as Asterion related these thrilling scenes.

" How did your Ethervolt sustain the fiery ordeal ?" asked Astronomer Solaris.

"Our brave Nai Taraza (Ship of the Stars) bore it well," Asterion replied, " but her brightness and beauty are gone forever," and a tear stood in his eye ; "every part of her surface is battered, scorched and blackened as if she had passed through the tempests of Infernus."

" Three cheers for our brave Asterion and his gallant Ship of the Stars," exclaimed Altfoura and the applause made the welkin ring. The Duke, accompanied by the Astronomer, ascended the platform and affixed a royal medal, blazing with jewels, to Asterion's breast, and other medals to Vidyuna and Bhuras, then the Astronomer, holding up a splendid memorial—

" The Royal Astronomical Society dedicates this to the Ship of the Stars. Our brave Interplanetary navigator shall, with due ceremony, affix it to her summit, and that gallant ship shall be awarded the highest place among the trophies of the Royal Observatory."

Asterion and his companions blushed like a trio of bashful school boys at the honors bestowed upon them, and Duke Oneigar made a speech of thanks in their behalf. Asterion then resumed.

" I now come to a subject of far greater importance, relating to our Moons, Aryuna and Rohanza."

At these words the assembly manifested earnest attention.

" Our planet, as you are aware, in its revolution around the Sun, annually encounters the showers from the great Meteoric belt, traversing its orbit. While the planet is in a measure protected by its atmosphere which consumes to ashes the greater part of the masses, before they reach the surface, and our cities are protected from the larger masses, by their screens. Our moons, having no atmosphere, are exposed to the full brunt of the bombardment and as time rolls on, the volumes and densities of their masses are necessarily increased. This, of course will have the effect, ultimately, of disturbing the harmonious adjustment of their centripetal and centrifugal forces,—the former gradually increasing, and the latter diminishing—the final result of which is known to us all,"—then addressing the Astronomer Royal,—

" What has been the amount of orbital disturbances during past ages ?"

" According to our astronomical records," replied he, " which extend back sixteen thousand years, our moons were more than twice their present distance and revolved much more slowly in their orbits. They were also much larger. Since that period many great volcanic outbursts have taken place, which by dissipating their materials into space, reduced their volumes to a very great degree. They were also subjected, during vast intervals of time, to extraordinary downfalls of meteors, which had the effect of retarding their velocities and gradually beating them downward toward the planet. About a thousand years ago, one of our Astronomers discovered, after a meteoric downpour of unusual severity that, Aryuna had descended two hundred miles, and Rohanza about one hundred. Two hundred years ago, after another similar downpour, the moons descended to their present position, with a corresponding increase of their orbital velocities, and a change of appearance."

" Has any appreciable descent been observed since that period ?" asked Asterion.

"My own observations, extending over a period of thirty years, show no deviation from their position, nor any increase in their orbital velocities."

"How often have you made these observations?"

"Four times each year."

"And the last?"

"A week ago."

"No deviation noticed?"

"Not the slightest."

"Did you notice any change in their appearance?"

"None whatever; Aryuna shone with the same mild radiance. Rohanza presented her usual dull red color. Why do you ask?"

"As I drew near our planet on my return this morning, I paused in my flight, ten thousand miles above the pole, to observe our moons as they revolved around the night side of the western hemisphere and I saw,—"

For a moment he paused—all bent forward in breathless attention.

"What saw you?" asked the Astronomer Royal.

"The long pent up fires of the lunar volcanoes are awakening!" he exclaimed, then pointing to the east, and in thrilling tones,—

"Look!—See for yourselves. Our moons are on fire!"

CHAPTER LIII.

MARS' MOONS ON FIRE.

" Belching outrageous flame far into Chaos."
Paradise Lost, Book X., Line 232.

It is impossible to describe the effect of these fearful words. Every man sprang to his feet ; the windows were thrown open and there, in that cloudless sky rolled the Moons, just above the horizon, Aryuna shining with a blazing light ; Rohanza wrapped in crimson flames. These phenomena of course, could not have been seen by day, under the bright light of the Sun.

" But the worst is yet to come," continued Asterion. " Nerve yourselves up to receive the news like men, with calmness and courage. I took their altitudes. Both Moons have sunk twenty miles below their former positions. If this goes on, destruction awaits our World."

Calmness and courage ? Great Heaven ! What assembly of men ; what kingdom or nation, could have received such appalling news with calmness ? 'Twas like the voice of the angel announcing the doom of the cities of the plain ; like the handwriting on the wall announcing the downfall of a kingdom ; like the Almighty voice foretelling the coming Flood, so this voice of Science revealed a far more awful fate, the destruction of a World ! The boldest scientists trembled ; strong and brave men staggered to their seats and bowed their faces on their hands ; not a sound escaped their lips ; every tongue seemed locked ;—the silence was profound.

The Astronomer Royal hurriedly entered an alcove

on one side of the room.   This was the telegraphic office.   An operator stood by the Opsiferon.

"Quick," said he, "signal my son at the Royal Observatory ; he is engaged in making observations on the rings of Saturn."

The operator touched a key, the next instant the bell sounded,—all listened—a voice issued from the instrument.

"Good evening, Father.   We are anxiously awaiting your return with news from the Asteroids ; all present wish me to convey their compliments and congratulations to our dear friend, Asterion."

"Leave Saturn ; take an observation of our Moons through the equatorial ; ascertain their exact altitude and azimuth, compare results with observations of last week ; note appearance of the satellites and report as quickly as possible."

The professors and scientists clustered around the alcove—the audience stood in groups awaiting the reply.

"This descent of the Moons was unquestionably caused by that severe meteoric shower on their surface," said one of the professors.

"Meteoric shower !" exclaimed Asterion.   "When and where ?"

"Last night," replied Solaris.   "Did you not see it on your return ?"

"See it ?   I was ten million miles from here."

Solaris related the phenomenon.

"From what quarter of the heavens ?" asked Asterion.

"The radiant point was from the west."

"This is extraordinary.   On my return, in passing through the meteoric belt in the south west quarter, we encountered showers of more than usual severity and I

noticed remarkable phenomena, evidently of a Cosmo-
electric origin, going on in certain parts of the belt."

"What did they seem like?"

"Undulatory movements almost of a convulsive
character, as if the main body was throwing off
detached portions from its mass."

"That shower was certainly a detached mass. Our
regular annual showers will not take place till fall."

"What could be the cause of this extraordinary disturbance?" asked one of the professors.

"It may possibly have been cometic;" replied Asterion. "I discovered one at a great distance in the west
quarter of the heavens. It was too far away and
faintly defined to be made out."

"Then it must be a new one," said Solaris. "All
our comets are catalogued, their elements and periods
of return calculated; none are due here so early in the
season."

"Hand me the table of logarithms, meteoroids and
periodic comets," said Asterion.

One of the professors placed the books on the table.
Asterion drew out his tablets and began to rapidly figure
up an intricate astronomical calculation. The bell of
the Opsiferon sounded—all bent forward in silence;
the voice of the Astronomer's son was heard:

"Observations completed,—Moons present a terrible
appearance,—large portions of Aryuna's surface enveloped with gaseous clouds in full combustion,—spectroscopic analysis shows burning hydrogen,—Rohanza's
fumeroles spouting torrents of volcanic lava, both Moons
have sunk twenty miles below former position, needles
of electro-magnetic apparatus violently agitated, showing great Cosmo-electric and magnetic disturbances.
Great Heaven! dear father, what does this portend?"

"Breathe not a word of what you have seen to any

one ; I will be with you by midnight ; have all instruments in readiness," replied Solaris.

Asterion finished his calculation, descended from the
platform and entered the alcove.

"Signal Ethervolt Station, No. 4, South Pole," said
he and the operator touched a key. The next instant
the bell sounded. Asterion spoke through the Opsiferon.

"Operator ?"

"Yes," was the reply.

"'Tis I, Asterion, at the Grand Duke's Palace.
Direct the superintendent to have my Ethervolt in
readiness—batteries in order—fresh supplies of food
and water—to morrow morning by 10 o'c. without fail."

"Aye, aye," replied the operator.

"What does this mean, Asterion ?" queried the Duke
in surprise.

"Your Highness will please direct the officers to
notify Capt. Volanto to have his air ship ready.   I leave
for the South Pole immediately."

"Nay ;—nay, Asterion.   Why this haste ?" exclaimed
several of the professors.

"I embark on my Ethervolt to-morrow morning for
a trip to the Meteoric belt, sixty million miles distant in
the west quarter, to ascertain the disturbances going on
there."

Exclamations of astonishment and dissent arose from
the assembly.

"Nay, Asterion, you must not go," said the Astronomer Royal—"you need rest,—"

"There's no rest for me while these meteoric offshoots are flying along the line of our orbit, ready to
spring on us unawares, like lions from their lairs,
spreading death and destruction around us and perhaps
beat our Moons down still further.   They may come

any moment, perchance to-morrow,—the next week, —the next month. Shall I dally here in ignoble ease in the face of this threatening danger? No, I must be up and about my business. I must haste to the field where these enemies are gathering; find out all I can, about their forces—calculate their distances— dimensions—speed and period of their assault. This accomplished, we are forearmed, and can make preparations for the protection of those near and dear to us."

"But why this haste?" exclaimed several. "You have had no rest for weeks."

"Nor for weeks to come, until these problems are solved. Delays are dangerous. Time presses, the events demand instant action;" then waving his hand, "Ho! there. My air ship!" he cried.

"'Tis in readiness," called out Capt. Volanto from the door.

"Farewell, gentlemen," said Asterion striding through the throng, Vidyuna and Bhuras by his side; "if it be the will of Heaven that I return, you shall know all."

"By Heaven! my friend, you shall not stir, this night," exclaimed Altfoura, advancing in front and laying his hand firmly on his shoulder, while the Dukes, Astronomer Royal and the professors, clustered around him.

Asterion glanced around with a proud smile.

"So you would detain me by force?"

"You shall not go!" replied Altfoura, firmly.

Asterion's brow grew dark,—for a moment it seemed as if he would scatter the throng like chaff. Many shrank back, overawed by his glance; suddenly there was a movement in the throng, and a sweet voice murmured,

"Will you not stay for my sake?" and the Princess Suhlamia, her countenance wreathed in a bright smile, stood before him.

This intrepid man, who had faced dangers and death in their most awful forms, and whose dauntless soul nothing in the heavens above or earth beneath, could for a moment appall, trembled, bowed his head, sank to his knee, pressed her hand fervently to his lips, while a faint blush mantled in his cheek.

"Princess," he murmured, "your slightest request is law to me; I will remain."

"'Twill give great joy to your friends," she replied, "and to all who esteem and love you."

The Astronomer Royal appointed a conference with the professors and scientists to be held the following day at the Royal Observatory, and the assembly departed.

"This startling phenomena," said one of the professors, "so contrary to all known experience of the past, seems to subvert our astronomical science and even incline us to doubt the immutability of the Creator's laws."

"The mercy of that Infinite Being who holds the Universe in the hollow of His hand is equal to His justice and power," said the Duke reverentially.

"I discover a ray of hope;" said Asterion. "Nature is eminently conservative, and what she loses at one point she gains in another. These outbursts of flame, by consuming and scattering into space, much of our Moons' materials, may, by reducing their volume and weight, stop their downward tendency."

We ascended to the balcony overlooking the splendid grounds of the palace. Asterion gazed long and earnestly at those fiery orbs, rolling in the skies, and casting their

lurid glare around. Then without a word we retired to
our apartments.

"The curtain has risen on the first act of this tremendous drama, and Heaven only knows how it will
end," I muttered as I threw myself on my couch.

An hour after, unable to sleep, I arose and passed
out on the balcony. It was one of the sweetest of summer nights. The glittering stars shone in the celestial
vault with a brilliancy unknown on Earth. The gentle
breeze sighed through the trees. The song of the
nightingale thrilled on the balmy air, mingled with the
rippling of fountains. The Moons had sunk below the
horizon, and high in the sky amid the starry orbs
gleamed the soft and mellow light of my dear Mother
Earth, with her companion, little snow white Luna,
close by her side. The window of Asterion's apartment
was open ; I glanced in. That intrepid voyager was
sleeping calmly as a little child on his couch, and as the
soft rosy light of that evening star gleaming through
the casement fell on his marble brow and noble countenance, they seemed illumined with an almost celestial
radiance.

CHAPTER LIV.

THE TERRIBLE COMET.

" The star which rules thy destiny
Was ruled, ere Earth began, by me :
It was a World as fresh and fair
As e'er revolved round Sun in air
Its course was free and regular,
Space bosom'd not a lovelier Star.
The hour arrived—and it became
A wand'ring mass of shapeless flame,
A pathless Comet, and a curse,
The menace of the Universe;
Still rolling on with innate force,
Without a sphere, without a course,
A bright deformity on high,
The monster of the upper sky."

Manfred. (*Seventh Spirit.*)—BYRON.

Next morning at break of day Asterion and his companions departed for the South Pole.

There was something almost superhuman in the inexhaustible energy, vitality and endurance of this extraordinary young man. He seemed insnsible to mental or bodily fatigue ; his physical resources were immense and he seemed to concentrate within himself the powers of twenty men. During his interplanetary journeys he would often pass days and nights without sleep, enduring a severe and unremitting brain and nerve strain that would drive the strongest Terrestrial man insane, yet a few hours' sleep would fully restore him. He seemed to derive the recuperation of his vital powers more from the Cosmic forces amid which he roamed, than aught else. His diet was simplicity itself ;

he never touched dainties or luxuries of any kind, nor the usual products of the *cuisine;* a few morsels of bread, fruits and a glass or two of milk was all ; he would not take in three days, what would barely suffice for the noon lunch of a Terrestrial gourmand, and often would go several days without touching a morsel. He never had an idle moment, continually on his journeys, or immersed in his scientific studies. Although only twenty six years of age, his scientific attainments were immense ; he was familiar with as many branches as professors who had spent their lives in mastering one single specialty. His knowledge of astronomy with all its intricate and abstruse calculations, involving the highest departments of mathematics, was profound, and whenever the Astronomer Royal and his colleagues were unable to solve a knotty problem, they would submit it to him and he would unravel it in a trice. He cared nothing for society, nor the usual recreations and pleasures that absorb the gay world. His character was simple and ingenuous ; he loved to commune with nature, the woods, birds and animals. His favorite pets were a donkey, an owl, a pig, a monkey and a pea-cock ; the first three, he was wont to say, were the best teachers of patience, wisdom and true philosophy. The last two, taught the vanity and frivolity of human affairs among man and womankind generally. He had an admirable fund of wit and sometimes indulged in a little dry humor. Several of his ancestors had lost their lives in the pursuit of their profession as Inter-planetary navigators, and he fully expected to meet the same fate, but was as indifferent about it as any sailor. Some elegant society exquisites, who led lives of ease and pleasure and took excellent care of their precious selves (of which a goodly number float around our Ter-restrial fashionable circles), once asked him,—

" Where did your father die, Asterion ?"

" Lost his life on one of these journeys."

" And your grandfather ?"

" Same way, and great-grandfather, ditto."

" We should think you would be afraid to go ; it's very dangerous for you."

" Where did your fathers die, gentlemen ?"

" In their beds."

" And your grandfathers ?"

" In their beds, also."

" And your great-grandfathers ?"

" In their beds, of course ; all our ancestors died in their beds."

" I should think you would be afraid to go to bed ; it's very dangerous for you."

He had been gone two weeks. One morning the following despatch was received by the Duke :

" Ethervolt Station ; South Pole.

" I have this moment returned ; have traversed part of meteoric belt crossing our orbit, several million miles in various directions. It is two million miles wide and a hundred thousand miles thick,—entire circuit probably over three thousand million miles. Numbers of isolated streams floating in outlying Space, dimensions from several thousand, to a million or more square miles in extent and moving irregularly in neighborhood of orbit ; densely packed with enormous bolides and uranolites like those of late shower. Have calculated elements of a few ; one is directly approaching ; sixty thousand miles long ; speed fifty miles a minute ; will pass equator two thousand miles above surface, 10 o'c. to-morrow night, will strike both Moons ;—bulk of shower will fall in Vodraga ocean. New Comet approaching from west quarter of heavens ; has probably passed through Asteroidal Zone ; Comet, sword shape,—sixty million miles long,—Coma a hundred thousand miles diameter ;—speed five million miles per day,—course directly toward meteoric belt,—will strike in seven days.. I predict extraordinary disturbances in belt—widespread scattering of meteoric streams and offshoots. Shall return immediately to resume observations on Comet—have communicated with Astronomer Solaris ;—watch moons to-morrow night at hour specified. ASTERION."

By 9 o'c. next evening our party repaired to the observatory. Several professors of the Royal University and members of the Academy of Sciences were assembled. Astronomer Solaris and his colleagues were at their posts in the great rotunda. The giant Equatorial was slowly revolved on its ponderous pedestal through the channel in the dome, and its enormous object glass levelled on the angry moons which were nearly in opposition with each other, and coursing low down over the southern horizon in the cloudless sky.

Never was an eclipse of Sun or Moon, occultation of Planet or Star, transit of Venus, or any other Celestial phenomenon, watched on Earth, with such intense and absorbing interest,—not to speak of anxiety—as was this approaching meteoric downfall, upon the results of which might remotely hang the fate of a World. Short tubes with eye pieces had been adjusted to the instrument which enabled several persons to view the phenomenon simultaneously.(1)

(1) The eye pieces of many Martian telescopes are arranged with adjustable tubes and reflecting lenses, by means of which several persons can view celestial phenomena at the same moment.

We counted the moments as they passed. 10 o'c. struck.

"Contact is beginning," said Astronomer Solaris.

Immediately in front of Rohanza, appeared a long, slender, conoidal shaped nebulous cloud, shining with a misty light, its apex pointing forward. It looked like some gigantic aërial shark suddenly sprung from the dark abyss to devour her. In a few moments the apex touched the orb, which seemed to be gradually drawn within the maw of the nebulous monster. The other moon, Aryuna, also disappeared. What convulsions these two moons endured, engulfed within the bowels of this meteoric tempest, eye hath never seen. Time passed on and they emerged from the base of the cloud. Their appearance was frightful. Rohanza, which had borne the full brunt of the bombardment, was spouting torrents of crimson lava, as if her life blood were oozing from every pore, while Aryuna seemed whirling in tornadoes of fire and smoke. The Cosmic monster now curved swiftly downward and plunged to the depths of Vodraga ocean.

Every man in that great rotunda grew pale ; not a word was spoken ;—not a sound was heard, save the measured ticking of the astronomical clock whose wheels silently revolve the huge telescope on its axis step by step, keeping its long tube parallel with, and its enormous eye fixed on the celestial body as it rolls along the heavens. The assistants, seated at their desks by their glimmering lights under the dark shadow of the lofty dome, silently worked at their calculations. The Astronomer Royal now approached the Grand Duke and Prince.

"As the full effect of this collision on our moons may not be manifested for many hours," said he, "I will communicate to Your Highness the results of our observations, soon as completed."

The assembly took their departure and it was doubtful whether, among them a single eye was closed in sleep that night, certainly not at the palace. Notwithstanding the anxiety caused by the terrible phenomenon, the cool headed Astronomer and his colleagues immediately went to work and after many hours' laborious calculation, confirmed the accuracy of Asterion's conclusions to the letter. How this extraordinary young man, shut up within the narrow confines of his Ethervolt car, whirled day and night amid these awful meteoric tempests, continually on the watch to avoid fatal collisions, and with the necessarily limited facilities for making such abstruse and careful investigations at hand, could correctly accomplish them, awakened the astonishment and admiration of the Astronomical Society. Had some terrestrial tourist, caught on the crater of Mount Vesuvius amid one of its most terrible eruptions, and running the gauntlet of its lava streams, and hottest scorial downpour, been able to solve a problem in integral calculus or conic sections, in the midst of it, the feat would not have been half so great.

The next day the following despatch from the observatory was received by the Duke :

"Aryuna has descended ten miles and Rohanza six miles below their former positions. Combustional action progressing with increased violence on both satellites ; no perceptible variation in their orbital velocities apparent.

"Solaris."

As the publication of this news would only serve to increase the general apprehension and alarm, it was decided by the astronomical society to withhold them from the public for the present.

The days passed on ; all were anxiously awaiting news from Asterion in relation to that most important event, the approach of the New Comet. The intrepid voyager was many million miles distant, watching its advent, calculating its elements, and the widespread perturbations it would produce in its rush through the Meteoric belt which our planet was steadily approaching. Such a phenomenon is certainly the most tremendous that could possibly take place in the vast abysses of Space,—the destruction of a World, perhaps, excepted.

This fiery Dragon of Chaos, seemingly endowed with infernal power and speed, its starry nucleus like a malignant Cyclopean eye encased in the centre of its Coma, a hundred thousand miles in diameter and throwing off its outer envelopes in successive layers, which form its train. This train sixty, to a hundred or more, million miles long, expanding at its extremity into the semblance of a gigantic broom,—bearing in its bosom the most inflammable of all gases,—saturated through its whole mass with the most combustible materials,— flying in its perihelion passage around the Sun at the rate of two hundred thousand miles per minute,—its tail lengthening out at the rate of twenty to thirty million miles per day.—This Empyreanic Monster, rushing headlong into a Meteoric belt two million miles wide and a hundred thousand miles thick, packed with countless millions of meteorites, bolides and uranolites, red and white hot,—clashing against each other and flying at the rate of fifty to a hundred miles per second ;—the mind is utterly overwhelmed at any attempt to conceive the tremendous horrors of the scene.

The Comet had now come in full view, visible all

over the planet every night from sunset to sunrise. Its dimensions were enormous, covering an arc of thirty degrees over the visible heavens. Its shape somewhat resembled a drawn sabre, its nucleus brilliant, and the stars shining through its thin, gauzy film. In these clear Martian skies its appearance was much more bright and beautiful than Comets seen from Earth. It was rapidly approaching the track of the Meteoric belt ; hourly watched by every observatory on Mars, and millions of people ; the results expected from its transit were looked forward to with great anxiety.

Seven days passed. The time for the collision was at hand. For several days extraordinary disturbances had been noticed in the aërial electric currents. Great magnetic storms had been seen on the Sun and changes also observed in the belts of Jupiter. These, however, were not deemed sufficient to produce the disturbances. The vicinity of the Comet was unquestionably the exciting cause. Telegraphic communications through the aërial currents had been greatly disturbed and during the last twelve hours were entirely cut off in the north west hemisphere. On the evening of the seventh day a violent storm took place accompanied with unusual thunder and lightning, which were almost incessant. We were assembled in the reception room. The storm increased in fury and violence. The rain fell in torrents ; the sky was black as midnight ; the thunder peals shook the palace to its foundations. Suddenly a loud crash was heard outside,—we sprang to our feet,— there was a clamor of voices,—the door burst open and Asterion rushed into the room,—his face pale as a corpse,—his hair dishevelled,—his eyes bloodshot,— his garments torn,—blood flowing from a deep wound in his forehead,—he staggered forward and feebly gasped out,—

"Comet dashed through belt last night !—tore part to fragments,—drew off clouds,—many offshoots follow in train,—Meteoric stream ninety thousand miles long coming ahead,—ten thousand miles a minute,—will strike Machival, and Puranthos by midnight.   Quick !— warn Polath,—Harovian,—if too late, millions will perish ;"—and he sank down insensible.

For a moment, all stood speechless with horror !

"Telegraphic communication is cut off," shouted the Duke.   "Haste !   Sound the alarm !   Out with the air ships !   Fly to the kingdoms of Polath and Harovian instantly !"

The whole palace was in confusion.   The alarm was sounded over the city ; in less than an hour a thousand air ships were flying swifter than the hurricane to the kingdoms of Polath and Prince Harovian, which were on the opposite side of the hemisphere, six and eight thousand miles distant, respectively.   It was 7 o'c. Could they reach them in time ?   No.   The swiftest ships at fullest power of speed could make only from two hundred and fifty to three hundred miles per hour. The only possible hope was, the shower might be delayed.   We bore the insensible Asterion to a private room and Dr. Hamival dressed his wound.   His ship had been broken in its impetuous downfall amid the trees.   Bhuras, Vidyuna, Capt. Volanto and crew were severely stunned.   Bhuras informed us they had been traversing the belt several million miles since last night. When the Comet struck the belt it tore a great gap strait through it, six million miles wide, scattering huge clouds of meteorites all around, and drawing immense streams of them in its train.   The sight was the most frightful ever seen.   Soon as he had discovered the great offshoot which was swiftly flying toward the planet, Asterion hastened his return, flying at the rate of two hundred thousand miles per hour ahead of it. Reaching the pole and finding telegraphic communication cut off, he mounted his air ship, shot her up ten miles in the air to the upper polar magnetic current and flew at the rate of fifty miles per minute. This terrible speed made the interior of the car so hot they were almost suffocated ; reaching the palace in the teeth of the tempest, they plunged down amid the trees regardless of safety.

" No ship but this could reach those kingdoms in time," said Vidyuna, " for none are provided with the magnetic motor and none but Asterion understands the working of it. Wherever that awful downfall strikes across those continents, not a soul will be left to tell the tale."

" Haste !" exclaimed Altfoura ; " order up another air ship and crew ; Asterion communicated the secret of his motor to me ; magnetic stations are erected near the palaces of King Polath and Prince Harovian. We'll fly there immediately."

The ship was brought up in the grounds. Altfoura carefully removed the motor from the broken ship and affixed it to the magnetic rod of the new one, and jumped aboard with the crew. The ship rose five miles above the surface into the region of calm, and sped toward the east at the rate of fifty miles a minute.

The hours dragged on ; the night was dark and the storm still raging, fit prelude to the awful tempest that would soon break on the other hemisphere of the Martian World.

The clock struck midnight.

" It is the hour," said Duke Athalton in a whisper.

We raised the windows, the sky had cleared, the wind moaned through the trees like a sad, wailing requiem. Low down in the eastern horizon appeared a long conical shaped nebulous mass. It resembled the Zodiacal light seen on our Earth before sunrise and sunset at certain seasons of the year, with its base toward the Sun and its apex toward the Zenith, and the exact nature of which is unknown. The apex of this conoidal mass stretched far out into space. It shone with a faint phosphorescent light. Now and then flashes of Cosmic lightning passed through its mass.

The blow had struck ; the awful tempest was falling on those doomed kingdoms. What untold agony, horror and despair, millions of our friends were now suffering.

The moments passed ; the cloud sank from view in the eastern horizon ; it was passing o'er the continents beneath us ;—soon it emerged on the west horizon and gradually disappeared in the far distant space ;—all was over and its fatal work was accomplished.

CHAPTER LV.

THE METEORIC TEMPEST.

" The strong cemented walls,
The tott'ring towers,—the pond'rous ruin falls.
The nations tremble at the dreadful sound.
Heav'n thunders,—tempests roar and groans the ground."
Joshua. (Fall of Jericho.)—HANDEL.

Too late ?—yes, alas ! too late for millions ; yet, not for many millions more. In great calamities like these, the universal horror and grief for the lost is mitigated by the joy over those who are saved. Of all those thousand swift ships that sped on their errand of warning, Altfoura's was the only one that reached those doomed kingdoms in time. He had raised that mighty motor to its fullest power, and drawn by the magnetic engines stationed in those kingdoms, his ship had sped through the upper aërial currents at the rate of seventy five miles a minute ! In this awful flight, every thing was swept from the deck, ornaments, railing and flag staff. The heat developed by its terrible rush through the air shrivelled the wood work of the cabin ; the metallic walls almost scorched the hand, and the air became suffocating. The crew were astounded at the audacious daring of the Prince in forcing a speed which Asterion himself would hardly have risked.

" 'Tis a race for life !" said he ; "millions of lives are at stake !—Have no fear ; many a knee is now bent in earnest prayer that we may be able to warn our friends in time, and on those prayers, our gallant ship and motor, we may safely rely."

He made that journey of four thousand miles, from one side of the planet's hemisphere to the other, in less than sixty minutes. Reaching the palace of Prince Harovian in Aliomador, the Capital City of Rohita-Savoyal, he paused only for a moment to sound the alarm ; then sped on to Machival Purantos, the realm of King Polath, two thousand miles further, reaching it just in time. As telegraphic communication had not been disturbed on that side of the hemisphere, the alarm flew through every city, town and hamlet in both continents and the vast, teeming populations, from the king on his throne, to the peasant in his cottage,—men, women and children, fled with tumultuous speed to their cellars under the great cities and the deep subterraneous excavations in the fields. In this mad rush of multitudes, thousands were trampled under foot or suffocated.

Precisely at noon, as Asterion had predicted, the cloud struck the planet, with no warning signal, as would have been seen by night, long beforehand. The sun was shining bright. At first, the sky became overcast with a thin cloudy film ; the sun became gradually obscured and changed to a dull red hue ; soon it totally disappeared ; the whole firmament was o'erspread with an infernal glare, and the downpour began.

With a rush and a roar as if heaven and earth were coming together,—amid explosions, thunders and lightnings,—compared with which the tornadoes that sweep o'er our Indian seas are but as gentle zephyrs,—countless myriads of bolides, uranolites and meteorites, of solid igneous metal or mineral, from hundreds of pounds to thousands of tons weight, half fused, red or white hot, and blazing with long trains of fire,—poured in one solid line over the doomed kingdoms, from west to east, four thousand miles long and two to six hundred miles wide.

Down sank the tall and powerful steel columns, pillars and arched networks covering the great linear cities. Down sank the lofty temples, castles, palaces and towers, the splendid mansions, châteaus and pavilions,—the bridges and ponderous walls of solid masonry. Down crushed, were the great forests,—blooming fields and gardens. Beneath the fury of this awful cataclysm everything was ground to powder, or consumed in whirlwinds of fire ! All nature seemed convulsed Cries and screams of agony, horror and despair, from millions, rose to the flaming heavens ! The whole face of the country where it fell, over mountains, valleys and plains was ploughed and torn in huge furrows, and ravines. Thousands of the deep underground cellars with their arches of solid masonry were crushed and the inmates miserably perished. Many small lakes were nearly filled up, and rivers dammed up, their overflowings producing widespread inundations. In many places covering hundreds of square miles, the bolides and meteorites spread in great fields many feet in depth, smoking like lakes of volcanic lava. As the tempest poured into Tanogar ocean ([1])—which at this point is over a thousand miles wide, the waters were turned into a vast boiling caldron of roaring billows, hissing steam and clouds of spray.

The downpour continued four hours. When all was over, the terror stricken multitudes issued from their places of refuge and toiled painfully over the burning marl to their homes, if homes they had. Multitudes were compelled to camp in the fields and forests. Seven million lives were lost. Thousands died of sheer fright and many became insane. The destruction of parts of the great linear cities, towns, villages, crops, property and domestic animals was incalculable.

It is impossible to describe the universal consternation and dismay that prevailed all over the Martian World. Men ran to and fro as if distracted. "When will the next tempest come?—Where will it fall?" was the universal question, and "God only knows;"—the only answer. The Astronomical world; all science, was utterly at sea. The only man to whom they could look with any confidence for the solution of this question, was hovering between life and death. Millions on their bended knees nightly prayed that his life might be spared. The first shock of horror passed, the sympathies of all the Martian kingdoms were awakened to the sad condition of the suffering ones. The coffers of wealth and stores of provisions were thrown open and freely distributed among countless thousands of suffering and destitute families. As the greater part of the

([1]) Corresponding to Kaiser sea on our Martian maps.

Capital City of Machival Purantos was destroyed,—
including the palace of King Polath and the mansions
of many of his suite and cabinet, Duke Athalton immediately extended the hospitalities of his kingdom, capital
and palace, and the King, royal family and many of his
court and suite, with their families, accepted. Duke
Oneigar also extended the same hospitalities to thousands of Prince Harovian's subjects ; their kingdom
had suffered the greatest loss of life and property but
the Capital had escaped. Diavojahr made no response
to the general appeal ; but nothing better was expected
of him and he was so universally detested that none
would have accepted any thing he might have offered.
A number of his boon companions, including Duke
Sybarite, Biborax, Gluttonog, Swaggerchop & Co.,
together with a bevy of swells and exquisites, had all
been crushed to a jelly while holding a dissolute orgie
on one of a beautiful group of islands owned by him in
Tanogar ocean, like the old Capri island in the days of
the Roman Emperors ; it was also a Pluto-Martian
Monte Carlo. Immense sums were squandered there
by the royal bloods, which supported the throngs of
gamblers, pimps and courtezans, as is usual in such
places. As many of these swells and exquisites were
professional female mashers, it seemed appropriate that
they also should experience a little mashing in their
turn. The untimely demise of these distinguished
ornaments of society had deeply affected His Royal
Highness and led him to suspect that the infernal gods
were beginning to turn up their noses at him. In the
mean time he had been crowned Emperor of his kingdom,
had formed a new Cabinet of his favorites (Eliff having
resigned and retired to his country seat), and being
occupied with the establishment of a new policy, involving increased taxation and oppression of the people, his

aspirations for the hand of the Princess of Mandal-Uttima, seemed to be lain aside for the present.

In the mean time Asterion had lain insensible for forty eight hours. The prolonged and terrible strain through which he had passed, combined with the severe wound, had proven too much for even his immense vitality, and his physical powers had suddenly given way. He passed from this, into a stage of violent fever and delirium, during which he seemed again to go through those awful scenes. Frequent ejaculations escaped his lips,—"Haste! O, haste, my brave ship;—speed on;—millions of precious lives are at stake!" Then in most touching accents he would implore heaven to aid him in his flight. Day and night we watched by his bedside with intense solicitude. The highest medical skill in the kingdom was summoned, and Dr. Hamival hardly left his side. Oft in the midst of his paroxysms of frenzy, the Princess Suhlamia would place her hand upon his fevered brow, her gentle touch and voice would always calm and soothe him to repose. Finally these dangerous symptoms passed away and he sank into profound sleep for three days and nights, during which perfect silence reigned in the palace, for this was the turning point in the disorder. From this he awoke, perfectly himself, though weak and exhausted, and greeted us with his usual pleasant smile and words of welcome. It is impossible to express our joy. The Astronomer Royal was seated by his side; for a while his memory seemed struggling to recall some event of the past;—then as if it had just dawned on his mind,—

"That shower ·—did,—did it—come?"

"It came;—" replied Solaris.

"At the time specified?"

"Exactly at the hour."

"What were the results?"

Solaris related the appearance and extent of the phe-nomenón, suppressing, however, any allusion to the dreadful loss of life.

"Seek not to conceal the facts from me,—" he replied, turning his eagle eye upon him. "When I saw that fiery messenger of destruction,—that Demon of the spheres, rushing through the Meteoric belt ;— when I saw that insatiate tiger of Chaos, the meteoric cloud—following hard upon my homeward track, I knew full well what was coming, and in the wild dreams of my delirium, those visions of horror were ever before me."

Altfoura related the awful details of the catastrophe, to which he listened with calmness.

"Had it not been for your wonderful magnetic motor and the magnetic stations you caused to be erected in the kingdoms of our friends, and which enabled our Prince to reach them in time, the loss of life would have counted up to scores of millions," said Solaris.

"I am deeply grateful that my little invention was put to such great use," replied Asterion.

"Come now, it's time for lunch ;" said Altfoura, touching a bell and an attendant entered with a well laden salver.

"Hand me my note book and astronomical tables ;" said Asterion. "I have a calculation to figure up."

"Nay, my friend ; no more Astronomical business at present ; you must take lunch."

"Hand me my tables," demanded Asterion imperi-ously.

"Gastronomics are the order of the day, and Astro-nomics must give way ;" emphatically replied the Prince, motioning the attendant forward with his salver.

"My tables ; I tell you. Do you hear ?" exclaimed Asterion, motioning the salver away with supreme disdain, and regarding Altfoura like an Oriental satrap giving his orders ; suddenly there was a movement in the throng and the Princess Suhlamia, glided to a seat by the cot and presented a delicious little *morceau* to his lips.

" I made it myself, expressly for you," said she.

That settled the question, and Asterion, after the first emotion of embarrassment at the distinguished honor, thankfully partook of the delicacy. The Princess was mistress of the situation and controlled affairs accordingly. Asterion yielded like a little child ; it did our hearts good to see our poor, dear friend eat ; and the Doctor and Astronomer blessed every morsel. The Princess fed him with her own fair hands right strait along.

" Yes," said the Prince ; " you haven't had a fair meal in months. We are completely out of patience with your starvation diet ;—dry bread ; grapes or apples, cold water and milk, flavored with science, calculations, and nothing else. We've got you in hand now, and we'll make you eat three full meals every day with lunches in between, for a long time to come. Do you hear, sir ?"

" If he objects, I shall be under the painful necessity of feeding him," remarked the Princess, quietly.

Asterion looked as if he hoped the Princess might occasionally be under the painful necessity. The repast concluded, he asked the Princess very submissively, if he might not be permitted to look at his tablets ; she handed them to him herself, with a strict injunction that he must not bestow over twenty minutes examination, which he faithfully promised, then bidding him adieu, she left the room. The tables were filled with abstruse problems in algebraic and mathematical symbols, known to no one but himself, and which he always carried in his pocket on his voyages. With a rapidity which astonished even Astronomer Solaris, he ran up a calculation ; at the conclusion, he grew suddenly pale, uttered a faint exclamation and sank back on his pillow. We bent anxiously over him, —his eyes were closed.

" What is it, Asterion ?"—asked Altfoura.

"A calculation," he murmured. " I had not finished when—when the blow struck me ;—but now—"

" What is there in the conclusion, that so agitates you ?" asked Solaris.

He hesitated, and an almost imperceptible shudder ran o'er him.

" Tell us, Asterion, we are prepared for anything now,—if you are."

" As the Comet plunged through the belt it drew in its train a Meteoric stream three hundred thousand miles long. I calculated its elements. It will separate from the Cometic train in ten days."

"And after separation ?" asked Astronomer Solaris.

" Being on a line with our orbit, it will gradually be drawn within the attraction of our planet."

" And then ?"

" Can you receive the news calmly ?"

After a pause—" We can."

" It will strike on the 40th parallel North Lat."

" What part of the hemisphere ?"

" On our beloved kingdom of Mandal-Uttima, and cut a path six hundred miles wide diagonally across the whole length of this continent, from the South West to the North East !"

" And our beautiful city, Elfrezulah ?" asked Altfoura, in tones that trembled.

" Lies right in its pathway."

For several moments there was a profound silence.

" Thank God for the warning ;" said Duke Athalton ; " we'll have time to sound the alarm, and the whole population of every city and town in its pathway can fly to distant parts of our kingdom."

" But this is not all ;" continued Asterion ; " more is yet to come."

" Great Heaven !" exclaimed all. " And has dire fate greater horrors in store for us ?"

" Aye ; the moons ! They will be on that part of our hemisphere, and receive the shower, which may so retard their orbital velocities, or beat them down so far, as will hasten their downfall."

A shudder ran through the room and many a cheek grew pale ; finally,—

" Have you calculated the time when the stream will strike our planet ?" asked Solaris.

" I have."

" When ?"

" In sixty days exactly ;—and far worse even than this may come."

For several moments all were silent, as if in terror to receive the frightful news.

" The central part of the stream, through its whole length is so densely packed with enormous meteorites that, should it pass lengthwise over the moons, the combined weight of the masses,—surpassing that of the satellites a hundred fold,—will hurl them down on our planet to its utter destruction !"

A groan of inexpressible horror ran through the room, then came deep silence,—all seemed absorbed in contemplation of the awful doom hanging over the Martian World.

" Great God !" exclaimed Altfoura in a burst of uncontrollable anguish. " Is our beautiful world indeed doomed to destruction and all whom we love and cherish thus to perish ?"

"We are in the hands of the Almighty Framer of the Universe," said the Astronomer in tones of deep reverence ; "and whate'er our fate may be, we must bend in humble submission to His Divine Will."

"There is one chance for escape, not for all, indeed, —but for many of us here," said Asterion.

"Escape ?—How ?—Where ?"

"By a flight to Earth !"

"A flight to Earth !" they all exclaimed in profound astonishment.

"Yes !" he cried, springing from his couch, his voice ringing like a clarion. "A flight to Earth. It is only one hundred and twenty million miles distant. I'll take a trip there immediately. Will make surveys over the Antarctic regions and parts of the Southern hemisphere, and note the best places of refuge for us all. In the meantime, My Lord Duke of Mandal-Uttima, you will issue instant orders for the Ethervolt car and air ship establishments to be increased a hundred fold and with armies of workmen ;—we can turn Ethervolts and ships out at the rate of twenty thousand per week ;—I'll instruct their captains and engineers, in battallions ;— erect fifty additional Ethervolt stations at the South Pole ;—this done, we can transport a million or more people to Earth every week and as facilities increase, in still greater numbers. Aye,—thus can we save our friends.—Away !—lose not a moment,—bring me my garments,—I must be up and about my business,—Ho ! —there—my air ship !—bring her up immediately."

It was impossible to restrain him,—he seemed inspired with the fiery ardor of a god ;—his swift orders were like the commands of Jupiter on the eve of battle with the Titans ;—he threw on his garments ;—the air ship came up ;—in company with the Duke, Prince and highest peers of the realm, he flew on the wings of the wind to meet the awful crisis that hung o'er the Martian World.

CHAPTER LVI.

THE DOOMED PLANET.

"And I will show wonders in heaven above and signs in the earth beneath, blood and fire and vapour of smoke. The sun shall be turned into darkness, and the moon into blood before that great and notable day of the Lord come."

"The sun shall be darkened and the moon shall not give her light, and the stars (meteors) shall fall from heaven, and the powers of the heavens shall be shaken."

Matt. XXIV : 29; Acts XI : 20.

The news of the expected downfall increased the universal terror. This predicted tempest might be the prelude to others yet to come at any moment, none could tell, when or where, and with it came the anticipation of far greater horrors. "The moons will fall !—Our World will be destroyed !"—went up in one dreadful cry of agony to the heavens. Had the trump of doom sounded, the widespread consternation could not have been greater. The whole Martian World presented a complete picture of that "distress and tribulation among the nations, with perplexity ;—men's hearts failing them for fear and for looking after those things which are coming "—described in the words of the Apostle as appearing in the last days of our Terrestrial World.([1]) This final catastrophe might long be

([1]) St. Luke XXI : 26.

delayed ;—might indeed never come ;—no diminution
of the moon's orbital velocities was yet apparent ;—the
meteoric bombardment falling on them might be com-
pensated by destructive combustions and dissipations of
their materials into space, thereby lessening their
densities.   With such reasonings as these, Astronomical
science sought to allay the public alarm.   But scientific
reasonings and probabilities were of no avail.   Business
of every kind—except providing the daily necessities of
life—was thrown aside.   Trade, commerce, internal
improvements ceased.   Vast fleets lay moored at the
docks deserted by their crews.

The great subject that absorbed the public mind was
the protection of life and property against the dreadful
catastrophies.   Sixty days was the limit within which
preparations could be accomplished.   Imagine such a
horror as this, impending over the nations and kingdoms of our globe.   What facilities, what measures
could we, with all our boasted achievements in mechanical science and machinery, adopt, to protect our populations against such a terrible catastrophe ?   None but
Martians are equal to such emergencies (the downfall
of her moons excepted).   The frameworks covering the
linear cities, effective as they might be in shielding
them from the usual annual showers, could afford no
protection against those tremendous downpours that
were to come ; neither could the under ground cellars.
The kingdom of Mandal-Uttima immediately went to
work with its gigantic and powerful machinery, engines
and millions of workmen over the whole continent at
points removed from the lines of the expected downfall.   The foundations of mountains and hills were
excavated in vast caverns extending scores of miles.
Thousands of deep and spacious cellars were dug all
over the plains and valleys in the vicinity of the cities

and towns, roofed with solid arches of metal or masonry, and covered with enormous embankments extending for miles, affording ample refuges for the entire populations and stored with abundant supplies of food and water. Every Martian kingdom engaged in this immense work and a great part of the surface of the planet was burrowed and excavated from equator to poles.

For protection against a possible downfall of the Moons, of course nothing could be done. The planet must take its chances. These enormous masses—of which Rohanza, at the lowest calculation weighs four trillion tons, and Aryuna ten times that weight,—with the immense momentum acquired by the speed of their downfall, the solid crust of the planet could no more resist the blow, than could the roof of a shed, the ball of a hundred ton Krupp cannon. The enormous heat produced by the impact would set those parts of the planet where they fell, on fire. They would certainly drive a huge gulf or shaft ten to twenty miles in diameter right into the very bowels of the planet, perhaps fly straight through it, like a grape shot through a pumpkin. The pent up fiery gases and incandescent vapors, the molten metals and minerals would gush out in torrents all over the surface, destroying all vegetable and animal life ; collapses of the crust, sinking of plains and mountains, dissipation of oceans and seas into vapor would speedily follow and the whole globe converted back into its primeval geological condition of a semi-fluid molten mass. Some held that the planet would be blown up, and the Terrestrians witness the production of a new belt of Asteroids revolving inside the old one. It may all be very well for us Terrestrians to complacently flatter ourselves as to the everlasting perpetuity of our own Terrestrio-Lunar affairs, but when we see through our great telescopes the extraordinary appearances and changes manifest on the surface of our brother World ; when we see its little Moons whirling around the orb at such a rate—the inner one, Phobos, three times in twenty four hours, and sixty times nearer to it than our moon is to us, it must be confessed that the perpetuity of Martio-lunar affairs look rather dubious in the remote future, and the same things happening with them, may possibly happen to us (1) 'Tis true, our Luna, like many a vain and pretty woman, has been keeping her bright side toward us ever since Astronomy found it out ; how she behaved herself in Adam and Eve's day we know not ; but she is certainly a very inconstant little coquette, calmly as she looks on lovers' vows. Perhaps she may take a notion some day, to solicit a near acquaintance with us, or show us her dark side, or dance around us as lively as her little Martian brothers around their own primary. Who can tell ? The inevitable results consequent upon such acts of inconstancy toward her old mother Terra, are not only well known to the Astronomical world, but have been graphically foretold by the old Hebrew prophets and Apostles ages ago.

Asterion's recovery was hailed with universal joy. He was the only man who dared roam among the realms of chaos, and who could, amid those terrible

(1) It has been thought by some Astronomers that the axis of Mars' rotation has changed its position during the last hundred years. Observations on the large white spot near the south pole may help to decide this point. Such a stupendous phenomenon could not occur by the action of any astronomical laws with which we are acquainted. Milton (Paradise Lost, Book X., Lines 668–671) describes the shifting of the poles of Earth by the Angels, at command of the Almighty, as one of the penalties visited on Nature in consequence of Adam's sin.

dangers, calculate the approach and accurately determine the downfall of these wandering clouds. But it was not to be expected that he could spend his whole life in an Ethervolt, playing the *rôle* of a detective on the look out for meteoric guerillas and tramps. He was now occupied with his plans for the trip to Earth and preparing for the great emigration that might possibly take place in the universal panic, and for which the government possessed ample facilities. Immense numbers of workshops were established for the construction of fleets of Ethervolts and air ships. Schools of instruction in the science of Interplanetary navigation for the captains, engineers and assistants— young men of ability and courage being selected for the profession, all under Asterion's supervision. The ships were to be transported to Earth in trains attached to the Ethervolts ; arriving there, the emigrants were to embark in them and fly to their various places of refuge around the South pole and different parts of the southern hemisphere ; supplies of food and water were to be conveyed. It was hoped that, their sojourn on Earth might after all, be only temporary, until the true state and prospects of lunar affairs were satisfactorily determined ; still, it was necessary to be in readiness for any event. The preparations for our trip to Earth were hastened. Two magnificent Ethervolt cars and air ships on improved patterns were made. The ships were spindle shaped, ninety feet long by thirty five abeam, constructed of the strongest combination of metals, equipped with batteries, machinery and wings of immense power and speed, fitted to encounter the vicissitudes and dangers of aërial voyages over the antarctic lands and seas of Earth, to breast the terrible polar storms and angry billows of these regions. Their interior arrangements were commodious and elegant.

The Ethervolts were taken to the south polar station to be put in readiness for our journey. Capt. Sussonac, an old and experienced aërial navigator, with a select crew, submitted both ships to a thorough test and pronounced them the finest he had ever commanded and that, it would afford him the greatest pleasure to circumvolate the Terrestrial globe with them. One having been selected, the ceremony of christening was delegated to the Princess Suhlamia. This took place in the grounds of the palace and was conducted with appropriate ceremonies. The Captain placed in her hands a bottle of finest crystal, filled with a rare and ruby wine. The prow of the ship was ornamented with the figure head of an albatross *volant*, and festooned with garlands. The Princess, standing on deck.

"I name thee Nai-Alavestron, or the 'Explorer.' Thou shalt traverse the vast and trackless realms of Space to another World. Thou shalt fly through the wind and storm,—the rain and snow, the mist and cloud, the lightning and thunder : I commit thee to the charge of the Great Creator. May His all-seeing eye watch over thee, and His protecting hand guard thee on thy perilous journey, and when thou hast reached that other World, which may perhaps become the final refuge of us here, may propitious winds waft thee o'er thy journeys there, and bring thee in safety to thy destined haven."

So saying the Princess broke the bottle over the prow and the wine ran down to the ground ; a short prayer was said and the ship was put in readiness for our departure.

Our party consisted of Asterion and his two assistants, Vidyuna and Bhuras, the former to take charge of the second Ethervolt. Altfoura, Capt. Sussonac, officers

and engineers, to take charge of the Terrestrial air ship ;
Capt. Fulminax, formerly of the Martian polar ice fleet ;
two telegraphic operators ; skilled air ship and battery
machinists. Dr. Hamival ; our renowned Leviathan
driver, Hartilion ; Corporal John and Commodore Jack
who positively refused to be separated from his master.

I have had a casket made to contain my journal, notes,
etc., taken during my sojourn on Mars. It is about two
feet in length, elliptical in shape, its two halves united
with a fine screw joint, impervious to water. It is constructed of a peculiar combination of Martian metals,
lighter than cork, stronger than our toughest steel. It
is encased with a network of strong cords to which
small buoys are attached. Should we suffer shipwreck
in our journey over the Oceans of Earth, it shall be
thrown overboard and perchance may be picked up by
some passing vessel, or washed to some shore, or near
some sea port, and our fate be made known to the world.
Tightly corked bottles, etc., containing papers announcing the distress, or loss of ships at sea, have not
unfrequently been thus discovered.

All being in readiness, the Duke, members of the
royal household and many friends were assembled in
the grounds to witness our departure. The Explorer
was mounted on its platform manned with Capt. Sussonac and crew. The mutual farewells were exchanged.
Suhlamia and I were in a little arbor embowered with
flowers. She plucked a forget-me-not and affixed it to
my breast, struggling to conceal her emotions, and in
trembling accents, "May our Heavenly Father watch
over and shield you from all shadow of danger shall be
my hourly prayer till we meet again. All angels bless
and guard you." Our parting was almost like the final
severing of hearts long united and that beat as one.

We quickly embarked ; the ship rose from the

grounds, swiftly flew over the city and kingdom of Mandal-Uttima, crossed the equatorial ocean, the lands and
seas of the Southern hemisphere and by evening of the
following day reached the South Pole.

---❖---

CHAPTER LVII.

FLIGHT TO EARTH.

" The affair cries haste,
And speed must answer it, you must away to-night."
Othello, Act I., Sc. 3.

We landed in the great amphitheatre of the station.
The magnificent Ethervolts which were to convey us
once more through the Realms of Space were resting on
their platforms. They were models of beauty, sixty
feet high by thirty wide, at the base, and glittered like
burnished silver. From their summits projected the
metallic staffs surmounted by the magnetic globes.
Their interiors were commodious and elegant, the circular door and windows with their telescopic lenses, the
air generators, calorific apparatus, instruments; ample
supplies of provisions, etc. Beneath the platforms were
the great polar magnetic batteries, manned by the
operators clad in their crystal armor.

Bhuras now took a small metallic casket, and accompanied by one of the telegraphic operators we entered the
private office of the station. He opened the casket and
carefully removing an exceedingly delicate and beautiful instrument placed it on the table. A brilliant and
highly sensitive dial plate of mingled steel and crystal,
was attached to the instrument, directly over the keys.

"Gentlemen," said Asterion, "I take pleasure in announcing to you the invention of our young friend, Bhuras."

"What is it?" we asked.

"The Interplanetary Telegraph."

The cheers that followed this announcement made the walls of the amphitheatre ring.

"By means of which messages can be sent from Mars to Earth, and back again through the Cosmo-magnetic currents running between them. I consider it the greatest invention of the age."

Bhuras blushed like a school boy at his master's compliment, and as we all shook him by the hand,—"I dedicate my little invention to Asterion," said he.

"If you don't look out, Asterion, Bhuras will strip you of your laurels," said Altfoura.

"O, I'm expecting it any day;—the sly dog. Before we took our Asteroidal trip, he used to sit cooped up in his corner in our workshop, pegging away at his machine day and night, without letting me know anything about it till it was finished."

"He's got something better than that, on hand,"—said Vidyuna.

"What?" we asked.

"An Interplanetary Opsiferon, or talking machine, by which the inhabitants of Mars and Earth can converse together as easily as if they were seated side by side in each others' parlors."

We all began to cheer louder than before.

"Please don't hurrah till the chicken is hatched,"—implored Bhuras. "Many an egg of invention turns out addled."

He now made the wire connections between the telegraph and the metallic rods which ran directly to the polar magnetic centre beneath the foundations of the station. Asterion then spoke to the operator.

" You will remain in this office day and night, taking your meals and sleeping here. When we reach the South pole of Earth, which will be within a week at farthest, unless unforeseen delays occur, Bhuras will set up his other instrument at the polar station and signal to you our arrival, which will appear on the dial plate written out in symbols. You will immediately transmit the same to the Duke at his palace, and send me his reply. Other instructions I will send you here-after. Bhuras will remain at the station there. Tele-graph to him immediately any news of importance you may receive."

We now passed out and ascended the platforms of the Ethervolts, one of which was in charge of Asterion, the other of Vidyuna. The contents of our air ship had been transferred to the cars, and Captain Sus-sonac and crew had fastened it by a long chain to Vid-yuna's car, its anti-gravitation batteries having been adjusted to the proper degree of tension for its journey through space. It was 10 o'c. at night ; the stars shone bright in the clear vault above, and among them gleamed the soft and rosy light of our dear Mother Earth, one hundred and twenty million miles away. I gazed on her with emotions of joy such as the traveller feels who sees the glimmering light of his far distant home ; yet with it were mingled feelings of awe, as I contemplated this perilous journey once more through the infinite Abysses of Space.

" Well, Lieutenant," queried Asterion, " do you feel as nervous about returning as you did about coming ?"

" I frankly confess, I don't see much difference about it," I replied.

" John,—how do you feel about it ?" asked he.

"O, me likee travellin' 'round among the stars big heap ;—nice fun ;—ain't that so, Jack ?"

"Fact ; d—d if 'tain't," replied the Commodore, perched on his shoulder.

"How is it with you, Hartilion ?"

"Well,—my great-great-great-grandfathers flew all the way from Pluto here, to get rid of a smash up there, and I don't see why their great-great-great-grandson shouldn't follow suit, to get rid of a threatened smash up here ;" replied the colossus with a grin. "By the way, Lieutenant, have you any big fellows over there like me, or any Leviathans I can ride over the sea ?"

I replied that we had a few giants, but the tallest could walk under his arm pits with their umbrellas over their heads, and there was nothing in the way of a sea horse for him to ride except a Greenland whale.

"I'll catch a young one and put him in training," said he.

"All aboard for Earth !"—called out Captain Sussonac.

We bade adieu to the superintendent and ascended the platforms. Half of our party headed by Asterion, entered one car, the rest, with Vidyuna, entered the other, and the doors were shut. The assistants took their positions. The operators worked the batteries beneath the platforms. A profound vibration seemed to arise from the solid ground and the granite walls of the amphitheatre trembled. Showers of electric sparks flew from the magnetic globes on the staffs. Both Ethervolts rose gracefully from their platforms, followed by the air ship attached by its chain. Enclosed within the mighty Cosmic streams we swiftly traversed the atmosphere and entered the gaseous envelope surrounding the planet. The moons came in full view ; their appearance was far more terrible than seen from the surface. Leaving Mars far behind, we entered the vast Interplanetary space amid the full glories of the heavens with their starry galaxies, constellations, suns and nebulæ, the Milky Way spreading its mighty arch over all.

" Look !"—said Asterion, pointing to the west— " there speeds the terrible Comet that dashed through our Meteoric belt."

We looked through the windows. Millions of miles distant, that dreadful messenger of destruction hung in the heavens, like the sword of Damocles. Here and there in the distance floated faint nebulous clouds.

" Those are some of the offshoots whirled out from the belt by the Comet," said Bhuras ;—" wretched tramps in this Celestial Universe, giving our planet and its poor little unoffending moons so much trouble. Of what use are they ?"

" In the economy of the Universe, nothing is made in vain, and every evil also has its corresponding good ; they are the materials of which Worlds are made," said Asterion.

" But these Comets," said I, " wandering Bedouins, in the Interplanetary desert. Of what use are they ?"

" They are helpers, and render valuable service in the manufacture of Worlds," replied he.

" Please explain."

" The rolling up of asteroidal and meteoric belts into solid planets is a slow process. The occasional advent of a Comet among them is necessary to stir them up to their work ; which it accomplishes by lashing them liberally with its tail."

I confessed that Asterion had thrown new and valuable light on the usefulness of Comets.

" This last one was evidently a new hand at the business," remarked Altfoura.—" Like an overbustling house wife, or raw chamber-maid, it raised a terrible dust with its broom while sweeping the celestial carpet."

"And that very dust has its uses, also," replied Asterion. "It teaches us the instability of planetary affairs, as well as the vanity of human affairs."

The moral lessons inculcated by Comets were satisfactorily demonstrated.

The meteoric cloud which was to strike Mars in sixty days, being many million miles distant, was invisible.

The batteries were now put to higher tension as we sped through space, and in two days we had advanced thirty million miles. We encountered no meteorites on the way, millions of them having been gathered up and swept away by the tail of the Comet. We had now reached that neutral point between Mars and Earth where their attractive forces mutually balance each other, where all gravitation ceases, and every thing weighs nothing. This point has no fixed position, but continually varies according to the ever changing distances of the planets from each other in their orbital revolutions. Asterion asked us with a grim smile if we would not like to indulge in the same terpsichorean performances we did before, but as we all declared we had enjoyed enough celestial waltzing to satisfy us for the balance of our lives, he shot the car past this seductive Interplanetary ball room like a flash of lightning.

Vidyuna's Ethervolt followed close in our wake several miles in the rear; the air ship fastened by its chain, speeding gracefully behind. In this empty space, where there is no resisting medium, and weight amounts practically to nothing, the slenderest filament of silk, or even a spider's web, could have drawn her. She looked like a tiny silver shuttle flying between the warp and woof of this Interplanetary carpet.

We now flew onward with tremendous speed and by night fall of the seventh day had flown the whole distance of a hundred and twenty million miles, and were nearing Earth. Its immense south polar disc spread beneath us, displaying in clear outlines and colors, the Antarctic continent, South Atlantic and Pacific Oceans, with their clusters of islands, the Southern extremities of Africa, Australia and South America. We swiftly traversed the gaseous envelope and atmosphere, and the same magnificent auroral display that commemorated our departure, greeted our return. In the very midst of the upshooting columns and spires of golden fire, the arches of crimson flame, which flashed up to the heavens, illumining them with brilliant hues—our two Ethervolts and air ship, slowly and gracefully descended side by side, to the bubbling circle of waters in the centre of the open polar sea. The doors were thrown open, Asterion fired off the signal gun, the superintendent and his assistants appeared on the platform, greeting our arrival with loud cheers. They put out boats and rowing swiftly through the waves, threw out ropes, bent to their oars and drew the Ethervolts and ship close to the shore.

"My own dear Mother Earth!" I cried, springing out upon the ledge—"my native World,—the land of my birth,—my home! O how my heart swells with joy as I greet thee once again,"—and overcome with my emotions I knelt and kissed the cold grey rock.

At this moment the clocks in the Ethervolts struck the hour that ushers in Christmas morning;—propitious omen!—With one accord we knelt and breathed our prayers of thanksgiving to that Almighty Father whose kind hand had shielded us on our perilous journey.

We landed on Earth, Sunday, Dec. 25th, 1892, Terrestrial time.

The Planets were all engaged in their various Zodiacal occupations. Vulcan, nearest the Sun, at his anvil, was forging the thunderbolts of Jupiter, and keeping an eye on his gay spouse, Venus. Mercury, the herald of the gods and the most slippery thief among them,(¹) was dodging around the Sun in his usual style. Venus had turned her back on Virgo, was now in Libra (the Scales), probably finding out her exact weight, avoirdupois. Our Luna was also in conjunction with her, which friendly association rarely takes place between rival beauties. Mars was in Aquarius, evidently taking a bath, while old Mother Terra—herself in Capricorn, attending to her goats—had planted herself in between them, as she generally is, or ought to be on such occasions. Jupiter, with his four well grown boys (a fifth one seems to have lately turned up), was in Pisces, catching fish for his Christmas dinner. The old dethroned monarch, Saturn—cannibalistic devourer of his own children,—was in Virgo, evidently trying to dazzle her eyes with a brilliant display of rings taken from the fingers of his dead wife Rhea. Poor old Uranus was wandering around in search of the bodies of his Titanic sons, slain by Jupiter. Neptune was coursing in his chariot and horses over the remotest bounds of the planetary ocean, while our great Solar luminary, mounted in Apollo's golden chariot was speeding along through the abysmal depths of space toward the constellation Hercules,(²) our whole family of planets, Earth included, following him.

(¹) He robbed Apollo of his quiver and arrows, Neptune of his trident, Venus of her girdle, Mars of his sword, and Jupiter of his sceptre.

(²) This astronomical fact, the movement of our Sun in

"A hundred and twenty million miles within seven days," said Asterion, glancing up at the ruddy Mars rolling amid the bright stars in the deep blue vault above. "Pretty fair time."

"Hi!" giggled John, "me muchee glad for to gettee home again, by Jingo!"

Jack flopped on top of the rock, flapped his wings, roaring out the most vociferous hurrahs that ever issued from a raven's beak,—

"Hurray! Hurray! Wish ye Merry Christmas. Never say die. All ri,'—" then began to utter peculiar sounds like the drawing of a cork out of a bottle, cocked his head on one side and winked one eye at John.

"Hello! Corp."

"Well, Commodore,—what's up?"

"Wish ye Merry Christmas."

"Thank ye, Commodore; wish you the same."

"Glass grog,—all 'round."

"By and by, Jack."

"All ri,'— hurry up. Cockadoodle-d-o-o-o-o!"

space, is of comparatively recent discovery; the whole ancient and modern world, before the period of Copernicus, held that the earth was fixed, and the Sun and Stars revolved around it according to the system of Ptolemy, but the movement of our luminary through the heavens is plainly expressed by the Psalmist (Chap. xix), "His going forth is from the end of the heaven, and his circuit unto the ends of it."

CHAPTER LVIII.

TELEGRAPH TO MARS.

" His lightnings enlightened the world. There is no speech nor language where their voice is not heard. Their line is gone out through all the earth, and their words to the end of the world."

Psalms xix : 3, 4 ; xcvii : 4.

" We will now lay the polar cable ;" said Asterion.

All went aboard the ship ; officers and crew took their stations ; she put off and sailed to the centre of the circle ; then lay to, heaving and tossing amid the swelling eddies and spouting foam. It seemed as if we were over the crater of a submarine volcano. This extraordinary phenomenon is caused by the magnetic currents streaming up from the polar axis. Beyond the circle, the whole sea surface was flat as a floor and smooth as a mirror, the horizon immensely extended as described in Chapter IX.

" Take soundings," ordered Captain Sussonac.

Thalek, the first officer, cast the sounding line, counting the fathoms as it sank beneath the waters. In a few moments it hung slack.

" Two hundred and sixty fathoms," he called.

The central polar sea is exceedingly shallow. The other Terrestrial oceans are from two to six miles deep in many places ; the Pacific deepest of all. Although the polar diameter of the globe is twenty six miles less than the equatorial,—the effect of rotation while in its primeval molten state—the Terrestrial crust is much thicker and more dense here than elsewhere, being composed of the heavier and more compact metals and minerals which form the crust. The thickness and density of the crust diminishes from the poles toward the equator. The physical and geological aspect of the Terrestrial surface plainly shows this. Only two active volcanoes are known near the poles ; Hecla, within seventeen hundred miles of the North, and Erebus within eight hundred miles of the South pole. The numerous clusters of islands lying in the equatorial regions of our planet, which are the denuded peaks of submerged mountain chains—many being of igneous or volcanic origin—show the great geological upheavals and submergences that have taken place in the relatively thinner parts of the Terrestrial crust, long ages ago.

Thalek now hauled in the line.

" What's the character of the sea bottom ?" asked Asterion.

Capt. Sussonac carefully examined the little instrument attached to the plummet which gathers up specimens of sea-sedimentary deposits of all kinds.

" No sediment whatever ;" he replied. " Sea bottom solid igneous rock, mingled with magnetic iron ore."

" The very best for the transmission of the magnetic currents ;" remarked Asterion. " Exactly the spot to lay the cable."

All the great Ocean beds of our World are covered with sedimentary deposits produced by the death and decay of countless myriads of infusoræ and animalculæ inhabiting them. In the early geological ages these formed the vast calcareous or lime stone deposits covering our continents, then submerged, but subsequently upheaved as the " dry land," and which deposits support all animal and vegetable life. The organic kingdoms of Nature owe their growth and support to the obscure and silent labors of these infinitesimal creatures. The coal that warms our habitations, the forests that clothe the landscape, the robes we wear, the food that supplies our tables, the flowers that bloom, are all originally the work of these humble little beings. This fact, however, touches not upon the original creation, nor evolution of any thing in this world; as Mivart properly says, the doctrine of Evolution is simply an attempt to guess at a developing process. It does not touch the Author of that process and never will.

The primeval, igneous and crystalline rocks, the granite, schists and quartzytes, and not the calcareous, prevail near the poles, and the seas in the immediate vicinity are comparatively free from these infusorial sedimentary deposits.

"Stand by to unloose and pay off cable;" ordered Captain Sussonac.

The men descended to the hold where the cable was coiled around its huge drum. It was composed of twisted strands of a peculiar magnetic metal, unknown on Earth, of a bluish color and enormous tensile strength far surpassing our finest steel. The free end was unrolled from the drum and securely fastened to a huge globe of a ton weight consisting of several metals welded together and possessing extraordinary electromagnetic properties. By the aid of a derrick it was raised from the hold, passed over the ship's prow and lowered slowly down in the centre of the bubbling circle, the men carefully unrolling the drum till the cable hung slack, announcing that the bottom was reached. This globe was an immense magnet.

" The globe is exactly over the centre of the polar axis," said Thalek, consulting an instrument attached to the derrick.

"Precisely where the Cosmo-magnetic currents are most powerful," said Asterion.

"'Bout ship,—pay off cable and make for the shore;" ordered Capt. Sussonac.

The ship veered about, the men carefully paying off from the drum as she advanced. Reaching shore, the cable was lifted from the hold and laid along a deep trench cut in the rock to the superintendent's house and passed through an opening in the wall to a private room. Bhuras removed his other telegraphic instrument from the casket, placed it on a table, made the connections with the cable and tested it, an electric spark shot from the key of the instrument.

"TELEGRAPHIC COMMUNICATION IS ESTABLISHED BETWEEN EARTH AND MARS!" said Asterion.

The cheers that greeted this important announcement were never heard over the poles of any planet in this Solar System before.

"And if Lieut. Hamilton will accept," said Bhuras, "he shall send the first message between our respective Worlds."

I considered this the highest honor that could be conferred on any Terrestrial man and accepted it accordingly. Bhuras had instructed me in the working of the instrument and I sat down by the table with the keys, dial plate and bell before me.

"Signal the operator at the South pole of Mars," said he.

I touched the key—the bell sounded the next instant.

"The operator is wide awake and attentive to business," said Asterion.

"Good Heavens!" I exclaimed. "My signal flashed across space, a hundred and twenty million miles and back again in less than half a second Were it possible to transmit the signal through the medium of sound, it would require about twenty five years to do it ;—could one of our telegraphic wires be stretched from our World to yours, the message would require several hours, and could it be sent on a beam of light it would take nearly twenty minutes. The reply to my signal seems to be almost instantaneous."

" Much quicker than that," Asterion replied. " It is not instantaneous, for that implies an appreciable interval of time—however brief ; neither can it be called a transmission, for that also implies movement and an interval of time. It is simultaneous,—if the term can be employed which implies no interval of time. It is an impact, which, when applied at one point of an interval of space—no matter what the distance between them may be—is simultaneously felt or perceived at the other. In our scientific terminology it is called.' Ama,' signifying ' together, or in unison, or company.' The Cosmic streams running between the poles of the planets are merely the mediæ through which this ' Ama' or impact takes place. When you speak of the speed of it—which is not a proper term to apply, for speed also implies time, it is like thought. The human mind, according to its breadth and development, can take in many things simultaneously, however different from each other, or widely separated in space they may be ; in fact can take in the whole Universe at a glance. We can think of Uranus and Neptune simultaneously. The distance between them when on opposite sides of the Sun, is about forty five hundred million miles, nearly fifty times the distance between your Earth and the Sun. It would take a beam of light about six hours to travel across this space. Could our telegraphic operators with their instruments be placed on both planets, the instant one touched his key, the impact would be simultaneously perceived on the key of the other."

" Many of our fixed stars," said I, " are so far distant from us that, their light requires hundreds, thousands and even millions of years to reach us, and if one of them should be blotted out from our sight to day, we should know the catastrophe took place millions of years ago."

" Exactly, but if one of our operators could be there with his instrument, he could tell us all about the details of the catastrophe while it was going on."

" I consider our friend Bhuras one of the most dangerous men in modern society," said I. " He is certainly the most terrible Nihilist ever heard of. His machines practically annihilate time and space, reducing those great worlds to nothing."

Bhuras bowed his appreciation of the compliment.

" Does this simultaneous impact take place through the medium of the Luminiferous ether which fills all space ?" I asked.

" No. It takes place through what you might call the Magnetic Ether, which is as much more ethereal than the luminiferous, as that is more attenuated than solid rock. It is the soul or life, so to speak, of that Ether, and bears the same relation to it that vital force or life does, to the human body. It pervades the whole Supernatural as well as the Natural world and is the foundation or substratum of the World of Thought. In our language it is called ' Omoiah,' or the All pervading."

" Really, my friend," interrupted Altfoura," if you go on etherealizing things much further, you'll finally reduce everything to nothing."

" And the whole visible Universe,—ourselves included, —will be reduced to one single, mathematical, hypothetical point," said I.

"Which will exist, not in space, nor in time, but simply in idea," replied Asterion with a grim smile.

"Which is much finer still," continued Altfoura. "Now as we don't care to be reduced to mere hypothetical idealities at present, suppose we leave philosophics, and attend to telegraphics."

"All right;" said I,—"here goes,"—and I again touched the key. My finger was still on it, when suddenly were flashed out in large letters on the dial plate :

"Signal received long ago ;—what are you Martian tourists about, over there ? Are you going to sleep ?— better send your message beforehand,—business before pleasure, always."

"A good rebuke from our operator," said Altfoura.

"Your Highness is right and I accept it," replied Asterion. "Go ahead, Lieutenant."

I again touched the keys.

"Make communication with private office of the Grand Duke at Palace."

"Communication is made ;" flashed out on the dial.

At this moment the clock struck six. I touched the keys.

"Dec. 25th, 1892, 6 o'c. A. M., Terrestrial time. To His Highness, Duke Athalton.

"Arrived all safe,—Earth sends her Christmas morning greeting to her dear brother Mars ;—extends to him both hands in friendship and hospitality, and begs him to accept, in fullest measure, the assurance of her sisterly love.   F. H."

A few moments passed, evidently required for the recipients to reflect upon the message, then the dial flashed out—

"September 22nd, 21992, 6 o'c. P. M., Martian time. (1)

"Message received.   Mars,—in this hour of his affliction,—gratefully receives the kindly salutation of his
dear sister Earth, and extends to her his New Year's
compliments and greetings.   He begs her also to
accept the full measure of his fraternal affection, with
sincere hopes that, this opening year may dissipate the
clouds of danger now hanging o'er him, and bring never
ending friendship and union, peace, happiness and
prosperity to both Worlds.

"S. T."

The reply was sent by the Princess Suhlamia, to
whom was delegated the first salute of Mars to Earth ;
an honor which the President of the United States or
Queen Victoria, or any monarch of Europe, might have
been proud to receive.

"Really," said Altfoura, "our Martian New Year,
and your Terrestrial Christmas, come pretty close
together."

"So much the better," I replied, "they are the most
joyous days in the calendar of time, and bring happiness
to countless millions of hearts on our World."

"But while it is evening with us, up there, it is morning with you down here."

"Our World, being about forty eight million miles
nearer the Sun than yours, we consequently get day
break twelve hours earlier."

Altfoura, Asterion, and the whole party began to
send messages to their families, friends and acquaintance, and such showers of salutations, compliments,
greetings and wishes for many happy returns, flashed
back and forth between Mars and Earth, as would

(1) The beginning of the Martian year corresponds to our
autumnal equinox.

have astonished the crabbed old monarch of Chaos and made him swear that a high class Christmas dinner party, and a New Year's reception, between denizens of different Worlds were simultaneously going on in his unsocial dominions.

Asterion placed his aërial telegraph on the table alongside the interplanetary instrument, then to Bhuras,—

"While we are on our journey in the air ship over these Antarctic regions, wherever we may be ; hundreds of miles away on land, or sea, any message you receive from Mars, or any news you may deem proper, to send yourself, transmit to me at once and my instrument in the ship's cabin will instantly receive it through the electric currents of this Terrestrial atmosphere."

We now left the house ;—our baggage, instruments, etc., were removed from the Ethervolts to the air ship,— Vidyuna and assistants remaining behind to look after the cars till our return. We got aboard ; the ship rose from the waters five hundred feet in air and flew over the open polar sea, due north, directly for Observatory island, five hundred miles distant. In two hours we reached it, descended to the pier, were received by the superintendent and assistants and escorted to the house where I had spent the previous winter and spring. We spent the day in arranging our plans for extensive surveys over the lands surrounding the pole. Next morning we re-embarked and coursed at high speed many hundred miles over these regions, noting on my geographical maps the most favorable places that could afford refuge to the throngs of Martians who might be compelled to fly to Earth from the threatened catastrophe. By nightfall our ship descended near the shores. We spent several days in these surveys and came to the conclusion that, these inhospitable and

barren regions, covered with boundless fields of snow
and ice, could afford but scanty shelter for the Martian
emigrants even during the summer months and that,
they would surely perish from the intense cold and
freezing tempests that prevail through the long polar
winter. It was therefore necessary to extend our surveys far beyond these regions, across the Antarctic
ocean to the South Atlantic and Pacific, among the
clusters of islands lying there and if possible to the
continents still further to the north. We sped swiftly
onward, passed the rocky ledge where my companions
and I had been thrown out from the ice berg prison the
year before, and the great glacier, along side which the
Albatross had been moored. We followed the shore
line of the great bay our ship had traversed on her
voyage, and reaching the 82° parallel, came in full view
of the great volcano, Mount Erebus, still spouting its
lofty columns of flame and smoke, while a stream of
red hot lava bubbling over the crater, ran down the
slope till it was lost in the glacier below. I now
described some of the celebrated volcanoes of our
planet to my friends.

"You should see the great volcanoes of Venus," said
Asterion. "Hundreds of them, from four, to six, and
ten miles high, whose eruptions are so terrible 'twould
seem as if they would almost tear open the very bowels
of the planet, and with rivers of lava pouring into the
oceans, converting them into boiling caldrons for miles
around."

We encountered no stormy weather nor adverse
winds, and sped swiftly over the snow clad plains, ice
barriers and mountain ranges of the continent. Late
in the evening, John, who was stationed at the dome,
suddenly called out,—

"Lookee yonder ! See big water !"

We looked through the windows. Under the bright moon light a broad expanse of foam capped billows extending on either hand as far as the eye could see, appeared in the northern horizon.

"What sea is that?" asked Asterion.

" 'Tis the great Antarctic ocean, which sweeps in a circle of twelve thousand miles around the south frigid zone of this World," I replied, then pointing to a snow capped rocky headland jutting out from the shore,—

"That is Cape North, the extreme northern boundary of this Antarctic continent."

We reached the Cape and discovered a quiet little cove penetrating the land. We lowered the ship to the water, moored to the ice bound shore, took supper, posted the deck watch, retired to our berths and sank to sleep in spite of the uproar of the sea.

CHAPTER LIX.

THE ANTARCTIC OCEAN.

"O Thou vast Ocean! ever sounding Sea!
Thou symbol of a drear immensity!
Thy voice is like the thunder, and thy sleep
Is as a giant's slumber, loud and deep."
The Ocean.—BARRY CORNWALL.

Early next morning we flew over the rocky cape and entered the great Antarctic Ocean. It was covered with enormous bergs and floes, heaving and tossing amid the billows.([1]) The sky was clear, the sun shone

---

([1]) The waves and icebergs of the Antarctic ocean are much larger than those of the North Polar Ocean. (See Sir Jas. Ross, Baron D'Urville, Capt. Cook, Scoresby, Beechy, Voyages, etc.)

bright and a brisk breeze blew from the west as we coursed o'er the sea. My Martian friends gazed with wonder on the scene.

"These skies are so different from ours," said Asterion. "Such a beautiful blue, and expanding to a far greater amplitude. The horizon sweeping around in a great circle, and this rolling ocean. It is magnificent. We have no such seas on Mars. Every thing is on a vast scale in your World."

"I wish we had old Leviathan here," said Hartilion, his countenance glowing with excitement. "By Pluto! How he would delight to breast these big billows."

"Lieutenant," said Capt. Sussonac, "your world is so different from ours in its physical and geographical appearance. We know nothing of your meteorological changes, storms, etc.; should tempests assail us, we will commit the guidance of our ship to you."

"To you, Captain, belongs the honor of navigating the first Martian air ship over this Terrestrial globe. I will act only as your pilot," I replied.

I now pointed out on the map the southern extremities of South America, Australia and Africa, which form three points of an irregular triangle surrounding the southern hemisphere. I described the physical and geographical divisions of those continents and the peoples inhabiting them ; New Zealand, lying off the east coast of Australia was the nearest land, being only about sixteen hundred miles distant.

We flew swiftly over the ocean, passing many islands and toward evening the long shore line of New Zealand came in view. It was skirted with rugged reefs and precipices. Passing Stewart island, we entered the interior country, coursing over its mountains, plains and cultivated fields, keeping the ship at a high altitude, which commanded a more extensive view. We decided not to land, being doubtful what reception we might meet with from the inhabitants. The superior personal appearance of my Martian friends, the gigantic stature and herculean frame of Hartilion, far surpassing any human being on Earth,—the sight of our glittering, six winged ship descending from the clouds, would certainly fill them with astonishment and alarm, and in their terror they might fire on us. We traversed the whole south island and by nightfall reached Cook's strait, separating it from North island. Its mouth is about thirty miles wide. Port Nicholson and Willington city lie to the north on the slope of the Tararua mountains. The moon shone brightly, illumining the landscape and we could plainly see the country beyond, the mountain slopes covered with fine trees, and in the valleys and meadows, cattle and sheep grazing, or reposing on the grass.

" This seems to be rather a fine country," remarked Asterion.

" Yes," said I, " it has excellent agricultural and mineral resources, climate fine and equable, numerous flourishing plantations, cities, towns and villages, inhabitants thrifty and industrious, good internal trade, and commerce with foreign ports. Many parts of it have magnificent and beautiful scenery, pretty lakes and countless streams of the purest water. It has the most wonderful collection of geysers, hot springs and mineral waters of any country in our world,—natural baths of clear blue colored water possessing remarkable medicinal properties, flowing in beautifully colored natural marble basins. Our friend John is lineally descended from one of the most distinguished warrior kings of the original Maori tribes."

John, who was quite familiar with all parts of his native land, assisted my description.

" Hi !—" said he, " me feel muchee big proud of great Tanehoka war chief what was me own great-great-grand-daddy. He killee, cookee and eatee heap big enemy chiefs in his day. By Jingo ! He huntee big bird twelve feet high, what hab no wings nor tail, lay egg big as bushel basket,—run swifter than race horse, fight like lion, rip any man or beast right open with one kick of his foot.(¹) Big war chief and big bird allee gone forever,"—and tears stood in his eyes. " Hab muchee funny little things in me country ; birds what hab no wings,—covered all over with hair like poodle, run terrible swift. Hab muchee big bat what suck blood from folks when go sleep,—fan 'em softly with their wings allee time, so canno' wakee up, sometimes never wakee up.(²) Hab big rat with long legs, can jumpee right up in second story window, terrible sharp teeth, gnaw hole strait through window glass, make teeth allee sharper. Hab little frog, what fly like bird, and cry like little pig ;—pretty little white mice what sing like bird. Hab queer little animal,—wool like sheep,—tail like beaver,—bill like duck,—webbed feet like goose,—poison claw on hind foot, live under water or on land allee same, bark like dog,—lay eggs like

(¹) The Dinoris giganteus, allied to the Æpyornis maximas of Madagascar, now extinct ; from the dimensions of the bones and fossil remains, the bird must have stood fourteen feet high. It was called the Moa. The natives of New Zealand waged a war of extermination against it. Nearly a hundred years ago, Captain Livingston, of the British Navy, was shown the spot where the last Moa was destroyed, after a tremendous battle in which numbers of the natives were killed. One of the eggs was used as a vessel for carrying water.—*Circle of Sciences.*

(²) Enormous Vampire bats are found in the forests and caves with wings two to three feet stretch.

hen, eat worms and fish.([1]) Hab no snakes in my country."([2])

" Quite a menagerie of natural curiosities," remarked Altfoura.

" It has an area of about a hundred thousand square miles, sixty million acres of land, and a population of about five hundred thousand people," said I.

" A very small population for a country of that size," replied Asterion. " In the event of an emigration from our planet, with our improved system of agriculture and chemical science as applied to it, the island could easily support a population of a hundred millions."

I now described Australia, lying twelve hundred miles to the west, in the South Pacific and Indian Oceans ; its area of three million square miles, about the size of the United States, and its population of nearly three millions.

"About as large as our kingdom of Mandal-Uttima, and under Martian cultivation could support a population of over a thousand millions," remarked Asterion.([3])

([1]) The duck billed Platypus.

([2]) A remarkable fact, in this respect resembling Ireland. Serpents cannot live on Irish soil.

([3]) Density of Population, England has a population of about 350, to the square mile. France, about 175 ; Germany, about 180 ; United States, about 120. An average of about 450, can easily be supported to the square mile (about one person to one and a half acres). This is a low estimate ; under higher cultivation two or three times that number can be supported. Of course, the sustenance capacity of a country depends on its soil, temperature and other climacteric conditions. North and South America with their islands, comprise an area of nearly fifteen million square miles. It follows that, if their natural resources were developed they could support a population of over four thousand millions, nearly four times as great as the entire population of the Globe. The United States alone could support nine hundred millions.—*Encyclop. Britt.*, 9th Ed.

" Let us pay the Australians a visit," said Altfoura looking at his watch. " It is now 9 o'c. P. M. We can reach it early to-morrow morning."

" Provided no storm arises," said I.

" Ho! For Australia !" exclaimed all.

CHAPTER LX.

THE SHIP ON FIRE.

" Hark! Hark! What was that? Hark, hark to the shout.
' Fire! Fire!' then a tramp, and a rush, and a rout ;
' Fire! Fire!' It is raging above and below.
The smoke and hot cinders all blindingly blow ;
The cheek of the sailor grows pale at the sight,
And his eyes glisten wild in the glare of the light ;
The flames in thick wreaths mount higher and higher,
O God !—It is fearful to perish by fire."

The Ship on Fire.—CHARLES MACKAY.

We sped rapidly through Cook's strait into the sea and had advanced about two hundred miles when John who was stationed in the dome suddenly called out,—

" Big light ahead !"

We rushed to the dome. About ten miles to the nor'-west was a great flaming light, now shooting up in lofty spires, then sinking down partially obscured by smoke.

" 'Tis a ship on fire !" said I. " Haste to the rescue of passengers and crew."

We flew swiftly onward and soon reached the burning ship. She was a three mast vessel about two thousand tons burden, all on fire, deck, masts, sails, rigging : the scene was appalling. Hanging to the deck railings, chain-wales, foot ropes and anchor chains, were crowds of people shrieking in agony, as scorched by the flames they let go their hold and fell one by one into the sea. The bowsprit and jibboom were thronged with others clinging to the fore-stays and martingales. Scattered over the waters were numbers clinging to spars, planks, boxes and bales of goods. Several boats crowded with passengers, and many clinging to the gunwales, were tossing in the waves ; many of them having no steersmen, ran foul of each other, or falling into the trough of the sea, capsized, and the wretched inmates were thrown pell-mell into the water and drowned. The smoke from the burning ship settled around, almost concealing the frightful scene.

" Her passengers are Chinese coolies, or the lower class of laborers, on passage to Australia or the West Indies," said I. " The ship has evidently been driven by stress of weather out of her course. I don't discover her Captain and officers. Our ship cannot hold one tenth of the poor creatures, but we must save all we can."

The ship was lowered to within a few feet of the water ; rope ladders were thrown out. The life-boat was got out, manned by Hartilion and some of the crew. We coursed to and fro among them, shouting and blowing the whistle, but the poor drowning wretches, as they caught glimpses of our ship sailing over their heads amid the smoke, and Hartilion towering in the life boat, and heard our shouts and the loud whistles, seemed frenzied with terror, refusing help ; some in the boats fired their revolvers or struck at us with oars and axes, and we were compelled to sheer off for safety and drew in the life boat.

"They are ignorant and superstitious," said I ; "we can do nothing to save them and must leave them to their fate."

All at once loud yells were heard some distance off, and hurrying to the spot we witnessed a sight that made our blood run cold. A large raft constructed with spars, planks and fastened together with cross-pieces and ropes, was tossing on the waves. It was so thickly crowded with coolies it had sunk almost knee deep below the surface and scores of others half immersed in the water, were clinging desperately to the timbers. Our ship advanced slowly and hung about a hundred feet above the raft, the smoke from the burning ship concealing it from the view of the people beneath.

A perfect pandemonium of blood and murder, amid yells, shrieks and curses, raved like a hell on board the raft. The coolies were massacreing the miserable wretches of their own race who clung to the timbers, and also fighting among themselves, plunging their long knives into each other, the stronger killing the weaker and flinging the dead bodies overboard by the score ; the raft being lightened, rose higher out of the water. On one side of the raft were clustered the Captain of the ship and a few of his crew making a desperate defence against the coolies who, brandishing their knives, charged upon them with loud yells. Fortunately the crew were armed with revolvers, cutlasses and axes. The Captain, a tall, athletic young man, was armed with a cutlass and half a dozen revolvers in his belt. As fast as the coolies charged they were shot, brained or slashed, their dead bodies lay in heaps, forming almost a rampart in front of the Captain and sailors.

"O, horrible ! Horrible !" exclaimed Altfoura. "Is

it possible that a common danger involving all, should arouse such murderous instincts ?"

At this moment the flames of the burning ship flared up, shedding a bright light over the faces of the Captain and sailors, hitherto concealed by the smoke.

" Great God !" I exclaimed ; " they are of my race,—white men,—quick,—lower the ship."

The coolies paused in their bloody work, drew back, dragging out the dead bodies of their companions which had obstructed their onset, and flinging them overboard, then rushed forward with loud yells, and amid the explosions of pistols and clash of cutlasses, the shriek of a woman rent the air.

" O haste ! Haste !" exclaimed Altfoura and Asterion.

Again the coolies were driven back, and we saw the prostrate form of a young woman, her fair hair streaming over the timbers of the raft, and clasping a young babe to her breast. Close by her side knelt the Captain, who had sunk wounded to his knee, holding aloft his blood dripping cutlass and pointing his last revolver at the coolies. The sailors were already dead.

" Fling out the rope ladder," shouted Hartilion. " I'll scatter that murderous gang like chaff."

Down rushed the ship,—the ladder was thrown out, —Hartilion and I grasping our cutlasses in our teeth, leaped over the railing followed by Altfoura and John, and sprang down the ladder to the raft.

" Hello !—You bloody devils ;" shouted Hartilion in a voice of thunder. " Fall back !"

The coolies heard that terrible voice and looked around. As they saw this tremendous giant towering in their midst and the great air ship hanging over their heads, they were frenzied with terror and rushed with loud cries to the further extremity of the raft, some leaping overboard. Hartilion pursued them like an incarnated spirit of vengeance, hewing off their heads, lopping off their arms and legs, shearing them from shoulder to hip with the blows of his terrible cutlass and in less than three minutes not a single coolie was left alive ; the surrounding waters were strewn with dismembered bodies and dyed with blood. In the mean time I raised the head of the dying Captain on my knee, staunched his bleeding wounds and administered a powerful stimulant. In a few moments he revived and looked wonderingly around.

"I'm an American," he feebly murmured. "My name William Allen,—my ship, the Plymouth,—my wife Marienne,—where ?—"

Hartilion laid her insensible form by his side ; he took her hand and pressed it to his lips. Altfoura took the babe and laid its little face close to his ;—his eyes brightened and he kissed its forehead and cheeks, then faintly murmured, "Marienne,—darling,—our dear little one,—farewell ;" then raising his rapidly glazing eyes upward,—"O ! God,—I commit them to thy care ;" his lips blanched, the blood gushed from his wounds,— he gave a few short gasps and expired, still clasping the hand of his unconscious wife in his own.

The gathering surges rolling over the raft, which, released from its human freight tossed on the waters, warned us to depart. Hartilion raised the dying mother gently in his arms, she also had been stabbed by the knives of the coolies. Altfoura took the babe ; we ascended to the ship and laid her on a couch. She was of beautiful form, lovely countenance, and apparently about eighteen years of age.

"How beautiful she is ;—so young to die ;—O, Frederick,—Doctor,—save her life for God's sake and her dear little child's," exclaimed Altfoura with streaming eyes.

We bound up her wounds and administered a strong stimulant, but it was too late ; her life blood had almost drained away. She opened her eyes, saw her little babe smiling by her side, and with a cry of pleasure feebly raised it in her arms and clasped it to her breast, " O, my darling little one," she murmured, pressed its lips, and in that last lingering kiss her soul took its flight.

We knelt around the couch where smiling infancy in the dawn of life lay side by side with youth and beauty wrapped in the cold embrace of death. Around her neck was clasped a locket containing a miniature photograph of herself and husband, with a lock of dark and golden hair entwined in a true lover's knot ; also a little cross with the engraved motto, " *Christus mea spes* " (Christ my hope) ; on her finger a plain gold ring engraved " William to Marienne, *Semper fidelis.*"

We cruised around in all directions ; the light of the burning ship illumining the sea to a great distance ; scanning the waters and blowing the whistle in hopes that we might discover some of the lost, but not a single boat or human form was seen. The fire by this time had reached the vessel's hold, where evidently gunpowder and spirits were stored with her cargo : a column of flame shot high in air,—there was a terrible explosion, the ship was blown to pieces and the fragments scattered over the deep. Of that good ship, thronged with its human freight treading the decks with strong and vigorous life, all were sunk beneath the waves, and naught was left but the helpless little babe, quietly sleeping in the arms of its lifeless mother.

We decided to hasten our journey to Australia and directed our course to the West.

We had noticed for some time past that, the powerful aërovolt batteries were unable to elevate the ship over five thousand feet in the air. Asterion and Thalek, after a thorough examination, announced that the electric currents traversing the Earth's crust were not near so strong as those on Mars, although our planet is more than six times its bulk and weight. They also found that, the currents diminished in intensity from the poles toward the equator, whereas on Mars they are of uniform strength all over the planet. Thalek decided that the cause of this difference was in the Martian metals, of which the batteries were made, but whatever it was, the unfortunate results that followed could not have been foreseen, nor averted.

We directed our course to Sidney, lying on the east shore of New South Wales in Botany Bay. In former years this was the old penal colony of Great Britain, but is now a really charming city, with a fine harbor and surrounding country. The wind, which had been steadily increasing, began to blow a gale, and the storm wings were got out. We had advanced about two hundred miles when a violent storm arose from the south west against which it was impossible to make headway, and the Captain gave orders to elevate the ship above the storm belt. The aërovolt batteries were put to their fullest tension but could not raise the ship to the necessary height. We were immersed in the storm clouds and the lightning flew around us in all directions.

"Captain," said Asterion, " we are not safe here ; the magnetic metals of our ship cannot throw off these Terrestrial thunderbolts as they can our Martian flashes. You had better descend to the sea."

Suddenly there was a tremendous thunder peal, and a long, zigzag lightning flash struck the bow, broke off one wing, dashed into the machine room knocking down three engineers and steersman. The ship reeled, almost capsized, and whirled to and fro like a leaf in the wind.

"Check off batteries,—furl wings,—get out propellers, and descend to the sea !" shouted Capt. Sussonac, as he sprang to the wheel.

The orders were quickly obeyed ; the ship righted, swiftly descended to the sea and sank beneath the waves into the region of aqueous calm. We attended to the prostrate men ; fortunately they were not injured, but severely stunned. The cabin lights, bow and stern electric reflectors were lit. We were fifty feet below the surface. The propellers drove the ship ahead and as she rushed through the waters the sound was like the roaring of the rapids of Niagara. The valves of the air generators were opened, letting fresh supplies of air into the cabin.

"How fast are we going ?" asked Altfoura.

"Forty miles per hour," replied the Captain, consulting his velocimeter.[1]

"We will continue our sub-marine journey till the storm blows over, then rise to the surface and resume the aërial," said Asterion.

"I rather prefer this mode of travel," said Altfoura. "'Tis a pleasant variety, and appears to be safer than by air, in these Terrestrial storms."

"Provided we do not run against something in the way," said I.

Suddenly there was a severe shock and the ship came to a dead halt as if she had run on a sand bar. Hartilion sprang to the dome.

[1] It has been mathematically demonstrated that a submarine ship can attain nearly double the speed of that on the surface with the same amount of motor power, against surface head winds or waves, this resistance not being encountered beneath the surface.

" By the great Timimgila and all the big fish of the
sea !" he shouted with a roar of laughter. " Our ship
has run her nose smack into the jaws of a whale."

It was true. An enormous fin-back,(¹) over a hundred feet long, attracted by the head light and taking it
for some new and appetizing morsel had, with his usual
voracity, opened his huge jaws and rushed forward to
swallow it. The sharp prow entered his maw, splitting
him up half the length of his body, and he hung with
his lacerated jaws clasped around the bow, feebly fluttering his tail. The propellers were reversed, but it
was impossible to extricate the ship from the huge
writhing mass that clung to her.

" Well ; Captain," laughed Altfoura ; " as the whale
has got us half way down, it looks as if he would soon
make a dinner of us."

"Give him a little emetic from the stomach pump,"
suggested Hartilion ; " I reckon he'll vomit us up like
the whale did Jonah, as John has told us all about."

" All right. I'll administer a dose which I fancy will
stir his whaleship up rather lively," said Capt. Sussonac, then to one of the gunners—

" Fire into him with the bow gun."

The gun was thrust from its port in the prow,
which was buried in the whale's belly and fired. There
was a dull explosion, the monster was blown to atoms
and the surrounding waters were dyed with blood.
Freed from the incumbrance, the ship sped onward for
an hour longer, when suddenly a loud crash was heard
at the stern. The half sunken mast of a wrecked ship
had become entangled in one of the propellers and
broke it from the shaft. As it was impossible to con-

(¹) This species of whale is found mostly in the Antarctic seas.
They attain a length of from ninety to a hundred feet, and are
exceedingly fierce and dangerous.

tinue our course, the Captain gave orders to ascend. The prow was directed upward and had scarce risen above water when Hartilion, stationed at the dome, shouted,—

"Back ! Back ! Ice berg right ahead !"

The propeller was reversed, but too late. The berg was close on us ; its lofty wall towered over the ship, and a long, sharp ice spur projecting from the low platform at its base, struck below the water line, crushing a great hole in her prow and driving her back. The water rushed into the cabin ;—in twenty minutes she would have sunk with all on board. Everything was in confusion,—Hartilion sprang up the ladder,—tore open the hatchway, and leaped from the deck on the platform of the berg, where the ship lay helpless. He braced his colossal limbs like pillars of iron against the berg, stooped his mighty shoulders under the prow, and heaving the ship up with the strength of ten Herculeses, swayed and shook her to and fro, tore her loose from the ice spur and flung her off ; then leaped into the billows, seized a rope and climbed to the deck, just as the almost doomed ship rose trembling from the waves, the water pouring in torrents from the hole.

" Brave !—Brave !—Hartilion !" exclaimed Altfoura and Asterion, clasping him in their arms. " You have saved our lives."

As the young and handsome giant smilingly received the heart felt thanks and applause of all on board, he looked the very Grecian hero himself, just released from sustaining the burden of Atlas on his shoulders.

" Really, Lieutenant ;—" said Captain Fulminax, " do you Terrestrians let your wrecked ships and ice bergs float promiscuously around your oceans, to endanger the safety of vessels in this manner ? Such culpable carelessness would never be permitted on our planet."

" If we should undertake to destroy the ice bergs that

infest our polar seas ;" I replied, " the whole combined navies of our World could not accomplish a ten thousandth part of it."

" If we had our little ice fleet down here, we could clear all your oceans of them in a single summer."

The ship was hovering above the waves, two storm wings only half way out their ports, to steady her. Being on the lee side of the berg she was partly screened from the storm. The berg was enormous, full five hundred feet high and half a mile long, and the waves dashed high up against the upright wall with thundering sound. In the mean time the crew were hard at work trying to close the hole in the prow with double folds of strong canvass wrapped around the outside with cords, and also trying to rigup a new wing, and extra propeller, but the work was difficult and dangerous from the continual pitching and rolling of the ship in the fierce gusts of wind that swept around the berg. We hoped, when repairs were completed, to descend to the water and weather it out till the storm blew over. The heavy clouds in the west now broke away, leaving a clear opening in the sky, through which the bright moon shone over the storm lashed ocean. John, who was stationed in the dome suddenly shouted,—

" There's a ship !—A ship !"

We rushed to the dome and looked out. About six miles to the north west was a three masted vessel scudding before the wind under close reefed topsails. I examined her with the glass.

" She is an American ;—" said I. " I know by the cut of her hull and style of her trimmings."

" Suppose we fire off the alarm gun ;" said Altfoura, " and make a dash for her. When we get near enough, throw out grapnel ropes and the crew will haul us aboard and take us to some near port, where we can lay to and repair our ship. We'll pay them well in Martian gold."

"Excellent," replied Asterion. "But I fancy, Terrestrial sailors are not familiar with Martian air ships. They would probably be frightened out of their wits, refuse to take us aboard, or perhaps fire on us."

"On the contrary," I replied, "our genuine American tars are the bravest in the world. They would hob-a-nob with Old Nick himself and dance a hornpipe with his imps. They are also the most generous and noble men you'll find afloat. When we get near enough I'll hail them; they'll take us aboard at once. As for air ships, plenty of Yankee inventors are exhibiting flying models of them everywhere, and they'll think ours is a perfected thing. I'll tell them we're taking a trip around the world; represent you Martians as natives of the Fiji islands, quite civilized, and Hartilion as a small boy from the mountains of the Moon, all expressly imported for the Zoo gardens in Washington; they'll take· it all as a matter of course, and give us hearty greetings and hospitalities."

These suggestions received the unanimous approval of all on board.

"Load up the alarm gun,—get grapnel ropes ready and steer for the vessel ;—" ordered Captain Sussonac.

The gun was loaded ; the ropes with their three pronged steel anchors to catch into the rigging of the vessel, were secured to the deck railing ;—the ship veered about, ready to dash out,—suddenly the bell of the telegraph sounded ;—the operator stationed at the instrument shouted,—

"DESPATCH FROM MARS!"

We rushed to the cabin,—on the dial of the telegraph was flashed out in letters of fire, shot a hundred and twenty million miles from Mars in less than a second.

CHAPTER LXI.

TERRIBLE NEWS.

"Ill news is wing'd with fate, and flies apace."
Threnodia Augustalis.—DRYDEN.

"Terrestrio-Martian Telegraph Station, South Pole.
"Tuesday, Dec. 27th, 1892, 11 o'c. P. M. Direct from
Ethervolt Station, No. 4, Mars.

"To HELIOS ZAR ASTERION :—King Diavojahr has surprised and captured this island and station with a fleet of air ships and troops. Lord Chumivant is with them, but is secretly on our side. He has privately informed me that Diavojahr will capture you on your return ; he is also organizing an immense fleet and land force to attack our kingdom immediately after the coming meteoric downfall while we are in confusion and unprepared. He will hold you prisoners subject to death, the price of your release to be the immediate delivery to him, and marriage consummation with, the Princess Suhlamia. He holds this menace over our kingdom that, in case his forces here are threatened by ours, he will destroy the station, cut off connection with the Cosmic streams, rendering your return impossible, or in case you start, you will be lost on the way. I have fled from the office with my instruments to the secret subterranean caverns underneath the amphitheatre, in the heart of the polar magnetic streams. The heat is almost suffocating and the atmosphere is saturated with electric and magnetic auras. I fear I cannot long survive ; but am willing to die at my post if need be, in the discharge of my duty. Lord Chumivant will privately report to me all the news and movements of Diavojahr.

"THORIDAL."

For a moment we were speechless with horror and the countenances of strong and brave men grew pale.

"God in Heaven!" exclaimed Altfoura, "what is to be done?"

Done? What could be done in this awful situation? A frightful tempest raging around us,—a broken and crippled ship,—unable to sail,—unable to rise above the storm,—almost unable to fly. Two thousand miles of a rough and stormy ocean,—a thousand miles of an ice clad continent, over which freezing winds and furious storms rage,—between us and the pole. Even if we reach it, which would be almost a miracle, what awaits us there? a long, lingering agony of suspense, with one horrible thought ever present, as the days and nights drag on. The dreadful tempest of meteors desolating our homes, the universal terror of our friends, from which scarce recovering, to encounter, unprepared, the merciless legions of that inhuman tyrant who would drench our fair fields in blood, and we, helpless prisoners on the lone and barren pole of another world, compelled to purchase our release by the sacrifice of a young and lovely life. Great God! What a hell of anguish, horror and despair raged in my soul. What could be done? Nothing. That demon had played a deep game, and we were in his power.

"By the infernal gods!" exclaimed Hartilion, grinding his teeth and raising his arms aloft with a terrible gesture, "if we ever reach home, I'll get an audience with that devil on his throne, he has often asked me to live in his palace. When I get my hands on him, I'll break every bone in his accursed body, I'll tear him limb

from limb before his whole court, and they may cut me
to pieces for it the next minute, for aught I care."

"Lieutenant," said Asterion, "show me your map of
this World."

I placed my geographical atlas and chart on the
table ; he closely scanned the general topography of
the oceans and continents, the parallels and meridians
of latitude and longitude, the Zones, climacteric and
isothermal lines, etc., then placing his hand over the
western hemisphere,—

"Here are two great continents reaching almost
from pole to pole. Their names ?"

"North and South America ; the longest continents
on our Planet," I replied.

"On South America I see a continuous range of
mountains running along the western coast, from the
southernmost point, through the several countries up to
this narrow isthmus connecting the two continents.
Its name ?"

"The Andes. They are nearly five thousand miles
long and from sixty to three hundred miles wide.
They contain some of the highest peaks on this planet."

"I see another chain running along the west coast
of North America from the isthmus up to within 20
degrees of the North Pole."

"They constitute our great Cordilleran system ; the
southern line running through Central America and
Mexico is called the Sierra Madre. The northern line
running through the west part of the United States is
called the Rocky Mountains. The two, constitute the
longest and most stupendous mountain range on this
planet."

"Above the 70th parallel, north lat., I see an ocean
interspersed with islands and a large peninsula on the
east."

"That is the Arctic Ocean and Archipelago, and the continent of Greenland."

"This continuous mountain chain, extending through both continents almost up to the north pole, will render us essential service in our journey home," said Asterion quietly.

"Journey home!" exclaimed all.

"Certainly. In view of the rather unpleasant state of political affairs on our Planet, I propose we give up our Australian trip and start for home."

"Home! How in the name of heaven are we ever to get there? and even if we should, by some miracle, there's Diavojahr's troops ready to capture us."

"Don't give yourselves any uneasiness about it, gentlemen, I beg of you. If agreeable, we'll start in half an hour, and provided no unforeseen accidents arise, I can safely guarantee we'll reach Mars and have a pleasant chat in the Duke's palace within a week at farthest, and laugh at the failure of King Diavojahr's shallow scheme," replied Asterion.

We gazed on him in blank astonishment.

"Listen. Here's my plan. We'll toss overboard every thing except just enough ballast to steady the ship, food for three days, and the bow gun. Relieved of this weight, she can ascend above the storm belt, fly strait to the south pole at the rate of four hundred miles an hour, arrive there in eight hours at latest. We'll re-supply and equip her, there, of which there is an abundance ;—man the Ethervolts with aërovolt batteries,—attach them to the ship,—ascend to the high aërial regions,—fly across the Antarctic continent and ocean to South America,—strike the Andes,—there we're all right. The electric currents traversing the earth's crust are most powerful and uniform along great mountain chains. Over the oceans they are much weaker,

nearly three fourths being absorbed by the water and
are also continually fluctuating, which explains why we
cannot rise. Over the Andes we can ascend to any
height. We'll follow their whole length, cross the
equator, up the Sierra Madre range, follow the Rocky
Mountains up to their terminus, fly across the Archipelago of the Arctic ocean to the North Pole, making the
whole trip of nearly fourteen thousand miles in thirty
six hours. We will lay to, right over the polar axis,
transfer our baggage from the ship to the Ethervolts,
take her in tow, get aboard, and taking the Cosmo-
magnetic current that runs to the north pole of our
planet, fly back to Mars at the rate of twenty million miles
per day, or if we wish to make quicker time, we'll lash
the Ethervolts together, put up my Cosmic motor, and fly
across the Interplanetary space of a hundred and twenty
million miles within ten minutes, and arriving at the
north pole of Mars, re-embark on the ship and reach
the Duke's palace, twenty five hundred miles distant
with my magnetic motor in less than sixty minutes.
How does my plan suit you, gentlemen ?"

The applause that followed this stupendous announcement would have startled old Occidentalis himself, who
was raging and howling for his anticipated prey, with
all his might and main.

"Captain," said Asterion, "you may as well begin to
lighten the ship."

"Stand by to heave every thing overboard but the
bow gun and ballast enough to steady her," shouted
Captain Sussonac to the crew.

We all went to work with a right good will. Up
went the windows, port holes and hatchway. Out went
all the pretty furniture, pictures and other elegant
appointments, divans, tables, chairs, pell-mell into the
sea. Hartilion lent his festive vigor to the business

and rushed among the heavy truck like a wild elephant on the rampage.   He tore the life boat from its tackle ;— ripped up propellers and shafts,—tore out anchors and chains,—upheaved the huge crates of iron ballast and flung them helter-skelter into the billows.   Such a speedy unlading of a ship's cargo was never seen before.

"Ship is cleared.   Every thing overboard from deck to keel," shouted the first officer.

The Nai-Alavestron shook herself almost joyously, like a fiery steed released from a heavy burden.   With a steady movement of her storm wings she hovered above the waves on the lee side of the berg.

"She can now rise ten miles in the air, if necessary," said Thalek.

"Shoot the ship above the storm belt, and make strait for the pole," ordered the Captain.

"Wait a moment, I would like to get my casket aboard that ship if possible," said I.

"All right, Lieutenant ;   when you're ready, let us know.   Soon as she comes within hail, we'll dash out and make strait for her," replied the Captain.

I had determined, in case we could board the vessel, to deliver my casket to the Captain with instructions, whatever port he reached, to forward it to the destination I should make known to him ; but if we failed to board her,—as it would be impossible for him to bring his vessel to, in this terrible gale, I would fling it on deck or in the rigging as we passed by, and it could be secured by the crew ; if we should be lost in the perilous journey before us, or never return to Earth, our fate might thus be known to my Terrestrial friends.   I quickly got it in readiness, placed my journal and notes within, together with a few letters I had written and directed to my friends ; affixed a few strong hooks to the buoy cords of the net work, so that it might catch in the rigging. I wrote a note addressed to the Captain of the vessel, wrapped in a piece of rubber cloth and affixed it to the network.

"Off west coast of New Zealand. Six hundred miles out. Tuesday night, Dec. 27th, 1892.

"DEAR CAPTAIN :—An aërial ship and crew, in distress, implores you, by all that is dear to the true sailor's heart, to take charge of this casket, and when, by the blessing of Almighty God, you reach port, if you will forward it with the contents inviolate, to either of the parties herein named in New York city, or Washington, D. C., U. S. A., you will receive the heart felt thanks of him who commits it to your care and of those who receive it, and also be liberally rewarded. That the hand of Almighty God may protect you, your crew and brave ship in this hour of peril, and bring you safe to port, is the earnest prayer of a brother sailor and his comrades."

I now rapidly take notes in short hand, of the events as they transpire, ready to place them in the casket and seal up at the latest moment.

The poor little babe, undisturbed by the tumult, is still quietly sleeping, nestled close to the breast of its lifeless mother.

CHAPTER LXII.

RETURN TO MARS.

"Through the black night and driving rain,
A ship is struggling all in vain,
To live upon a stormy main,
Miserere Domine!"

The Storm.—ADELAIDE PROCTOR.

The tempest is increasing. Our ship is tossed in the tremendous gusts that sweep around the lee side of the berg. It is difficult to keep her in position. The thunder peals shake the heavens and the lightning flashes cast a lurid glare o'er the storm lashed sea.

My companions stand silent, almost spell bound, as they gaze upon the terrible sight;—the grand lines of Byron come to my mind—

"Thou glorious mirror, where the Almighty's form
    Glasses itself in tempests; in all time,
Calm, or convulsed—in breeze, or gale, or storm,
    Icing the pole, or in the torrid clime,
    Dark-heaving; boundless, endless and sublime,
The image of Eternity;—the throne
    Of the Invisible. Even from out thy slime
The monsters of the deep are made;—each Zone
Obeys thee; thou goest forth, dread, fathomless, alone,"

"How awful,—yet how sublime the scene!" exclaimed Asterion. "The ocean tempests of our World show nothing like this."

"Our globe being twice the circumference of yours, our oceans have far greater sweep," said I. "You should witness some of our equinoctial storms on the Atlantic, the cyclones of our Indian oceans or the hurricanes of the Tropics. We may encounter some of them on our aërial voyage over the World."

The American vessel is now plainly seen by the lightning flashes, swiftly scudding over the waves and heading for the north. She careens almost to her beam ends ; now proudly mounting the foam crested billows, and now sinking down, deep, in their dark and fathomless gulfs.

"Great Heaven !" exclaimed Altfoura. "She cannot live through this terrible sea. She will be lost !"

"I think she'll weather it," I replied. "She's a fine sailer, trim built and splendidly handled—she rides the waves like a sea gull,—is manned with American sailors, the best in the World."

"Heaven grant she may safely reach port," said Asterion.

"It will be impossible for us to board her," said I, "neither can she lay to as we approach. Our ship will be driven right over her masts. I must go up on deck and throw my casket in her rigging as we pass over."

"Let me attend to that," said Hartilion. "No man on this ship but I, can keep his foothold for a moment on this deck when we fly out from the berg. I have been whirled up and down amid the waves many a time when mounted on my Ocean steed. Have you forgotten Leviathan's battle with the sword fish ; how I clung to the saddle and whipped them to pieces with my cat-o'-nine-tails ? By Pluto ! How I wish he was here now. We'd get aboard, ship and all, and he'd carry us safely through this tempest. I'll go up on deck and when all's ready, pass the casket up to me, I'll fling it in the vessel's rigging as we pass over," and Hartilion ascended the companion way.

"And when 'tis done," said Capt. Sussonac, "I'll shoot the ship above the storm belt and fly strait to the South pole."

The furious howling of the tempest now rises high above the dreadful roaring of the sea. The storm driven vessel comes in full view, plainly visible by the light of her deck lanterns. Her masts, yards and rigging curved stiffly forward, as she flies madly on, the billows chasing her like hungry tigers their prey. The whirling foam sweeps o'er her decks. Two steersmen are lashed to the wheel,—their hair flying in the wind—their eyes fixed ahead—every nerve and muscle strung to its highest tension as they hold that wheel with a grasp of iron. Here and there a sailor is lashed to the railing or shrouds. High in the foretop is another sailor lashed to the cross trees. He is the lookout, watching with eagle eye far ahead, ready to shout his warning cry, should the fatal ice berg loom up amid the darkness.

Hartilion now calls out from the hatchway,—

"Ship close at hand ;—when she comes near, I'll give the signal ;—fire the bow gun—dash out from the berg—I'll hail her,—have casket ready."

"Aye ! aye !" replied Capt. Sussonac.

The moments pass ;—she is now within three cable lengths.

"Fire !" shouts Hartilion.

The gun is discharged,—the man on the lookout turns his face toward us,—the lightning flashes show his countenance blanched with terror,—he has discovered our ship, like some vast aërial monster amid the darkness.

"All's ready !" calls out Hartilion.

"Make for the vessel," orders Capt. Sussonac.

One turn of the rudder,—one lash of the storm wings and like an eagle from her eyrie, our ship dashes out, right into the heart of the tempest.

"Ship ahoy !—" rings out the mighty voice of Hartilion ; its clarion tones rising high above the awful din.

Reeling—staggering—trembling—our brave ship drives on through the darkness.—Hark ! a heavy trampling resounds from the deck, mingled with the loud rattling of a ponderous chain.

"Great God !" exclaims Altfoura looking through the dome. "Hartilion will be thrown overboard."

"Not he ;" replies Asterion. "See how he holds to that chain with a grasp of iron."

"Be all ready, Lieutenant," Hartilion cries. "We'll fly over the masts in three minutes."

The moment has come. I will now place my tablets within. Will my friends of Earth ever see these lines ? Will they ever know, while gathered around their cheerful firesides that, on this dark and stormy night, o'er this wild raging sea, an aërial ship, bearing in her bosom a band of brave men from another World, is making her desperate struggle to return to that far distant orb, o'er which the star of a dark and awful fate now hangs impending ? Will we ever reach that World, rolling in the vast abysses of space millions of miles away ? Shall I ever re-visit this, my native Earth,—ever again view the scenes of my youth,—ever again look upon the faces and hear the voices of those I love ?

"Quick !—The casket," Hartilion cries. "We're almost over the masts !"

I will now place it in his hands;—at this awful moment amid the lightning flashes and rolling thunders methinks a gentle voice whispers to my soul,—the same that cheered me in my prison cell,—the voice of one far away,—

"Courage !—Hope !—Trust in God."

THE END.